Roanoke County Public Library
Hollins Branch Library
6624 Peters Creek Road
Roanoke, VA 24019

S0-BAI-479

THE ROYAL PALACE

Goong

vol. 3

Park SoHee

NO LONGER
PROPERTY OF
ROANOKE COUNTY LIBRARY

Yen
Press

PROVINCE OF ONTARIO PUBLIC LIBRARY
LIBRARY
O
8

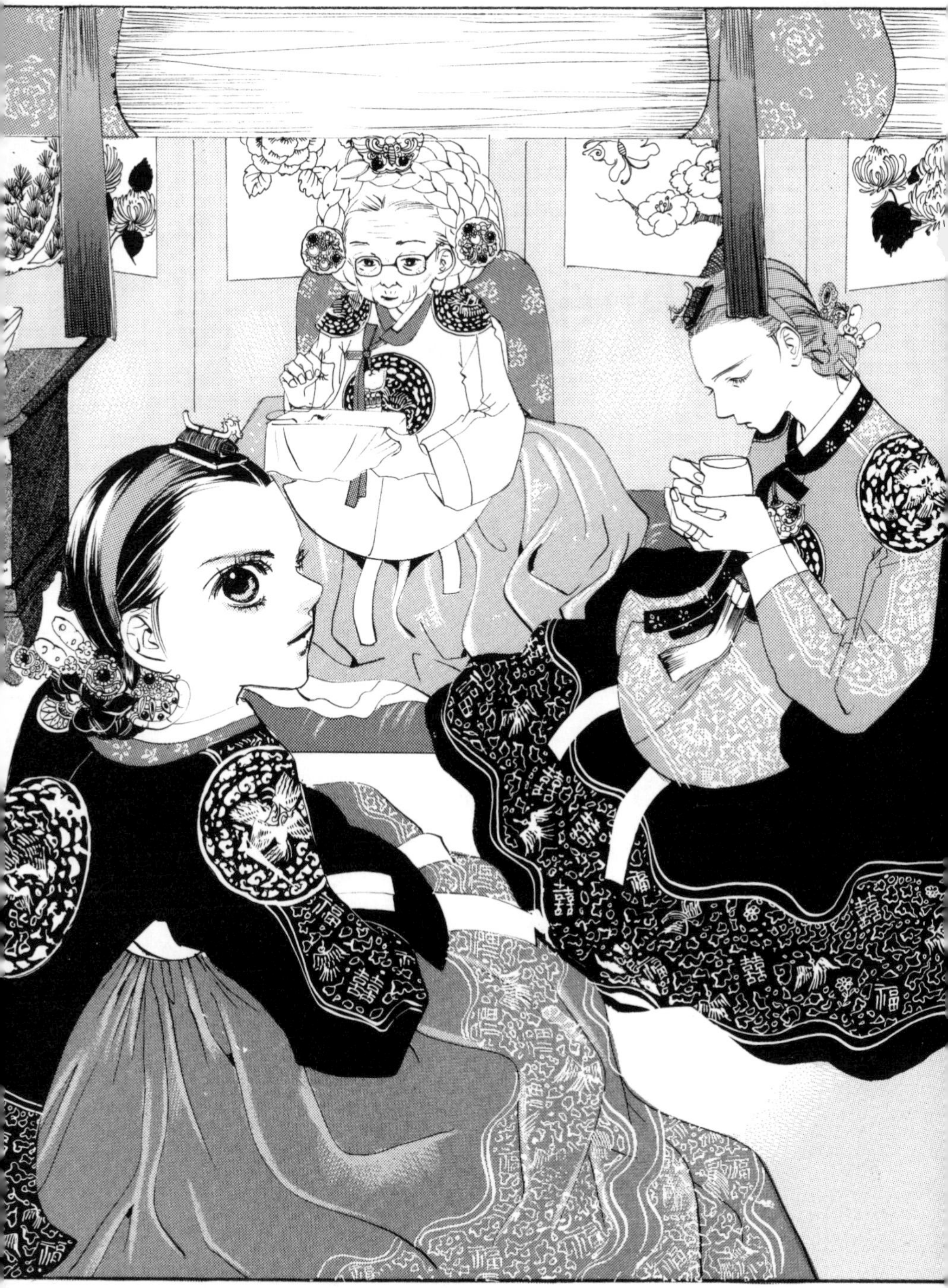

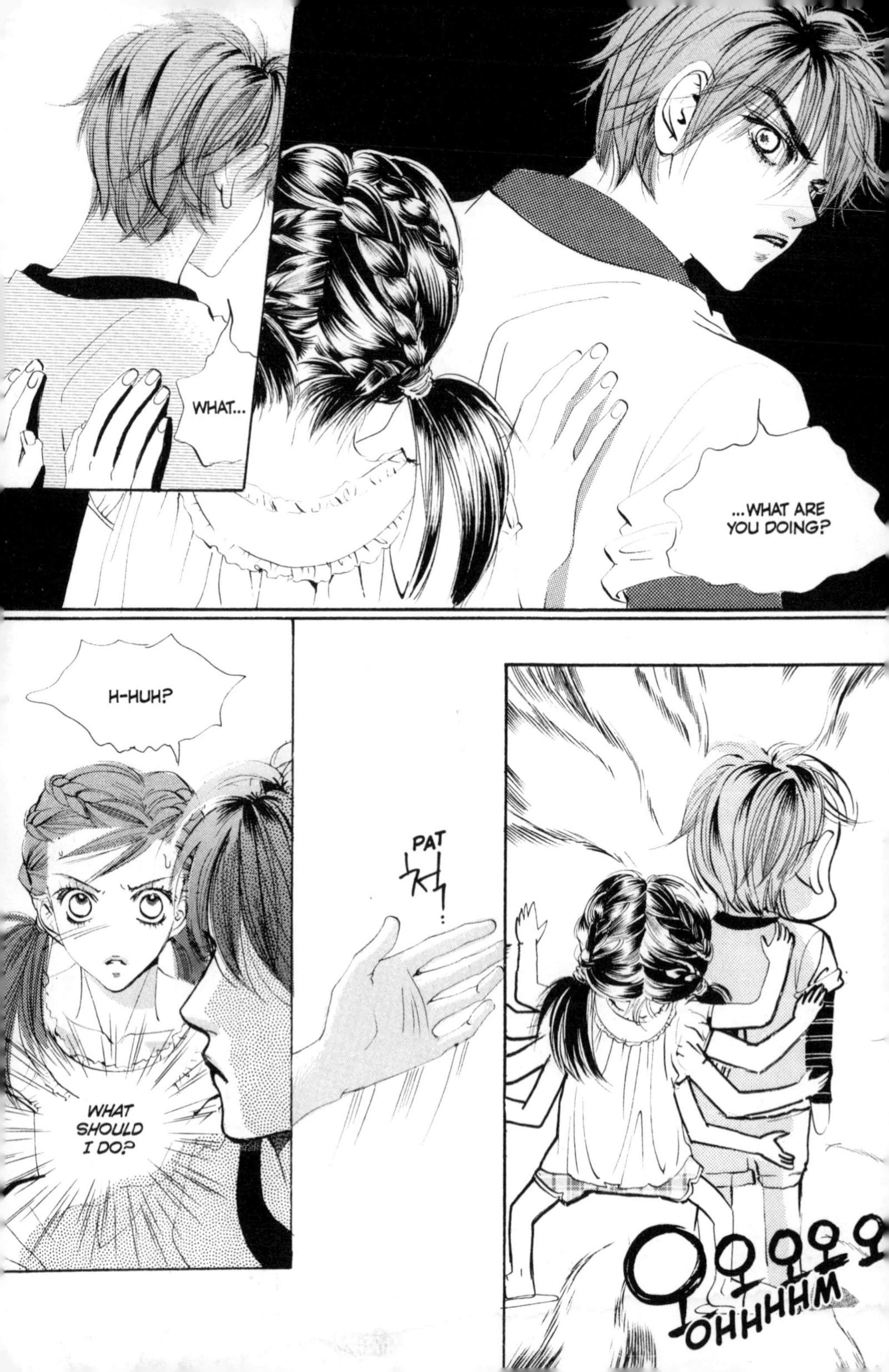
WHAT...
...WHAT ARE YOU DOING?
H-HUH?
WHAT SHOULD I DO?
PAT
척
오오오오오
OHHHHHM

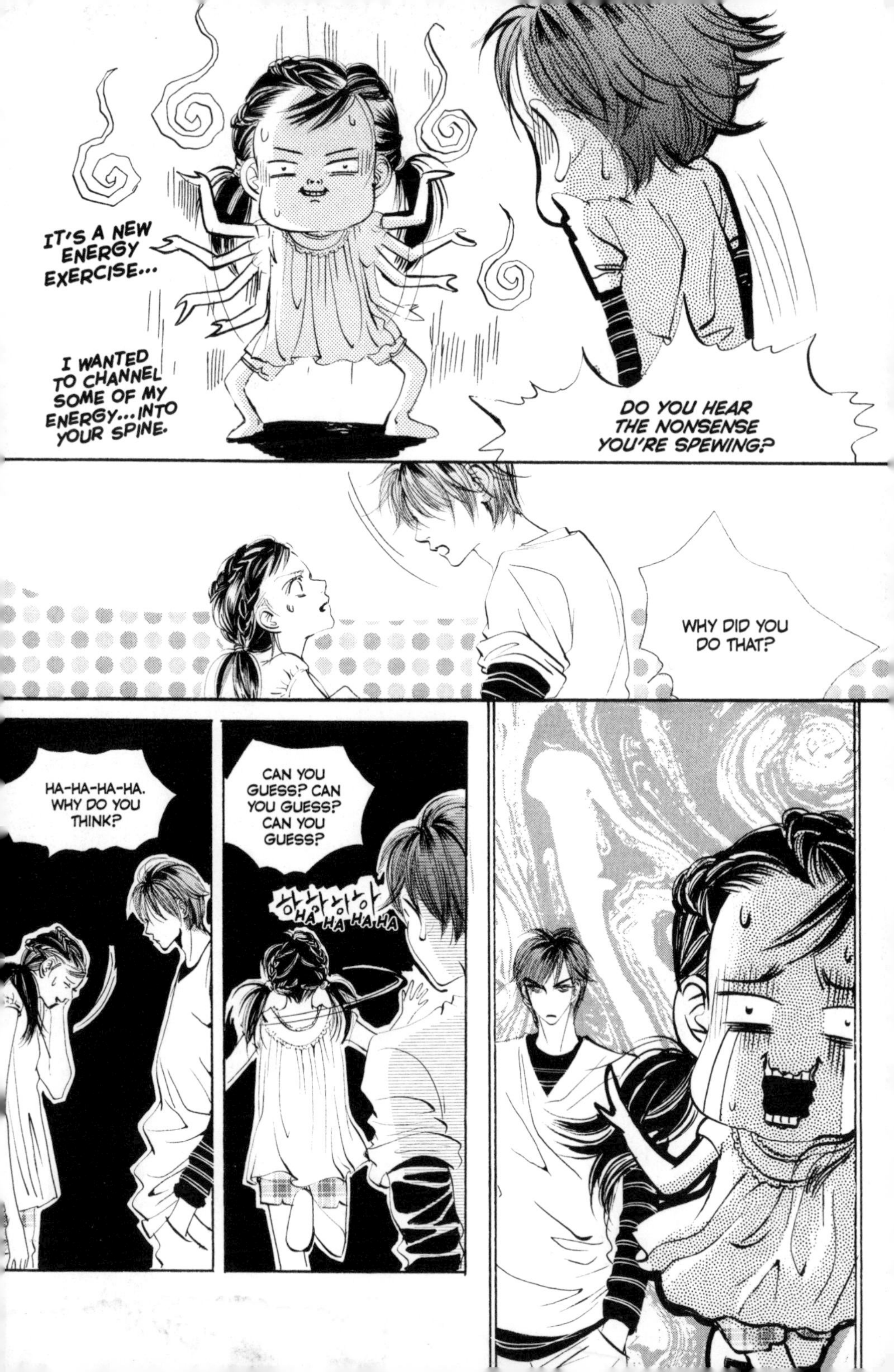

IT'S A NEW ENERGY EXERCISE...
I WANTED TO CHANNEL SOME OF MY ENERGY...INTO YOUR SPINE.
DO YOU HEAR THE NONSENSE YOU'RE SPEWING?
WHY DID YOU DO THAT?
HA-HA-HA-HA. WHY DO YOU THINK?
CAN YOU GUESS? CAN YOU GUESS? CAN YOU GUESS?
하하하하
HA HA HA HA

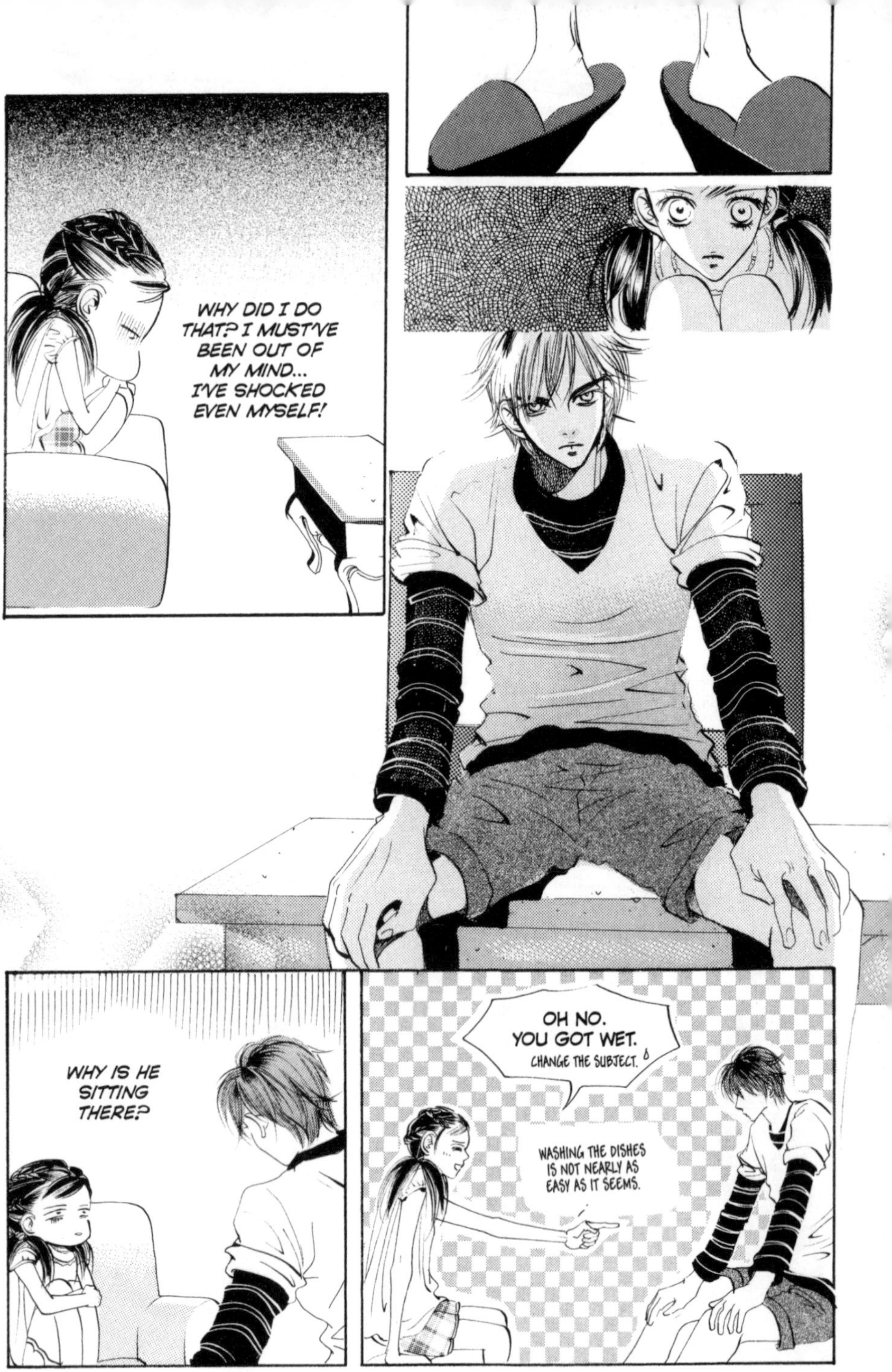
WHY DID I DO THAT? I MUST'VE BEEN OUT OF MY MIND... I'VE SHOCKED EVEN MYSELF!
WHY IS HE SITTING THERE?
OH NO. YOU GOT WET.
CHANGE THE SUBJECT.
WASHING THE DISHES IS NOT NEARLY AS EASY AS IT SEEMS.

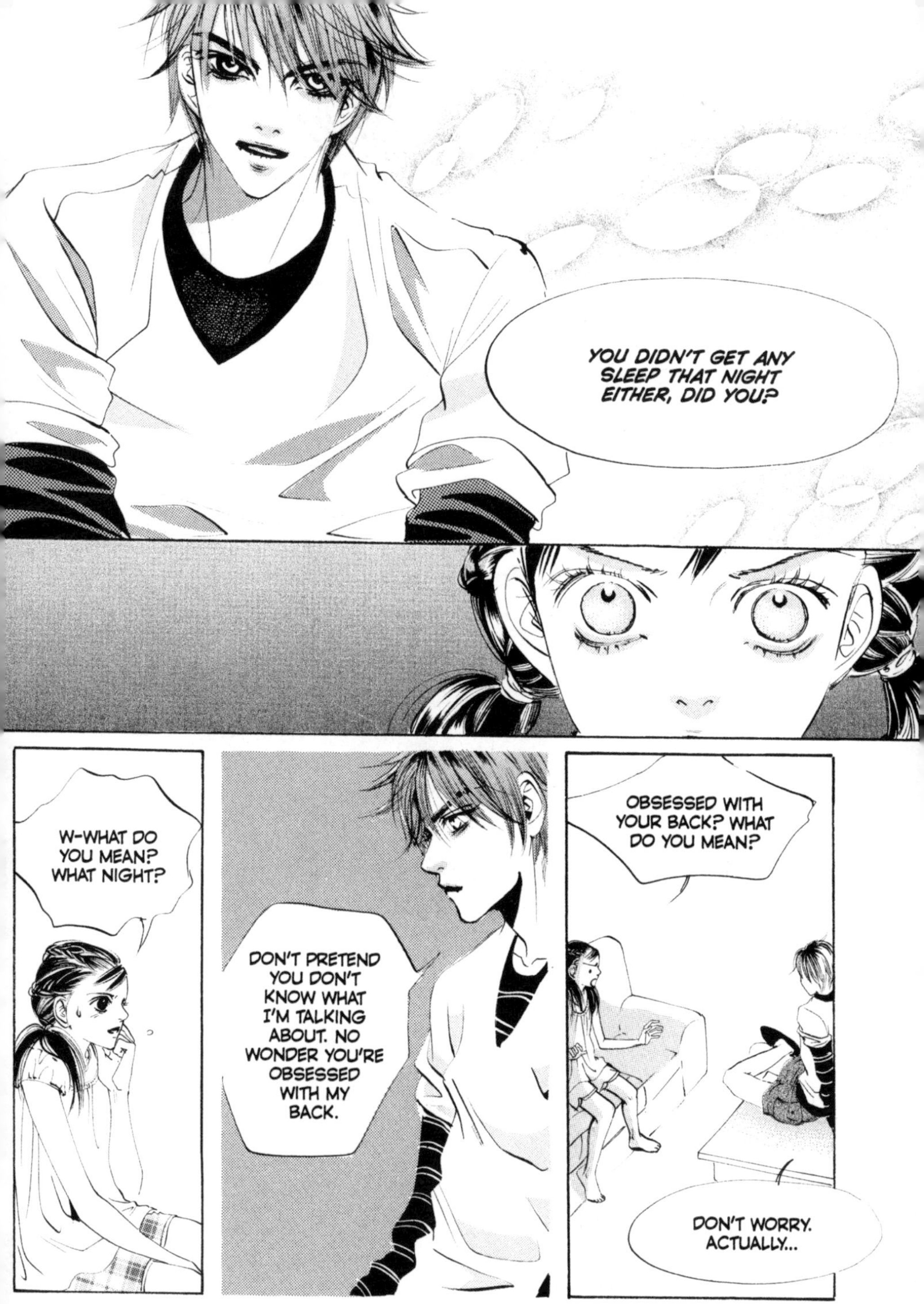
YOU DIDN'T GET ANY SLEEP THAT NIGHT EITHER, DID YOU?
W-WHAT DO YOU MEAN? WHAT NIGHT?
DON'T PRETEND YOU DON'T KNOW WHAT I'M TALKING ABOUT. NO WONDER YOU'RE OBSESSED WITH MY BACK.
OBSESSED WITH YOUR BACK? WHAT DO YOU MEAN?
DON'T WORRY. ACTUALLY...

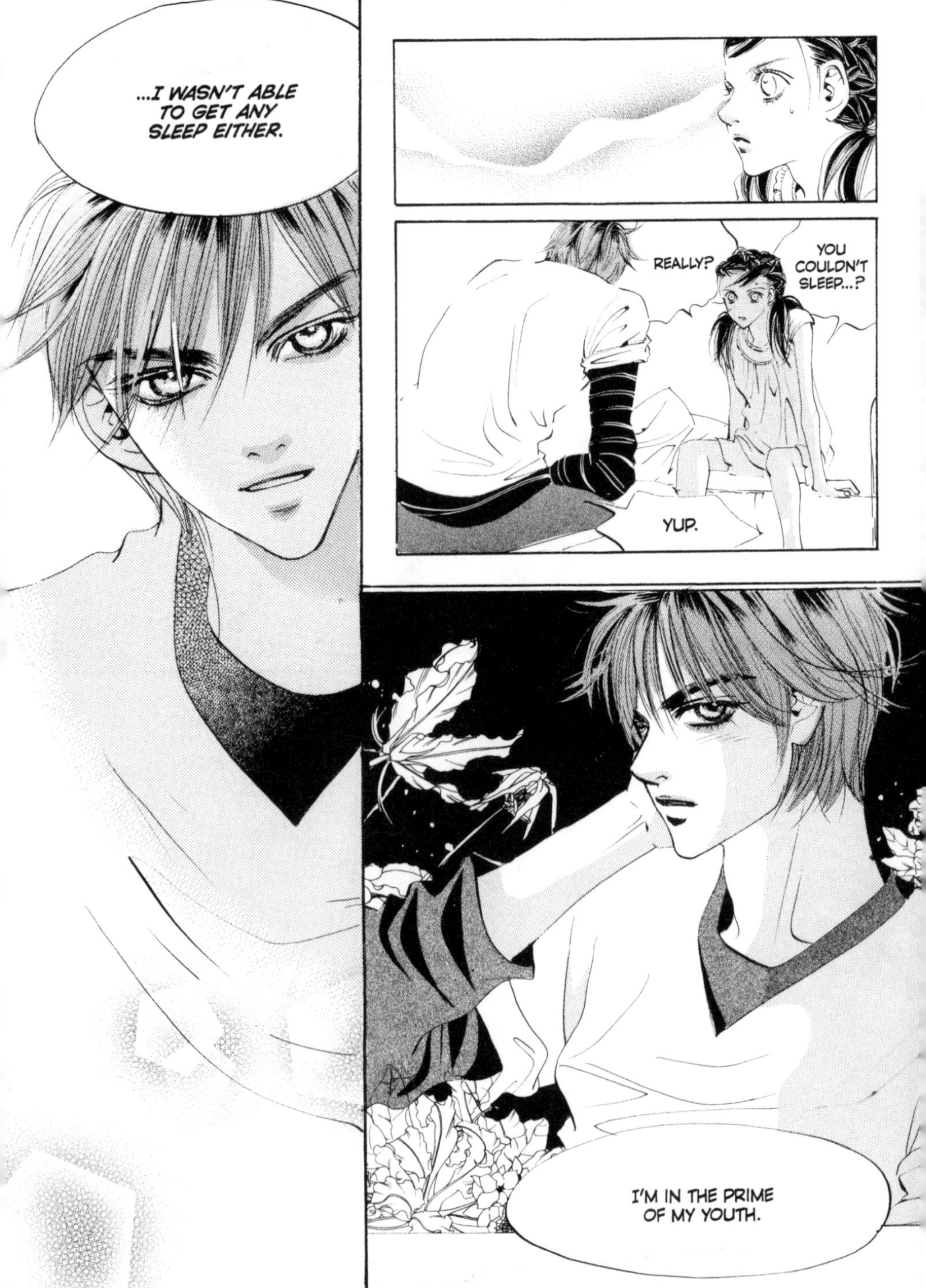
...I WASN'T ABLE TO GET ANY SLEEP EITHER.
REALLY?
YOU COULDN'T SLEEP...?
YUP.
I'M IN THE PRIME OF MY YOUTH.

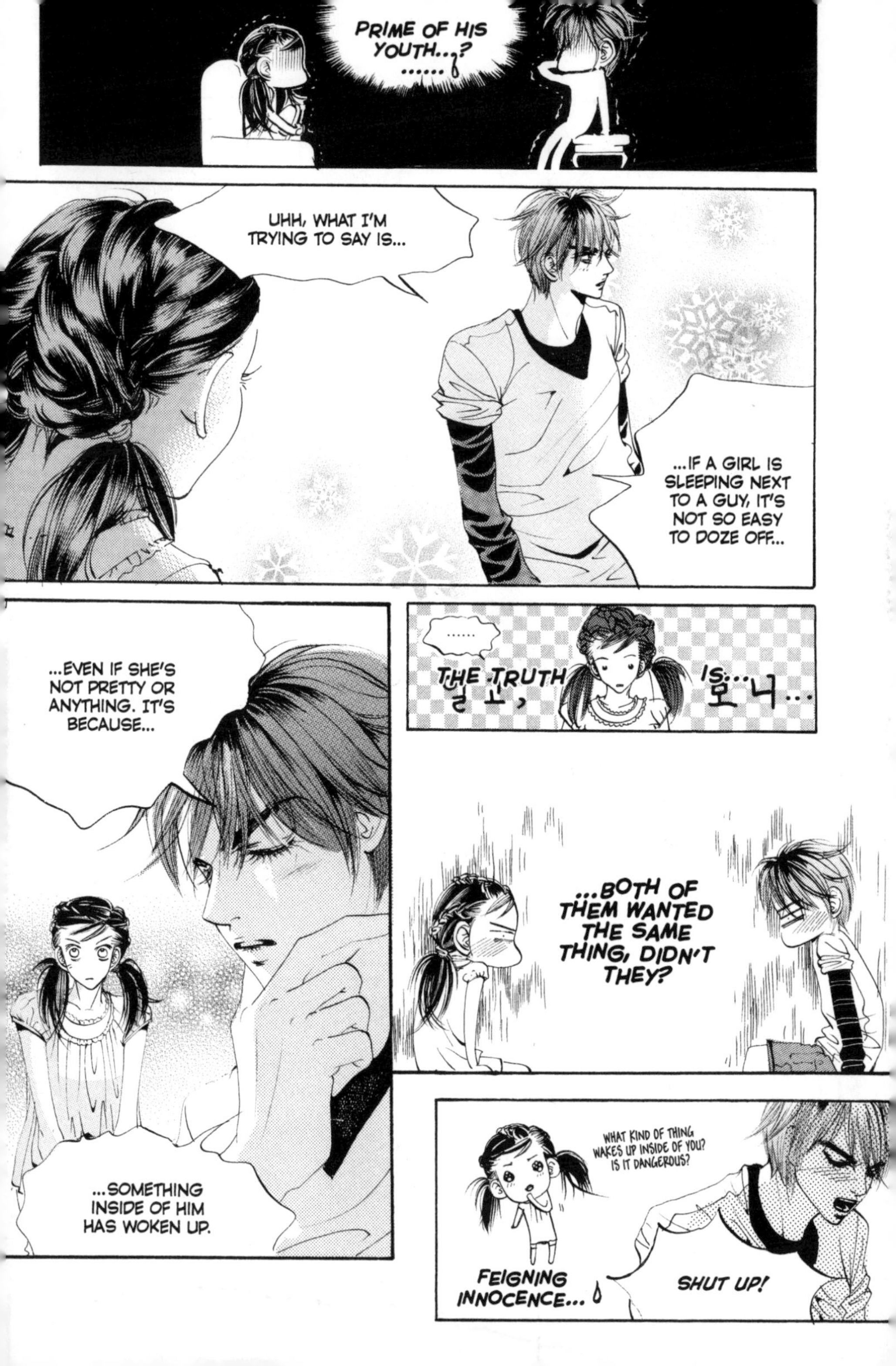
PRIME OF HIS YOUTH...?
......
UHH, WHAT I'M TRYING TO SAY IS...
...IF A GIRL IS SLEEPING NEXT TO A GUY, IT'S NOT SO EASY TO DOZE OFF...
...EVEN IF SHE'S NOT PRETTY OR ANYTHING. IT'S BECAUSE...
...SOMETHING INSIDE OF HIM HAS WOKEN UP.
......
THE TRUTH IS...
...BOTH OF THEM WANTED THE SAME THING, DIDN'T THEY?
FEIGNING INNOCENCE...
WHAT KIND OF THING WAKES UP INSIDE OF YOU? IS IT DANGEROUS?
SHUT UP!

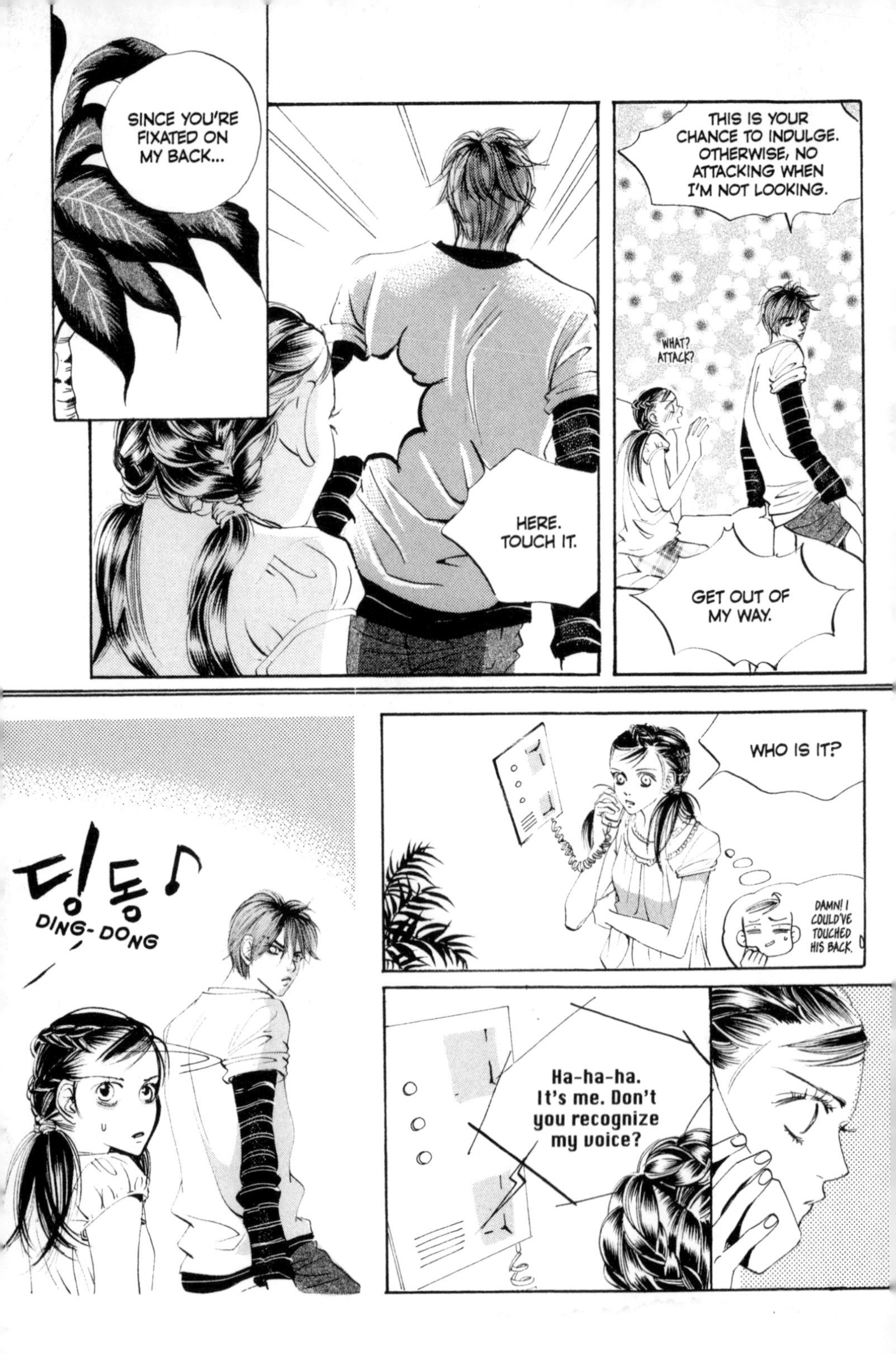
SINCE YOU'RE FIXATED ON MY BACK...
HERE. TOUCH IT.
THIS IS YOUR CHANCE TO INDULGE. OTHERWISE, NO ATTACKING WHEN I'M NOT LOOKING.
WHAT? ATTACK?
GET OUT OF MY WAY.
딩동♪
DING-DONG
WHO IS IT?
DAMN! I COULD'VE TOUCHED HIS BACK.
Ha-ha-ha. It's me. Don't you recognize my voice?

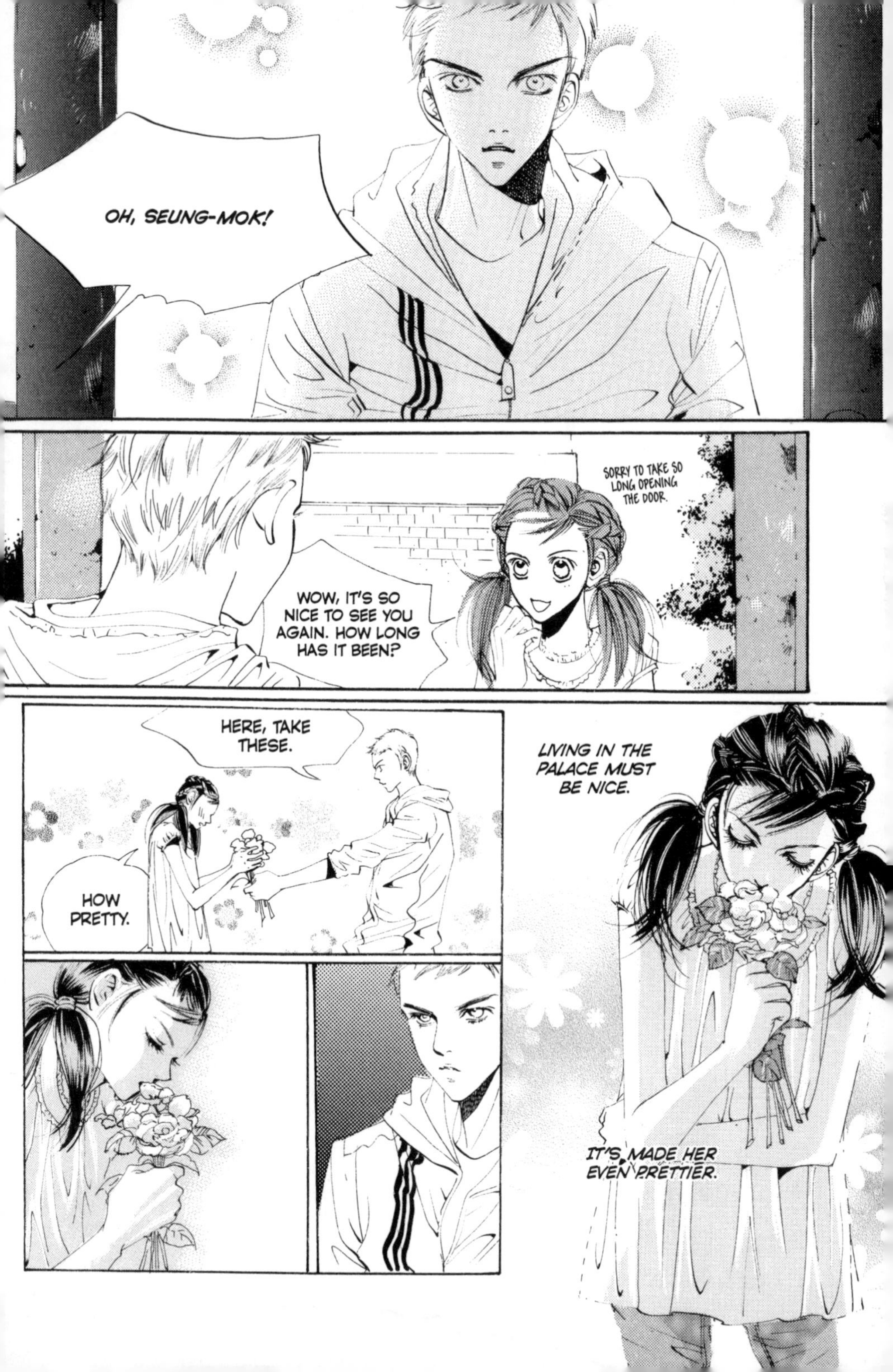
OH, SEUNG-MOK!
SORRY TO TAKE SO LONG OPENING THE DOOR.
WOW, IT'S SO NICE TO SEE YOU AGAIN. HOW LONG HAS IT BEEN?
HERE, TAKE THESE.
HOW PRETTY.
LIVING IN THE PALACE MUST BE NICE.
IT'S MADE HER EVEN PRETTIER.

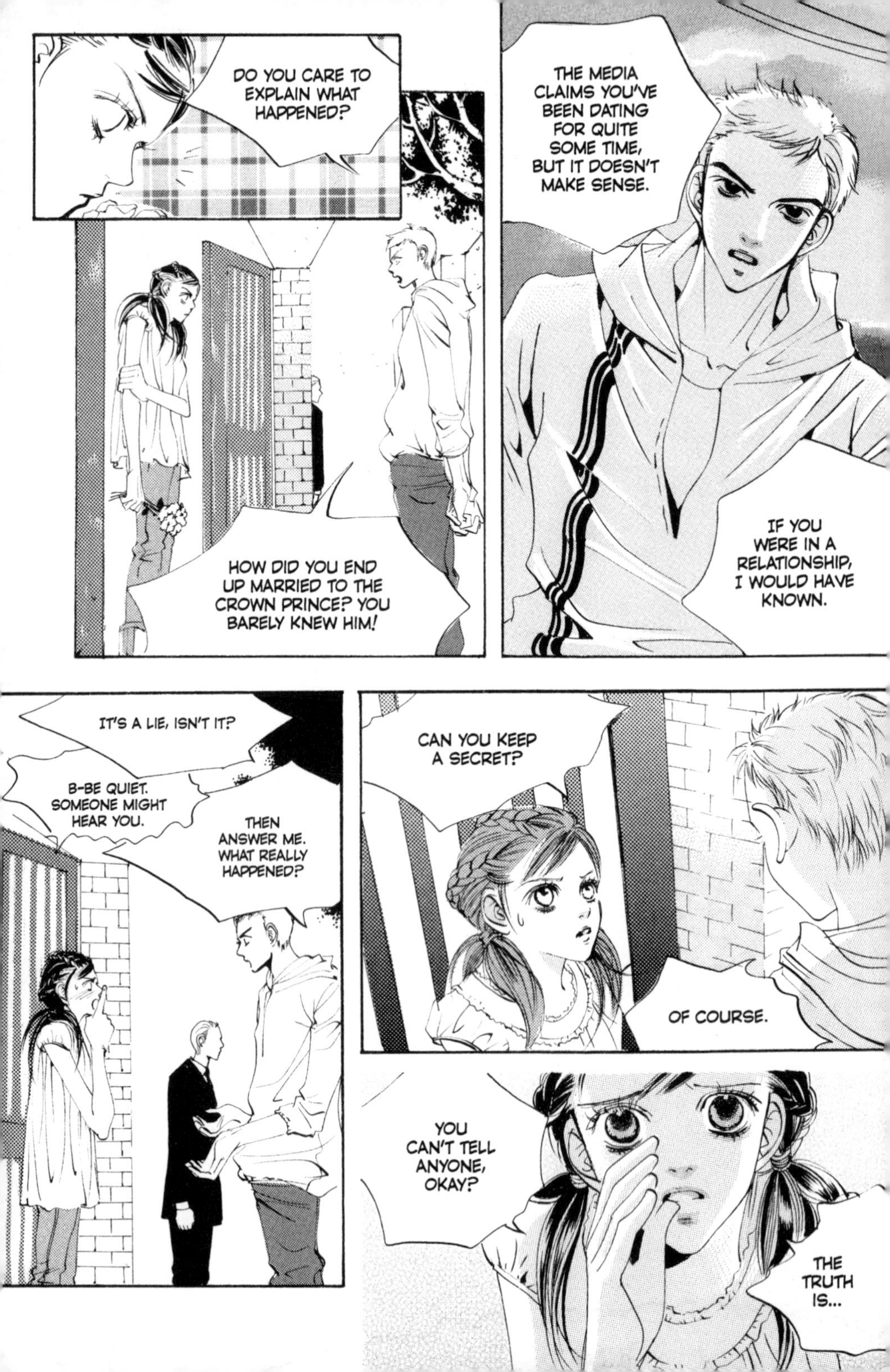
DO YOU CARE TO EXPLAIN WHAT HAPPENED?
HOW DID YOU END UP MARRIED TO THE CROWN PRINCE? YOU BARELY KNEW HIM!
THE MEDIA CLAIMS YOU'VE BEEN DATING FOR QUITE SOME TIME, BUT IT DOESN'T MAKE SENSE.
IF YOU WERE IN A RELATIONSHIP, I WOULD HAVE KNOWN.
IT'S A LIE, ISN'T IT?
B-BE QUIET. SOMEONE MIGHT HEAR YOU.
THEN ANSWER ME. WHAT REALLY HAPPENED?
CAN YOU KEEP A SECRET?
OF COURSE.
YOU CAN'T TELL ANYONE, OKAY?
THE TRUTH IS...

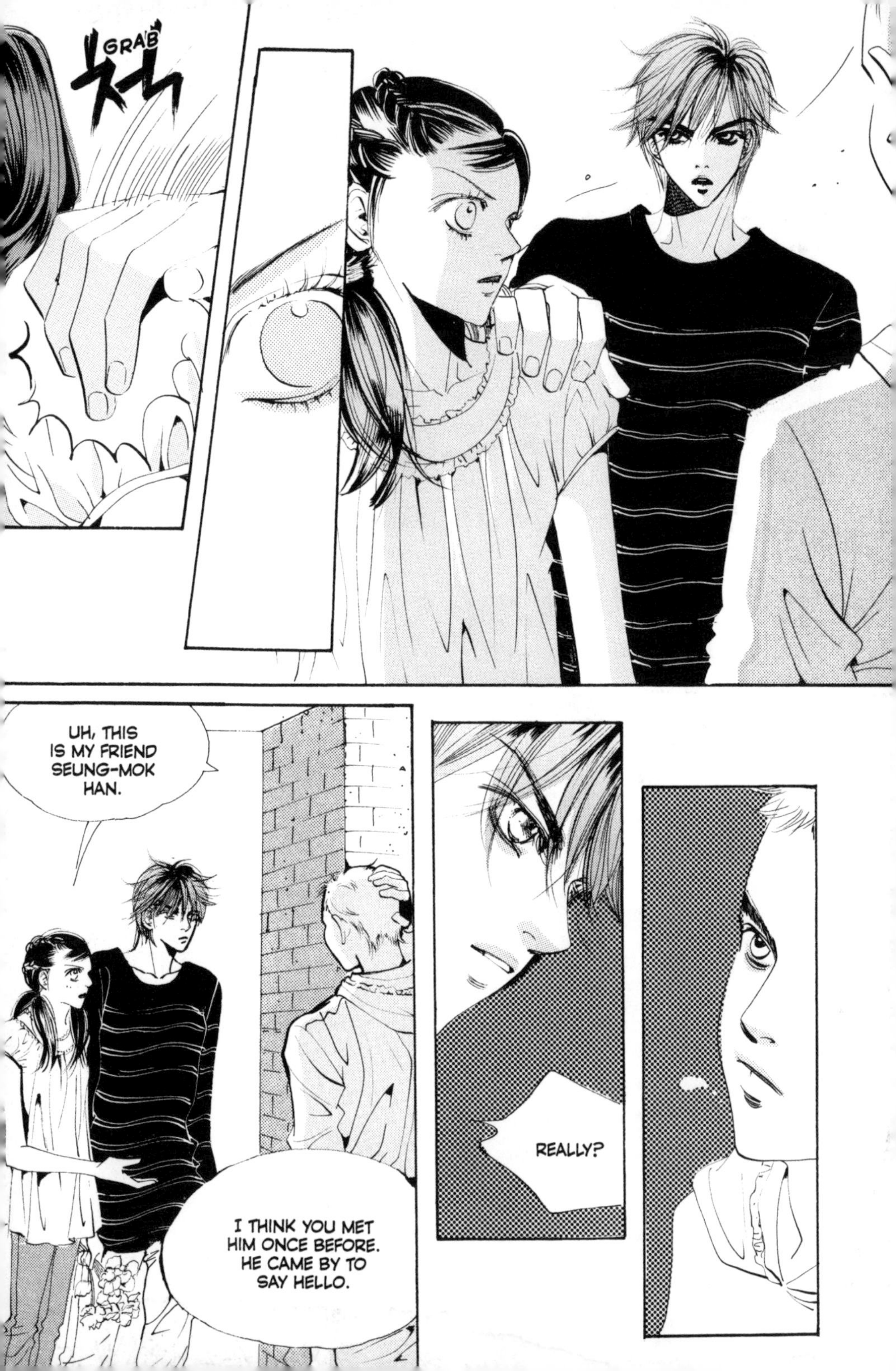
GRAB
UH, THIS IS MY FRIEND SEUNG-MOK HAN.
I THINK YOU MET HIM ONCE BEFORE. HE CAME BY TO SAY HELLO.
REALLY?

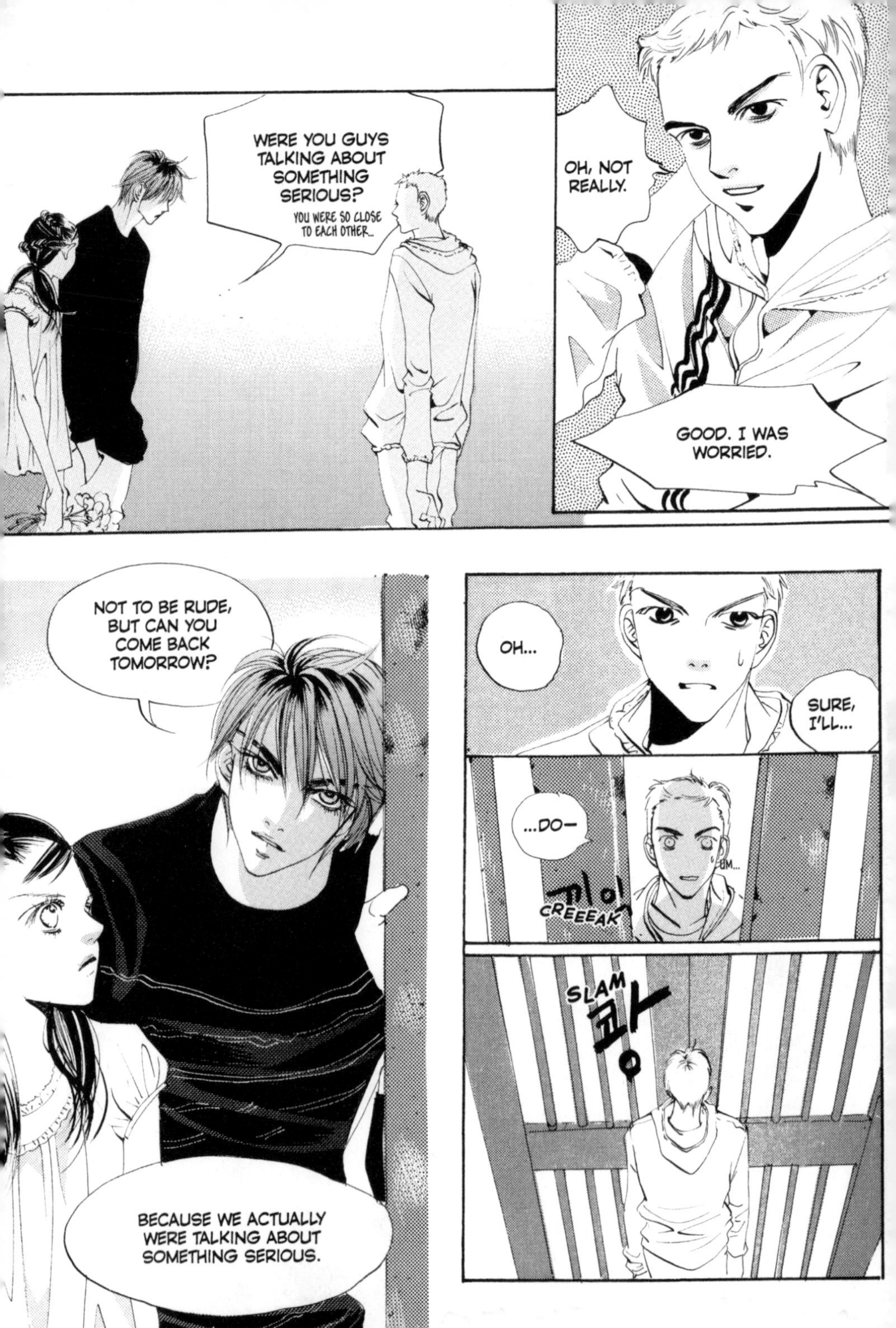
WERE YOU GUYS TALKING ABOUT SOMETHING SERIOUS?
YOU WERE SO CLOSE TO EACH OTHER...
OH, NOT REALLY.
GOOD. I WAS WORRIED.
NOT TO BE RUDE, BUT CAN YOU COME BACK TOMORROW?
BECAUSE WE ACTUALLY WERE TALKING ABOUT SOMETHING SERIOUS.
OH...
SURE, I'LL...
...DO—
UM...
끼이
CREEEAK
SLAM
쾅

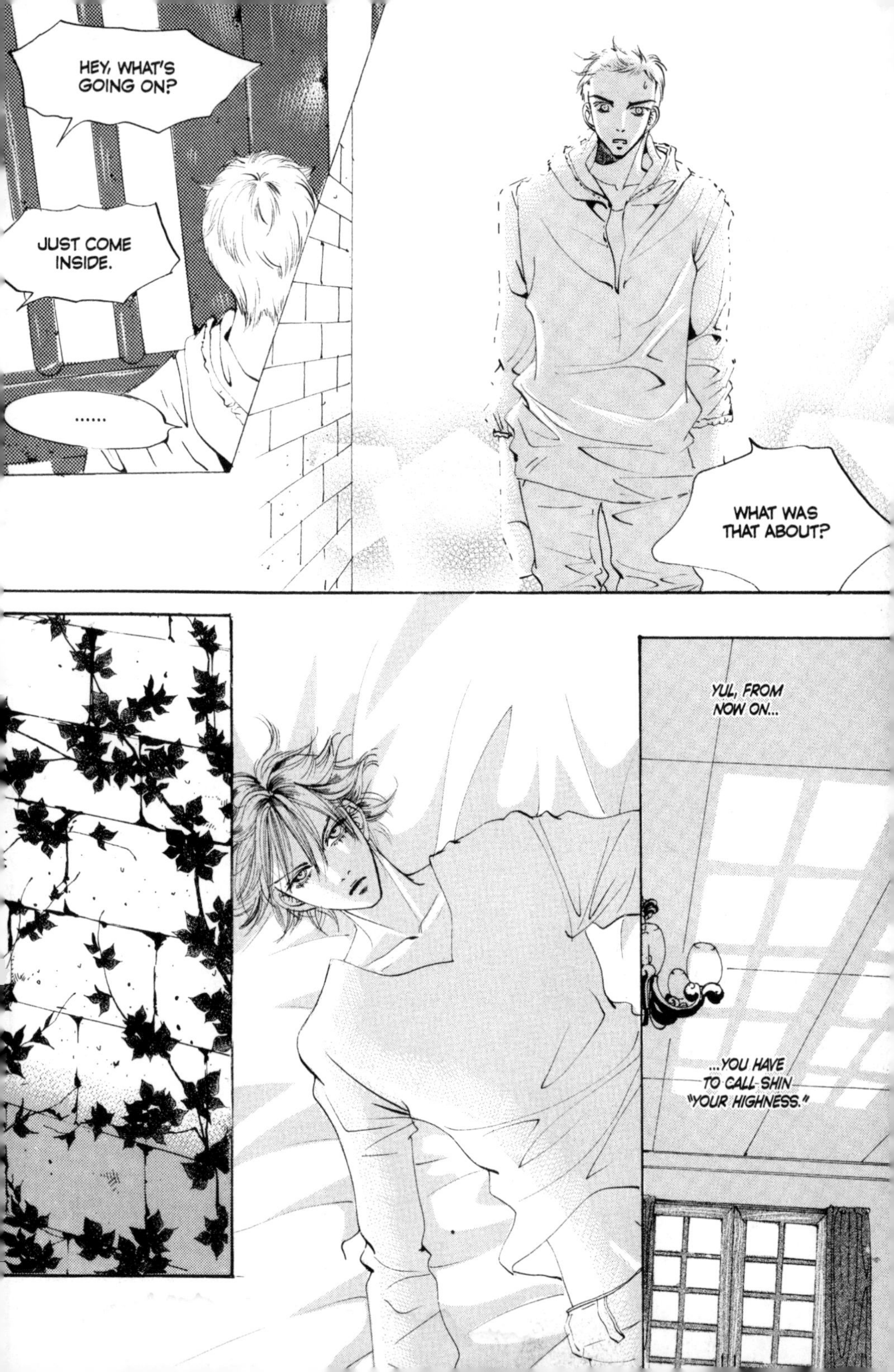
HEY, WHAT'S GOING ON?
JUST COME INSIDE.
......
WHAT WAS THAT ABOUT?
YUL, FROM NOW ON...
...YOU HAVE TO CALL SHIN "YOUR HIGHNESS."

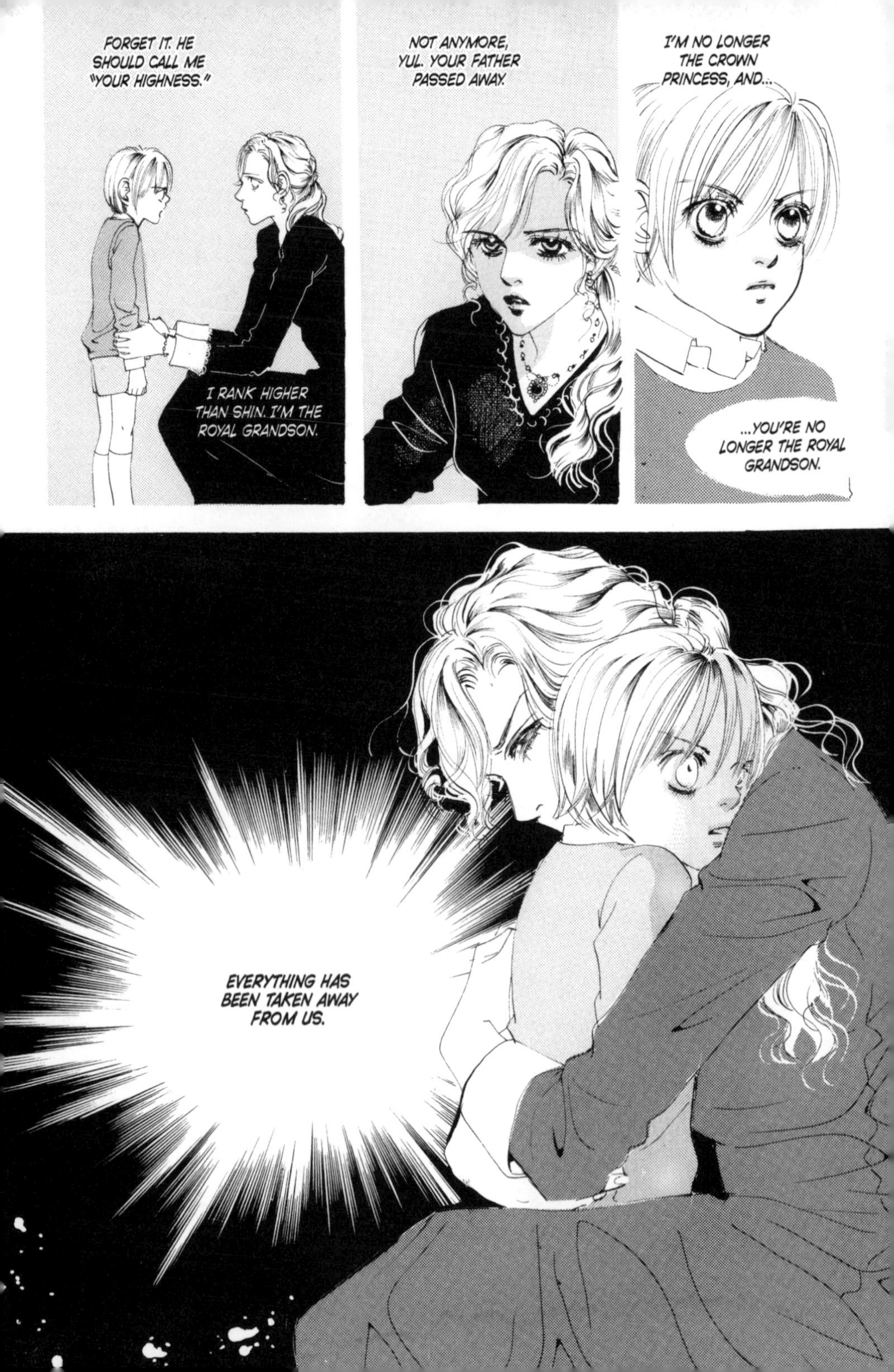
FORGET IT. HE SHOULD CALL ME "YOUR HIGHNESS."
I RANK HIGHER THAN SHIN. I'M THE ROYAL GRANDSON.
NOT ANYMORE, YUL. YOUR FATHER PASSED AWAY.
I'M NO LONGER THE CROWN PRINCESS, AND...
...YOU'RE NO LONGER THE ROYAL GRANDSON.
EVERYTHING HAS BEEN TAKEN AWAY FROM US.

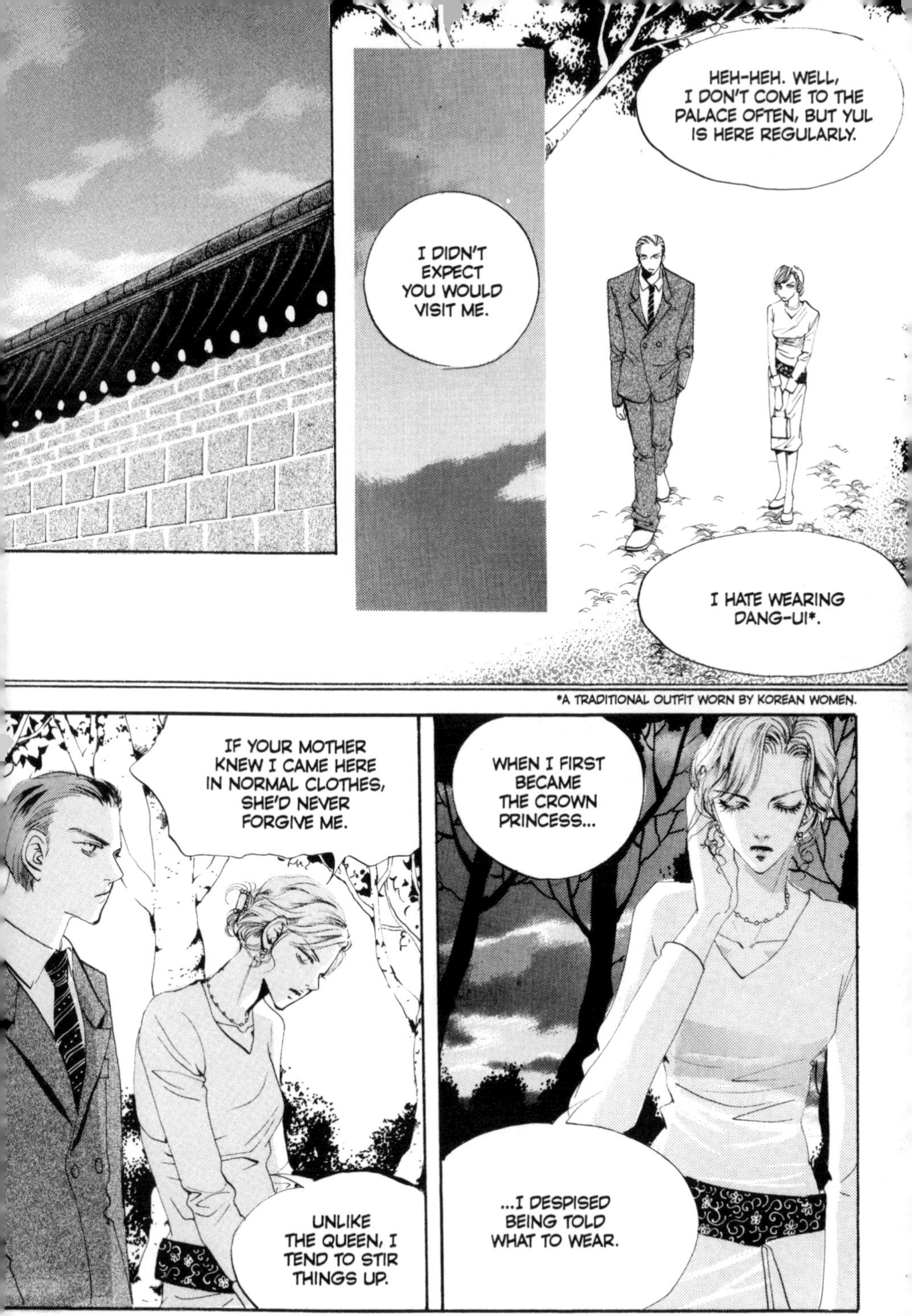
I DIDN'T EXPECT YOU WOULD VISIT ME.
HEH-HEH. WELL, I DON'T COME TO THE PALACE OFTEN, BUT YUL IS HERE REGULARLY.
I HATE WEARING DANG-UI*.
IF YOUR MOTHER KNEW I CAME HERE IN NORMAL CLOTHES, SHE'D NEVER FORGIVE ME.
UNLIKE THE QUEEN, I TEND TO STIR THINGS UP.
WHEN I FIRST BECAME THE CROWN PRINCESS...
...I DESPISED BEING TOLD WHAT TO WEAR.

*A TRADITIONAL OUTFIT WORN BY KOREAN WOMEN.

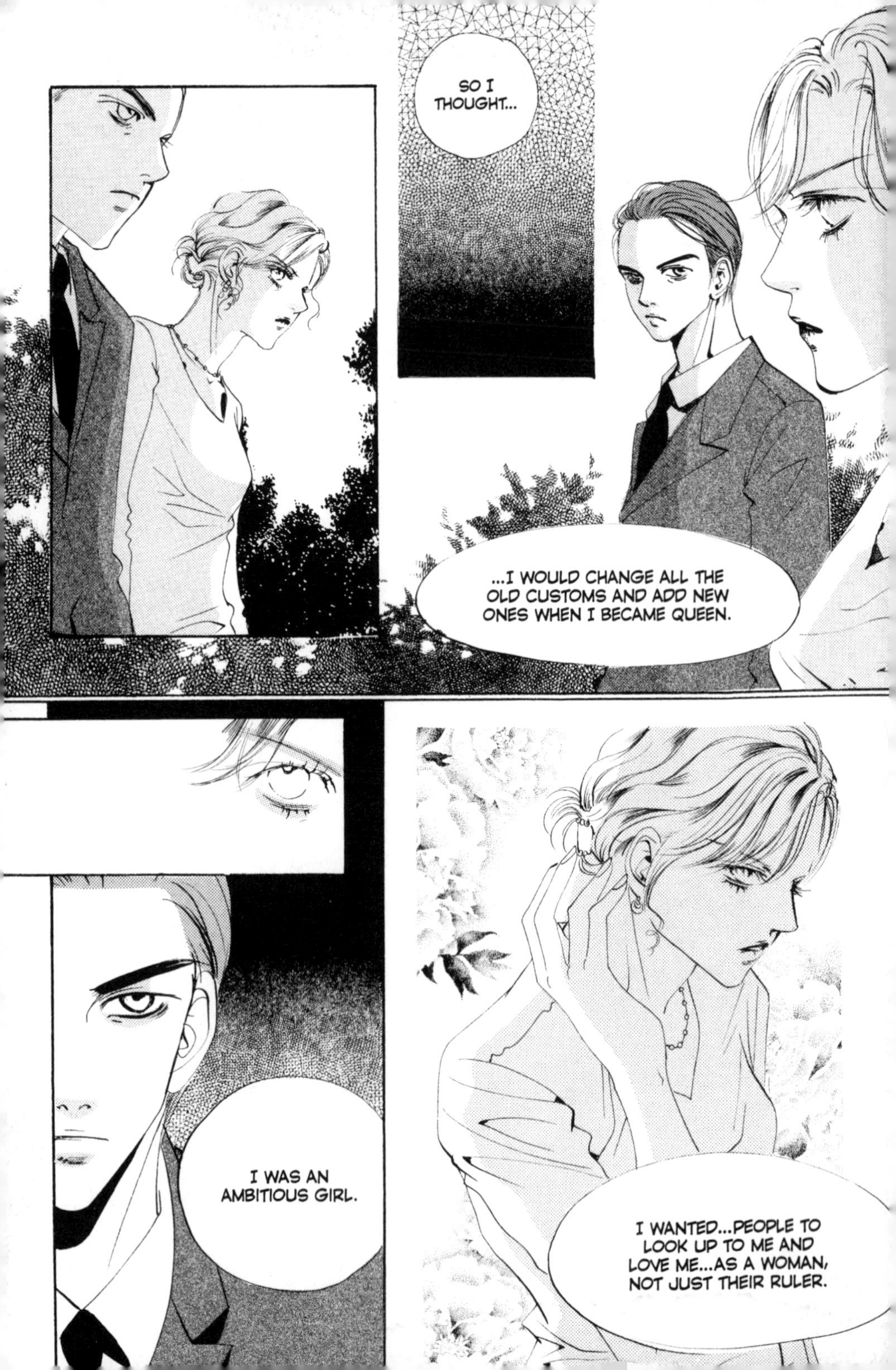
SO I THOUGHT...
...I WOULD CHANGE ALL THE OLD CUSTOMS AND ADD NEW ONES WHEN I BECAME QUEEN.
I WAS AN AMBITIOUS GIRL.
I WANTED...PEOPLE TO LOOK UP TO ME AND LOVE ME...AS A WOMAN, NOT JUST THEIR RULER.

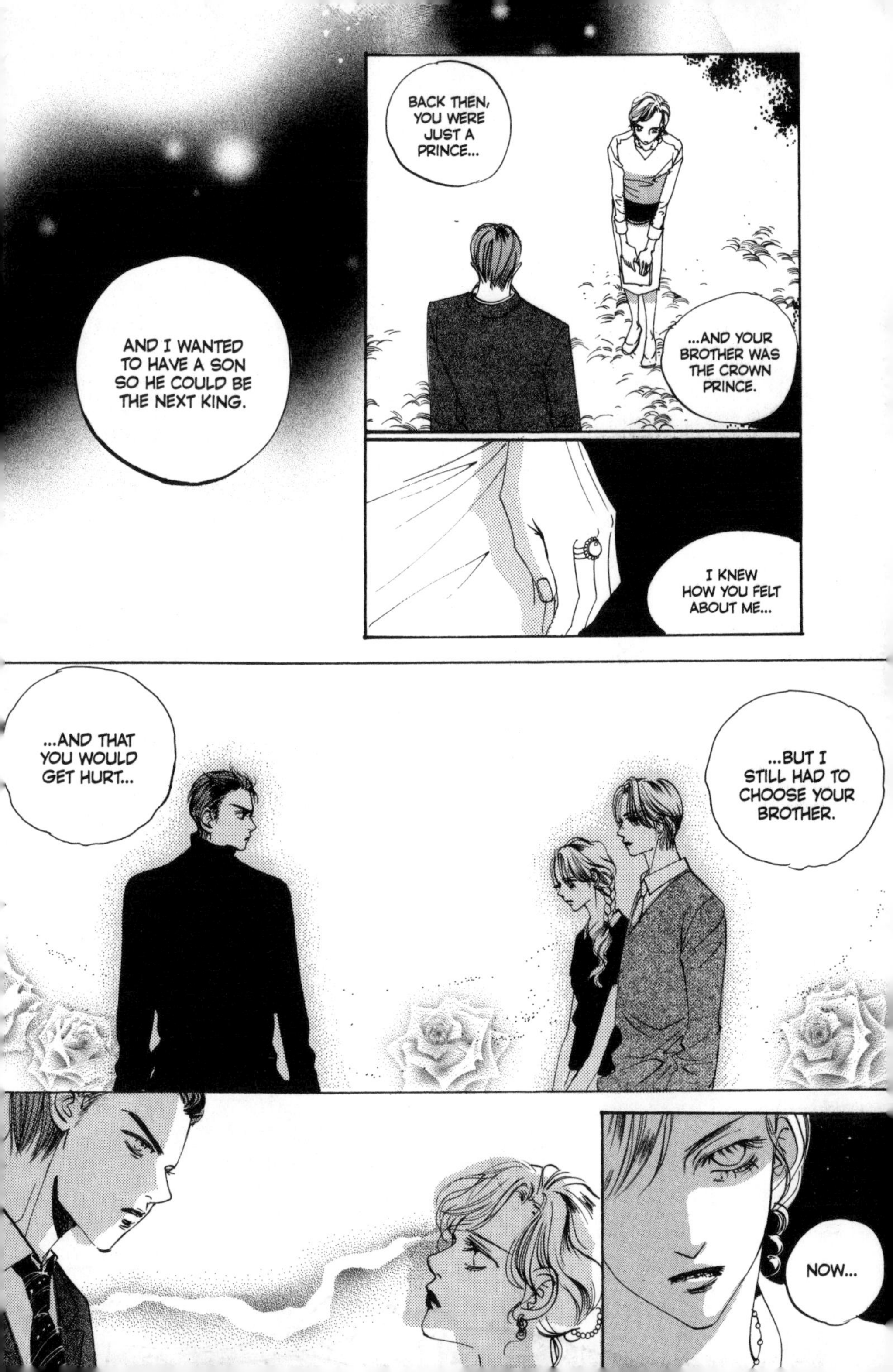
AND I WANTED TO HAVE A SON SO HE COULD BE THE NEXT KING.
BACK THEN, YOU WERE JUST A PRINCE...
...AND YOUR BROTHER WAS THE CROWN PRINCE.
I KNEW HOW YOU FELT ABOUT ME...
...AND THAT YOU WOULD GET HURT...
...BUT I STILL HAD TO CHOOSE YOUR BROTHER.
NOW...

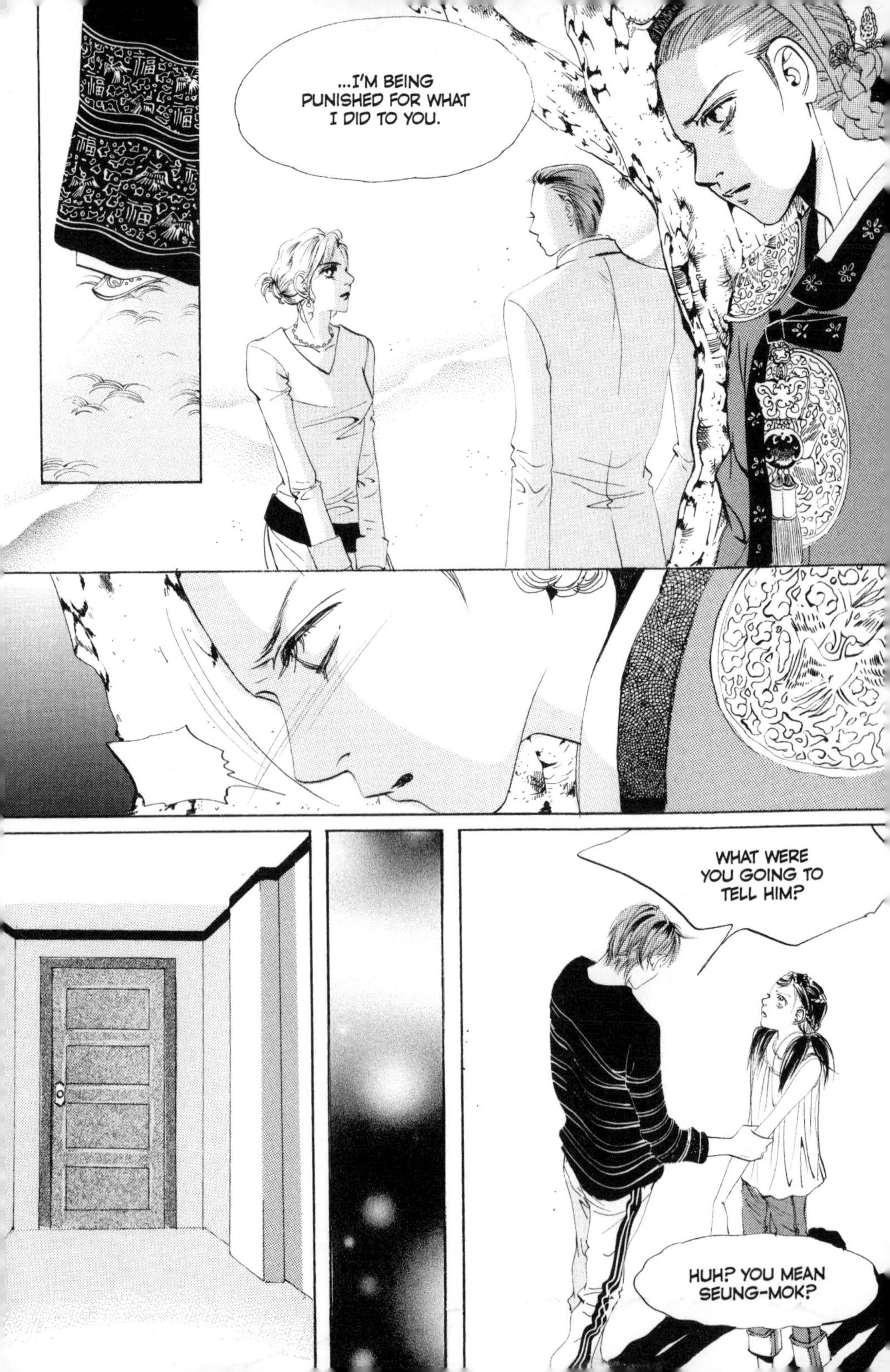
...I'M BEING PUNISHED FOR WHAT I DID TO YOU.
WHAT WERE YOU GOING TO TELL HIM?
HUH? YOU MEAN SEUNG-MOK?

HE WANTED TO KNOW HOW I ENDED UP MARRIED TO YOU.

AND YOU WERE GOING TO TELL HIM THE TRUTH?

HE KEPT ASKING ME.

THE NEWS MEDIA IS REPORTING THAT WE HAD A LONG-TERM RELATIONSHIP. YOU KNOW THAT, RIGHT?

IF PEOPLE FIND OUT THE TRUTH BECAUSE OF YOUR BIG MOUTH, WE'LL BE A LAUGHINGSTOCK.

LAUGHING-STOCK?

DON'T YOU THINK IT'S STUPID THAT WE GOT MARRIED BECAUSE OUR GRANDFATHERS MADE A DEAL WHEN WE WERE BABIES? IT'S LIKE SOME NONSENSE OUT OF A CHEESY FAIRY TALE.

BEAUTY

HEY, YOU JERK!

W-WELL, I GUESS... YOU'RE RIGHT.

SEUNG-MOK HAS A BIG MOUTH TOO.

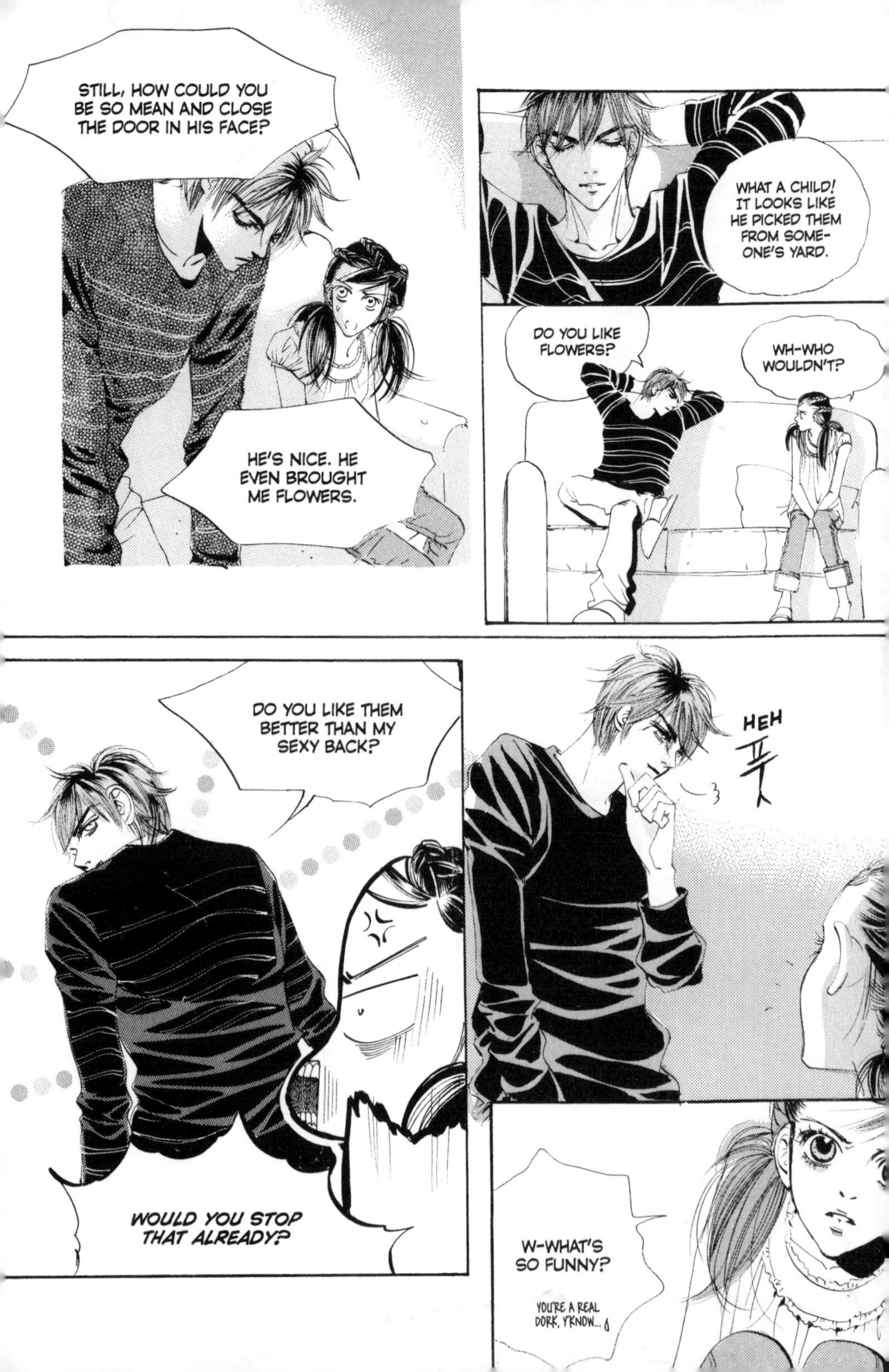
STILL, HOW COULD YOU BE SO MEAN AND CLOSE THE DOOR IN HIS FACE?
HE'S NICE. HE EVEN BROUGHT ME FLOWERS.
WHAT A CHILD! IT LOOKS LIKE HE PICKED THEM FROM SOME-ONE'S YARD.
DO YOU LIKE FLOWERS?
WH-WHO WOULDN'T?
DO YOU LIKE THEM BETTER THAN MY SEXY BACK?
WOULD YOU STOP THAT ALREADY?
HEH
W-WHAT'S SO FUNNY?
YOU'RE A REAL DORK, Y'KNOW...

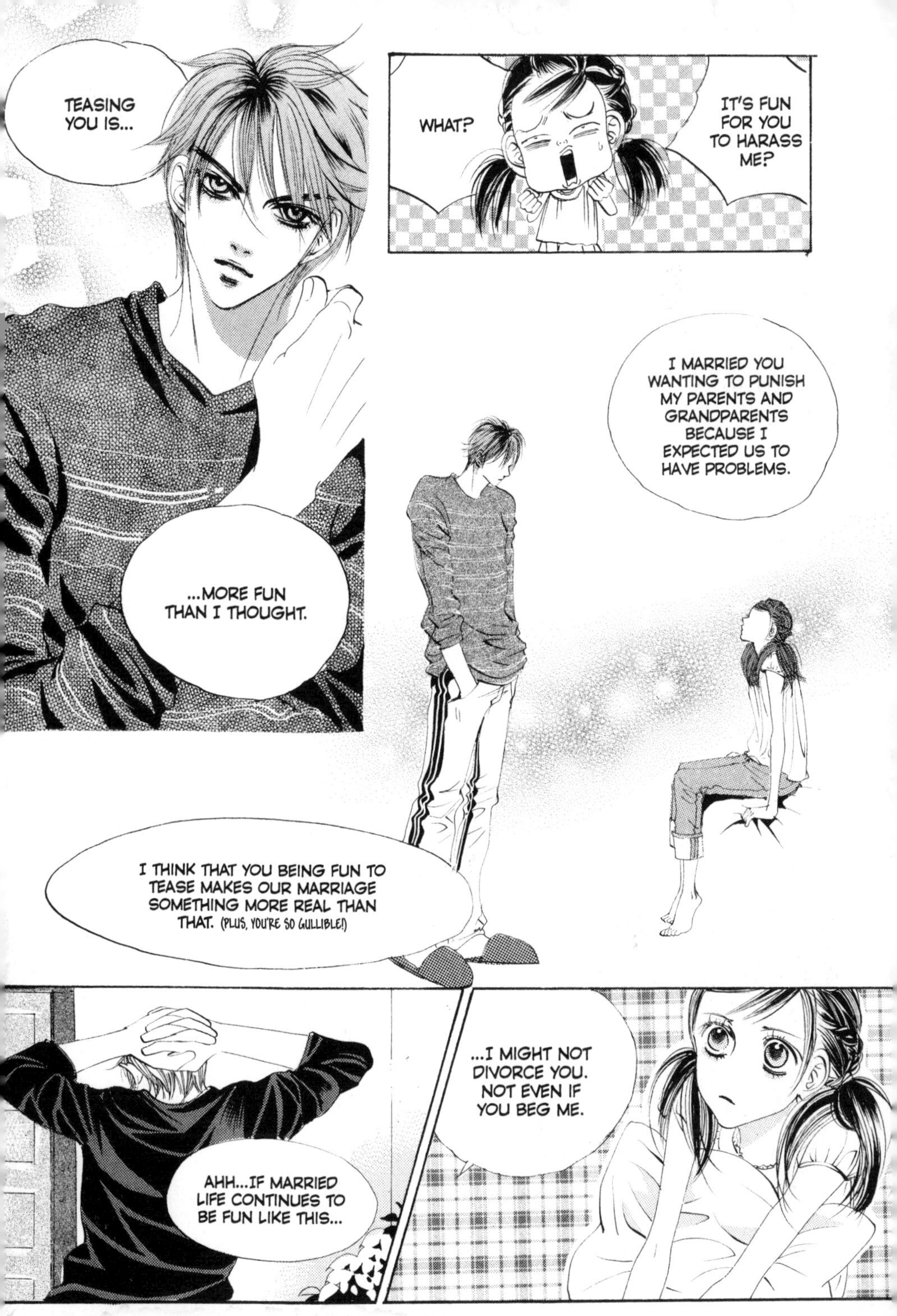
TEASING YOU IS...
...MORE FUN THAN I THOUGHT.
WHAT?
IT'S FUN FOR YOU TO HARASS ME?
I MARRIED YOU WANTING TO PUNISH MY PARENTS AND GRANDPARENTS BECAUSE I EXPECTED US TO HAVE PROBLEMS.
I THINK THAT YOU BEING FUN TO TEASE MAKES OUR MARRIAGE SOMETHING MORE REAL THAN THAT. (PLUS, YOU'RE SO GULLIBLE!)
AHH...IF MARRIED LIFE CONTINUES TO BE FUN LIKE THIS...
...I MIGHT NOT DIVORCE YOU. NOT EVEN IF YOU BEG ME.

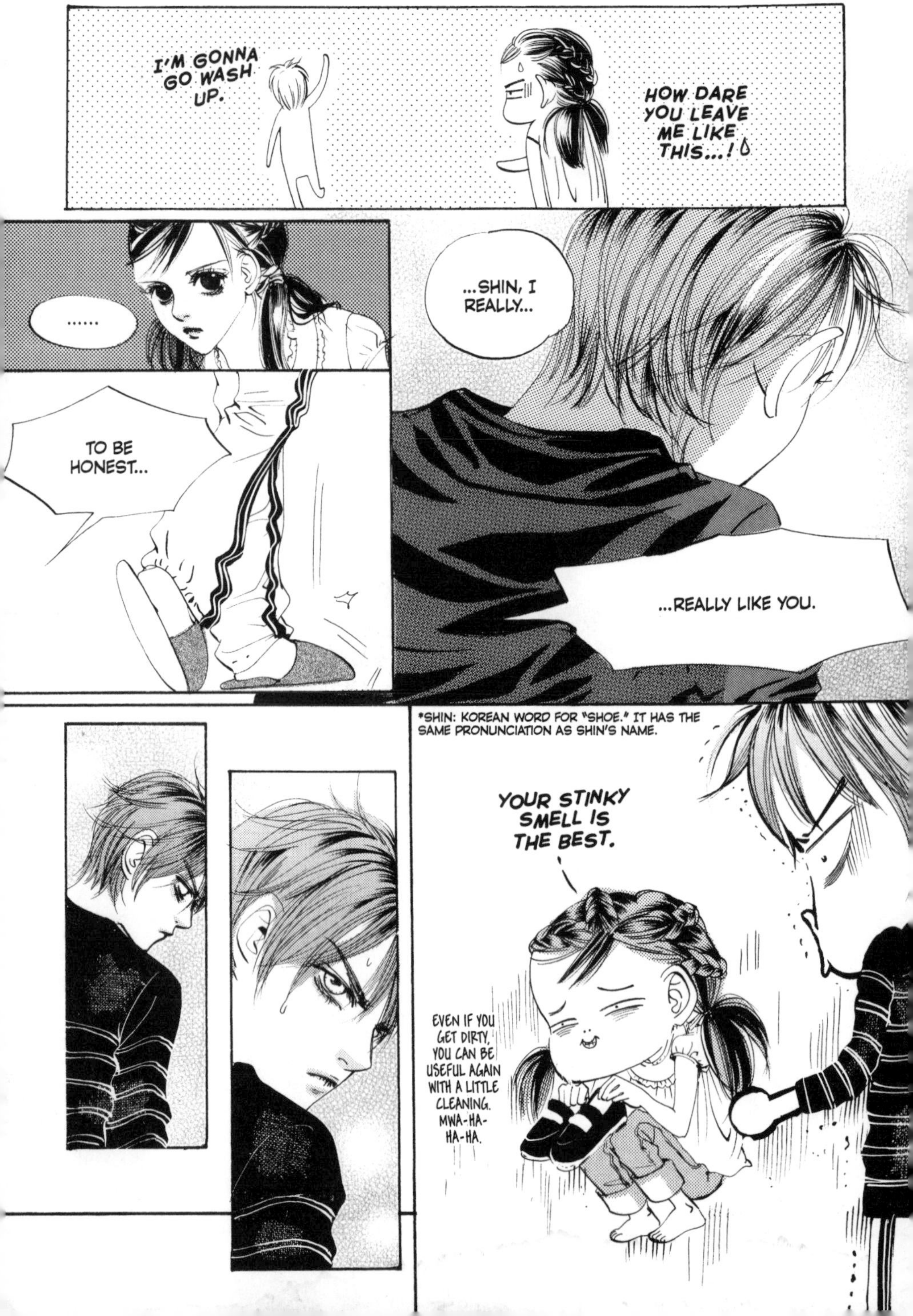
I'M GONNA GO WASH UP.
HOW DARE YOU LEAVE ME LIKE THIS...!
......
...SHIN, I REALLY...
TO BE HONEST...
...REALLY LIKE YOU.
*SHIN: KOREAN WORD FOR "SHOE." IT HAS THE SAME PRONUNCIATION AS SHIN'S NAME.
YOUR STINKY SMELL IS THE BEST.
EVEN IF YOU GET DIRTY, YOU CAN BE USEFUL AGAIN WITH A LITTLE CLEANING. MWA-HA-HA-HA.

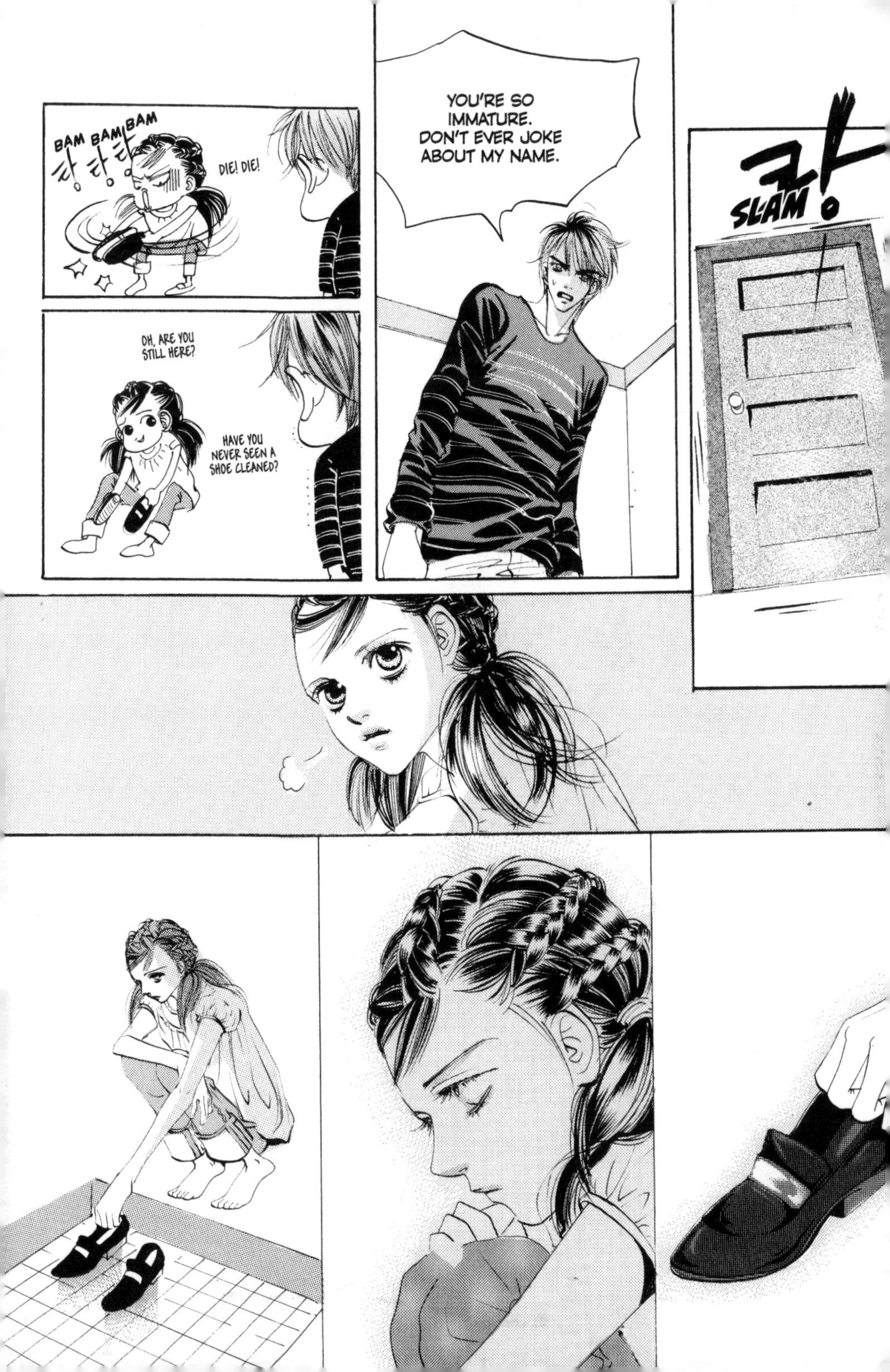

BAM BAM BAM
탕 탕 탕
DIE! DIE!
OH, ARE YOU STILL HERE?
HAVE YOU NEVER SEEN A SHOE CLEANED?
YOU'RE SO IMMATURE. DON'T EVER JOKE ABOUT MY NAME.
쾅!
SLAM!

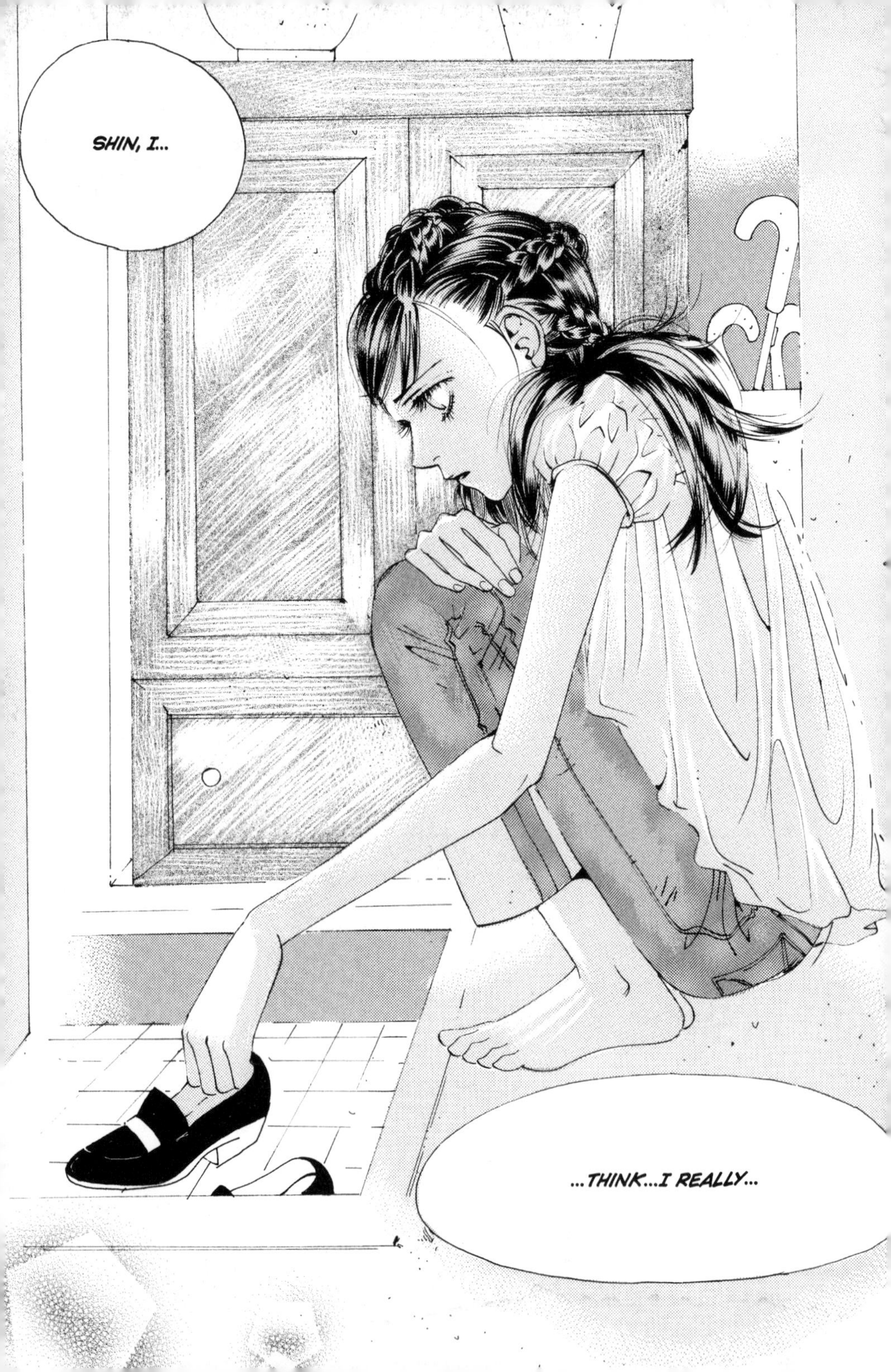
SHIN, I...
...THINK...I REALLY...

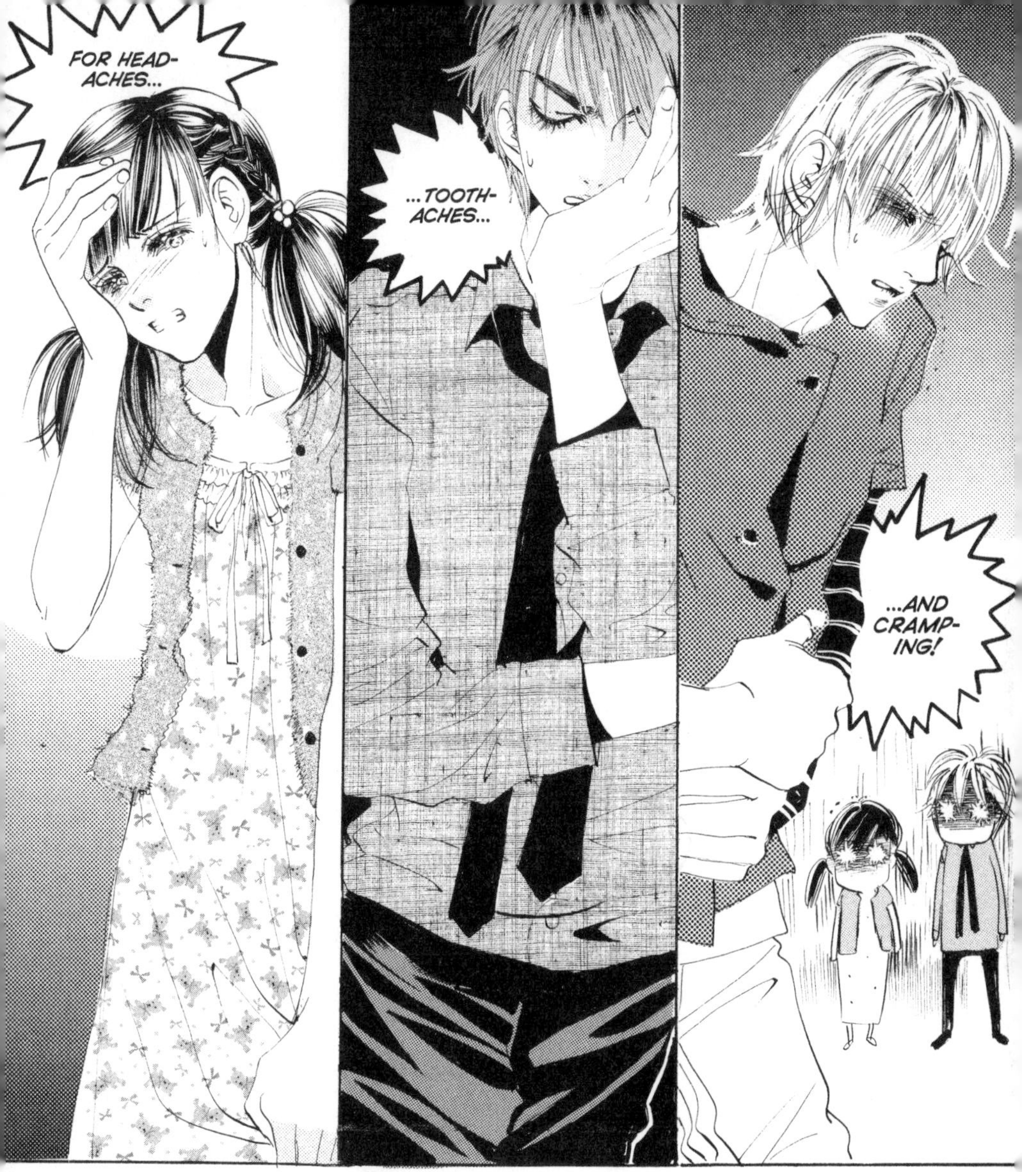
FOR HEAD-ACHES...
...TOOTH-ACHES...
...AND CRAMP-ING!

THE ROYAL PALACE
Goong

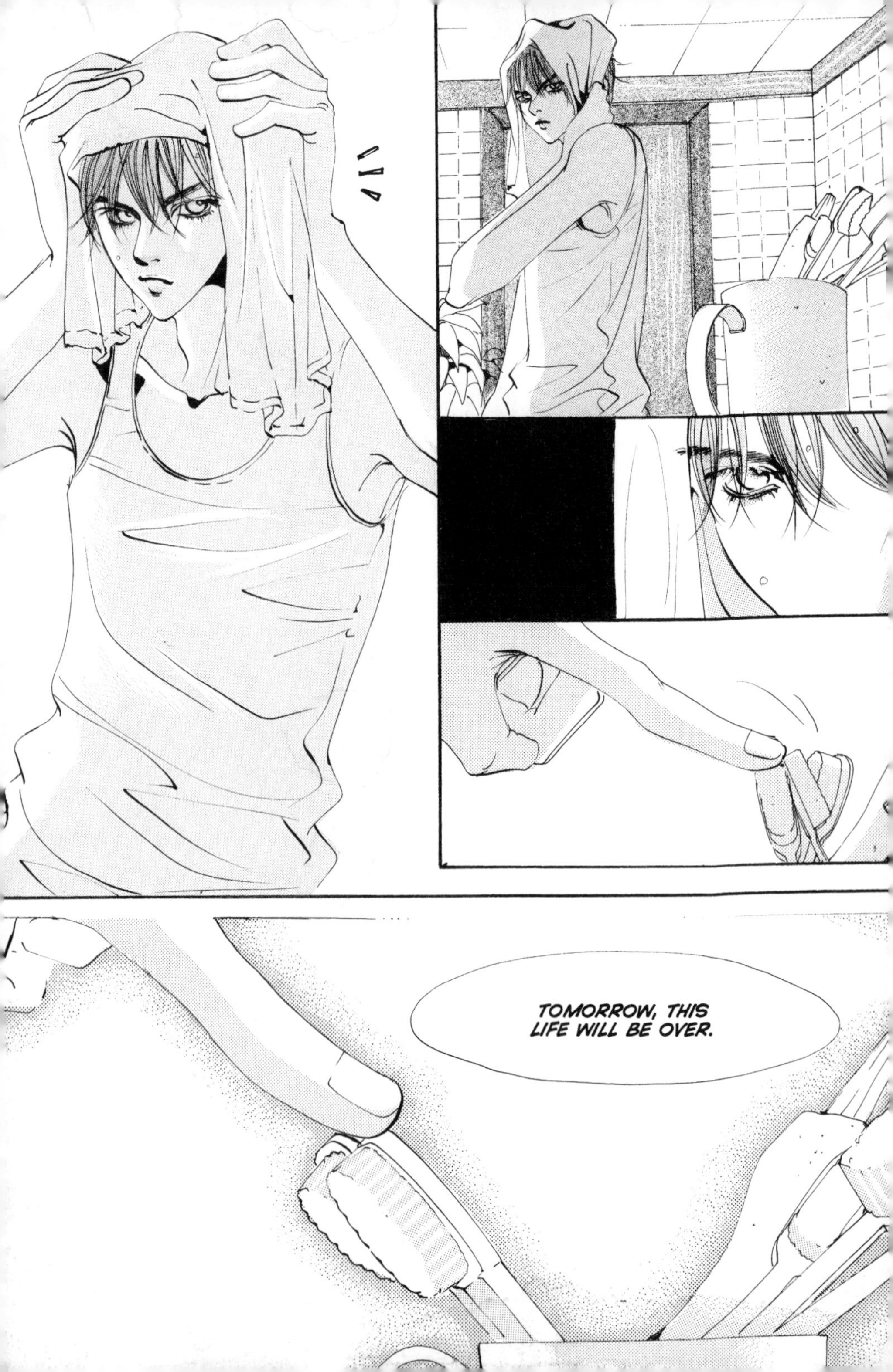
TOMORROW, THIS LIFE WILL BE OVER.

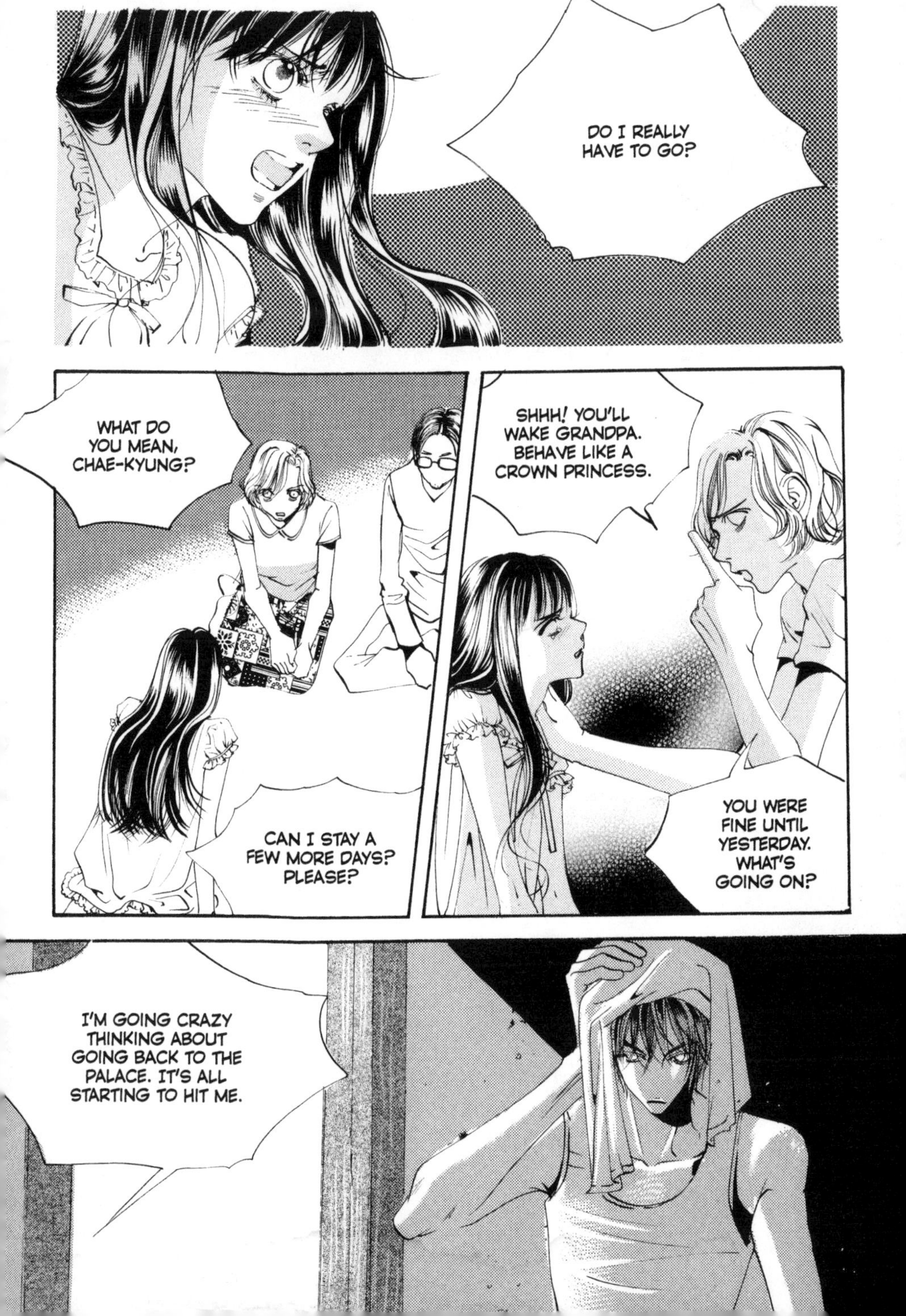
DO I REALLY HAVE TO GO?
WHAT DO YOU MEAN, CHAE-KYUNG?
CAN I STAY A FEW MORE DAYS? PLEASE?
SHHH! YOU'LL WAKE GRANDPA. BEHAVE LIKE A CROWN PRINCESS.
YOU WERE FINE UNTIL YESTERDAY. WHAT'S GOING ON?
I'M GOING CRAZY THINKING ABOUT GOING BACK TO THE PALACE. IT'S ALL STARTING TO HIT ME.

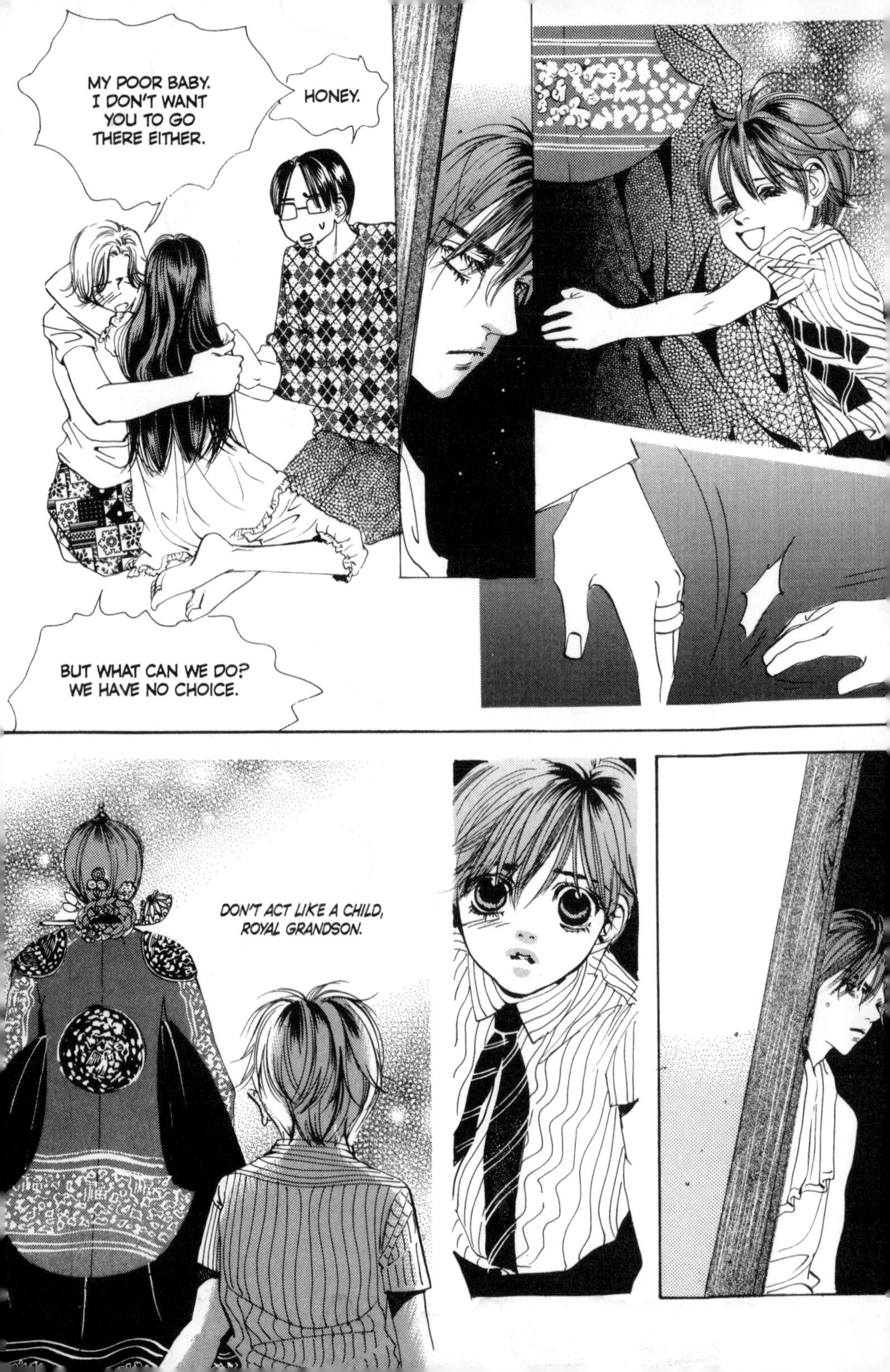
MY POOR BABY.
I DON'T WANT
YOU TO GO
THERE EITHER.
HONEY.
BUT WHAT CAN WE DO?
WE HAVE NO CHOICE.
DON'T ACT LIKE A CHILD,
ROYAL GRANDSON.

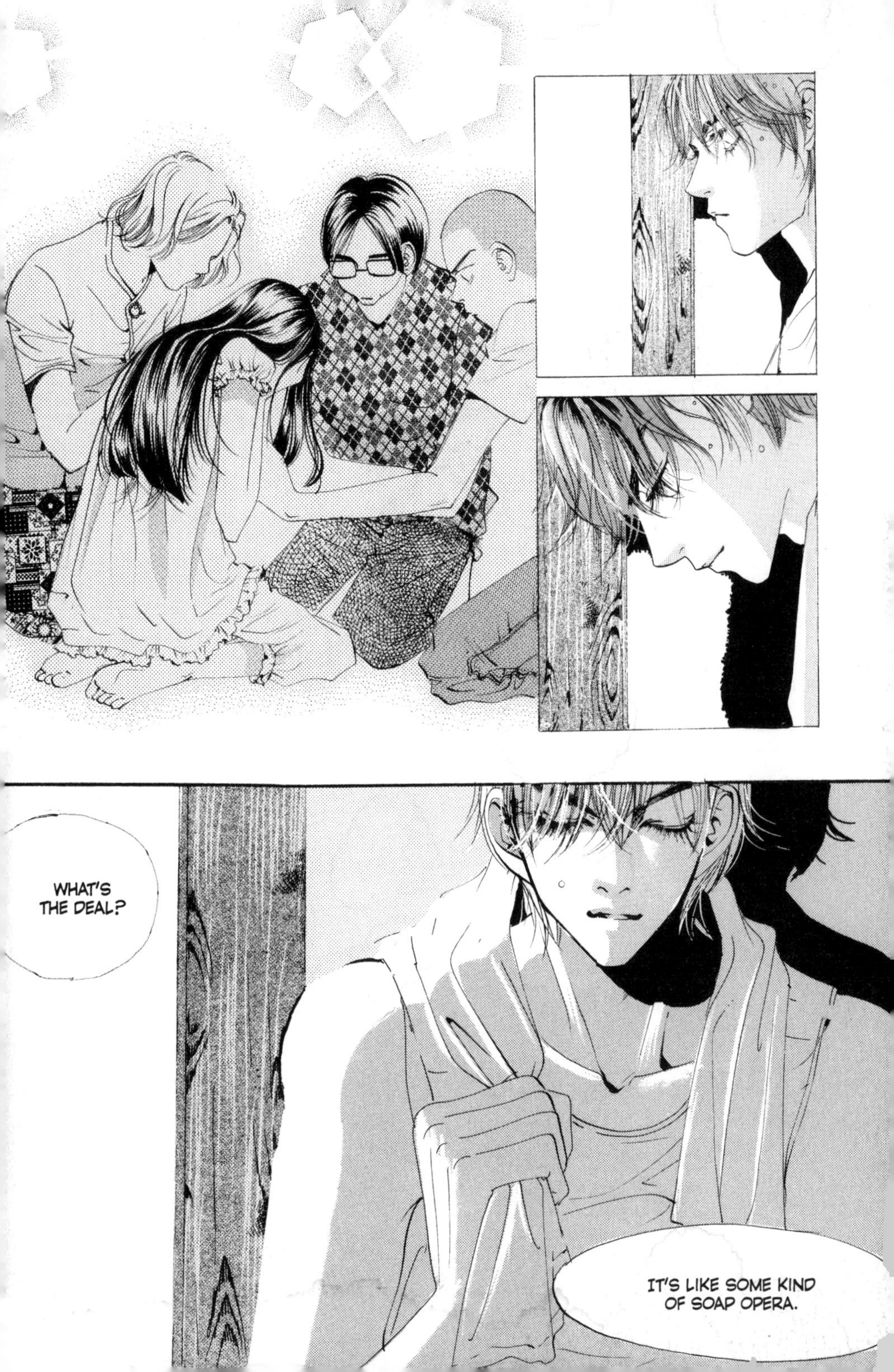
WHAT'S THE DEAL?
IT'S LIKE SOME KIND OF SOAP OPERA.

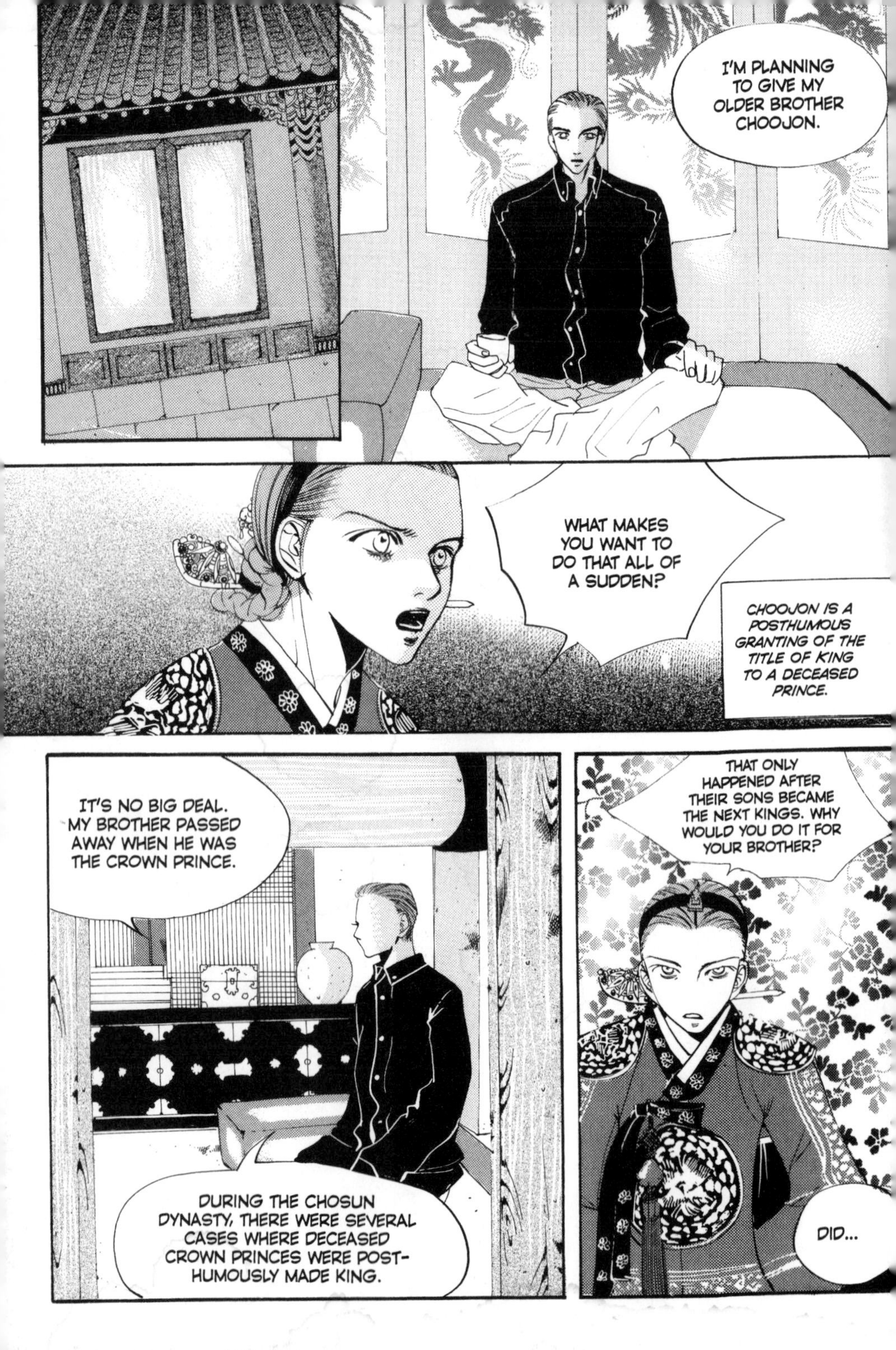
I'M PLANNING TO GIVE MY OLDER BROTHER CHOOJON.
WHAT MAKES YOU WANT TO DO THAT ALL OF A SUDDEN?
CHOOJON IS A POSTHUMOUS GRANTING OF THE TITLE OF KING TO A DECEASED PRINCE.
IT'S NO BIG DEAL. MY BROTHER PASSED AWAY WHEN HE WAS THE CROWN PRINCE.
DURING THE CHOSUN DYNASTY, THERE WERE SEVERAL CASES WHERE DECEASED CROWN PRINCES WERE POST-HUMOUSLY MADE KING.
THAT ONLY HAPPENED AFTER THEIR SONS BECAME THE NEXT KINGS. WHY WOULD YOU DO IT FOR YOUR BROTHER?
DID...

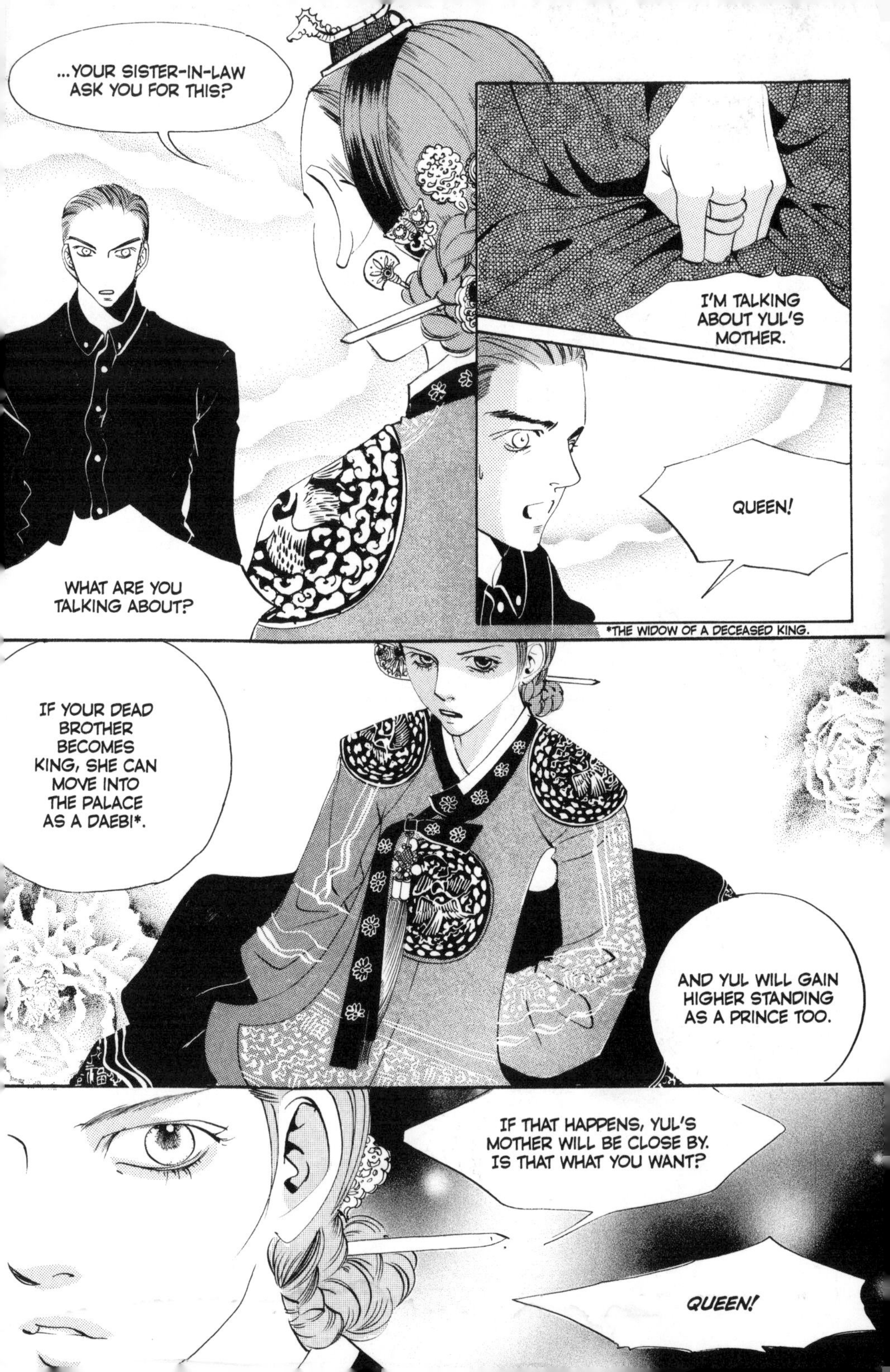
...YOUR SISTER-IN-LAW ASK YOU FOR THIS?
WHAT ARE YOU TALKING ABOUT?
I'M TALKING ABOUT YUL'S MOTHER.
QUEEN!
*THE WIDOW OF A DECEASED KING.
IF YOUR DEAD BROTHER BECOMES KING, SHE CAN MOVE INTO THE PALACE AS A DAEBI*.
AND YUL WILL GAIN HIGHER STANDING AS A PRINCE TOO.
IF THAT HAPPENS, YUL'S MOTHER WILL BE CLOSE BY. IS THAT WHAT YOU WANT?
QUEEN!

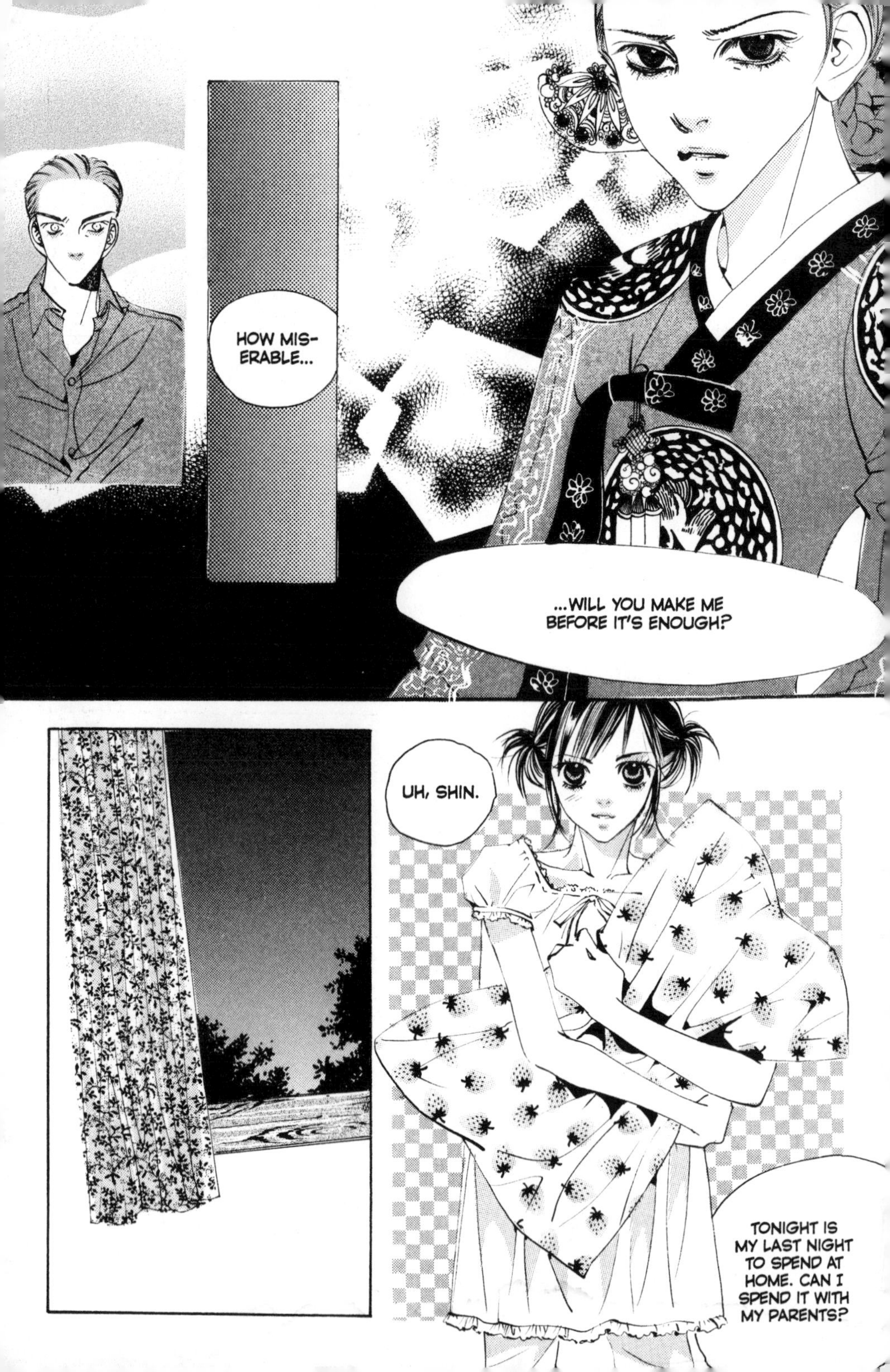
HOW MIS-
ERABLE...
...WILL YOU MAKE ME
BEFORE IT'S ENOUGH?
UH, SHIN.
TONIGHT IS
MY LAST NIGHT
TO SPEND AT
HOME. CAN I
SPEND IT WITH
MY PARENTS?

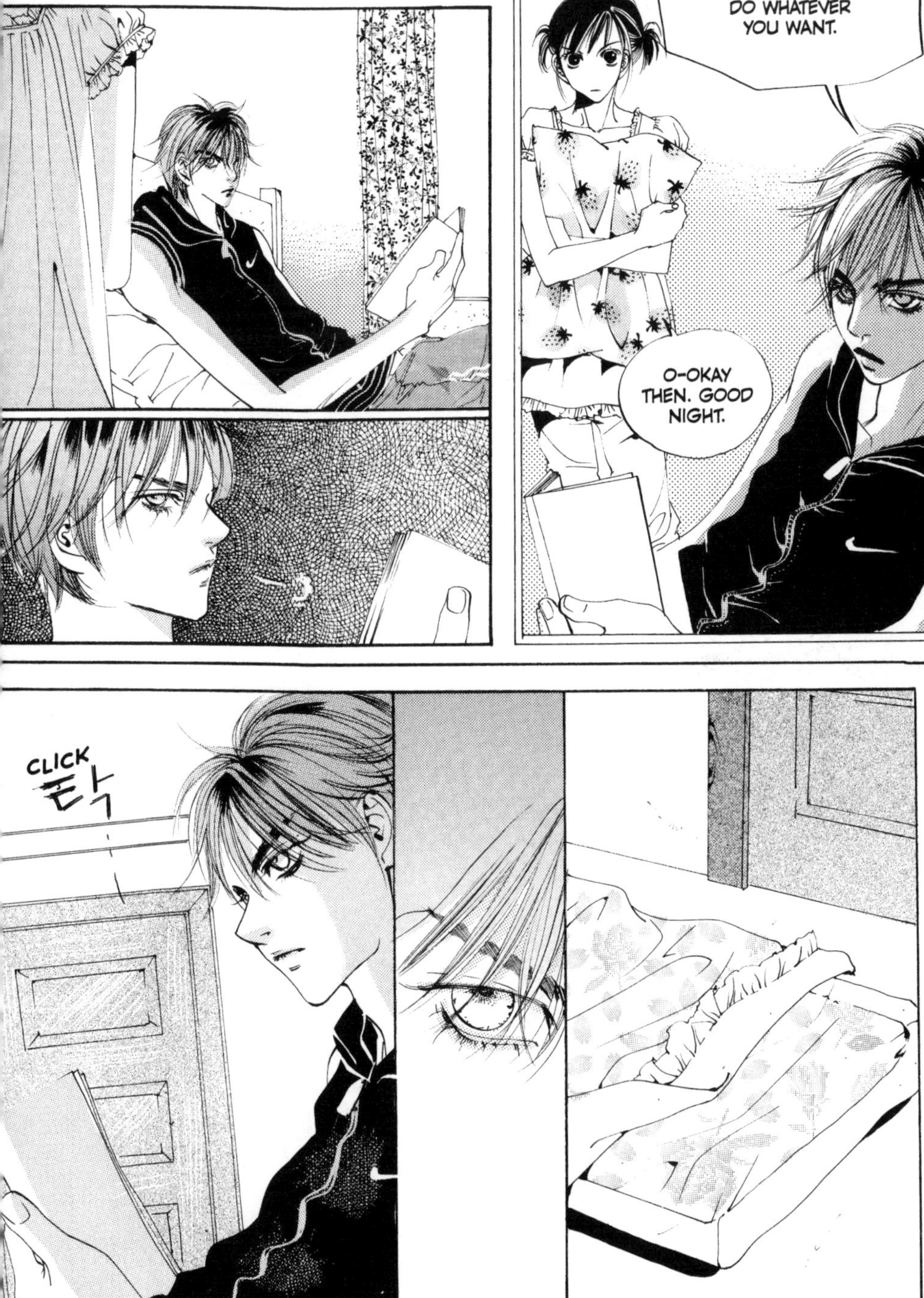
DO WHATEVER YOU WANT.
O-OKAY THEN. GOOD NIGHT.
CLICK
탁

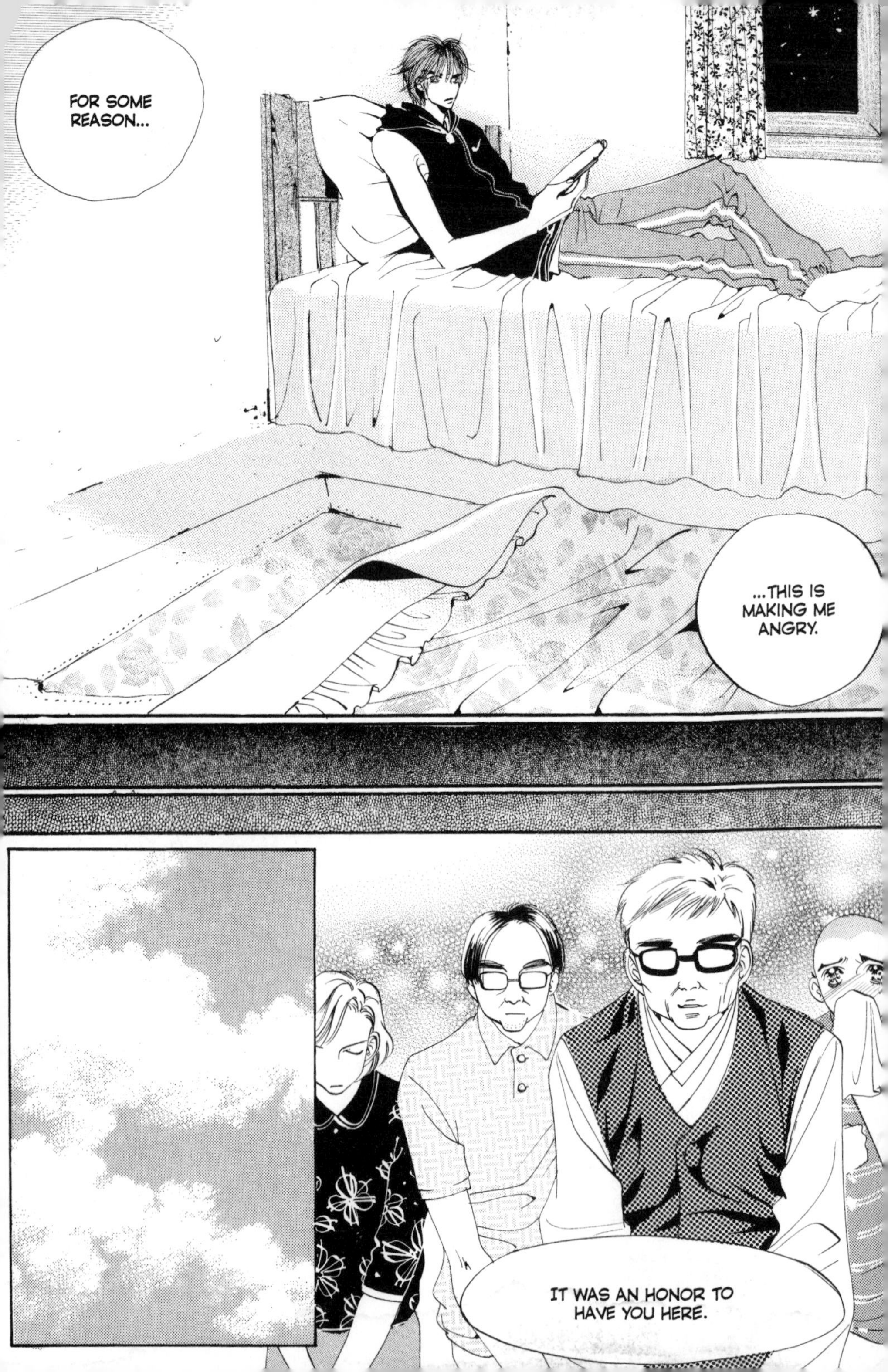
FOR SOME REASON...
...THIS IS MAKING ME ANGRY.
IT WAS AN HONOR TO HAVE YOU HERE.

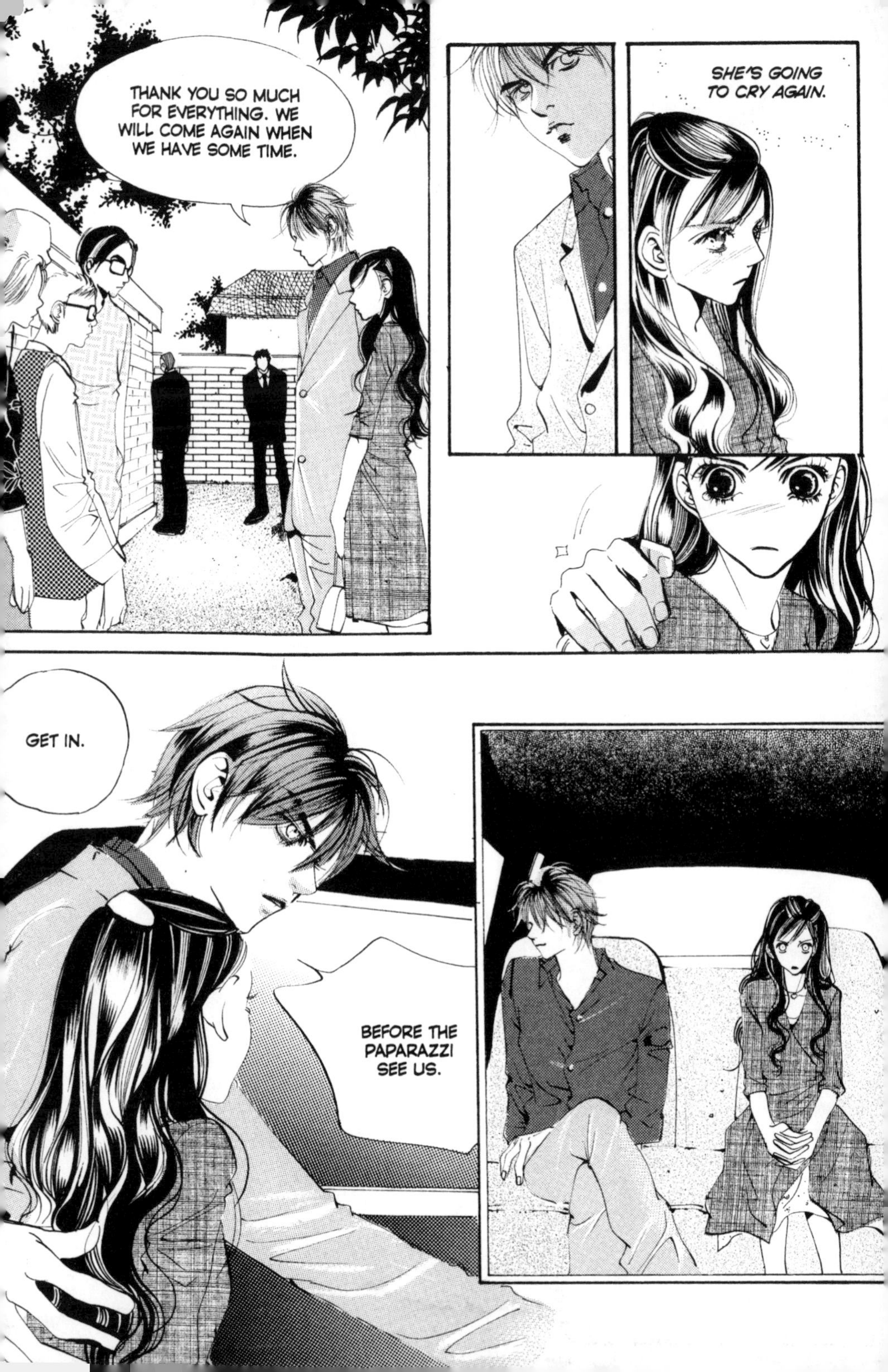
THANK YOU SO MUCH FOR EVERYTHING. WE WILL COME AGAIN WHEN WE HAVE SOME TIME.
SHE'S GOING TO CRY AGAIN.
GET IN.
BEFORE THE PAPARAZZI SEE US.

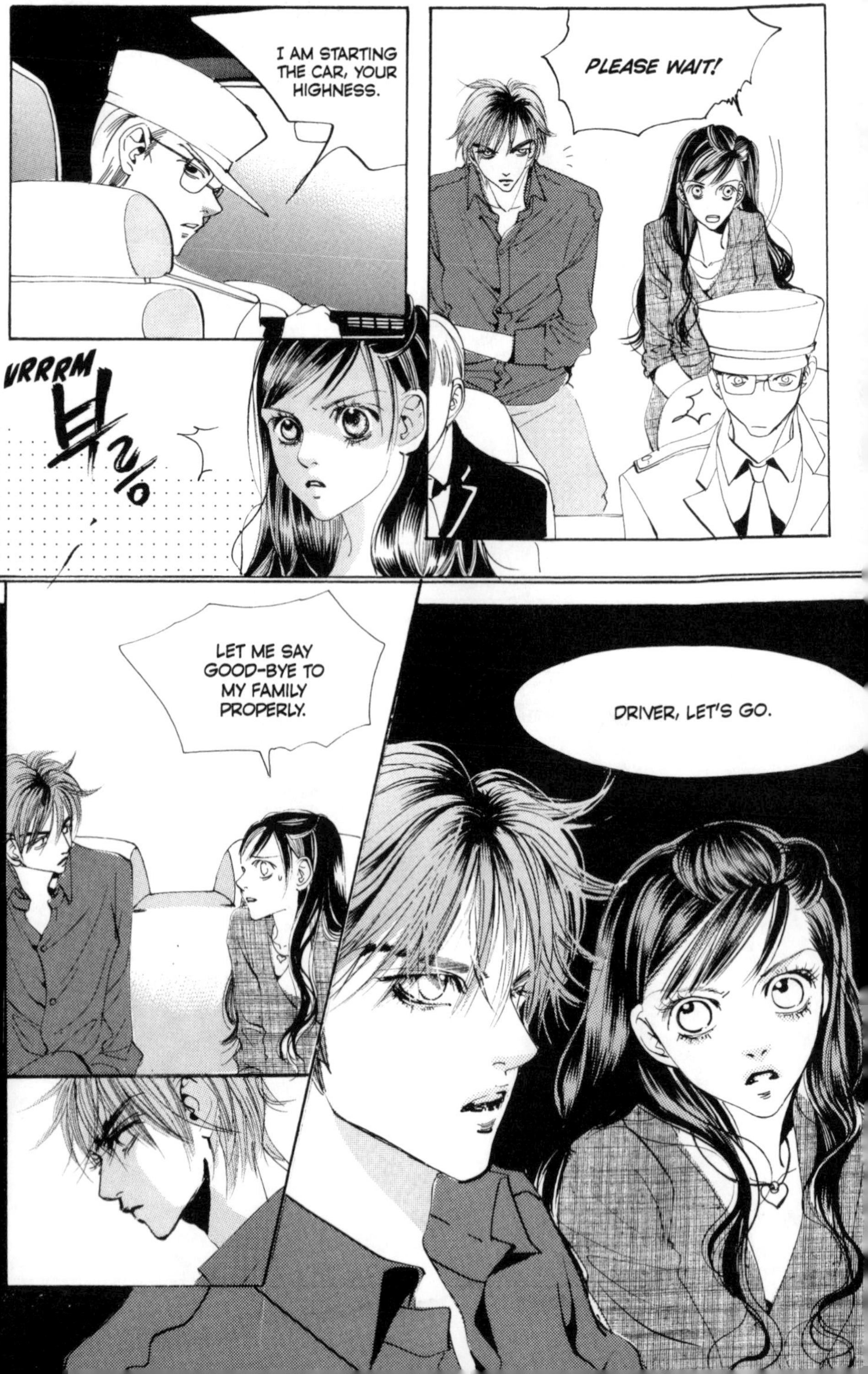
I AM STARTING THE CAR, YOUR HIGHNESS.
PLEASE WAIT!
VRRRM
LET ME SAY GOOD-BYE TO MY FAMILY PROPERLY.
DRIVER, LET'S GO.

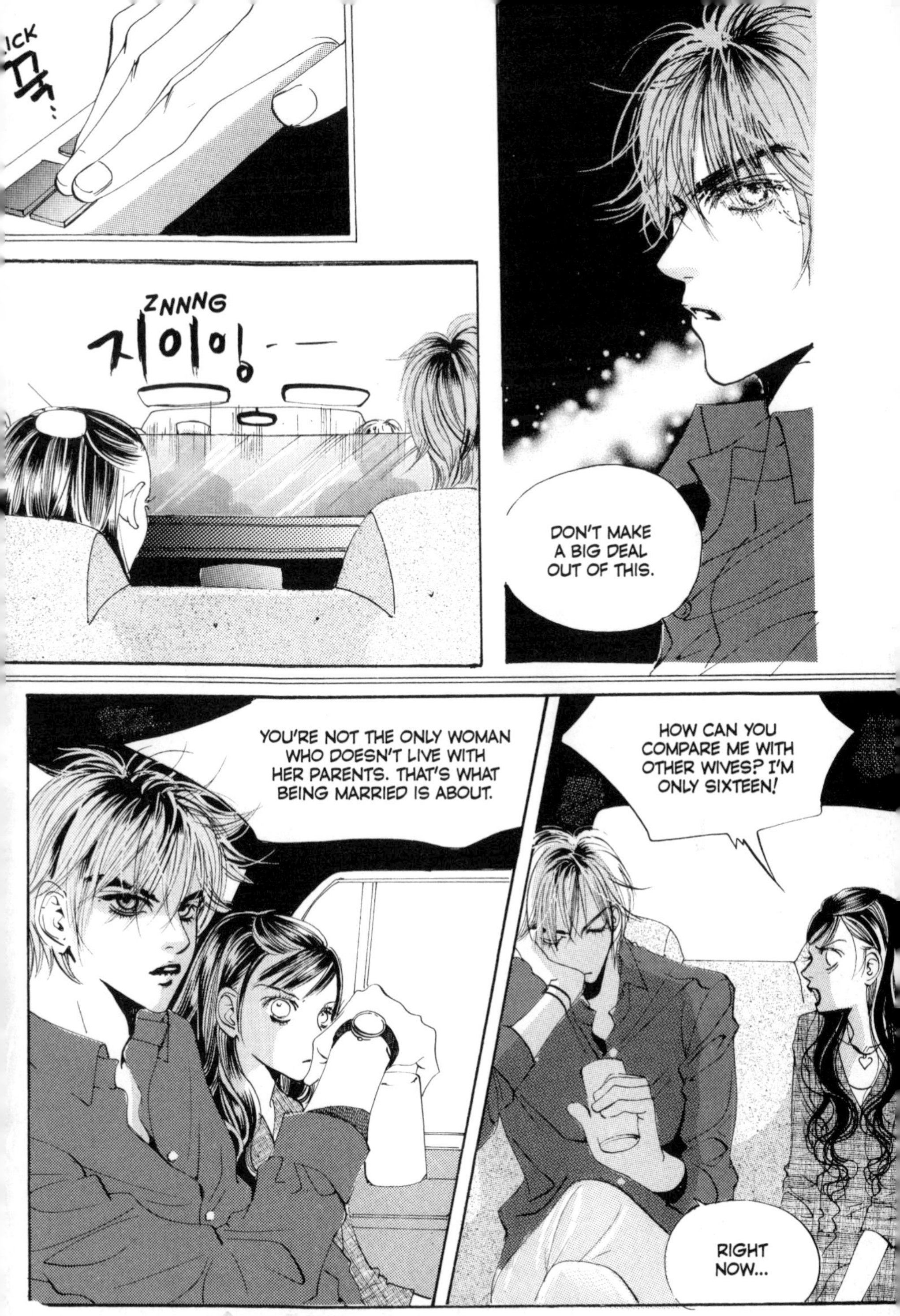

ICK
ZNNNG
지이잉
DON'T MAKE A BIG DEAL OUT OF THIS.
YOU'RE NOT THE ONLY WOMAN WHO DOESN'T LIVE WITH HER PARENTS. THAT'S WHAT BEING MARRIED IS ABOUT.
HOW CAN YOU COMPARE ME WITH OTHER WIVES? I'M ONLY SIXTEEN!
RIGHT NOW...

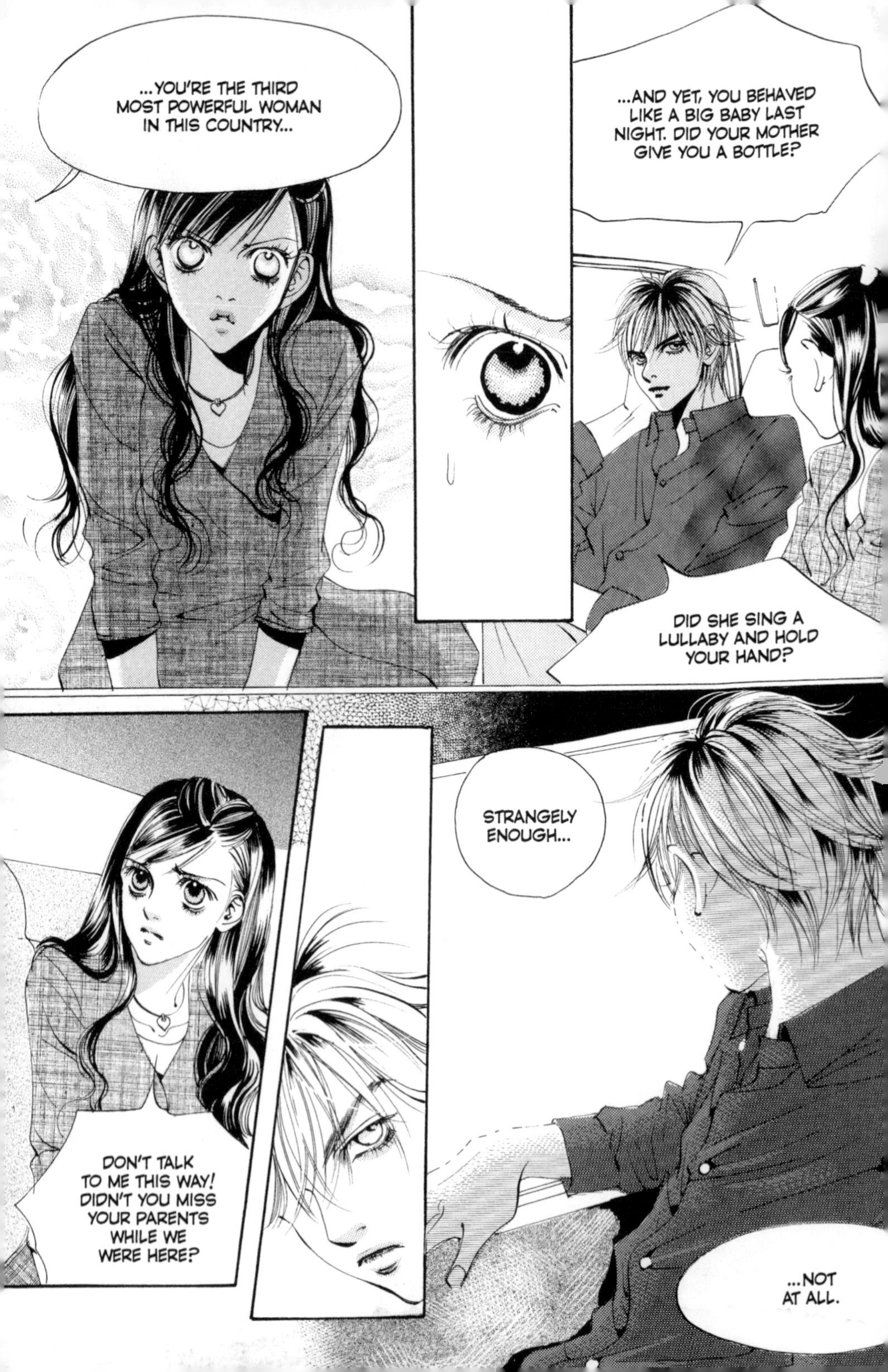
...YOU'RE THE THIRD MOST POWERFUL WOMAN IN THIS COUNTRY...
...AND YET, YOU BEHAVED LIKE A BIG BABY LAST NIGHT. DID YOUR MOTHER GIVE YOU A BOTTLE?
DID SHE SING A LULLABY AND HOLD YOUR HAND?
DON'T TALK TO ME THIS WAY! DIDN'T YOU MISS YOUR PARENTS WHILE WE WERE HERE?
STRANGELY ENOUGH...
...NOT AT ALL.

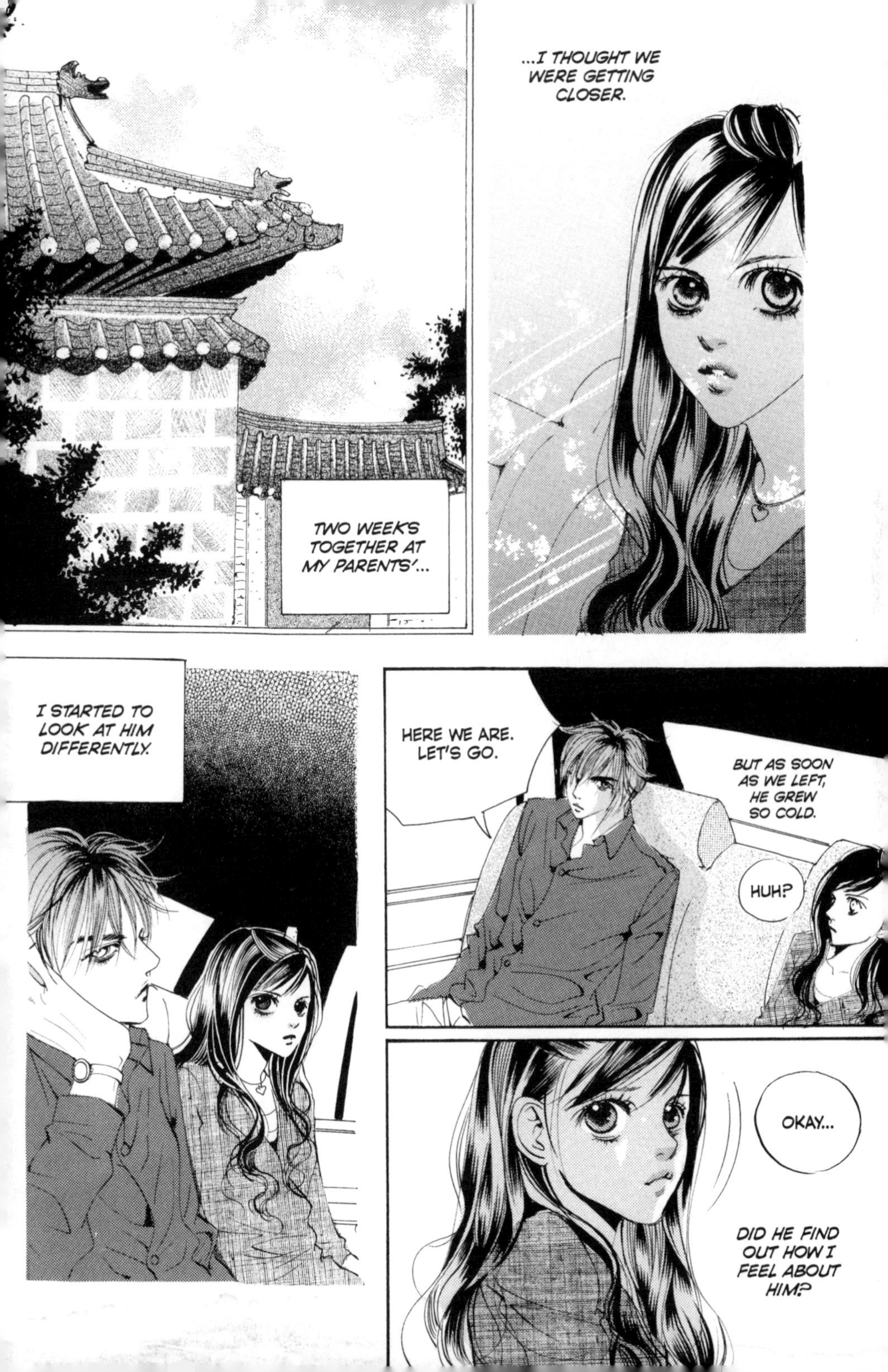
TWO WEEKS TOGETHER AT MY PARENTS'...
...I THOUGHT WE WERE GETTING CLOSER.
I STARTED TO LOOK AT HIM DIFFERENTLY.
HERE WE ARE. LET'S GO.
BUT AS SOON AS WE LEFT, HE GREW SO COLD.
HUH?
OKAY...
DID HE FIND OUT HOW I FEEL ABOUT HIM?

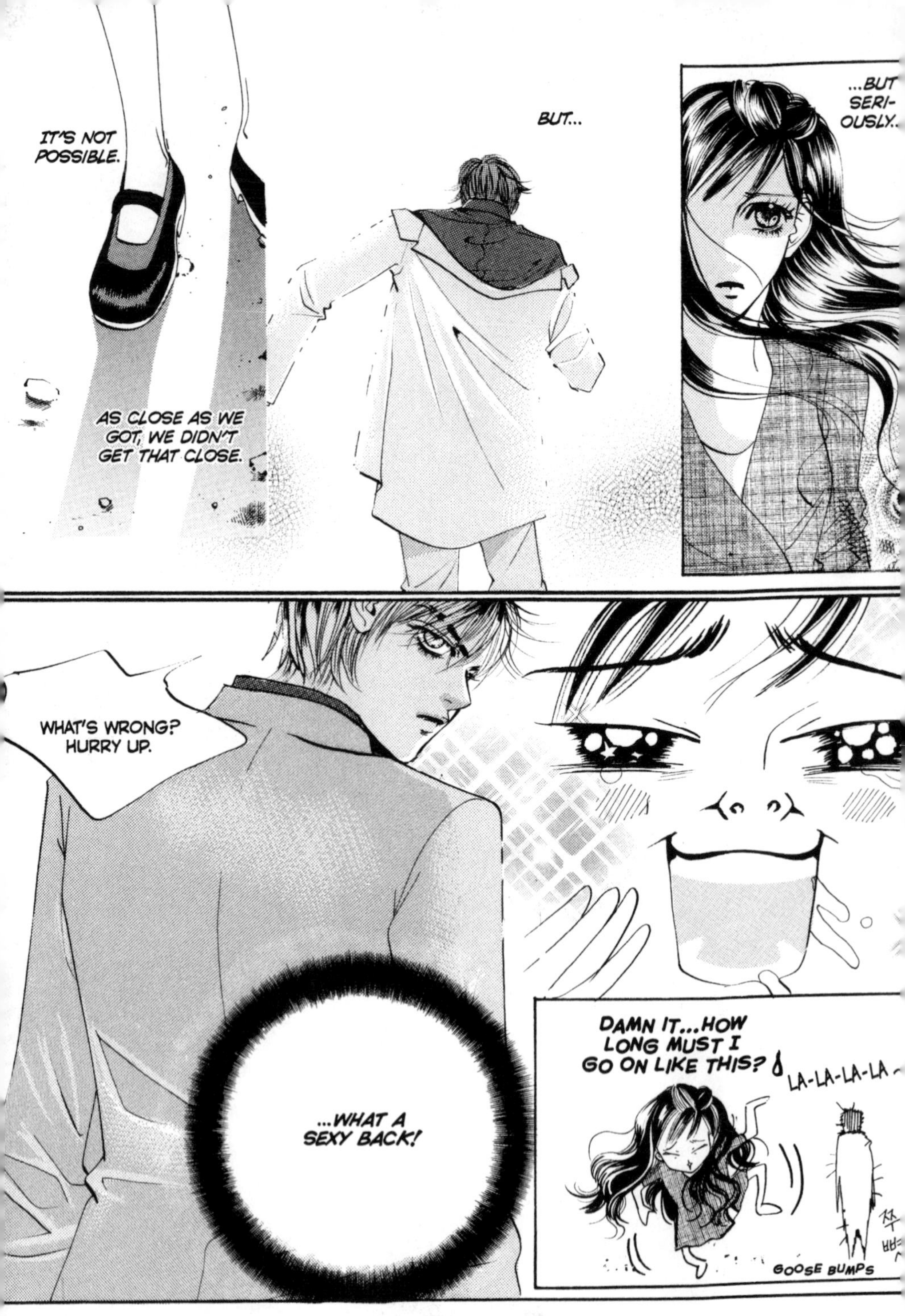
IT'S NOT POSSIBLE.
AS CLOSE AS WE GOT, WE DIDN'T GET THAT CLOSE.
BUT...
...BUT SERI-OUSLY...
WHAT'S WRONG? HURRY UP.
...WHAT A SEXY BACK!
DAMN IT...HOW LONG MUST I GO ON LIKE THIS?
LA-LA-LA-LA
GOOSE BUMPS

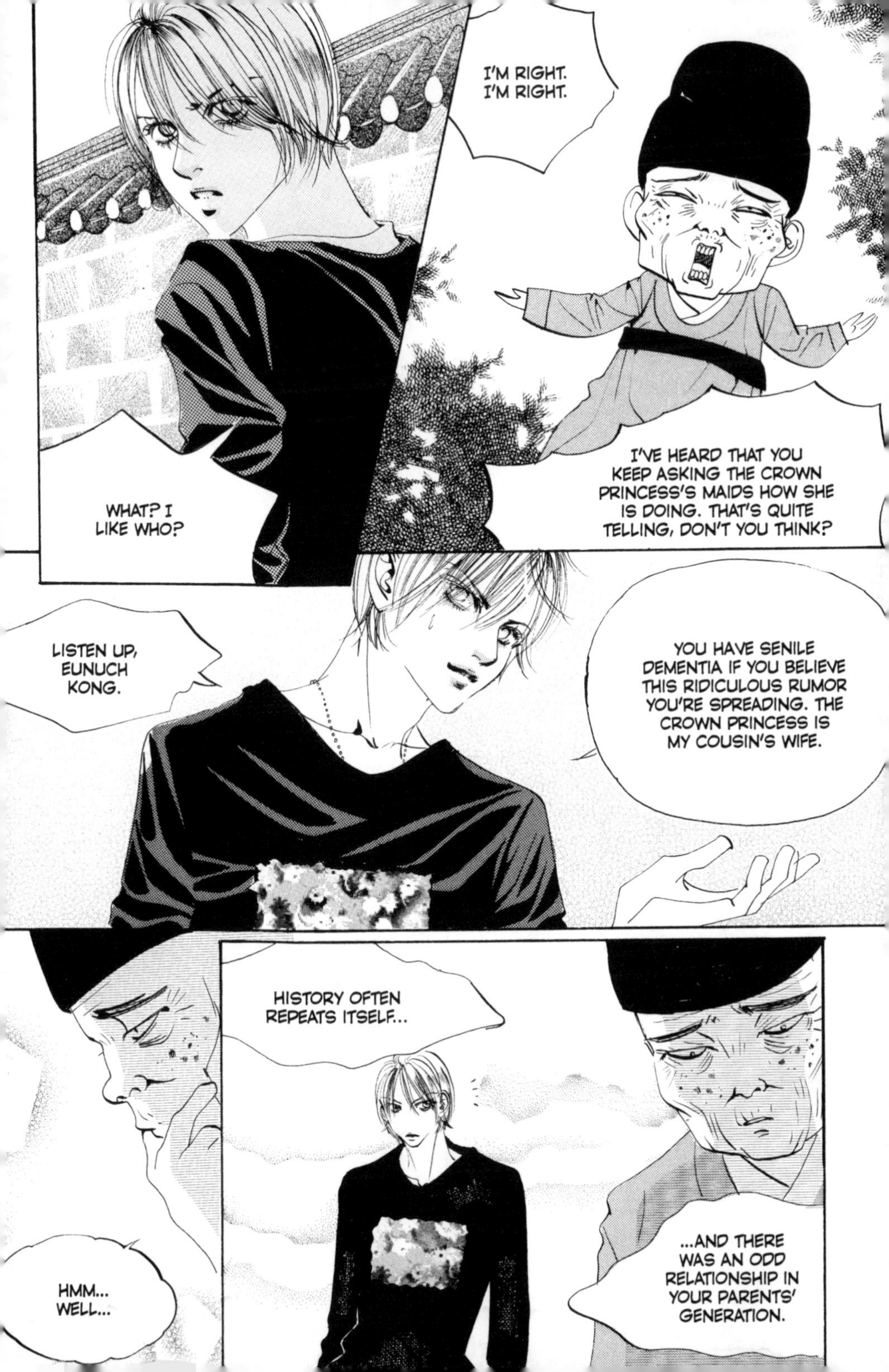
WHAT? I LIKE WHO?
I'M RIGHT. I'M RIGHT.
I'VE HEARD THAT YOU KEEP ASKING THE CROWN PRINCESS'S MAIDS HOW SHE IS DOING. THAT'S QUITE TELLING, DON'T YOU THINK?
LISTEN UP, EUNUCH KONG.
YOU HAVE SENILE DEMENTIA IF YOU BELIEVE THIS RIDICULOUS RUMOR YOU'RE SPREADING. THE CROWN PRINCESS IS MY COUSIN'S WIFE.
HMM... WELL...
HISTORY OFTEN REPEATS ITSELF...
...AND THERE WAS AN ODD RELATIONSHIP IN YOUR PARENTS' GENERATION.

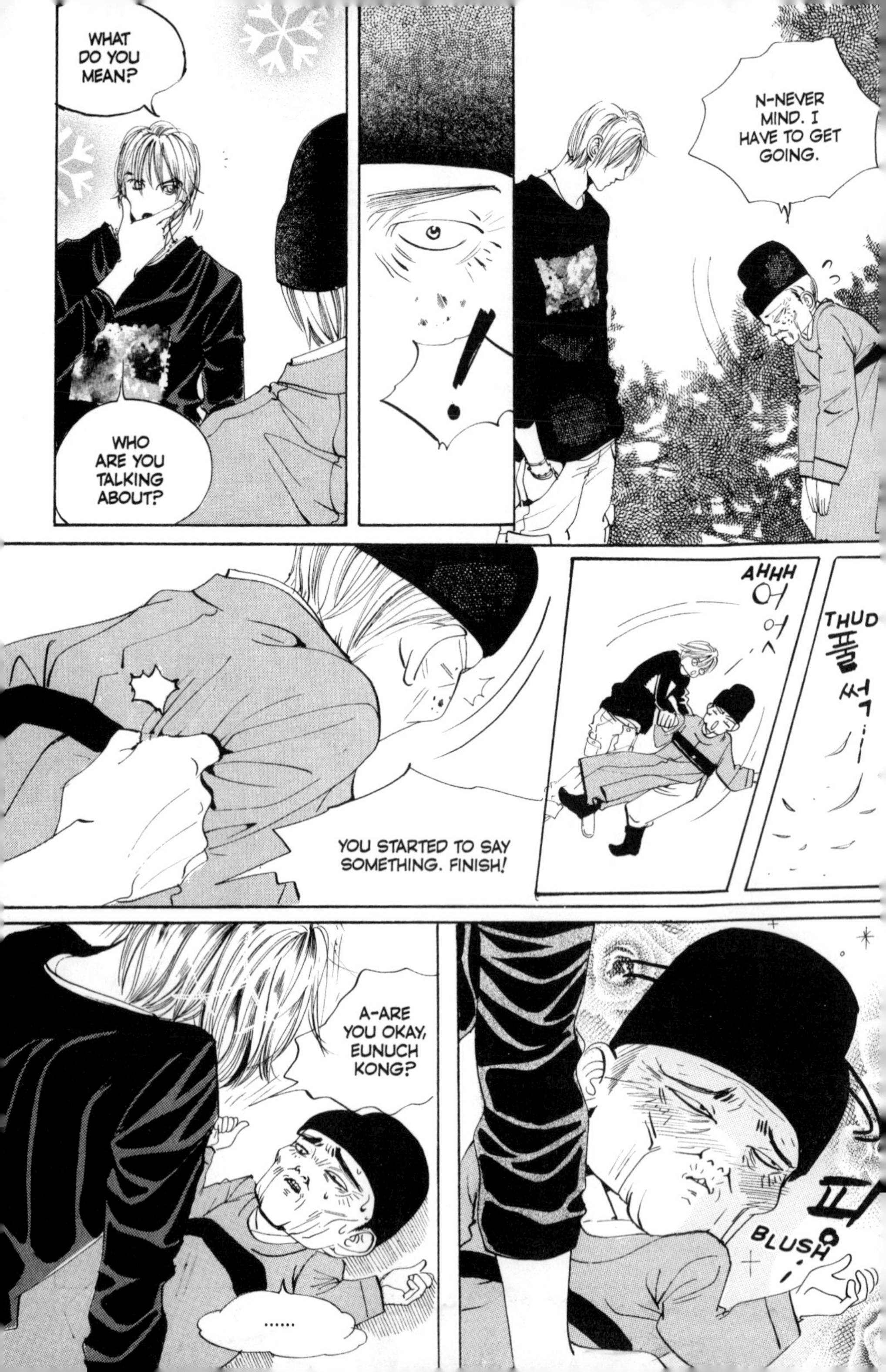
WHAT DO YOU MEAN?
WHO ARE YOU TALKING ABOUT?
!
N-NEVER MIND. I HAVE TO GET GOING.
YOU STARTED TO SAY SOMETHING. FINISH!
AHHH
어엇...
THUD
풀썩...!
A-ARE YOU OKAY, EUNUCH KONG?
......
BLUSH

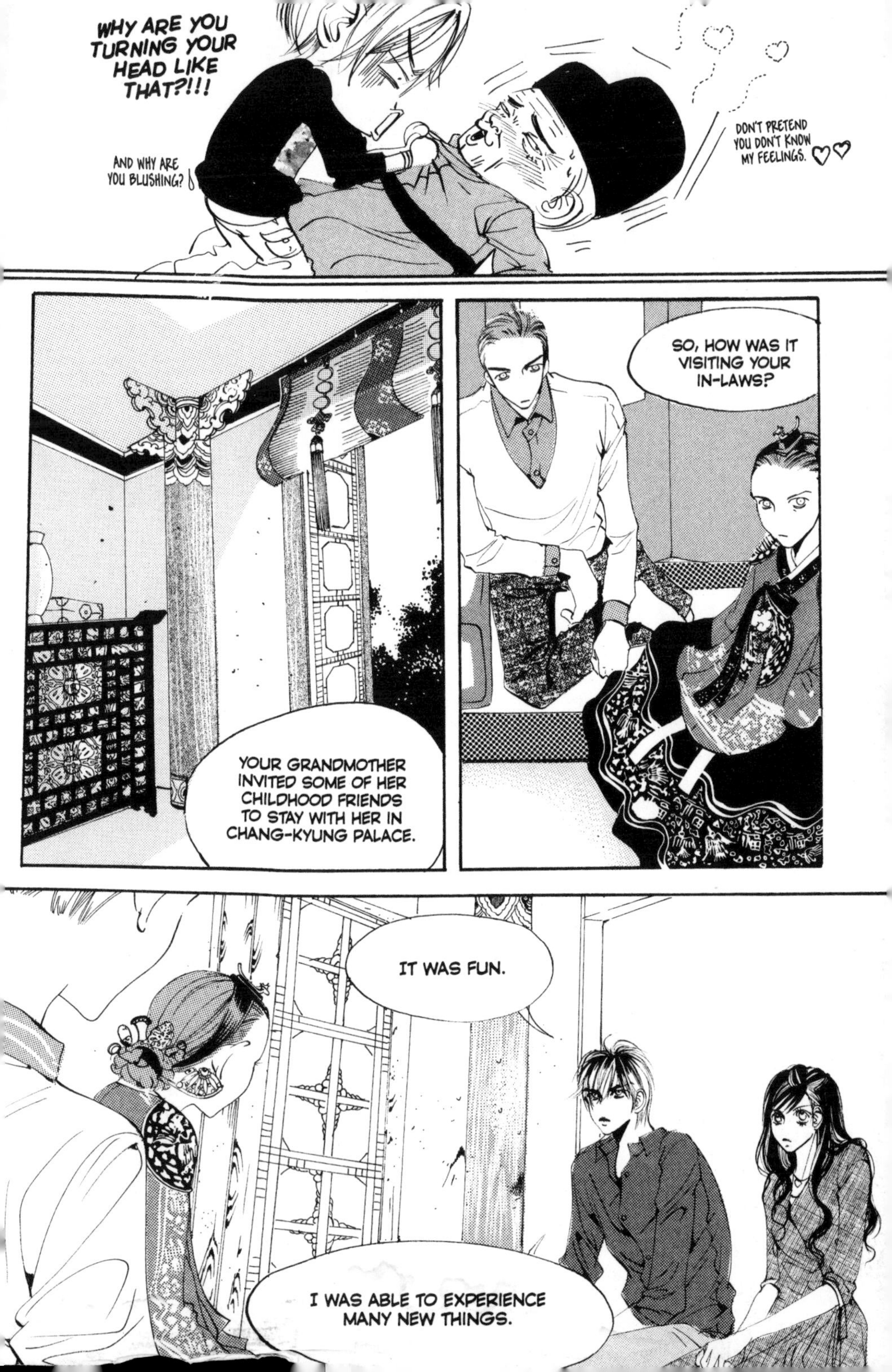
WHY ARE YOU TURNING YOUR HEAD LIKE THAT?!!!
AND WHY ARE YOU BLUSHING?
DON'T PRETEND YOU DON'T KNOW MY FEELINGS.
YOUR GRANDMOTHER INVITED SOME OF HER CHILDHOOD FRIENDS TO STAY WITH HER IN CHANG-KYUNG PALACE.
SO, HOW WAS IT VISITING YOUR IN-LAWS?
IT WAS FUN.
I WAS ABLE TO EXPERIENCE MANY NEW THINGS.

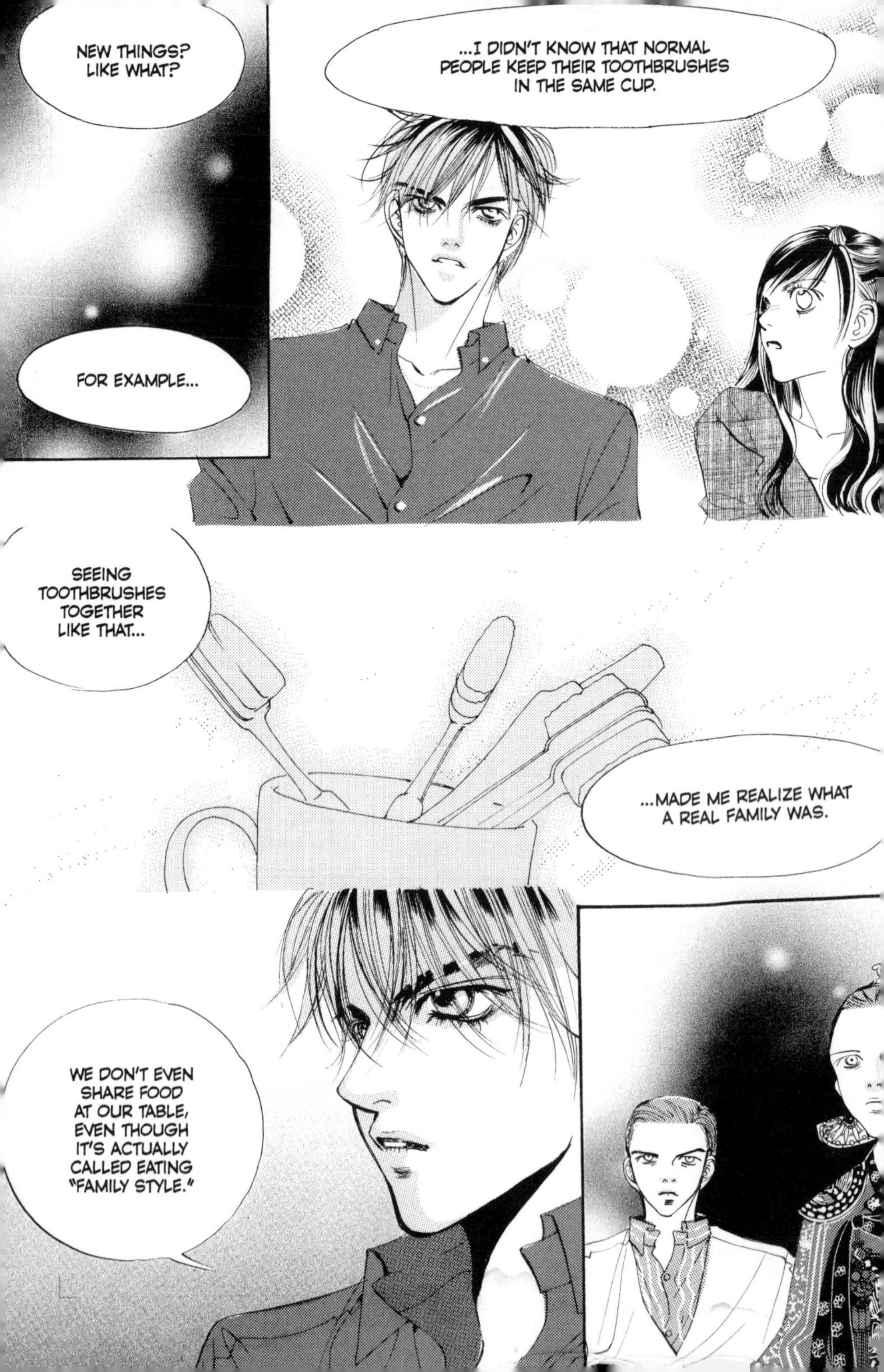
NEW THINGS? LIKE WHAT?
...I DIDN'T KNOW THAT NORMAL PEOPLE KEEP THEIR TOOTHBRUSHES IN THE SAME CUP.
FOR EXAMPLE...
SEEING TOOTHBRUSHES TOGETHER LIKE THAT...
...MADE ME REALIZE WHAT A REAL FAMILY WAS.
WE DON'T EVEN SHARE FOOD AT OUR TABLE, EVEN THOUGH IT'S ACTUALLY CALLED EATING "FAMILY STYLE."

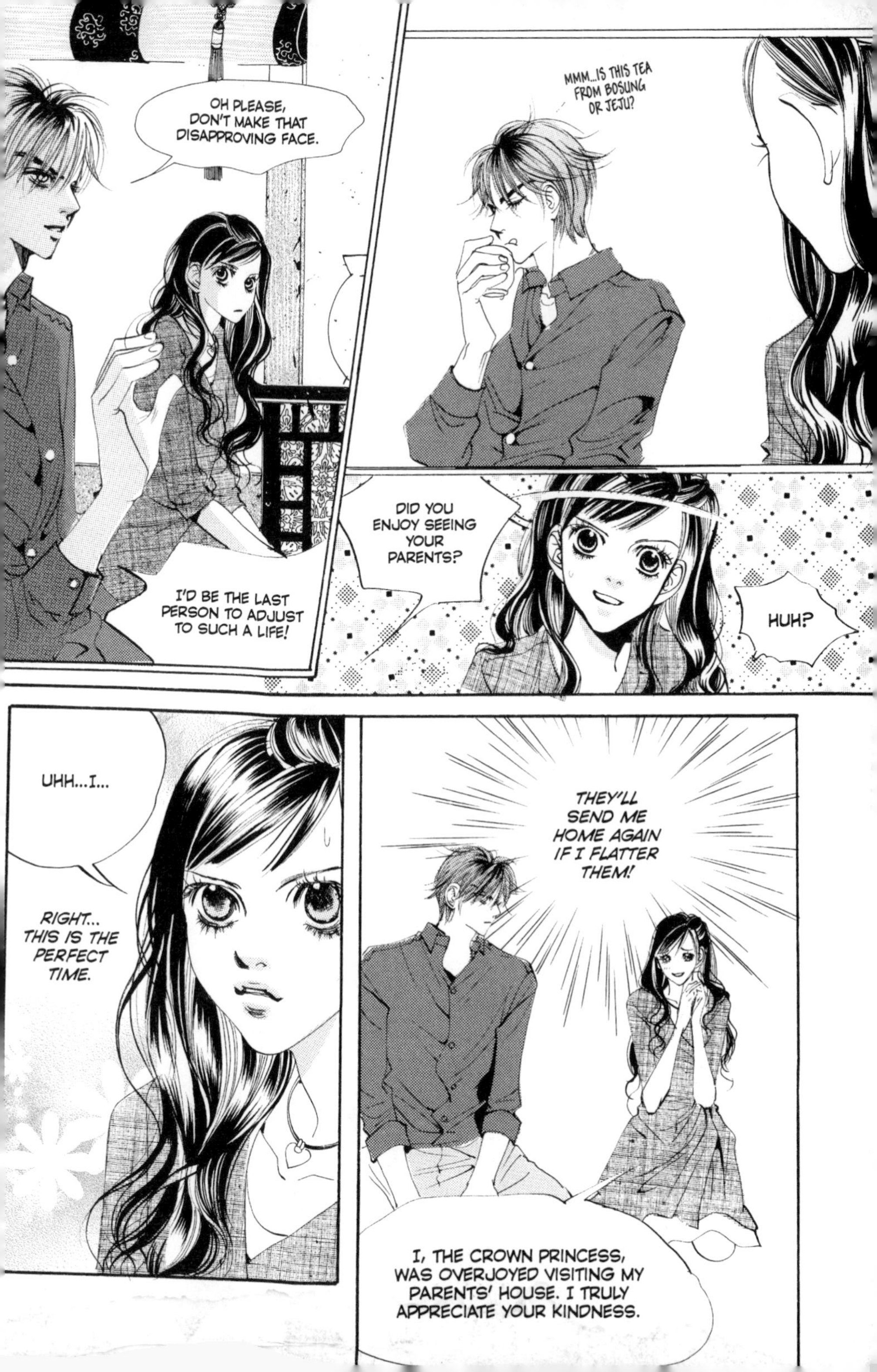
OH PLEASE, DON'T MAKE THAT DISAPPROVING FACE.
I'D BE THE LAST PERSON TO ADJUST TO SUCH A LIFE!
MMM...IS THIS TEA FROM BOSUNG OR JEJU?
DID YOU ENJOY SEEING YOUR PARENTS?
HUH?
UHH...I...
RIGHT... THIS IS THE PERFECT TIME.
THEY'LL SEND ME HOME AGAIN IF I FLATTER THEM!
I, THE CROWN PRINCESS, WAS OVERJOYED VISITING MY PARENTS' HOUSE. I TRULY APPRECIATE YOUR KINDNESS.

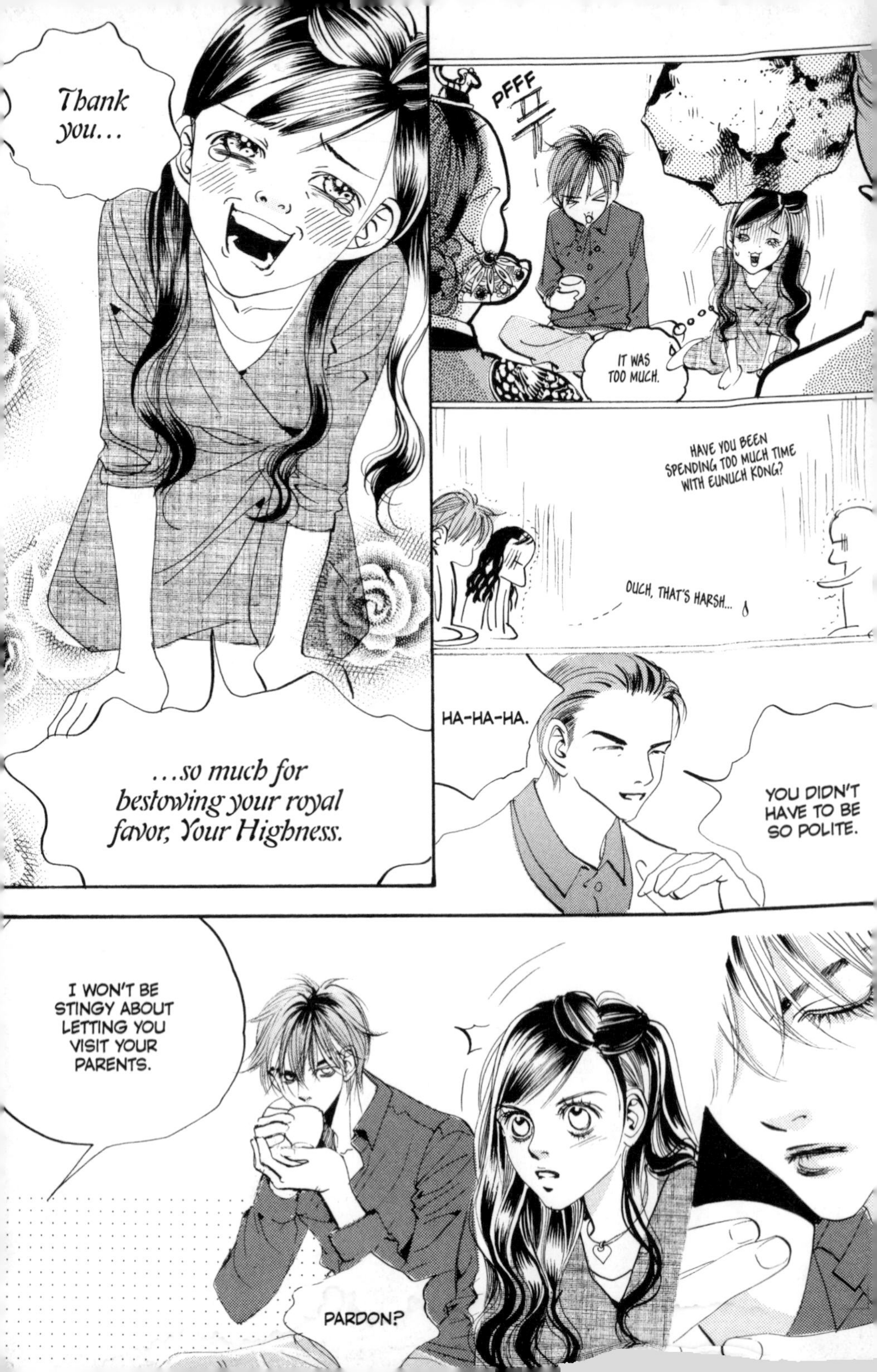
Thank you…
…so much for bestowing your royal favor, Your Highness.
PFFF
IT WAS TOO MUCH.
HAVE YOU BEEN SPENDING TOO MUCH TIME WITH EUNUCH KONG?
OUCH, THAT'S HARSH…
HA-HA-HA.
YOU DIDN'T HAVE TO BE SO POLITE.
I WON'T BE STINGY ABOUT LETTING YOU VISIT YOUR PARENTS.
PARDON?

MOTHER WASN'T EVEN ABLE TO GO HOME WHEN GRANDFATHER PASSED AWAY TWO YEARS AGO.

*THE CROWN PRINCE'S PALACE.

EVEN THOUGH I AM YOUNG, I AM THE HEAD OF MY HOUSEHOLD.

I AM MARRIED NOW.

DON'T I HAVE THE RIGHT TO DECIDE WHAT HAPPENS IN DONGGOONG-JUN*?

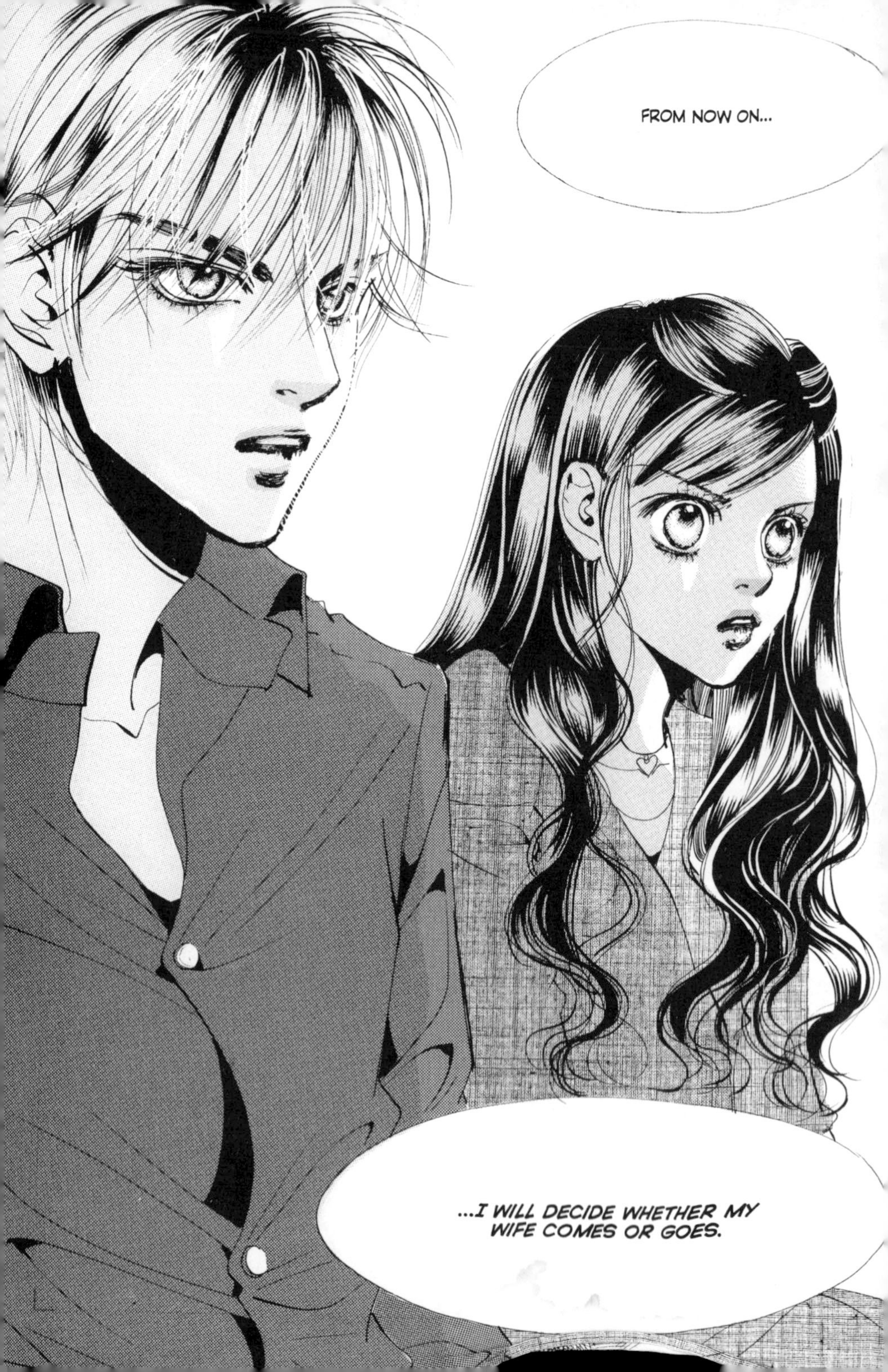
FROM NOW ON...
...I WILL DECIDE WHETHER MY WIFE COMES OR GOES.

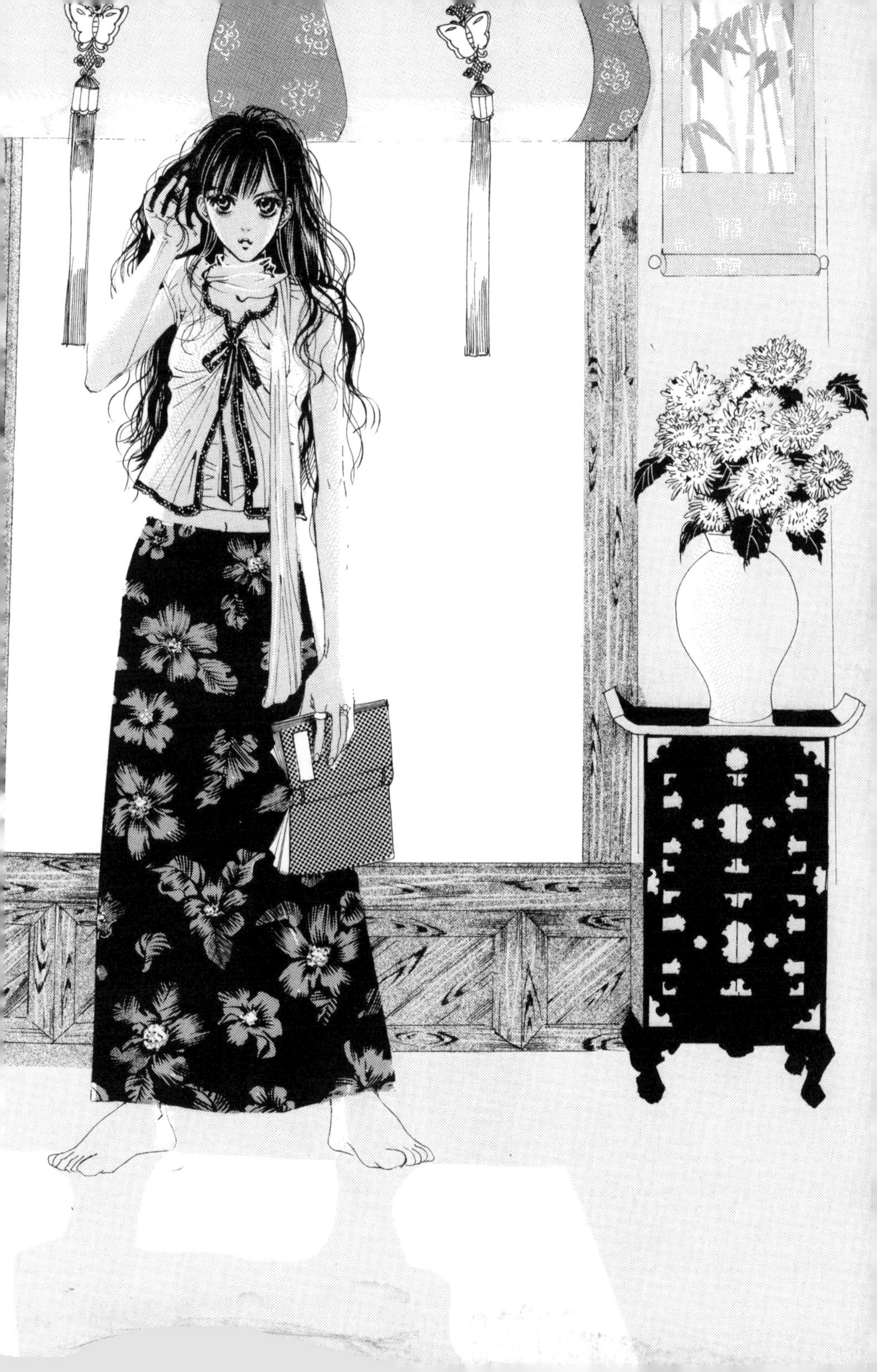

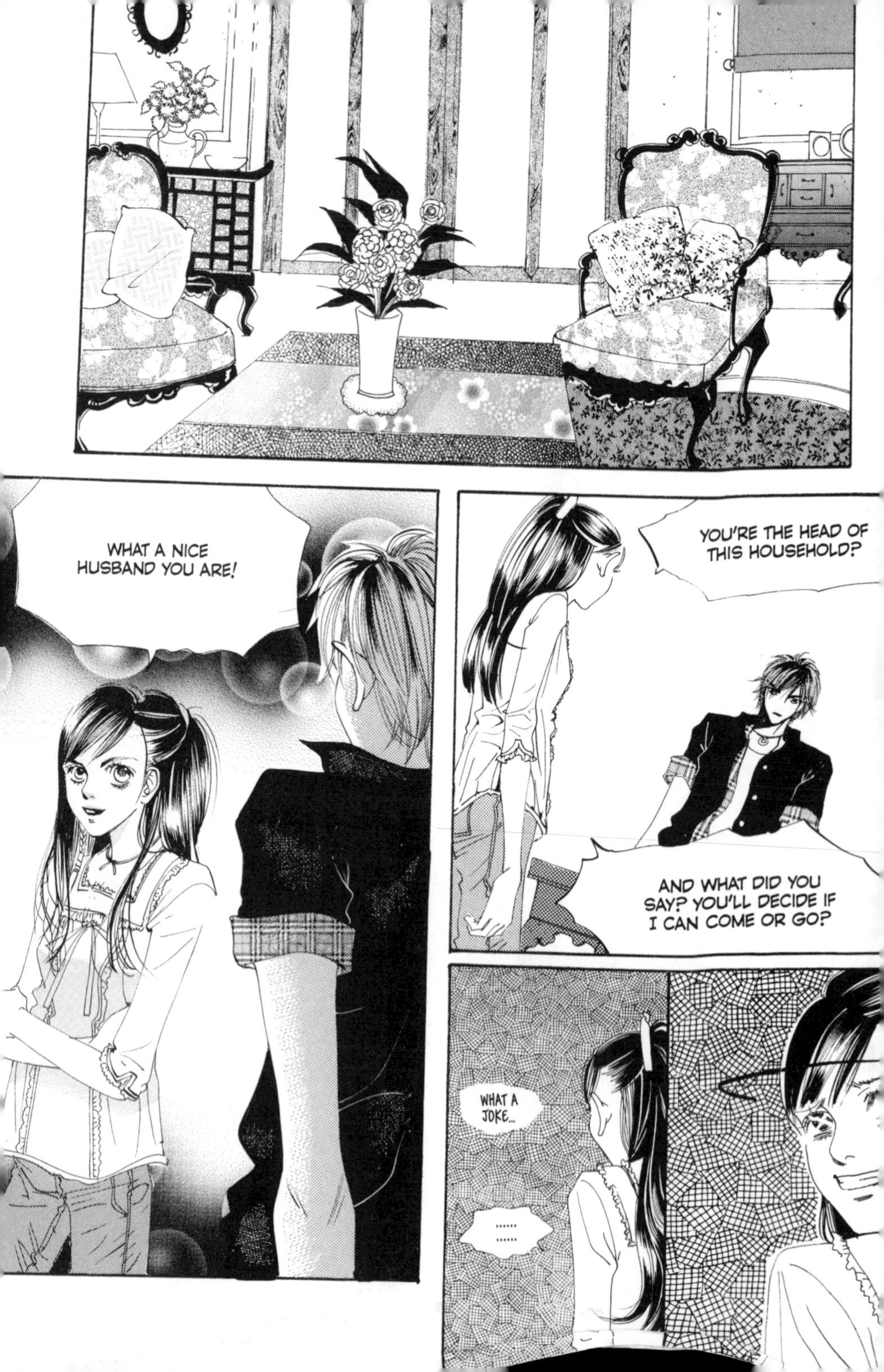
WHAT A NICE HUSBAND YOU ARE!
YOU'RE THE HEAD OF THIS HOUSEHOLD?
AND WHAT DID YOU SAY? YOU'LL DECIDE IF I CAN COME OR GO?
WHAT A JOKE...
......
......

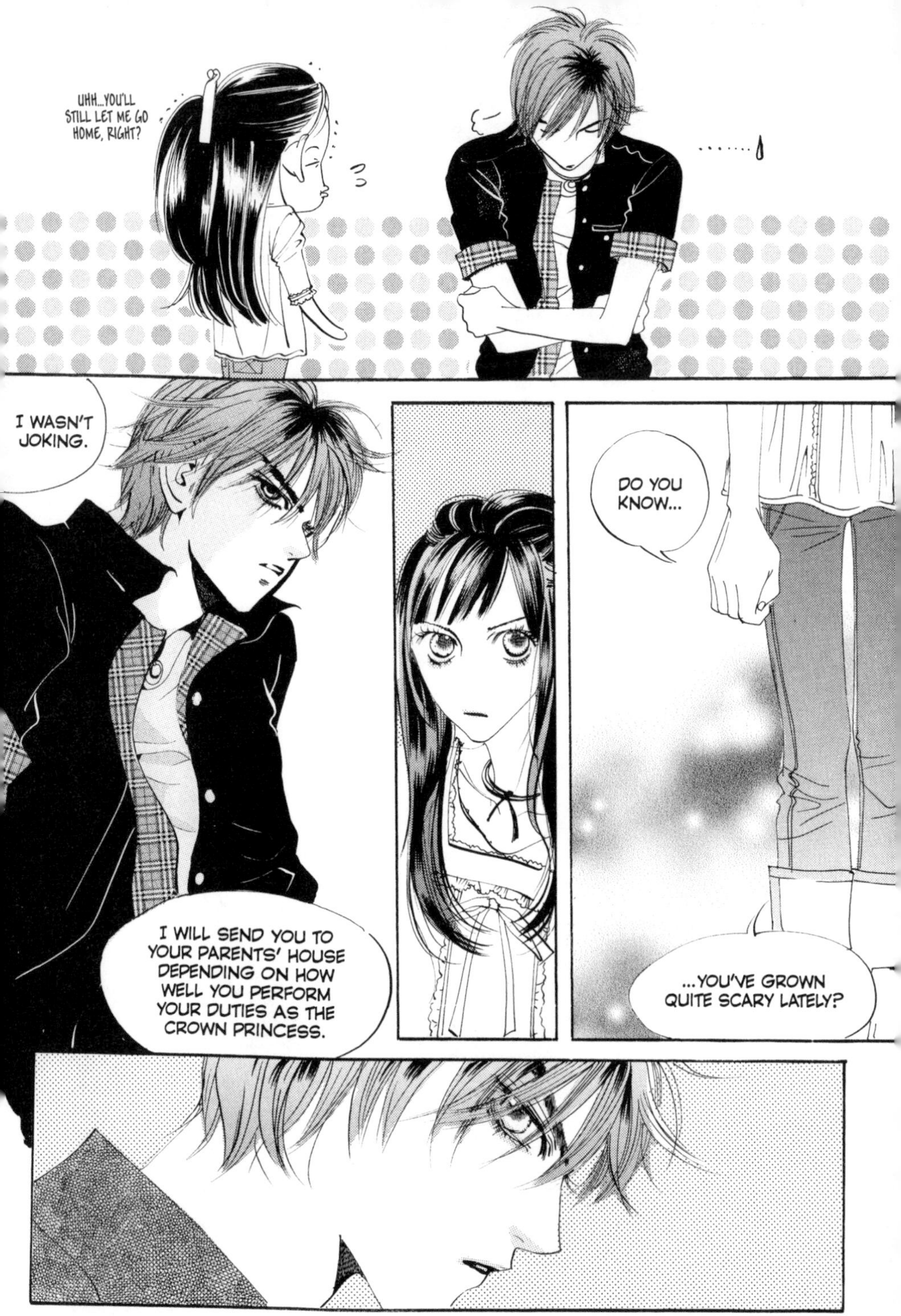
UHH...YOU'LL STILL LET ME GO HOME, RIGHT?
....
I WASN'T JOKING.
I WILL SEND YOU TO YOUR PARENTS' HOUSE DEPENDING ON HOW WELL YOU PERFORM YOUR DUTIES AS THE CROWN PRINCESS.
DO YOU KNOW...
...YOU'VE GROWN QUITE SCARY LATELY?

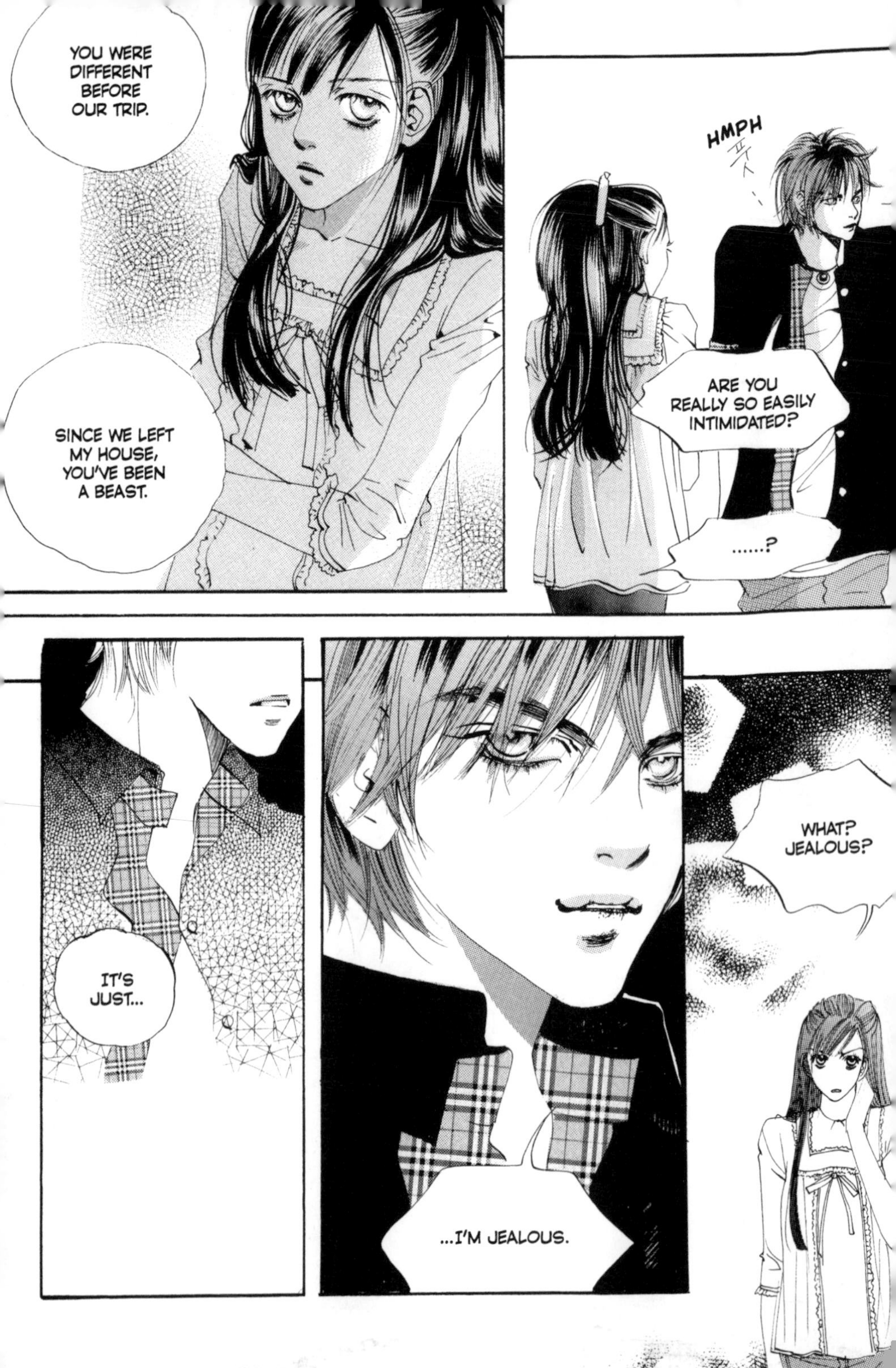

YOU WERE DIFFERENT BEFORE OUR TRIP.
SINCE WE LEFT MY HOUSE, YOU'VE BEEN A BEAST.
HMPH
ARE YOU REALLY SO EASILY INTIMIDATED?
......?
IT'S JUST...
...I'M JEALOUS.
WHAT? JEALOUS?

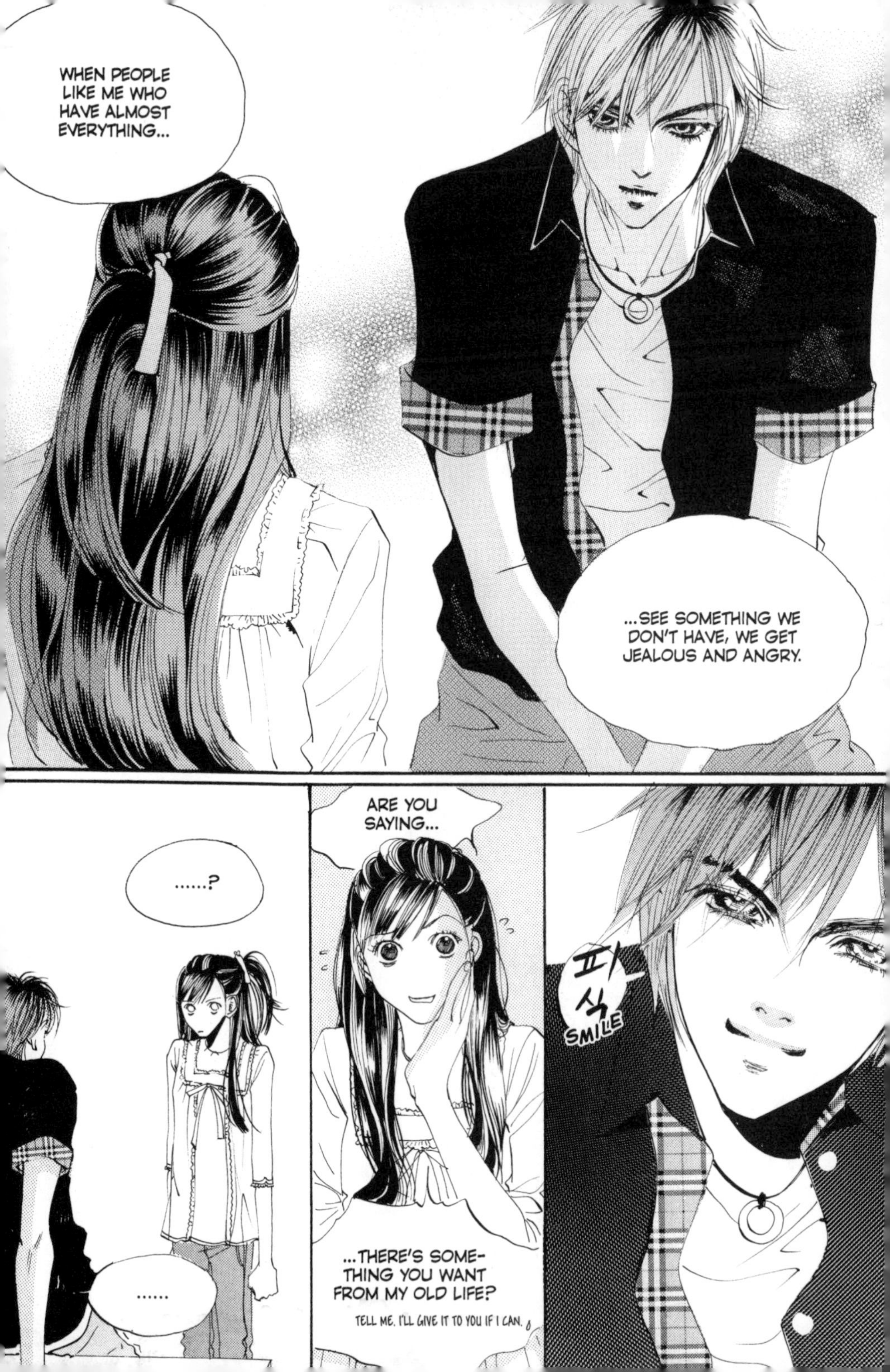
WHEN PEOPLE LIKE ME WHO HAVE ALMOST EVERYTHING...
...SEE SOMETHING WE DON'T HAVE, WE GET JEALOUS AND ANGRY.
......?
......
ARE YOU SAYING...
...THERE'S SOME-THING YOU WANT FROM MY OLD LIFE?
TELL ME. I'LL GIVE IT TO YOU IF I CAN.
피식
SMILE

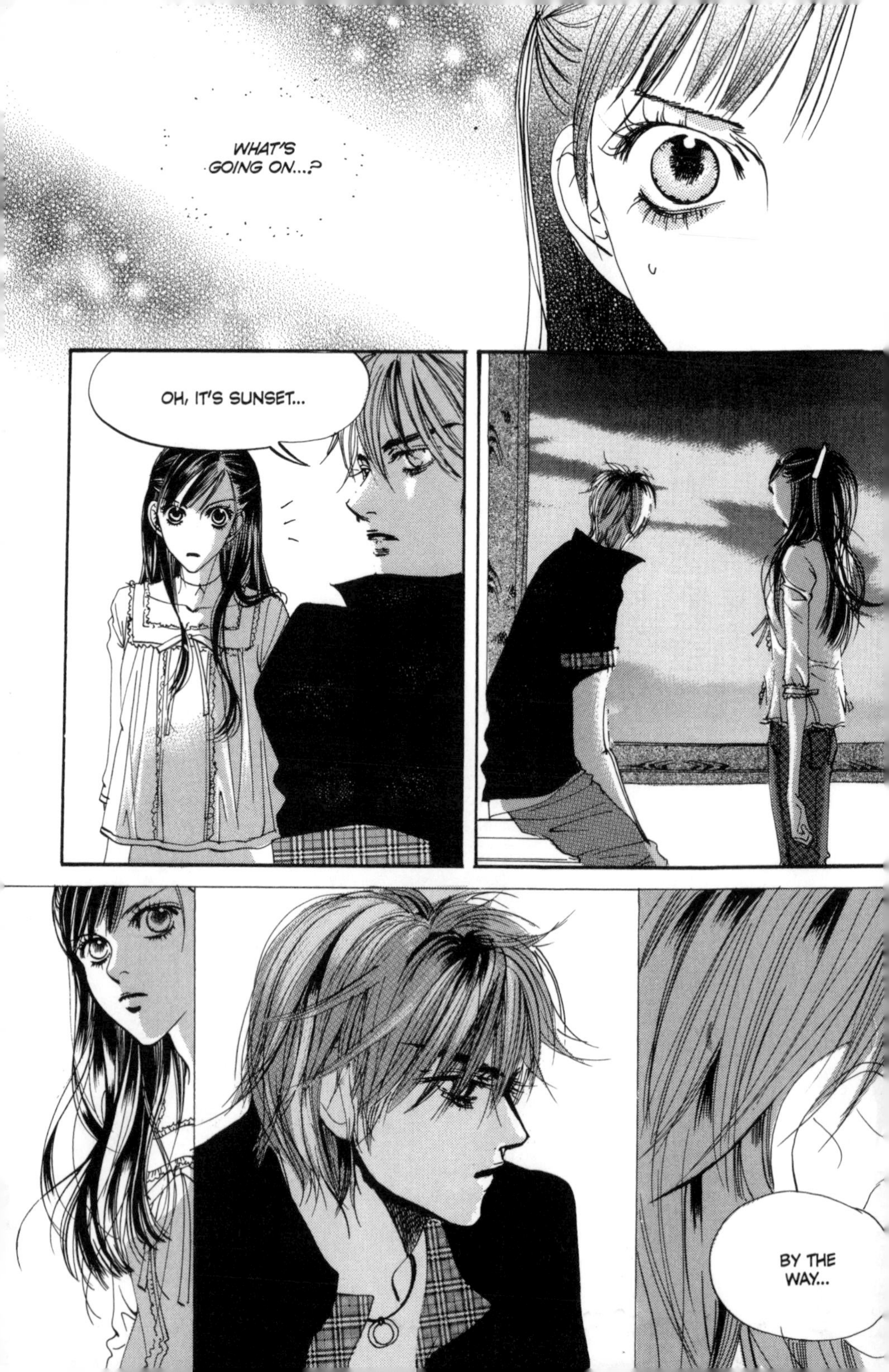
WHAT'S GOING ON...?
OH, IT'S SUNSET...
BY THE WAY...

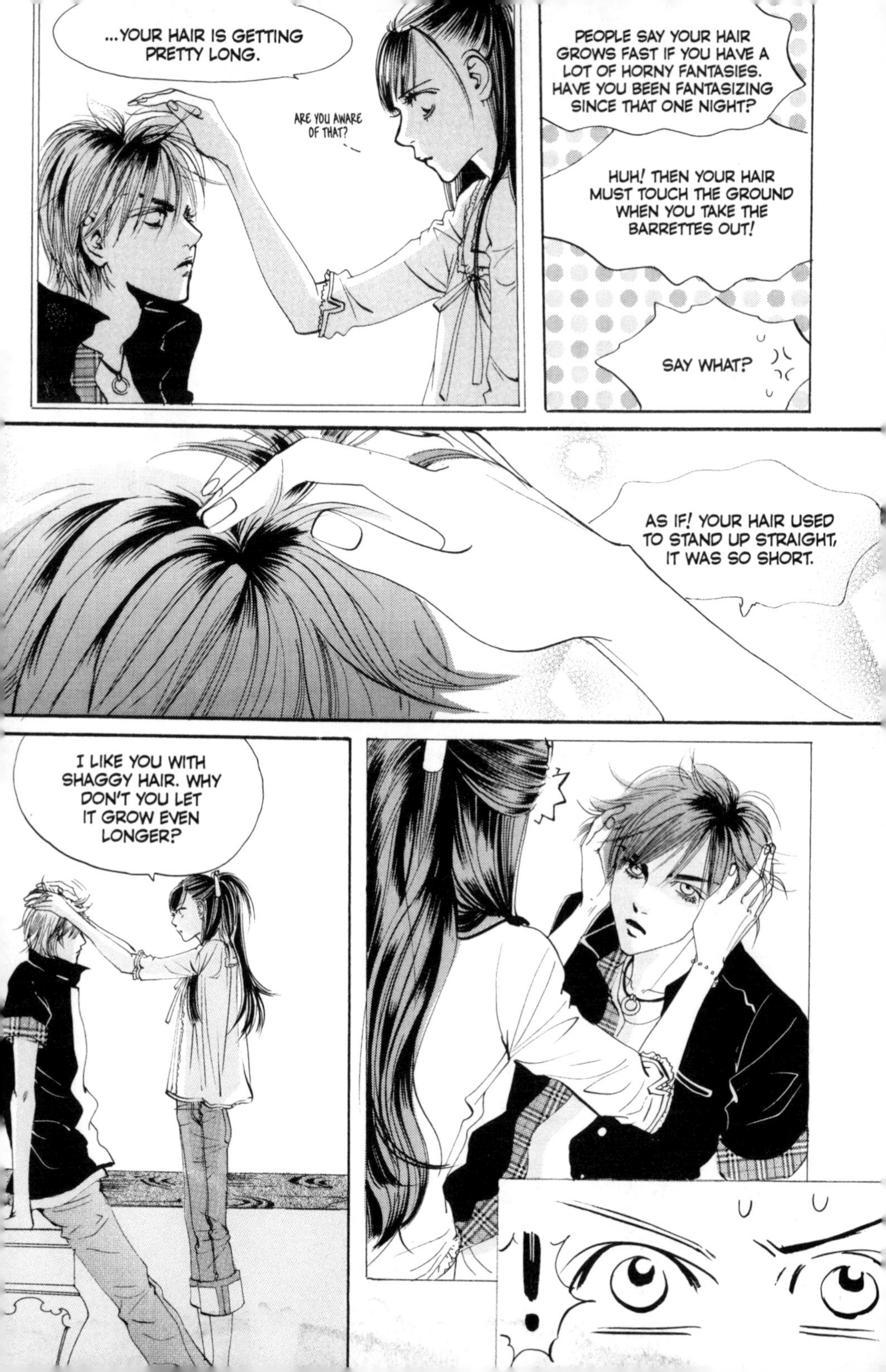
...YOUR HAIR IS GETTING PRETTY LONG.
ARE YOU AWARE OF THAT?
PEOPLE SAY YOUR HAIR GROWS FAST IF YOU HAVE A LOT OF HORNY FANTASIES. HAVE YOU BEEN FANTASIZING SINCE THAT ONE NIGHT?
HUH! THEN YOUR HAIR MUST TOUCH THE GROUND WHEN YOU TAKE THE BARRETTES OUT!
SAY WHAT?
AS IF! YOUR HAIR USED TO STAND UP STRAIGHT, IT WAS SO SHORT.
I LIKE YOU WITH SHAGGY HAIR. WHY DON'T YOU LET IT GROW EVEN LONGER?
!

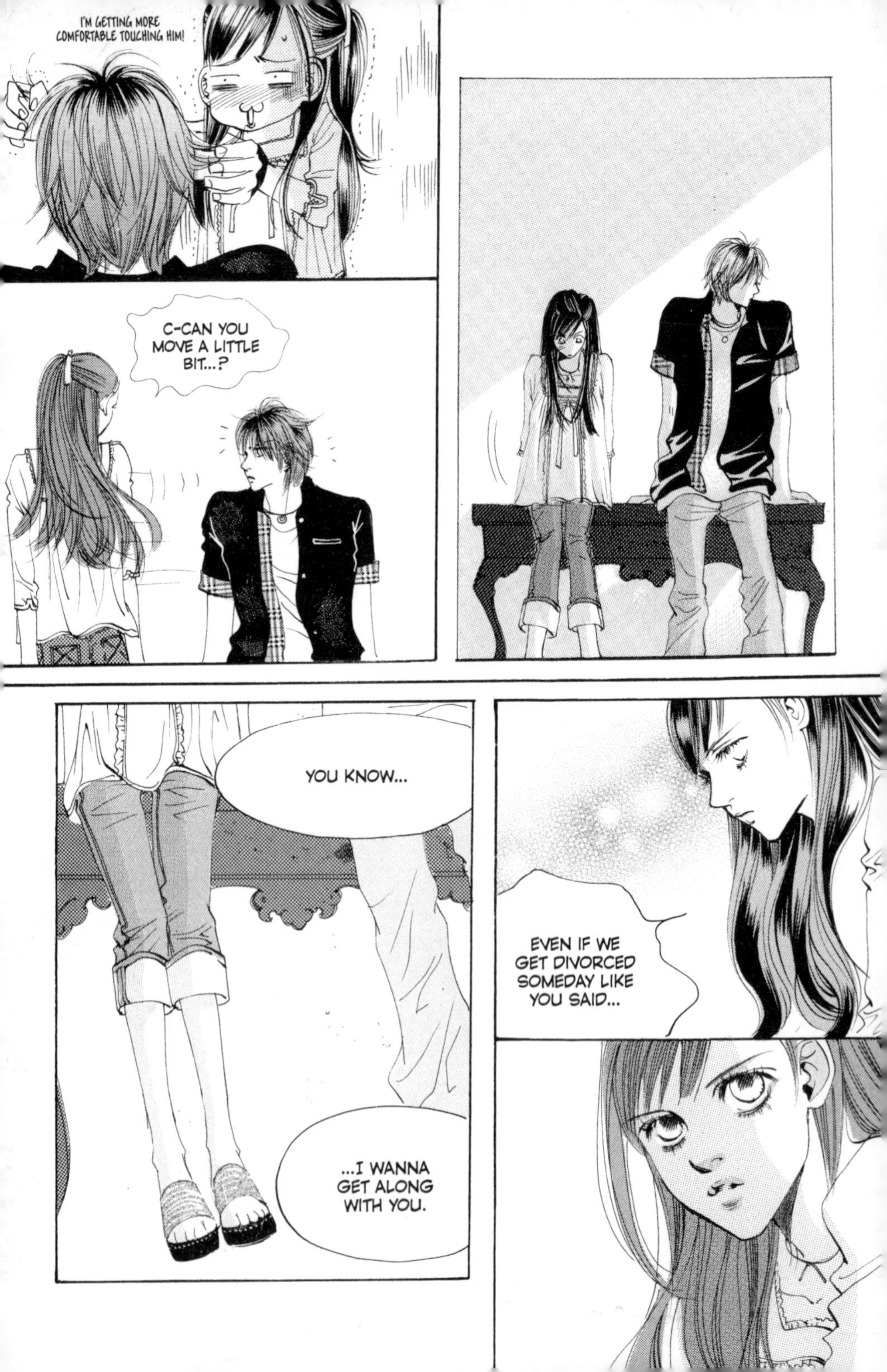
I'M GETTING MORE COMFORTABLE TOUCHING HIM!
C-CAN YOU MOVE A LITTLE BIT...?
YOU KNOW...
...I WANNA GET ALONG WITH YOU.
EVEN IF WE GET DIVORCED SOMEDAY LIKE YOU SAID...

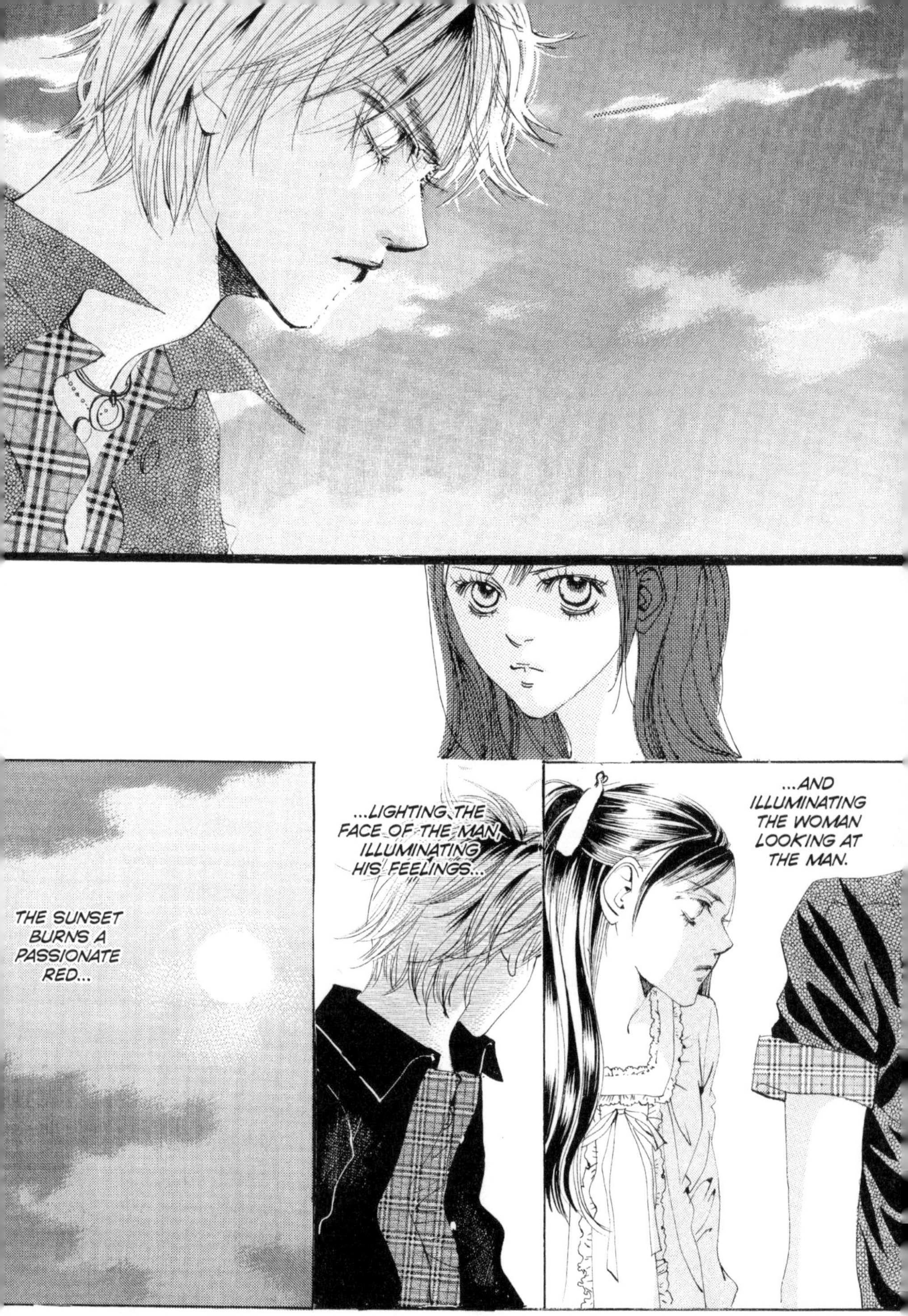
THE SUNSET BURNS A PASSIONATE RED...
...LIGHTING THE FACE OF THE MAN, ILLUMINATING HIS FEELINGS...
...AND ILLUMINATING THE WOMAN LOOKING AT THE MAN.

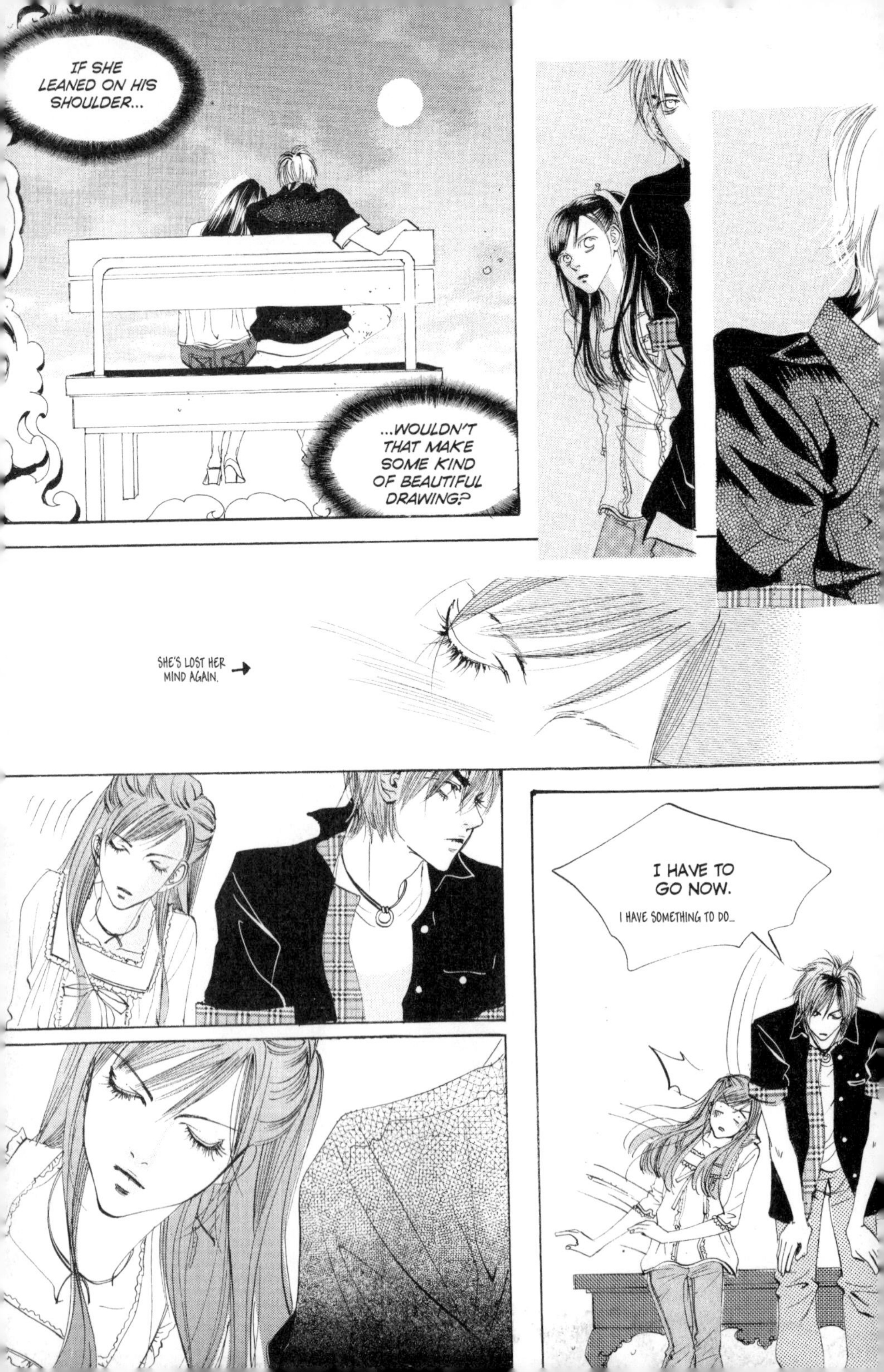
IF SHE LEANED ON HIS SHOULDER...
...WOULDN'T THAT MAKE SOME KIND OF BEAUTIFUL DRAWING?
SHE'S LOST HER MIND AGAIN.
I HAVE TO GO NOW.
I HAVE SOMETHING TO DO...

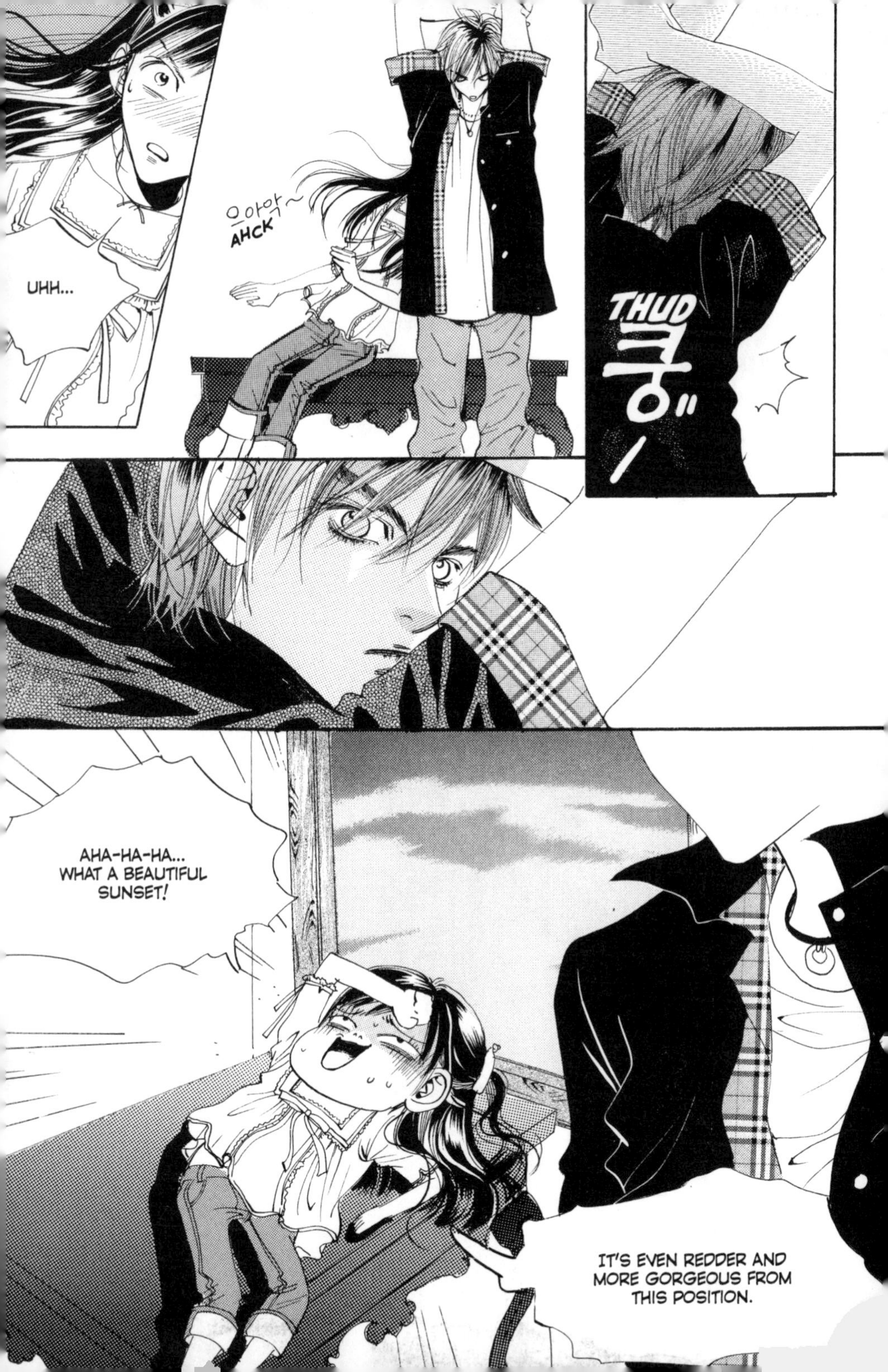

UHH...
으아악~
AHCK
THUD
쿵
AHA-HA-HA... WHAT A BEAUTIFUL SUNSET!
IT'S EVEN REDDER AND MORE GORGEOUS FROM THIS POSITION.

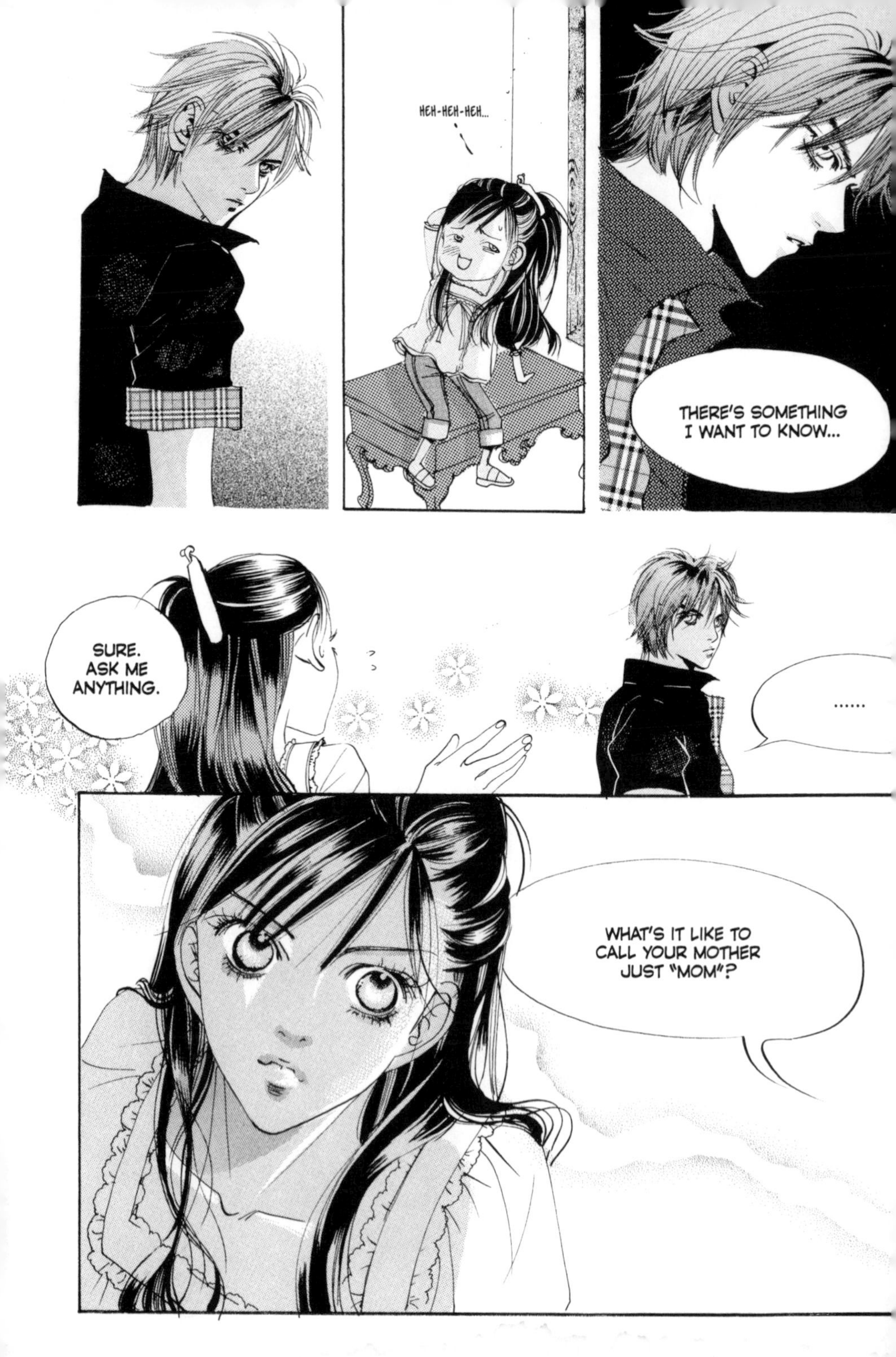
HEH-HEH-HEH...
THERE'S SOMETHING I WANT TO KNOW...
SURE. ASK ME ANYTHING.
......
WHAT'S IT LIKE TO CALL YOUR MOTHER JUST "MOM"?

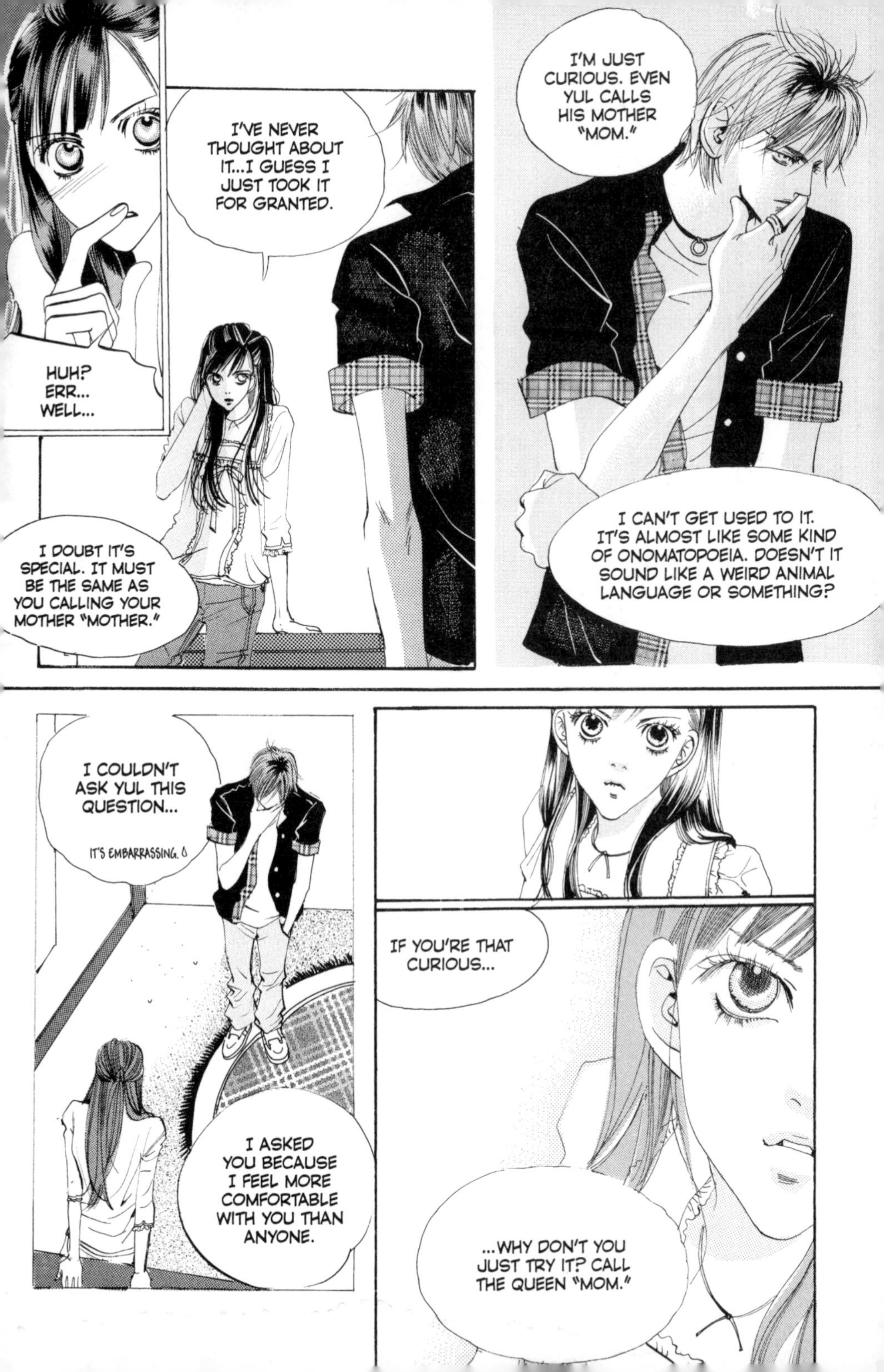
HUH? ERR... WELL...
I'VE NEVER THOUGHT ABOUT IT...I GUESS I JUST TOOK IT FOR GRANTED.
I DOUBT IT'S SPECIAL. IT MUST BE THE SAME AS YOU CALLING YOUR MOTHER "MOTHER."
I'M JUST CURIOUS. EVEN YUL CALLS HIS MOTHER "MOM."
I CAN'T GET USED TO IT. IT'S ALMOST LIKE SOME KIND OF ONOMATOPOEIA. DOESN'T IT SOUND LIKE A WEIRD ANIMAL LANGUAGE OR SOMETHING?
I COULDN'T ASK YUL THIS QUESTION...
IT'S EMBARRASSING.
I ASKED YOU BECAUSE I FEEL MORE COMFORTABLE WITH YOU THAN ANYONE.
IF YOU'RE THAT CURIOUS...
...WHY DON'T YOU JUST TRY IT? CALL THE QUEEN "MOM."

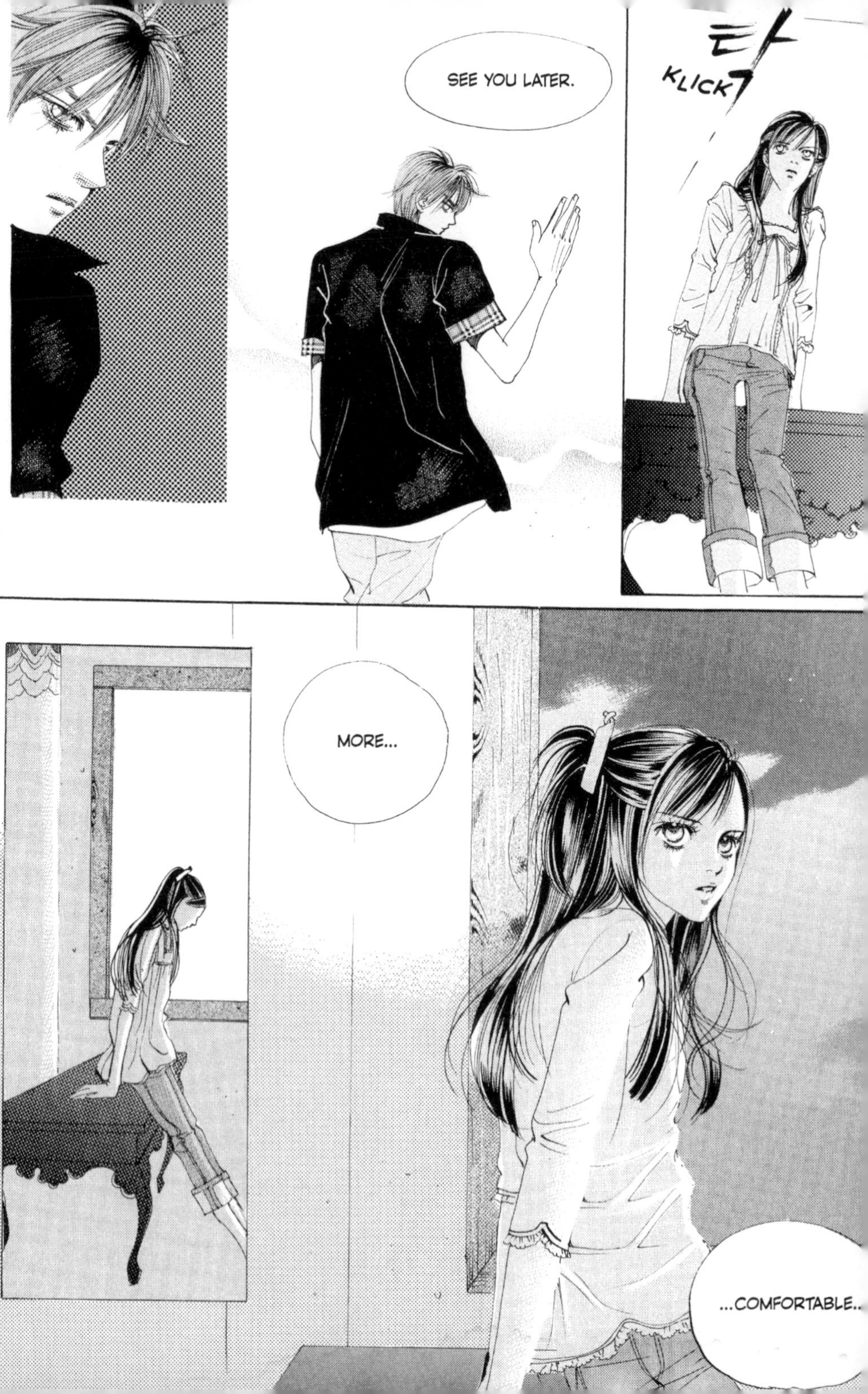
SEE YOU LATER.
KLICK
MORE...
...COMFORTABLE..

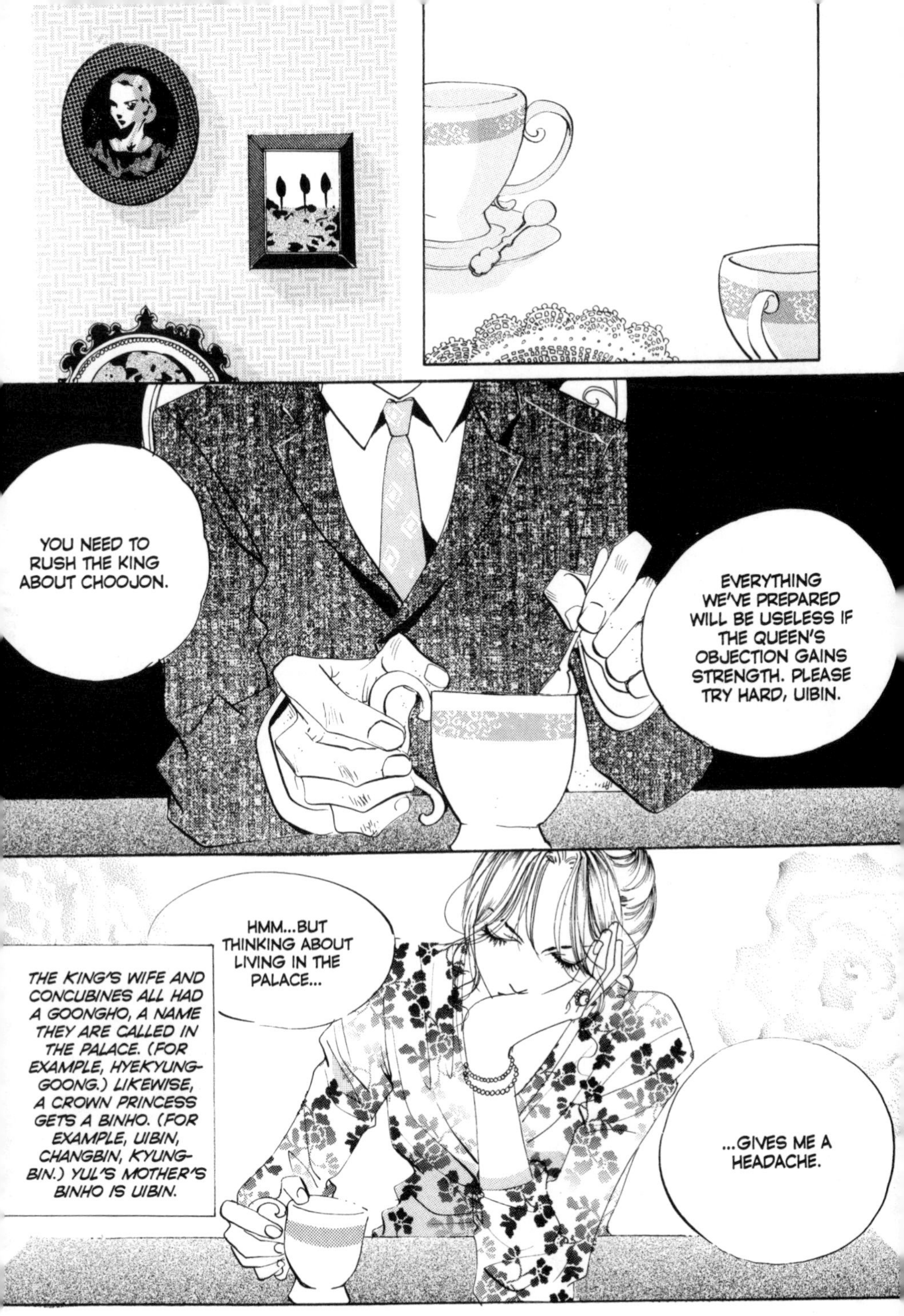
YOU NEED TO RUSH THE KING ABOUT CHOOJON.
EVERYTHING WE'VE PREPARED WILL BE USELESS IF THE QUEEN'S OBJECTION GAINS STRENGTH. PLEASE TRY HARD, UIBIN.
THE KING'S WIFE AND CONCUBINES ALL HAD A GOONGHO, A NAME THEY ARE CALLED IN THE PALACE. (FOR EXAMPLE, HYEKYUNG-GOONG.) LIKEWISE, A CROWN PRINCESS GETS A BINHO. (FOR EXAMPLE, UIBIN, CHANGBIN, KYUNG-BIN.) YUL'S MOTHER'S BINHO IS UIBIN.
HMM...BUT THINKING ABOUT LIVING IN THE PALACE...
...GIVES ME A HEADACHE.

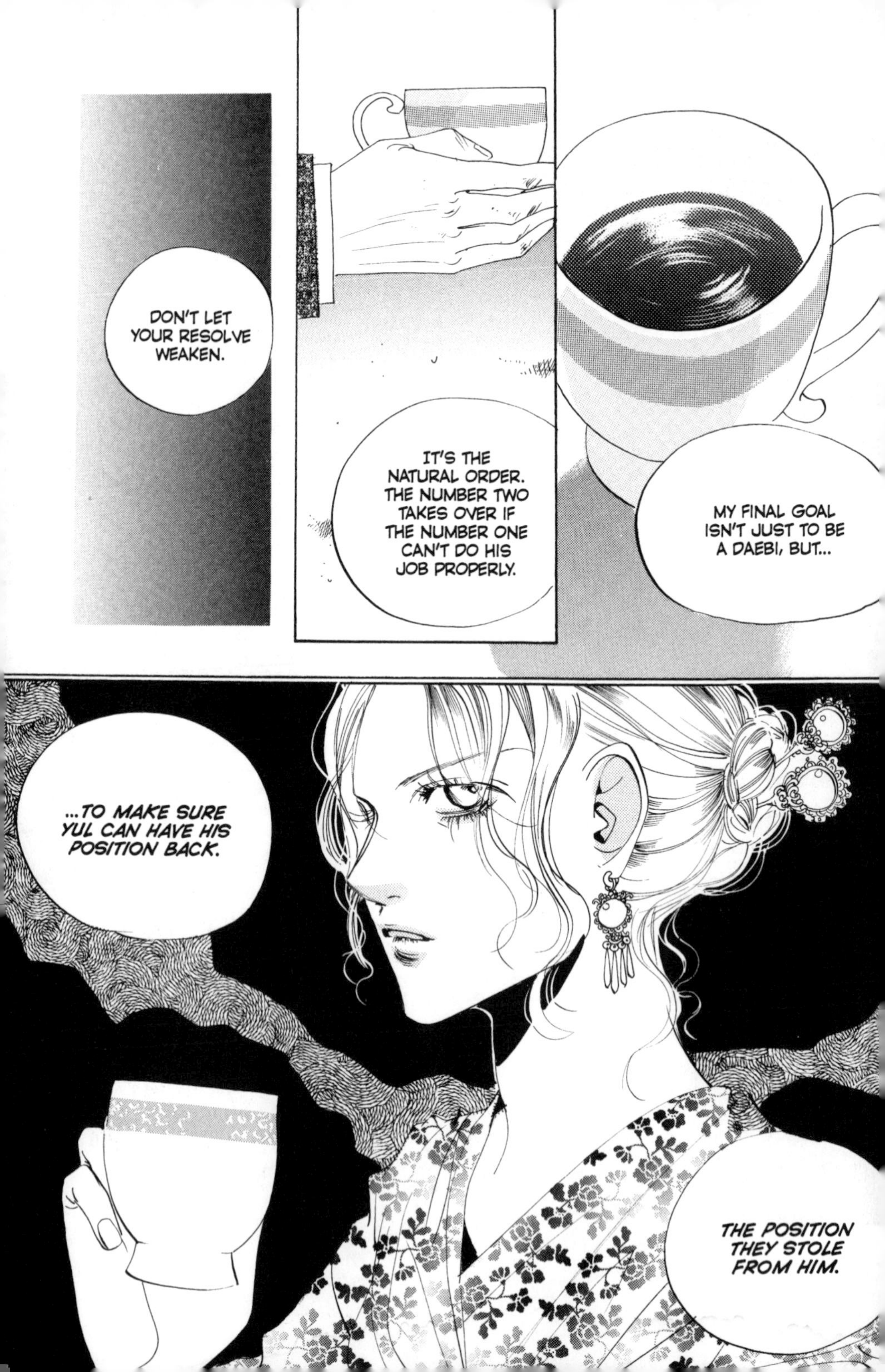
DON'T LET YOUR RESOLVE WEAKEN.
IT'S THE NATURAL ORDER. THE NUMBER TWO TAKES OVER IF THE NUMBER ONE CAN'T DO HIS JOB PROPERLY.
MY FINAL GOAL ISN'T JUST TO BE A DAEBI, BUT...
...TO MAKE SURE YUL CAN HAVE HIS POSITION BACK.
THE POSITION THEY STOLE FROM HIM.

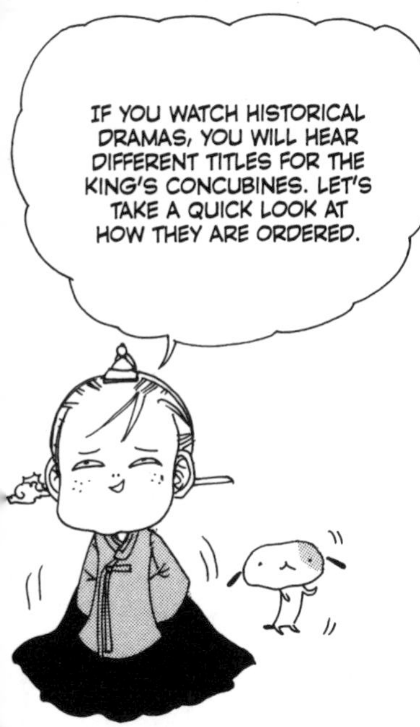
IF YOU WATCH HISTORICAL DRAMAS, YOU WILL HEAR DIFFERENT TITLES FOR THE KING'S CONCUBINES. LET'S TAKE A QUICK LOOK AT HOW THEY ARE ORDERED.

KING'S CONCUBINES

BIN – JUNG POOM 1
GUIIN – JONG POOM 1
SOUI – JUNG POOM 2
SUKUI – JONG POOM 2
SOYONG – JUNG POOM 3
SOOKYONG – JONG POOM 3
SOWON – JUNG POOM 4
SOOKWON – JONG POOM 4

CROWN PRINCE'S CONCUBINES

YANGJE – JONG POOM 2
YANGWON – JONG POOM 3
SEUNGHUI – JONG POOM 4
SOHOON – JONG POOM 5

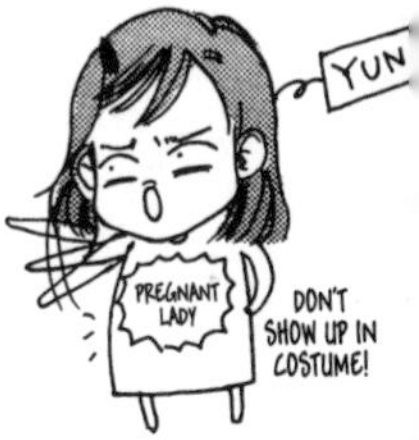
YUN
PREGNANT LADY
DON'T SHOW UP IN COSTUME!

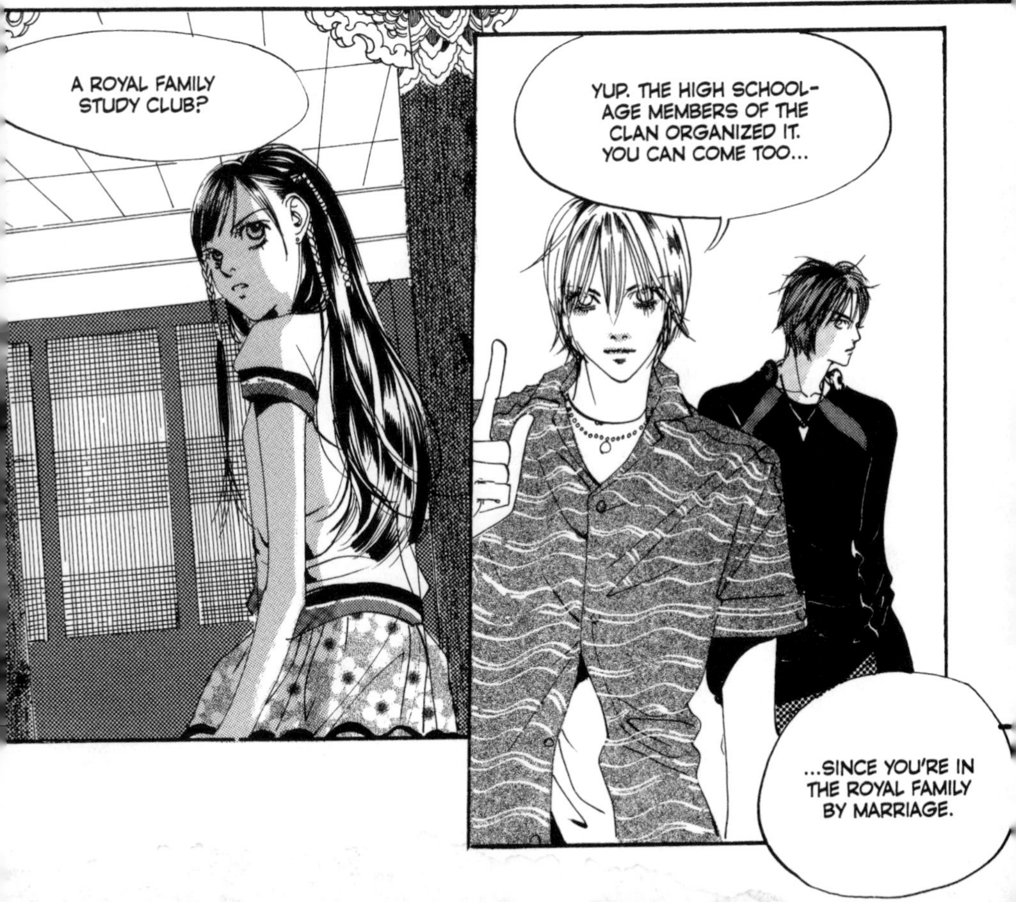
A ROYAL FAMILY STUDY CLUB?
YUP. THE HIGH SCHOOL-AGE MEMBERS OF THE CLAN ORGANIZED IT. YOU CAN COME TOO...
...SINCE YOU'RE IN THE ROYAL FAMILY BY MARRIAGE.

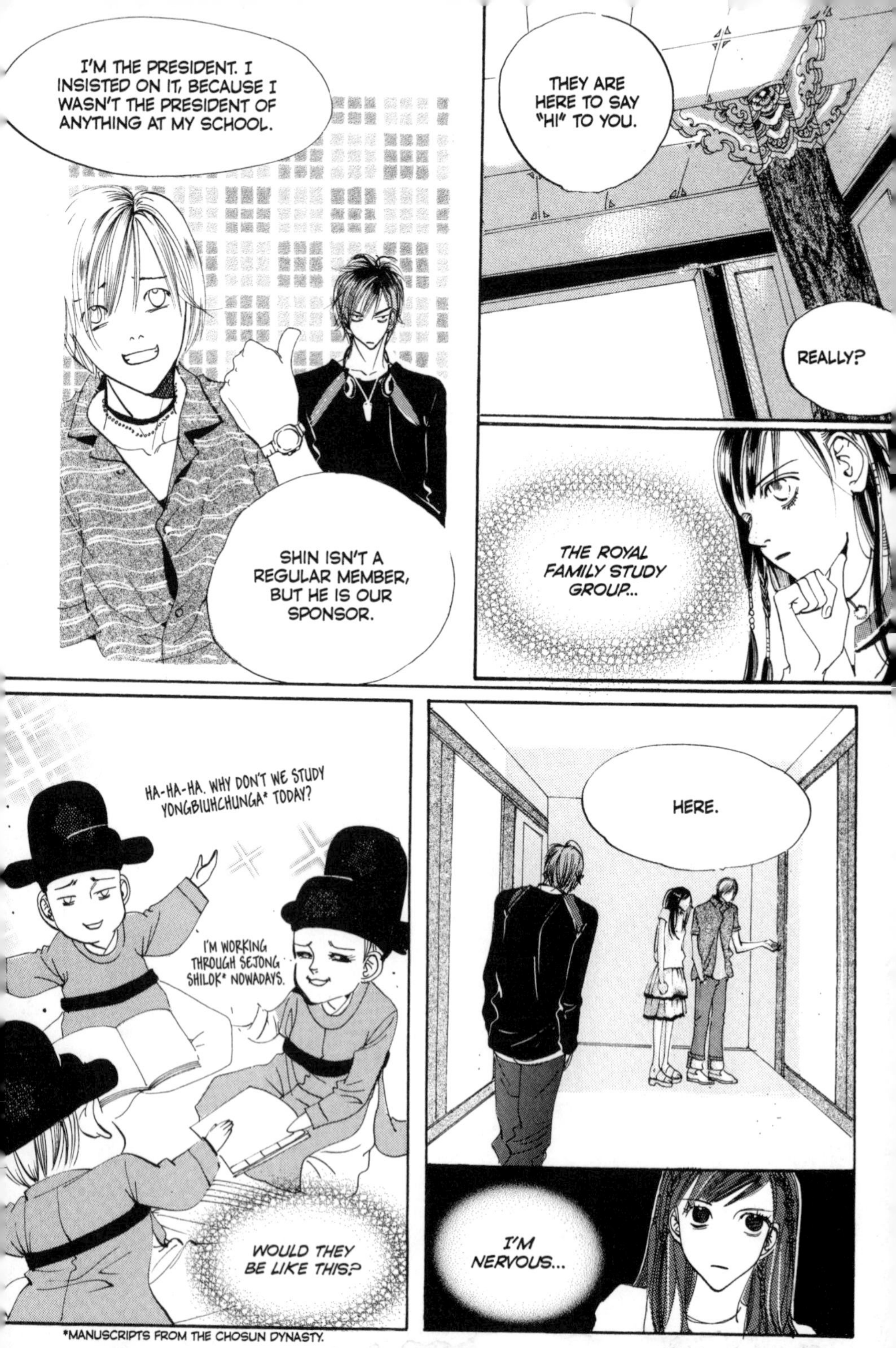
I'M THE PRESIDENT. I INSISTED ON IT, BECAUSE I WASN'T THE PRESIDENT OF ANYTHING AT MY SCHOOL.
SHIN ISN'T A REGULAR MEMBER, BUT HE IS OUR SPONSOR.
THEY ARE HERE TO SAY "HI" TO YOU.
REALLY?
THE ROYAL FAMILY STUDY GROUP...
HA-HA-HA. WHY DON'T WE STUDY YONGBIUHCHUNGA* TODAY?
I'M WORKING THROUGH SEJONG SHILOK* NOWADAYS.
WOULD THEY BE LIKE THIS?
HERE.
I'M NERVOUS...

*MANUSCRIPTS FROM THE CHOSUN DYNASTY.

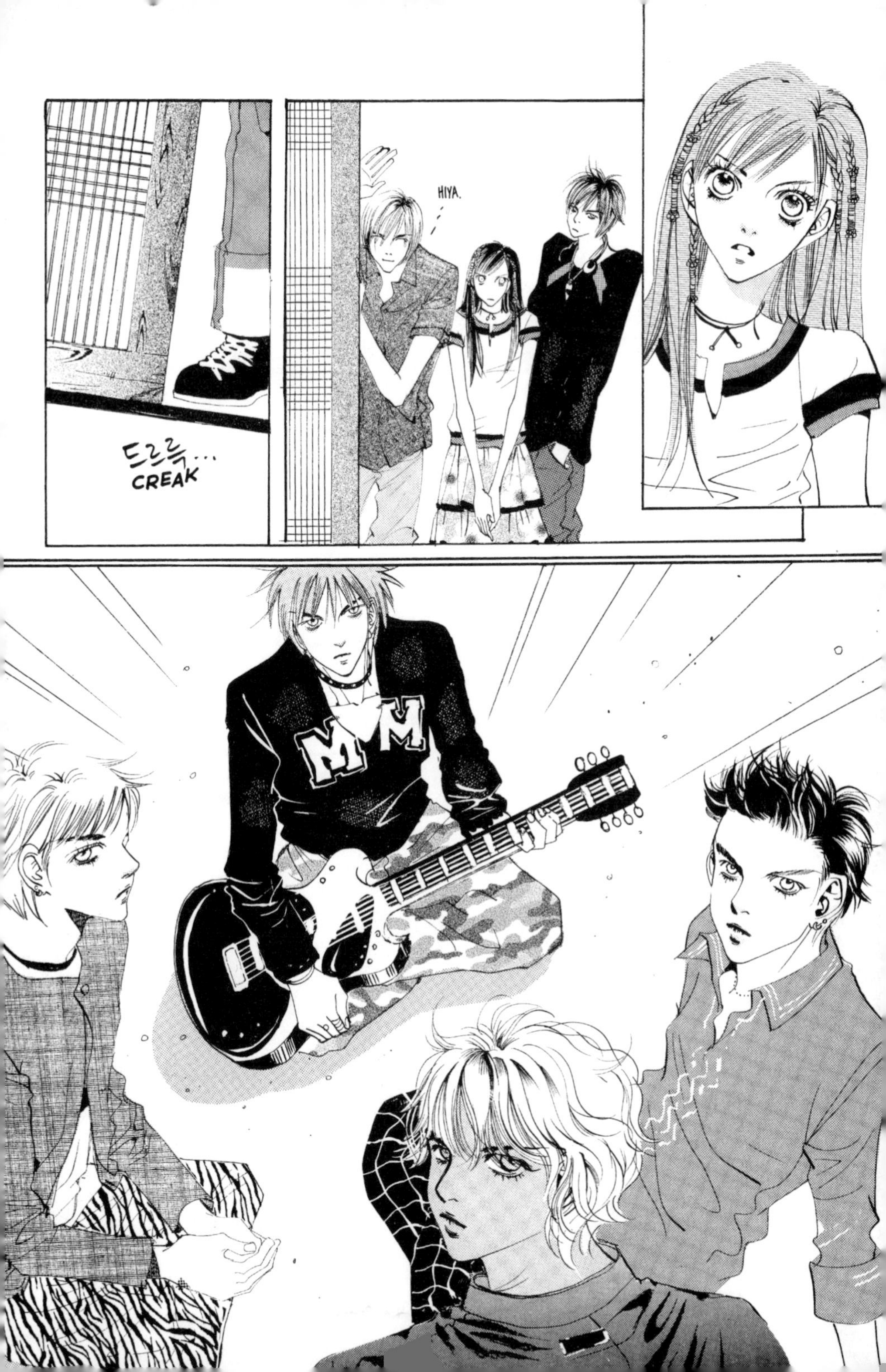

드르륵...
CREAK
HIYA.

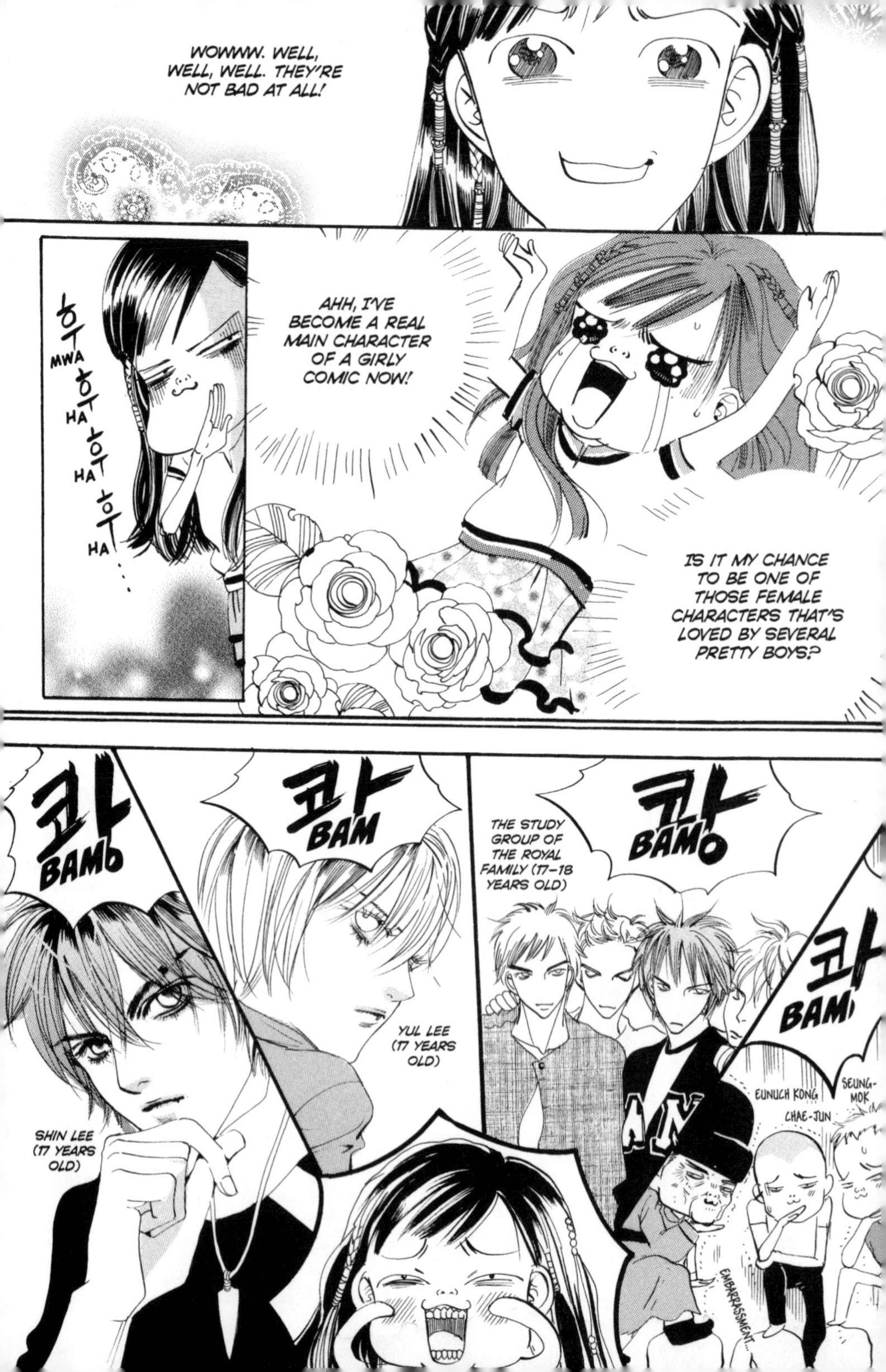
WOWWW. WELL, WELL, WELL. THEY'RE NOT BAD AT ALL!
호 MWA
호 HA
호 HA
호 HA...
AHH, I'VE BECOME A REAL MAIN CHARACTER OF A GIRLY COMIC NOW!
IS IT MY CHANCE TO BE ONE OF THOSE FEMALE CHARACTERS THAT'S LOVED BY SEVERAL PRETTY BOYS?
쾅 BAM
SHIN LEE (17 YEARS OLD)
콰 BAM
YUL LEE (17 YEARS OLD)
쾅 BAM
THE STUDY GROUP OF THE ROYAL FAMILY (17–18 YEARS OLD)
콰 BAM
EUNUCH KONG
SEUNG-MOK
CHAE-JUN
EMBARRASSMENT...

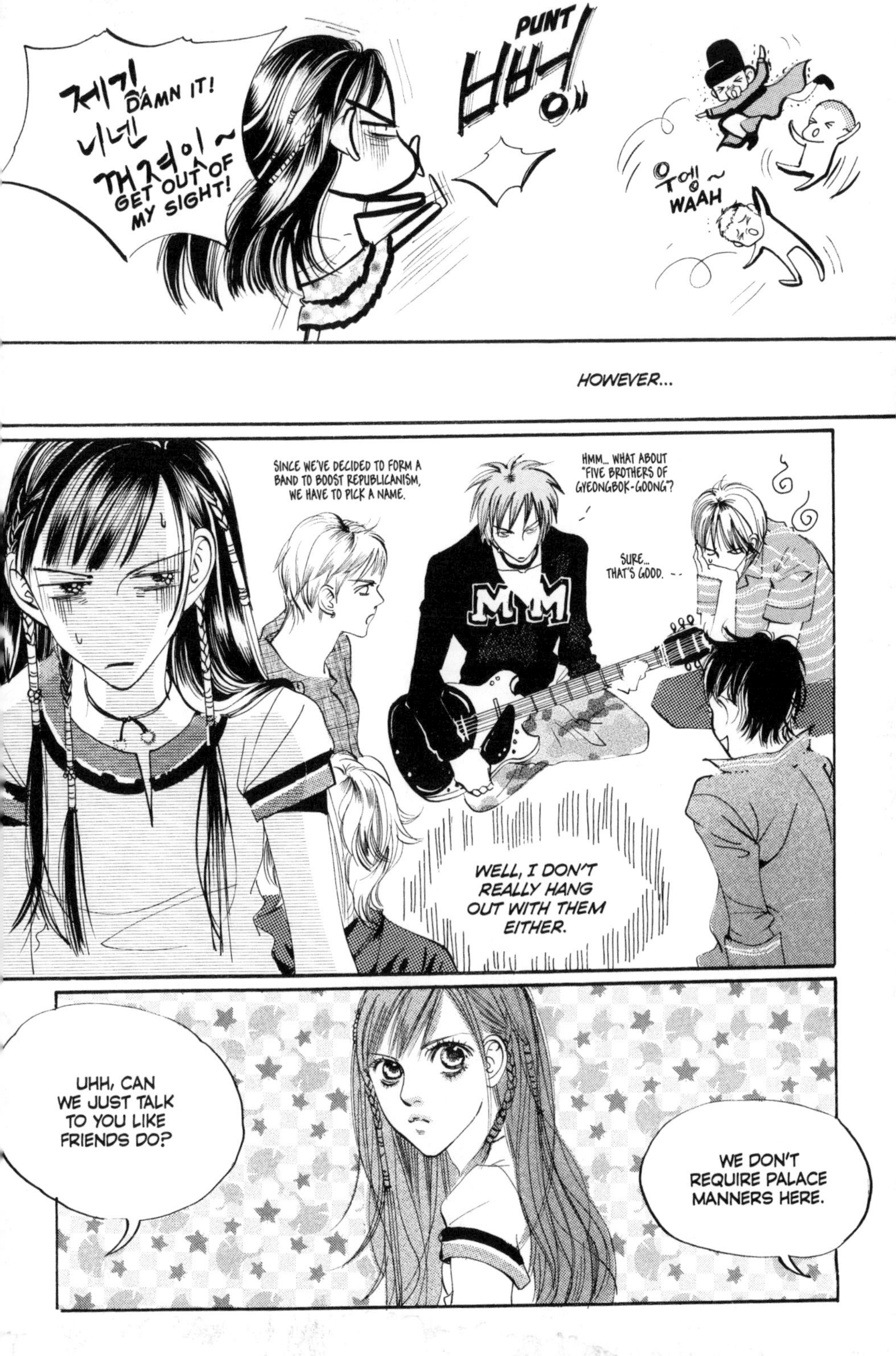
제기 DAMN IT!
니넨 꺼져이~ GET OUT OF MY SIGHT!
PUNT 뻥
우엥~ WAAH
HOWEVER...
SINCE WE'VE DECIDED TO FORM A BAND TO BOOST REPUBLICANISM, WE HAVE TO PICK A NAME.
HMM... WHAT ABOUT "FIVE BROTHERS OF GYEONGBOK-GOONG"?
SURE... THAT'S GOOD.
WELL, I DON'T REALLY HANG OUT WITH THEM EITHER.
UHH, CAN WE JUST TALK TO YOU LIKE FRIENDS DO?
WE DON'T REQUIRE PALACE MANNERS HERE.

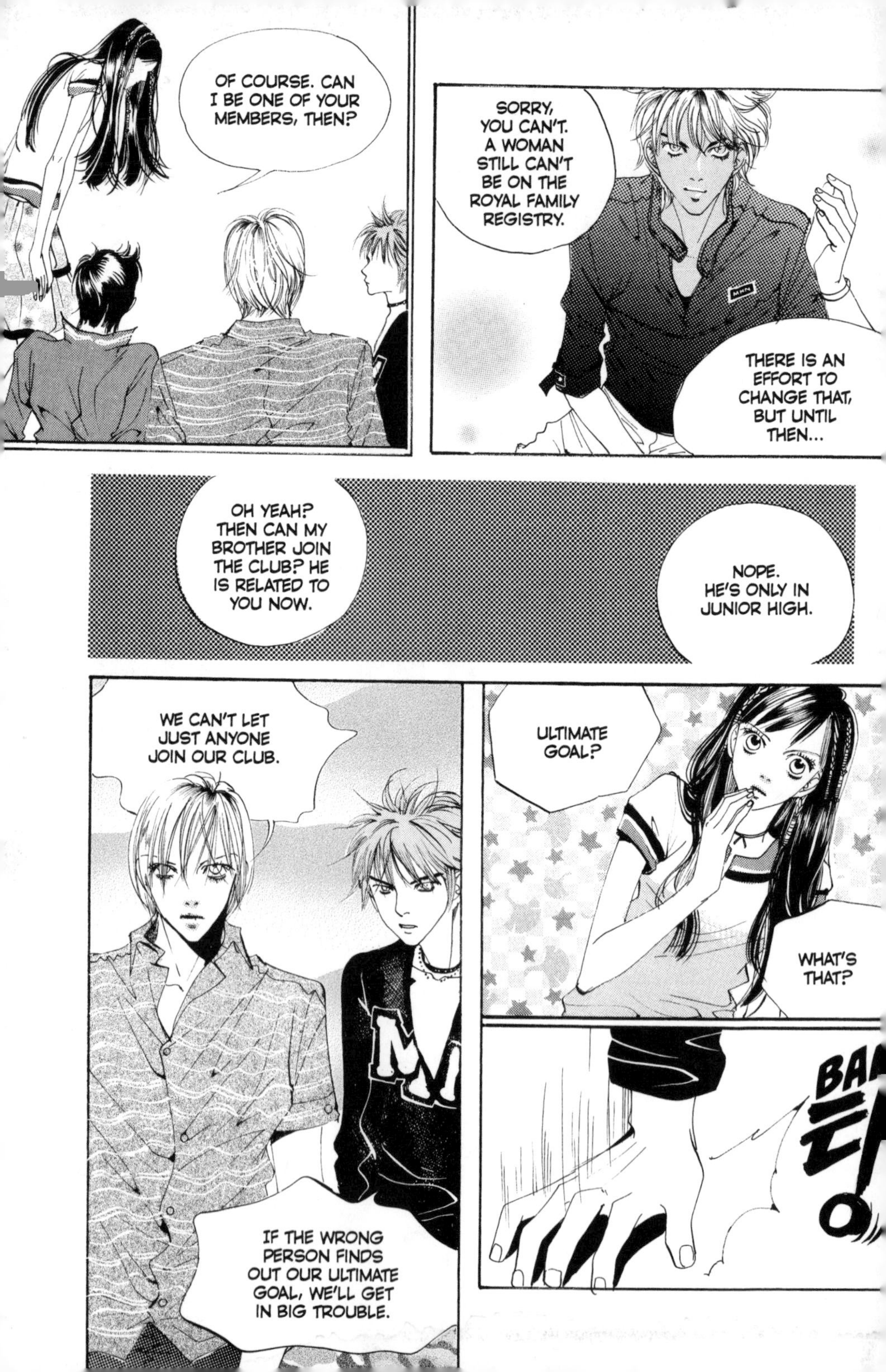
OF COURSE. CAN I BE ONE OF YOUR MEMBERS, THEN?
SORRY, YOU CAN'T. A WOMAN STILL CAN'T BE ON THE ROYAL FAMILY REGISTRY.
THERE IS AN EFFORT TO CHANGE THAT, BUT UNTIL THEN...
OH YEAH? THEN CAN MY BROTHER JOIN THE CLUB? HE IS RELATED TO YOU NOW.
NOPE. HE'S ONLY IN JUNIOR HIGH.
WE CAN'T LET JUST ANYONE JOIN OUR CLUB.
IF THE WRONG PERSON FINDS OUT OUR ULTIMATE GOAL, WE'LL GET IN BIG TROUBLE.
ULTIMATE GOAL?
WHAT'S THAT?
BA

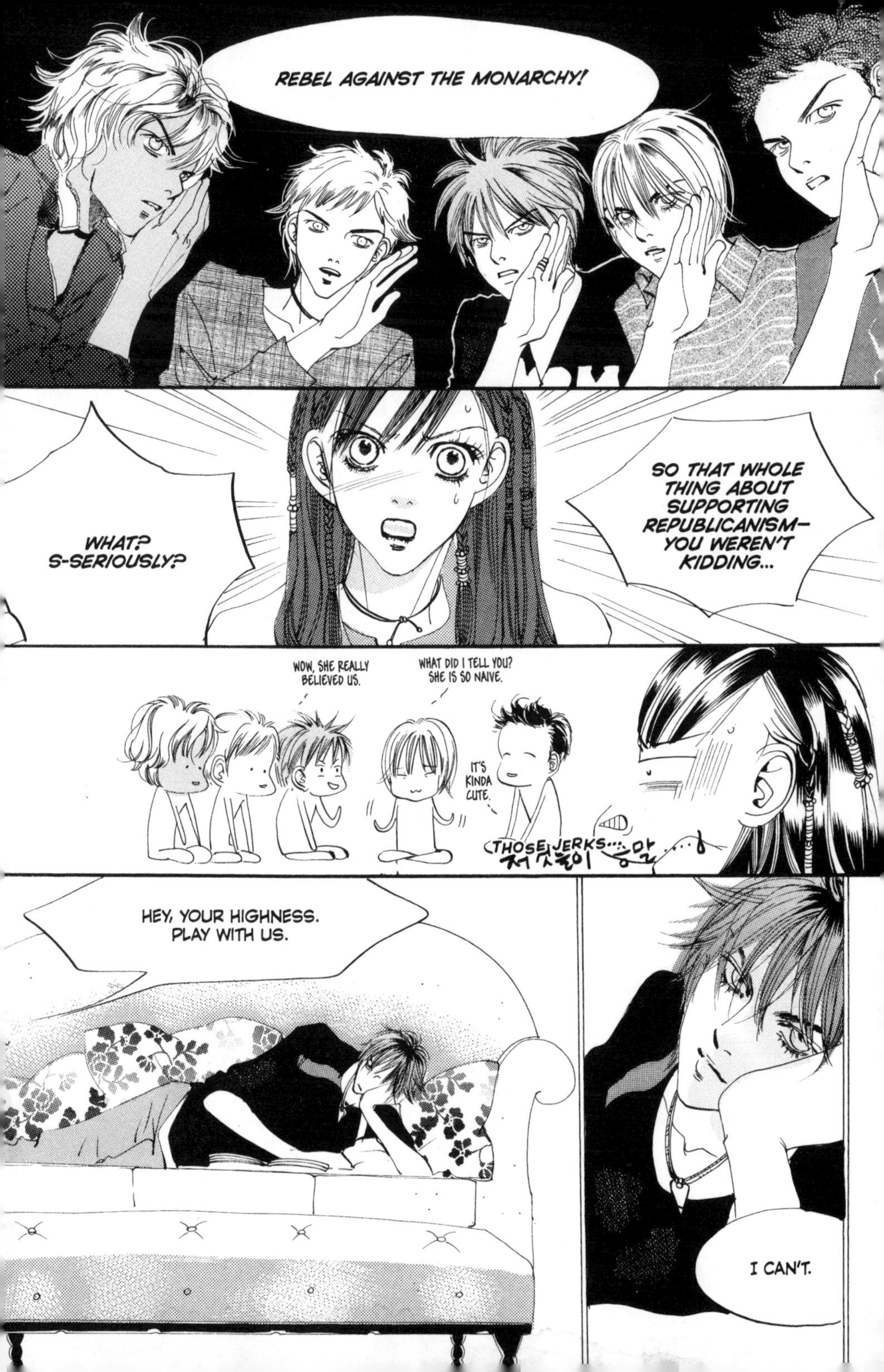
REBEL AGAINST THE MONARCHY!
WHAT? S-SERIOUSLY?
SO THAT WHOLE THING ABOUT SUPPORTING REPUBLICANISM—YOU WEREN'T KIDDING...
WOW, SHE REALLY BELIEVED US.
WHAT DID I TELL YOU? SHE IS SO NAIVE.
IT'S KINDA CUTE.
THOSE JERKS....
HEY, YOUR HIGHNESS. PLAY WITH US.
I CAN'T.

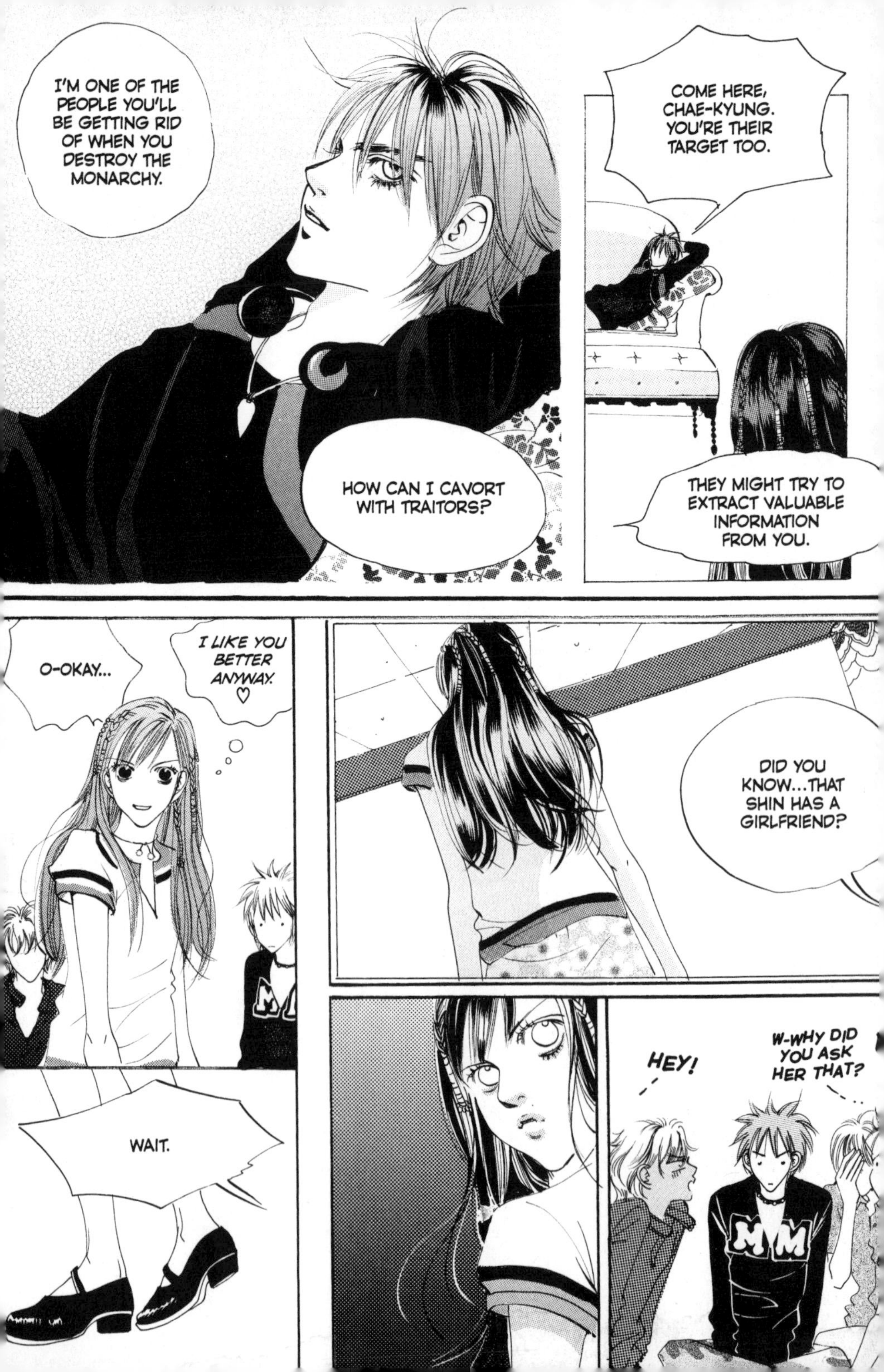
I'M ONE OF THE PEOPLE YOU'LL BE GETTING RID OF WHEN YOU DESTROY THE MONARCHY.
HOW CAN I CAVORT WITH TRAITORS?
COME HERE, CHAE-KYUNG. YOU'RE THEIR TARGET TOO.
THEY MIGHT TRY TO EXTRACT VALUABLE INFORMATION FROM YOU.
O-OKAY...
I LIKE YOU BETTER ANYWAY. ♡
DID YOU KNOW...THAT SHIN HAS A GIRLFRIEND?
WAIT.
HEY!
W-WHY DID YOU ASK HER THAT?

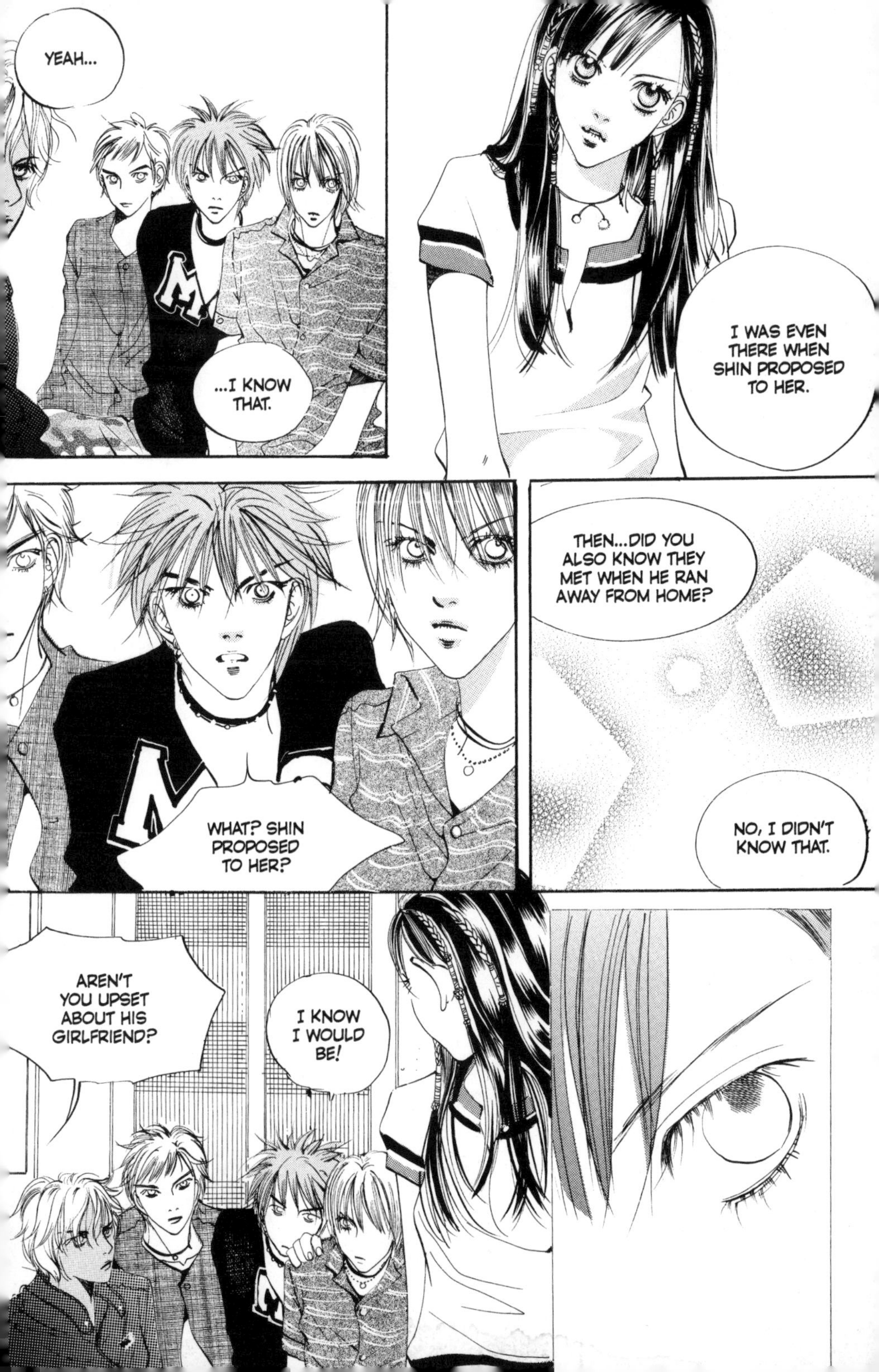
YEAH...
...I KNOW THAT.
I WAS EVEN THERE WHEN SHIN PROPOSED TO HER.
WHAT? SHIN PROPOSED TO HER?
THEN...DID YOU ALSO KNOW THEY MET WHEN HE RAN AWAY FROM HOME?
NO, I DIDN'T KNOW THAT.
AREN'T YOU UPSET ABOUT HIS GIRLFRIEND?
I KNOW I WOULD BE!

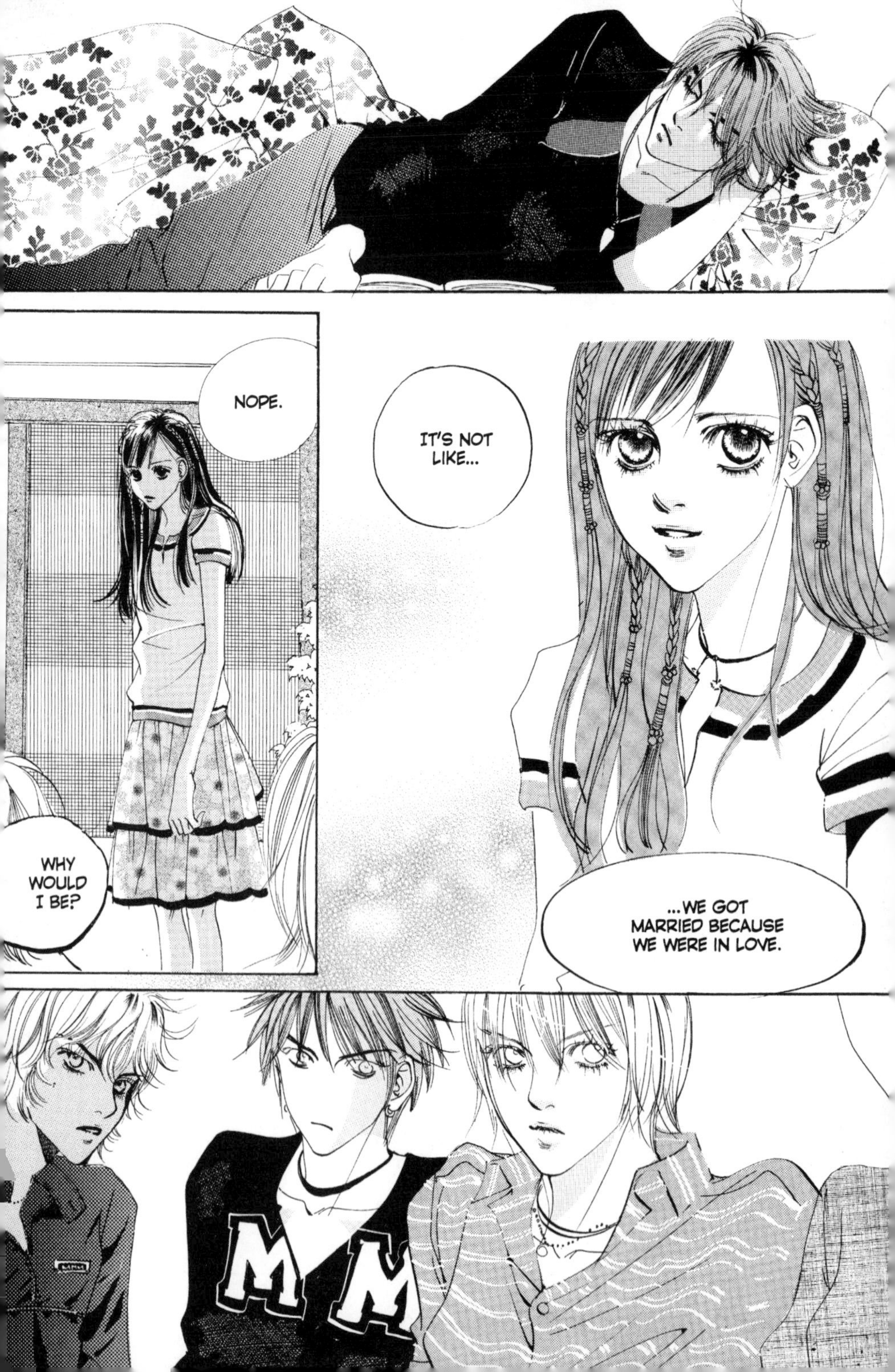
NOPE.
WHY WOULD I BE?
IT'S NOT LIKE...
...WE GOT MARRIED BECAUSE WE WERE IN LOVE.

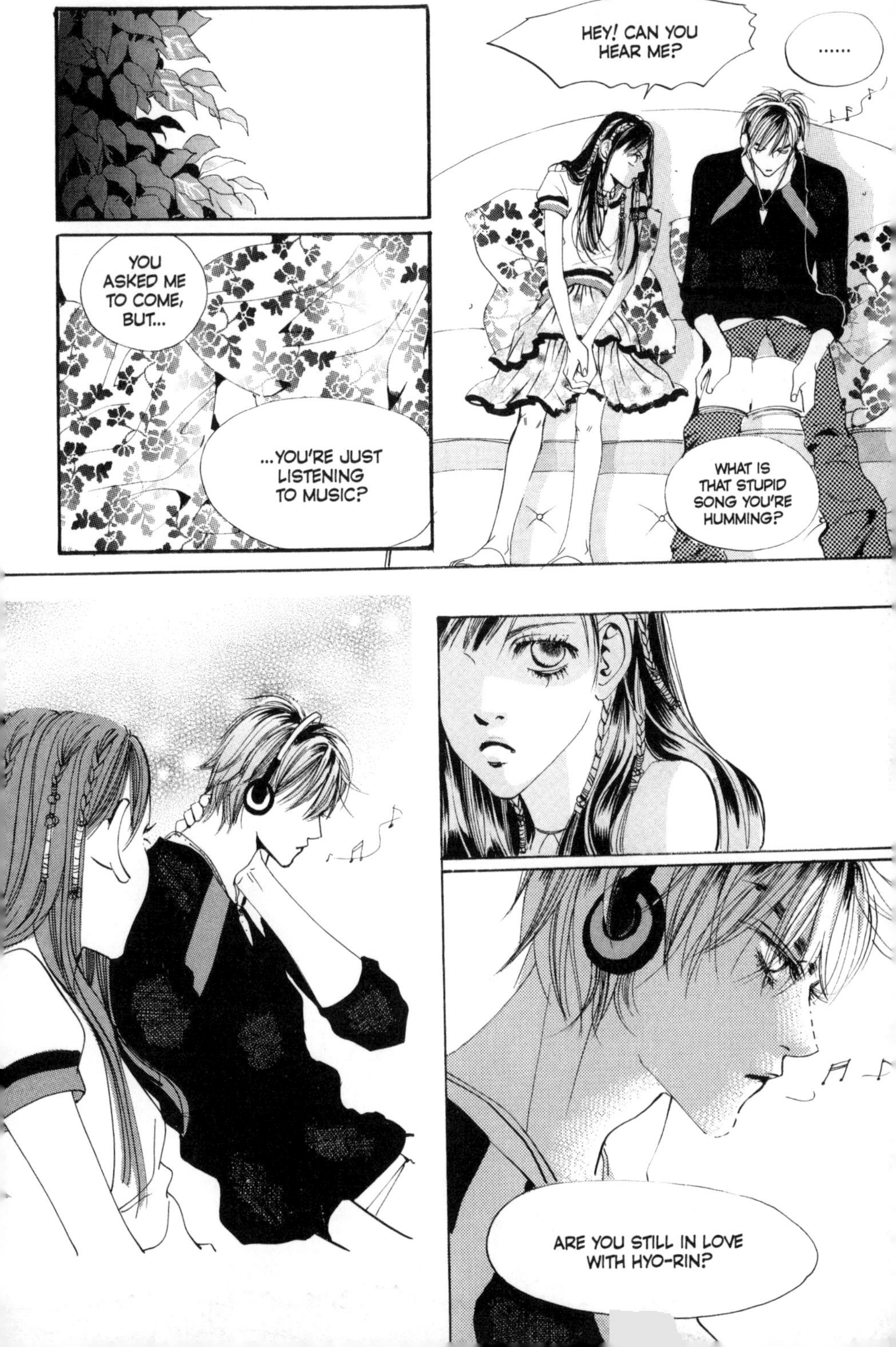
YOU ASKED ME TO COME, BUT...
...YOU'RE JUST LISTENING TO MUSIC?
HEY! CAN YOU HEAR ME?
......
WHAT IS THAT STUPID SONG YOU'RE HUMMING?
ARE YOU STILL IN LOVE WITH HYO-RIN?

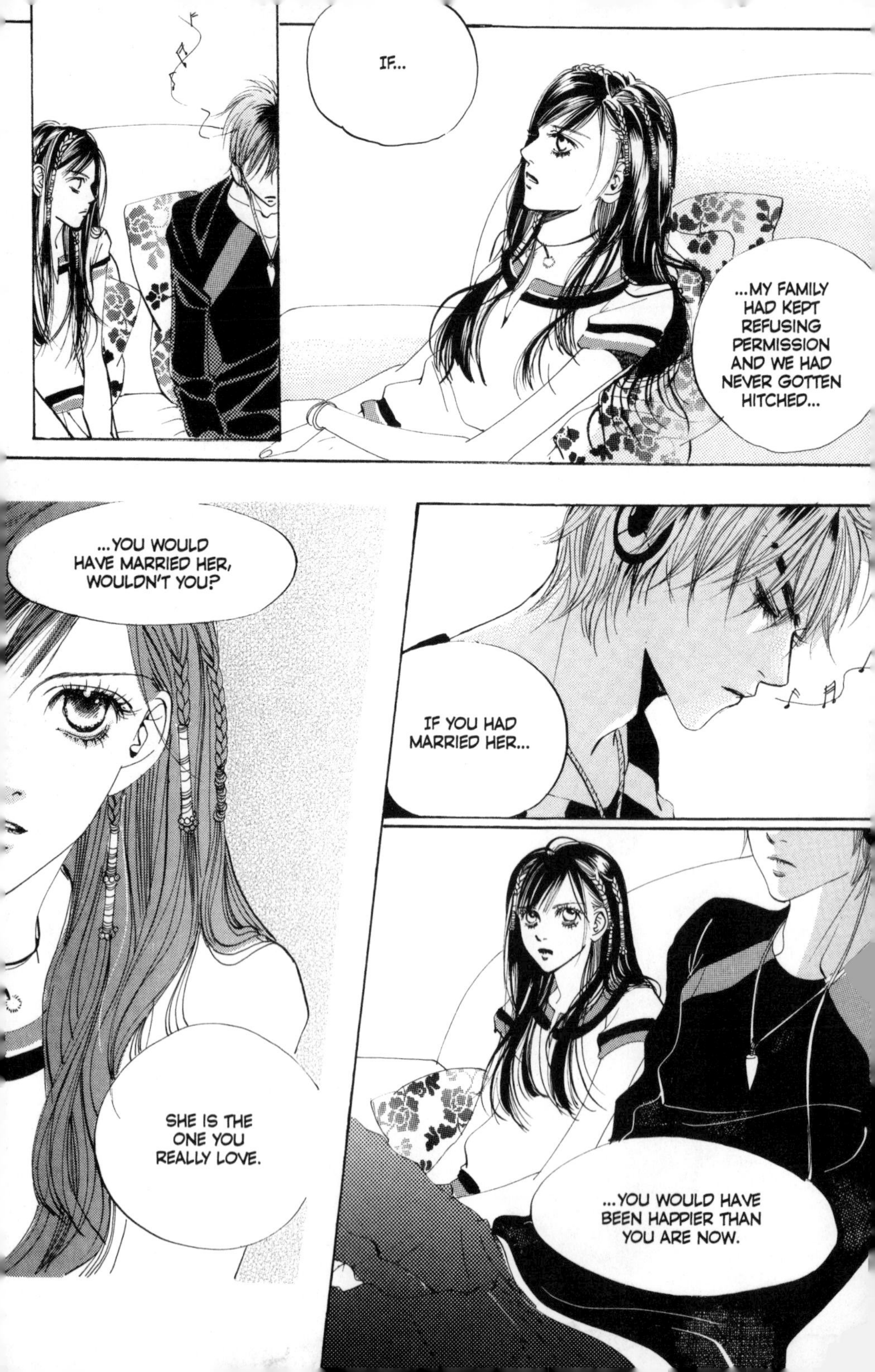
IF...
...MY FAMILY HAD KEPT REFUSING PERMISSION AND WE HAD NEVER GOTTEN HITCHED...
...YOU WOULD HAVE MARRIED HER, WOULDN'T YOU?
SHE IS THE ONE YOU REALLY LOVE.
IF YOU HAD MARRIED HER...
...YOU WOULD HAVE BEEN HAPPIER THAN YOU ARE NOW.

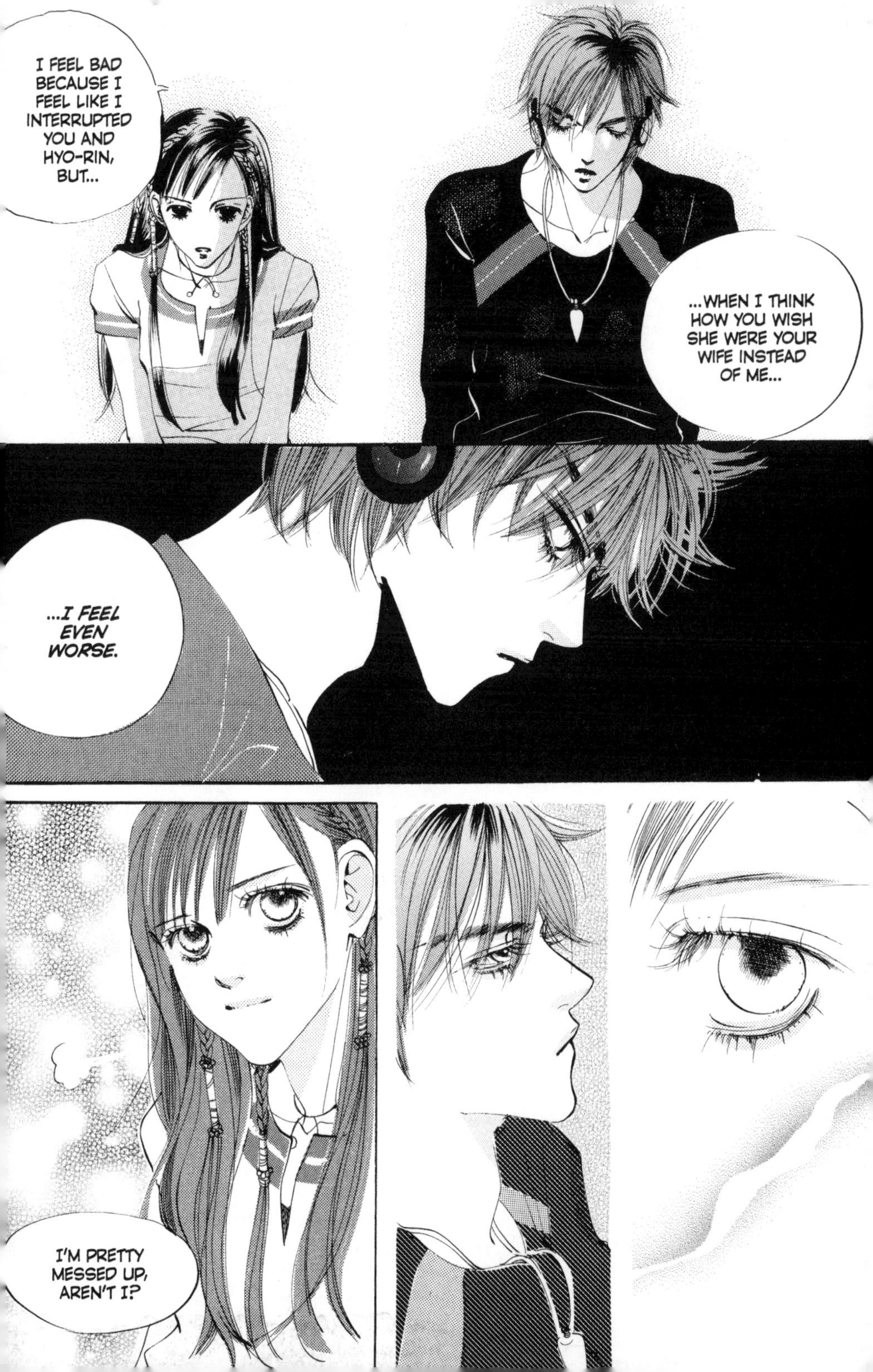
I FEEL BAD BECAUSE I FEEL LIKE I INTERRUPTED YOU AND HYO-RIN, BUT...
...WHEN I THINK HOW YOU WISH SHE WERE YOUR WIFE INSTEAD OF ME...
...I FEEL EVEN WORSE.
I'M PRETTY MESSED UP, AREN'T I?

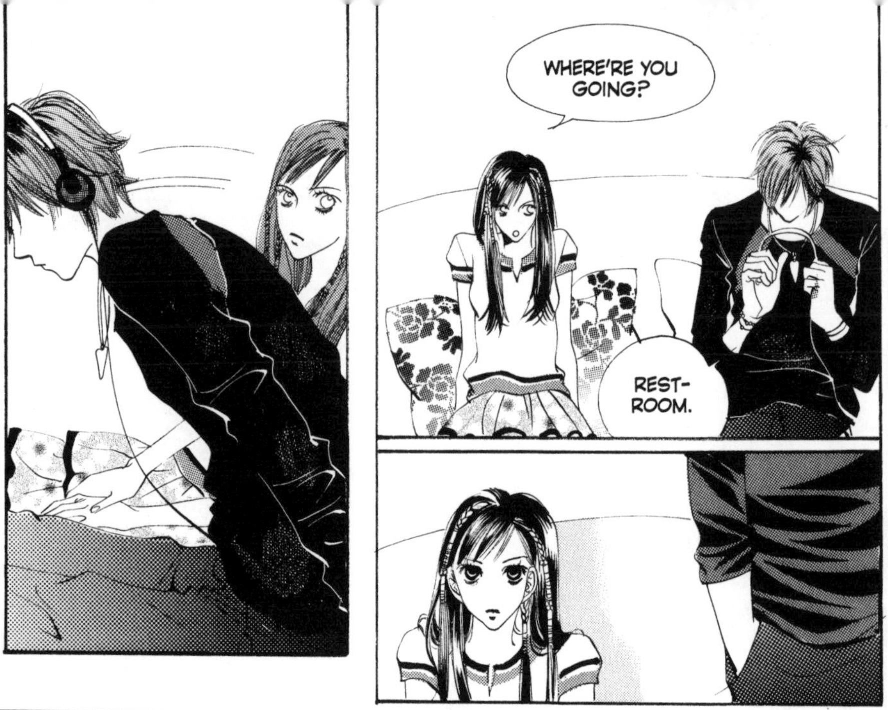
WHERE'RE YOU GOING?
REST-ROOM.
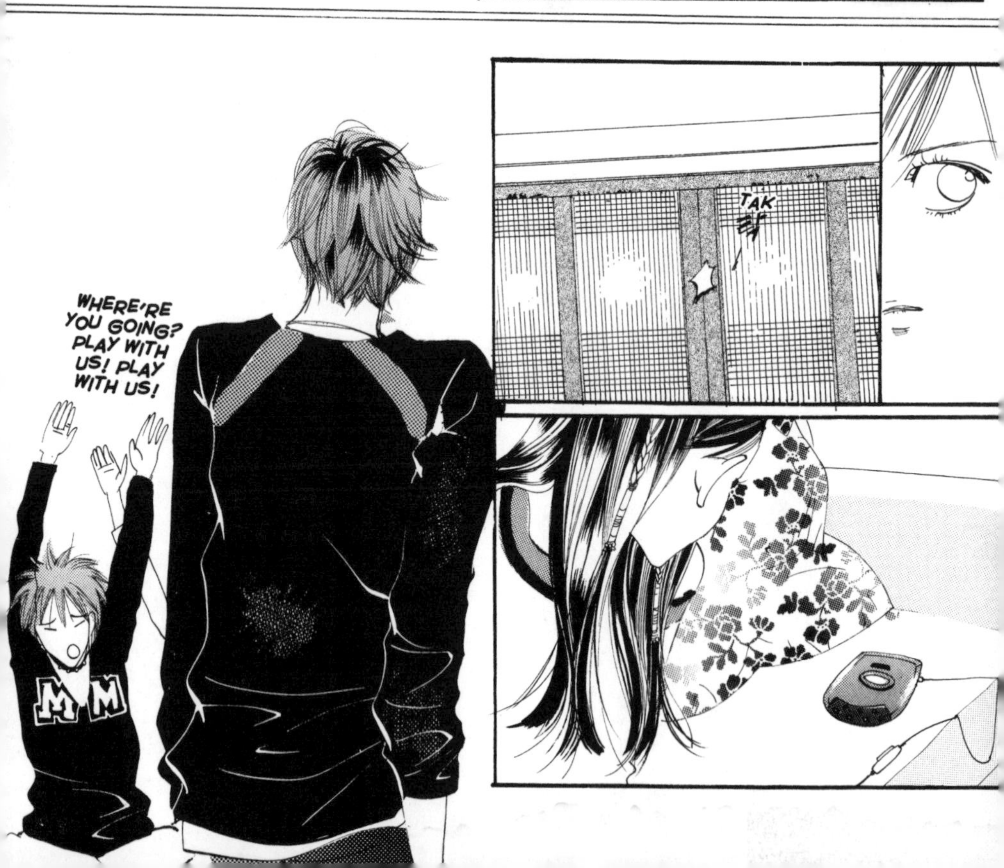
WHERE'RE YOU GOING? PLAY WITH US! PLAY WITH US!
TAK

WHAT WAS HE LISTENING TO?

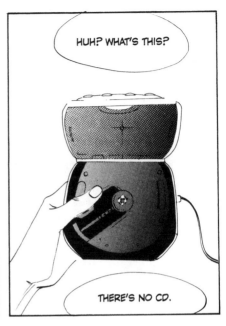

HUH? WHAT'S THIS?

THERE'S NO CD.

THIS CD PLAYER DOESN'T HAVE A RADIO...

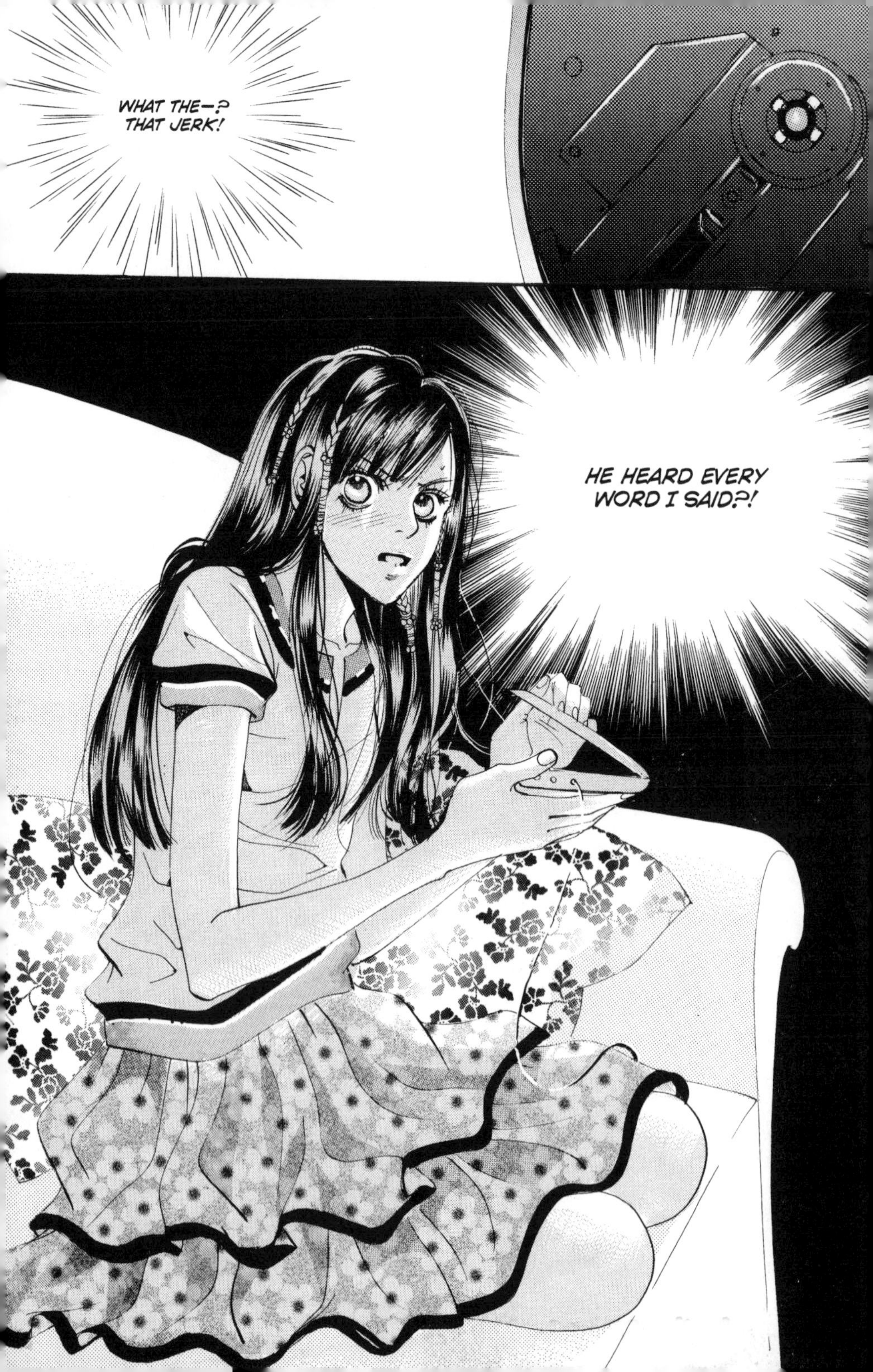
WHAT THE—? THAT JERK!
HE HEARD EVERY WORD I SAID?!

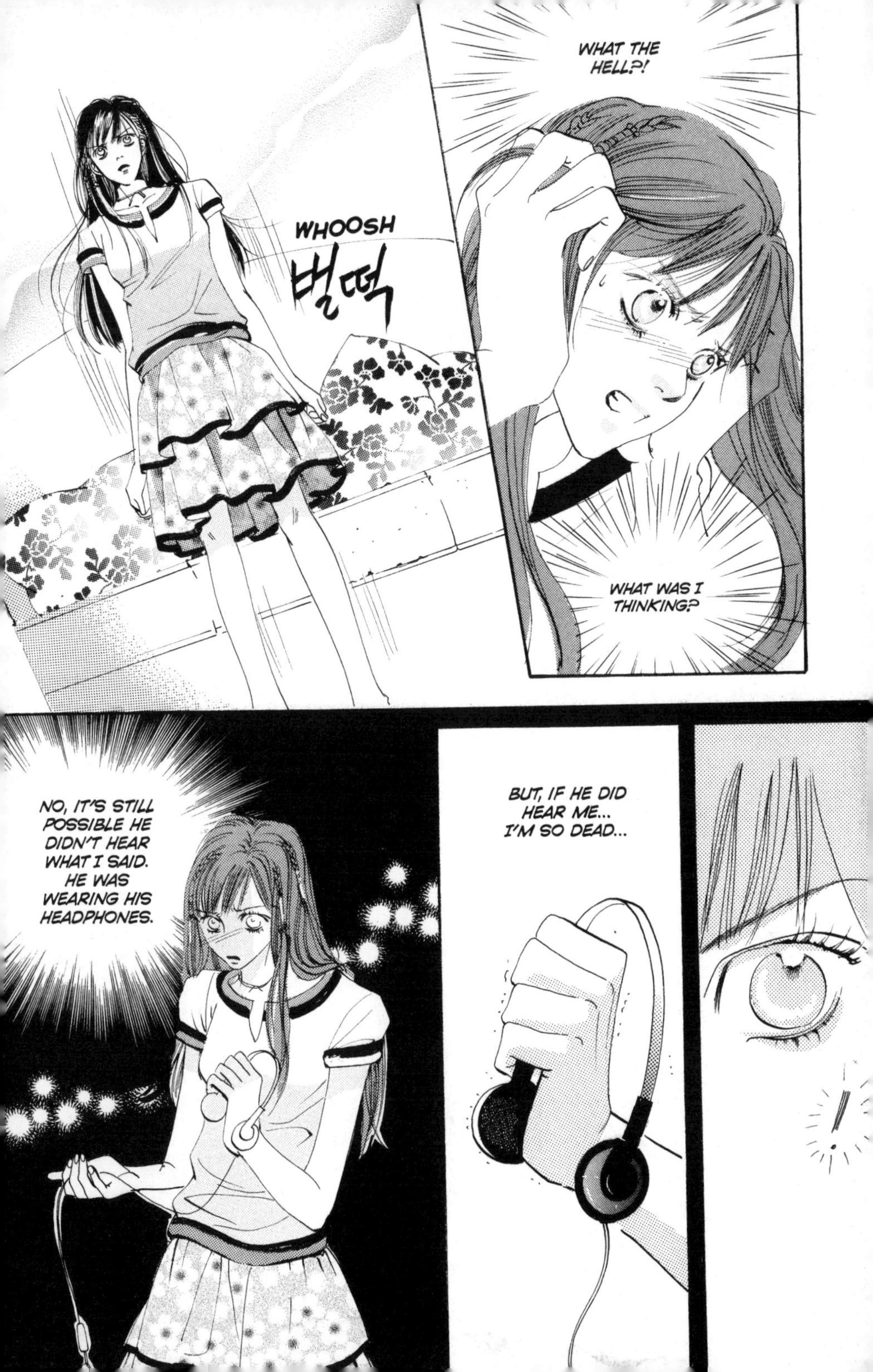
WHOOSH
벌떡
WHAT THE HELL?!
WHAT WAS I THINKING?
NO, IT'S STILL POSSIBLE HE DIDN'T HEAR WHAT I SAID. HE WAS WEARING HIS HEADPHONES.
BUT, IF HE DID HEAR ME... I'M SO DEAD...
!

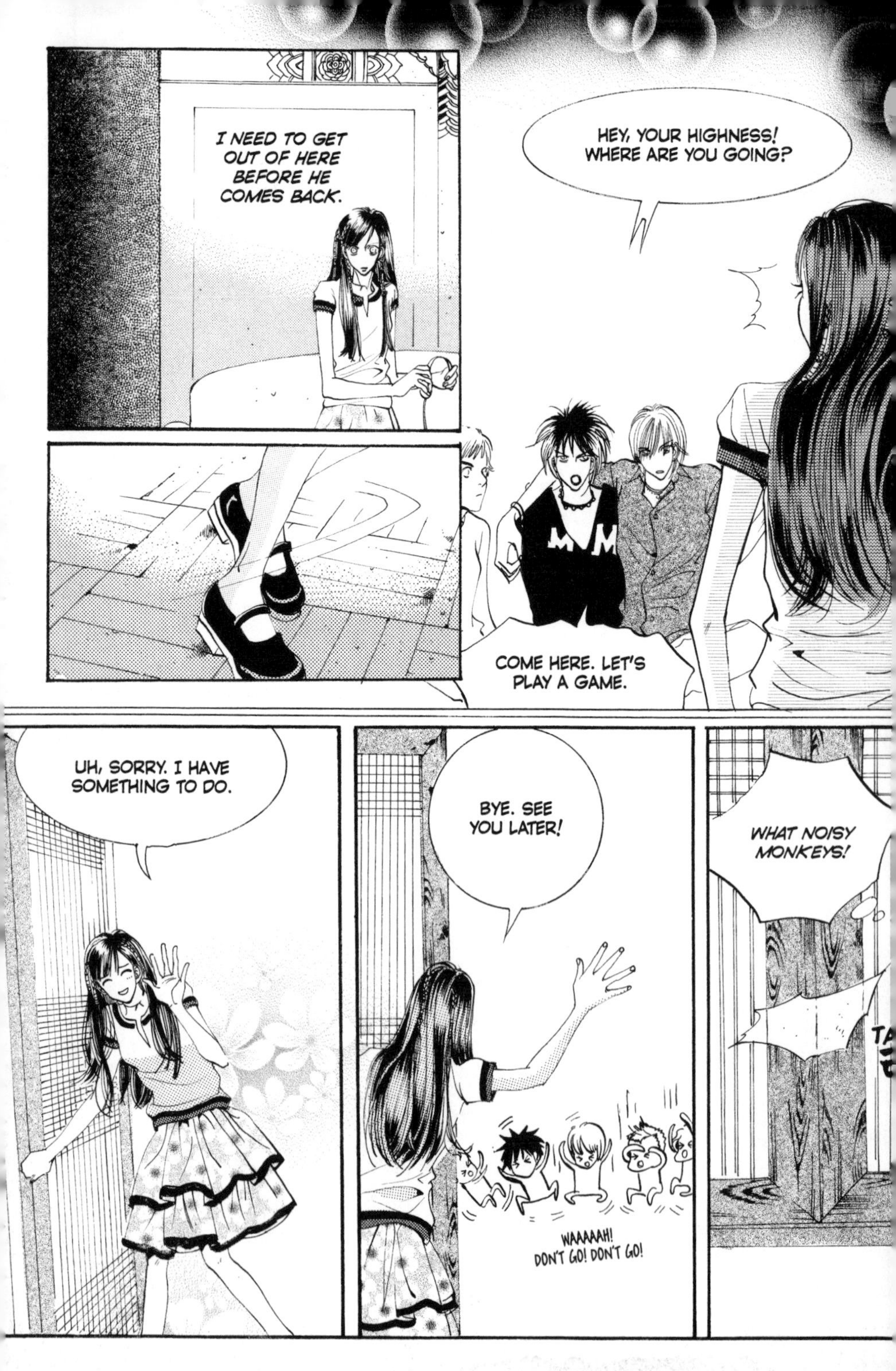
I NEED TO GET OUT OF HERE BEFORE HE COMES BACK.
HEY, YOUR HIGHNESS! WHERE ARE YOU GOING?
COME HERE. LET'S PLAY A GAME.
UH, SORRY. I HAVE SOMETHING TO DO.
BYE. SEE YOU LATER!
WAAAAAH! DON'T GO! DON'T GO!
WHAT NOISY MONKEYS!

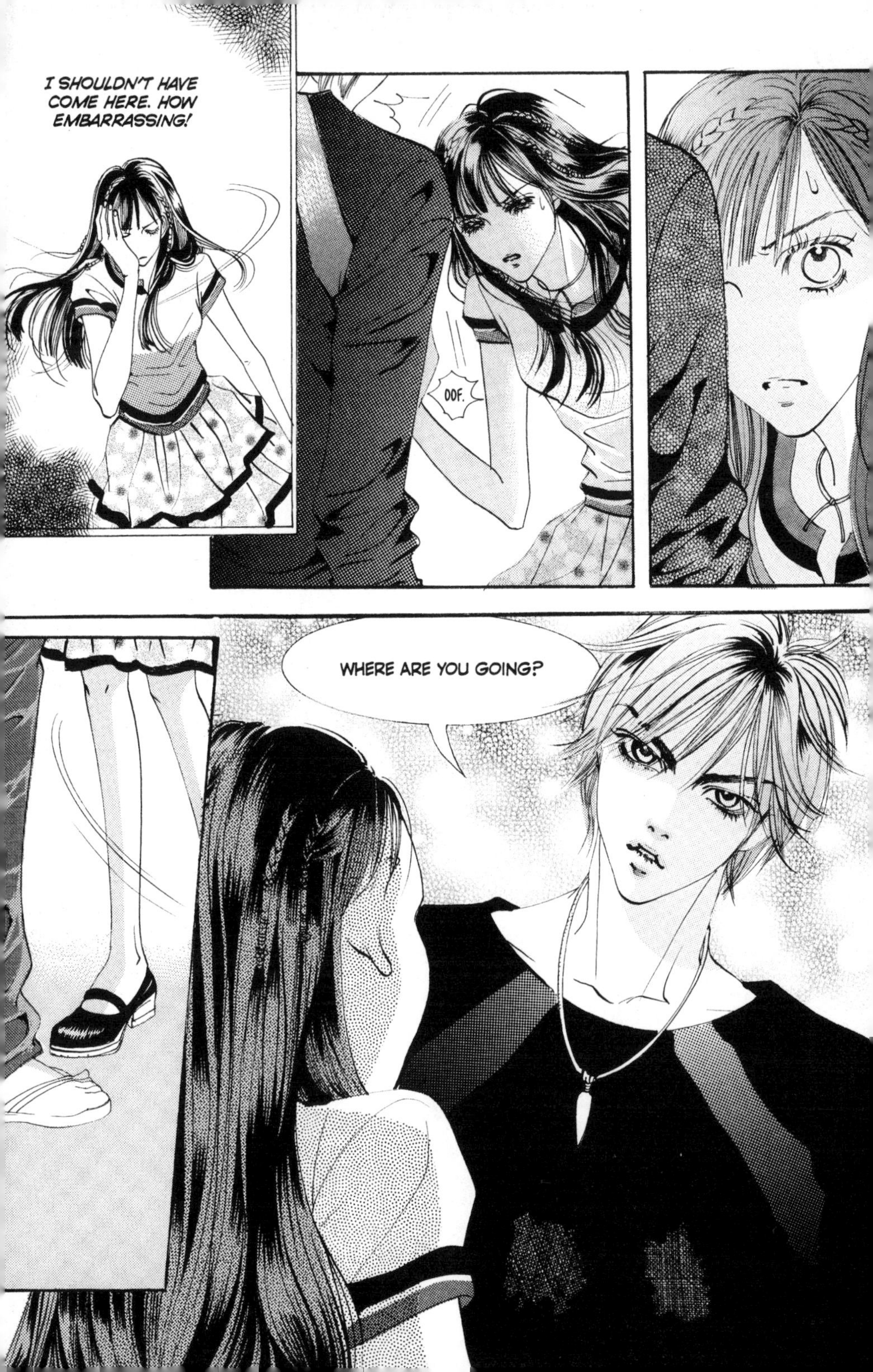
I SHOULDN'T HAVE COME HERE. HOW EMBARRASSING!
OOF.
WHERE ARE YOU GOING?

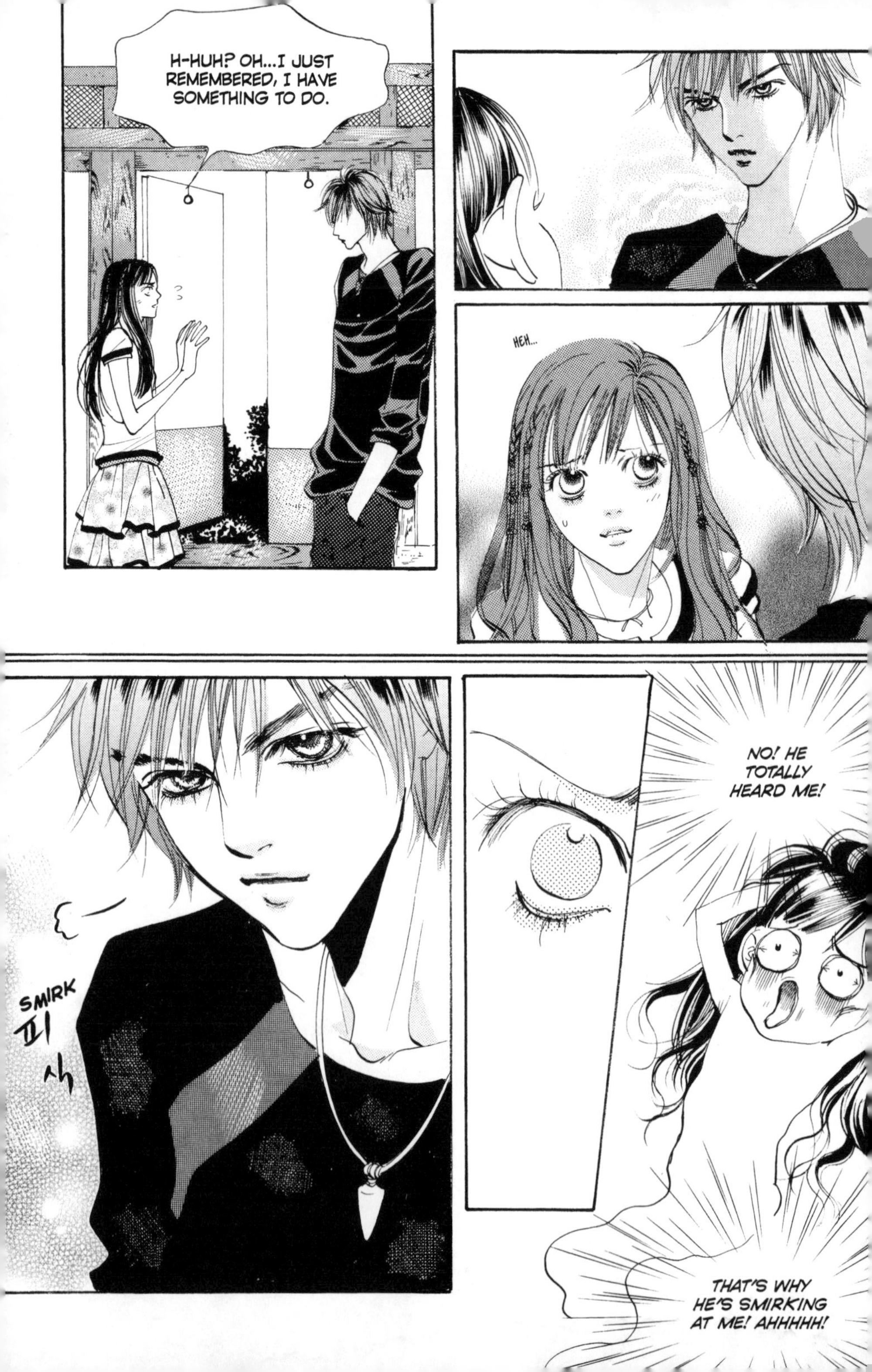
H-HUH? OH...I JUST REMEMBERED, I HAVE SOMETHING TO DO.
HEH...
SMIRK
피식
NO! HE TOTALLY HEARD ME!
THAT'S WHY HE'S SMIRKING AT ME! AHHHHH!

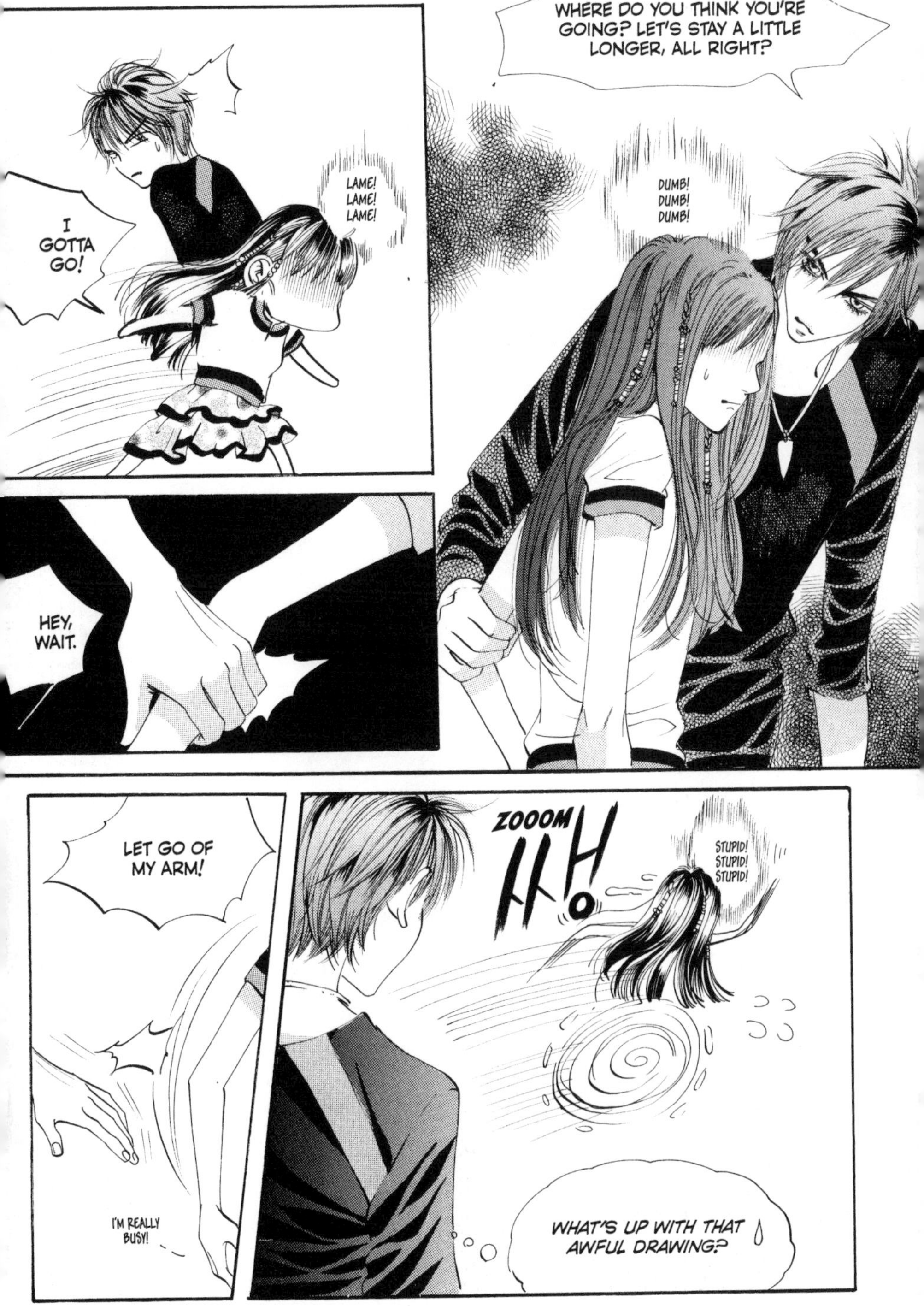
I GOTTA GO!
LAME! LAME! LAME!
HEY, WAIT.
WHERE DO YOU THINK YOU'RE GOING? LET'S STAY A LITTLE LONGER, ALL RIGHT?
DUMB! DUMB! DUMB!
LET GO OF MY ARM!
I'M REALLY BUSY!
ZOOOM
STUPID! STUPID! STUPID!
WHAT'S UP WITH THAT AWFUL DRAWING?

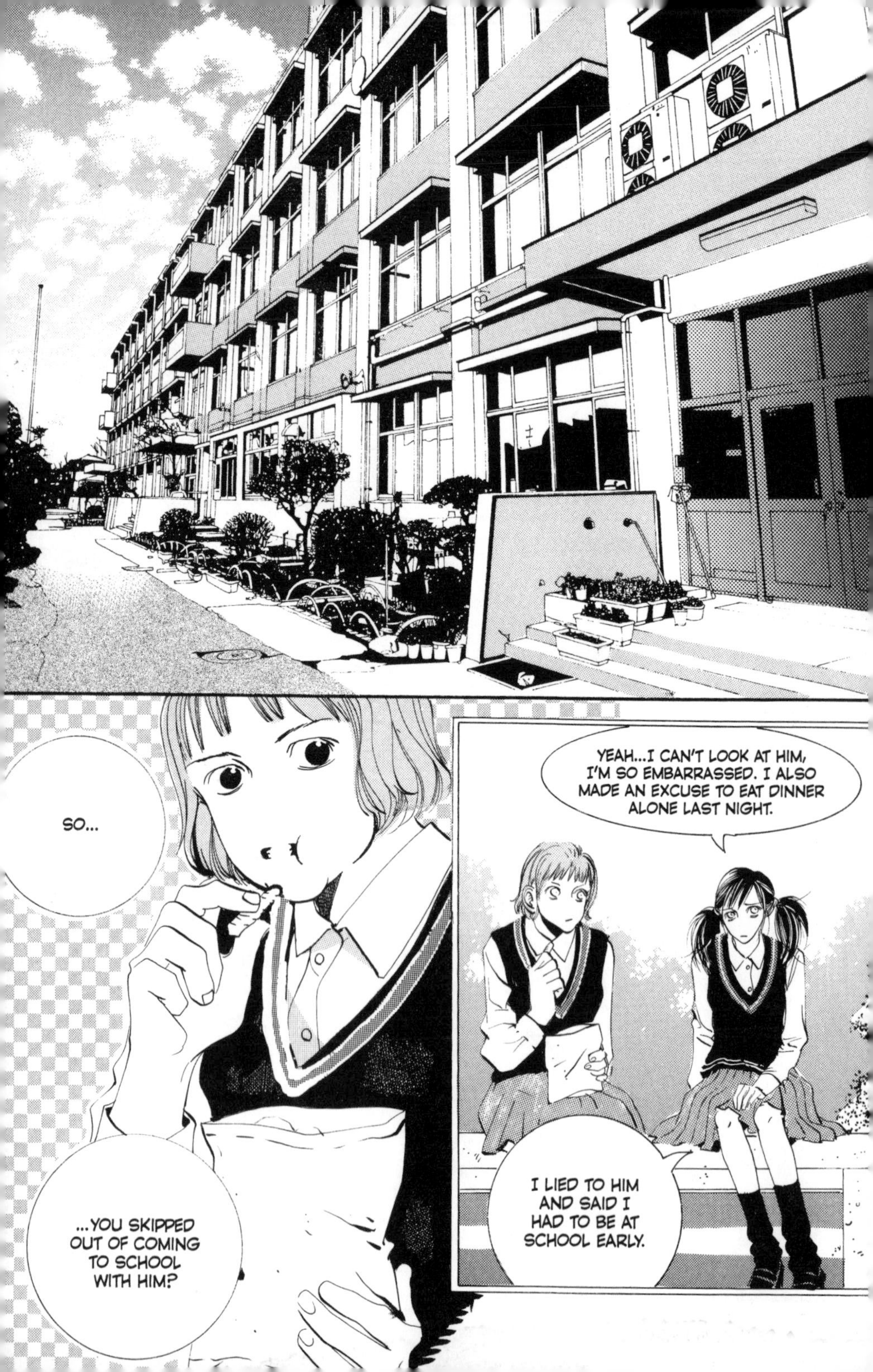
SO...
...YOU SKIPPED OUT OF COMING TO SCHOOL WITH HIM?
YEAH...I CAN'T LOOK AT HIM, I'M SO EMBARRASSED. I ALSO MADE AN EXCUSE TO EAT DINNER ALONE LAST NIGHT.
I LIED TO HIM AND SAID I HAD TO BE AT SCHOOL EARLY.

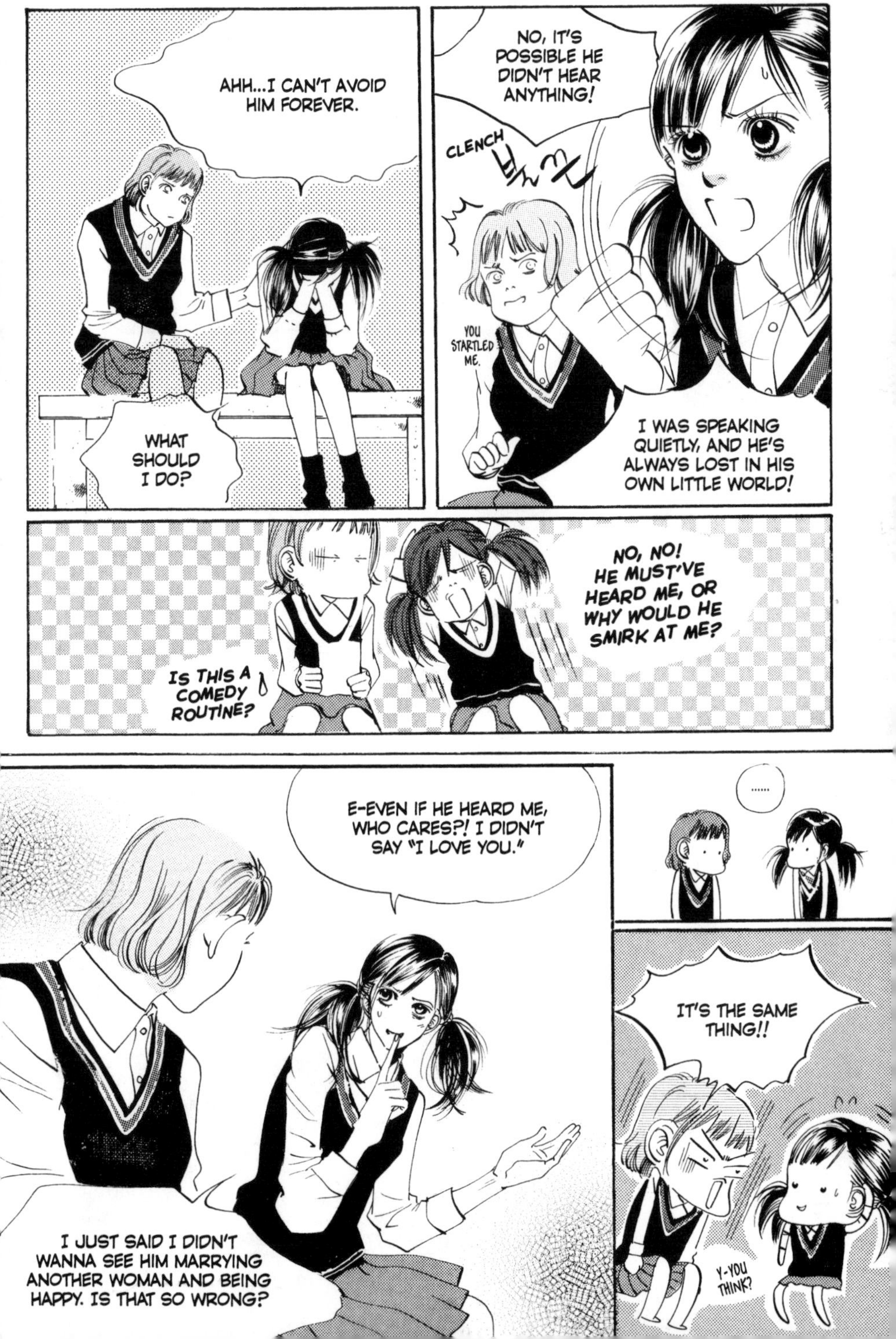
AHH...I CAN'T AVOID HIM FOREVER.
WHAT SHOULD I DO?
NO, IT'S POSSIBLE HE DIDN'T HEAR ANYTHING!
CLENCH
YOU STARTLED ME.
I WAS SPEAKING QUIETLY, AND HE'S ALWAYS LOST IN HIS OWN LITTLE WORLD!
NO, NO! HE MUST'VE HEARD ME, OR WHY WOULD HE SMIRK AT ME?
IS THIS A COMEDY ROUTINE?
E-EVEN IF HE HEARD ME, WHO CARES?! I DIDN'T SAY "I LOVE YOU."
I JUST SAID I DIDN'T WANNA SEE HIM MARRYING ANOTHER WOMAN AND BEING HAPPY. IS THAT SO WRONG?
......
IT'S THE SAME THING!!
Y-YOU THINK?

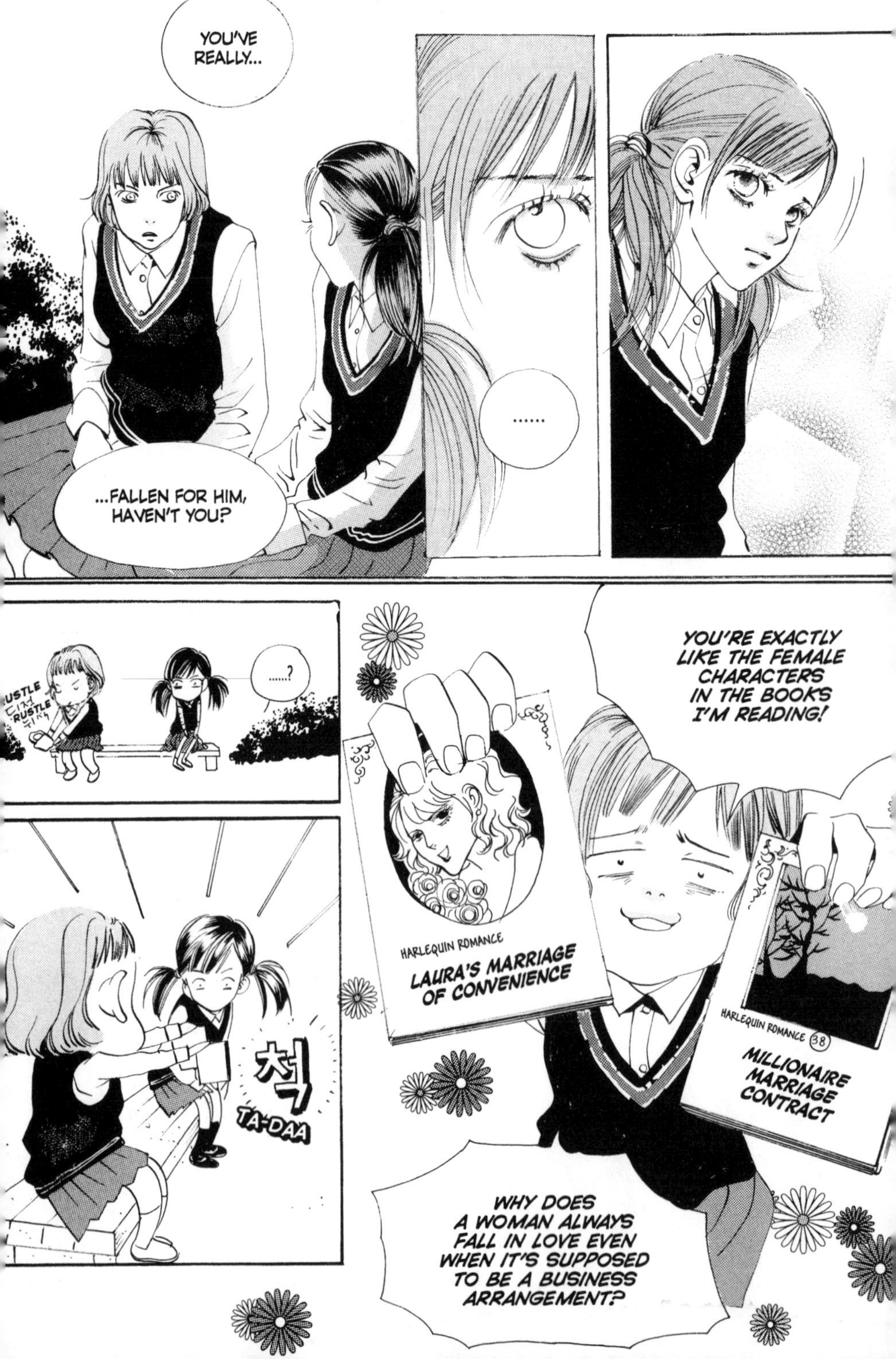
YOU'VE REALLY...
...FALLEN FOR HIM, HAVEN'T YOU?
......
RUSTLE
RUSTLE
......?
척
TA-DAA
YOU'RE EXACTLY LIKE THE FEMALE CHARACTERS IN THE BOOKS I'M READING!
HARLEQUIN ROMANCE
LAURA'S MARRIAGE OF CONVENIENCE
HARLEQUIN ROMANCE 38
MILLIONAIRE MARRIAGE CONTRACT
WHY DOES A WOMAN ALWAYS FALL IN LOVE EVEN WHEN IT'S SUPPOSED TO BE A BUSINESS ARRANGEMENT?

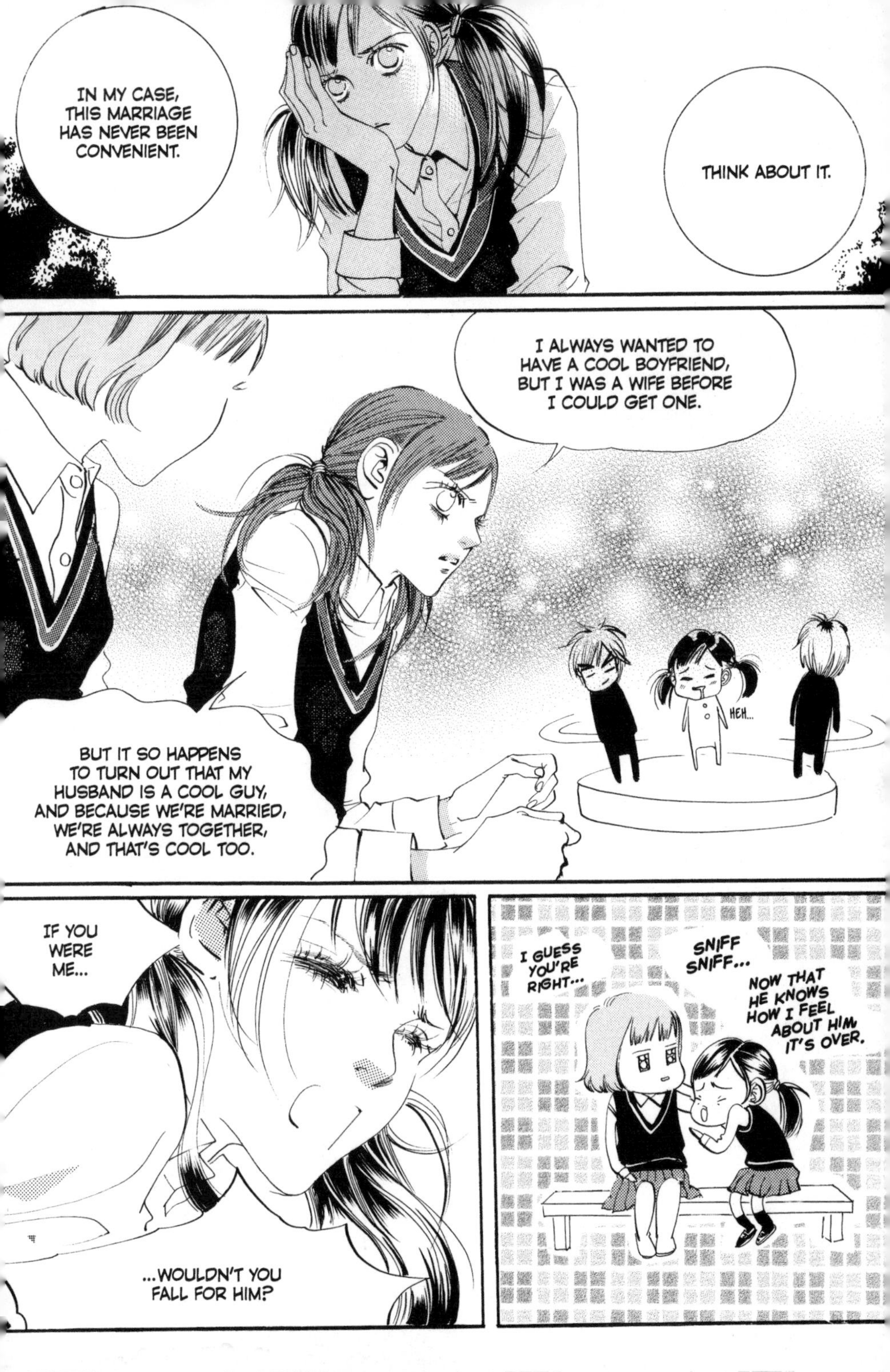
IN MY CASE, THIS MARRIAGE HAS NEVER BEEN CONVENIENT.
THINK ABOUT IT.
I ALWAYS WANTED TO HAVE A COOL BOYFRIEND, BUT I WAS A WIFE BEFORE I COULD GET ONE.
HEH...
BUT IT SO HAPPENS TO TURN OUT THAT MY HUSBAND IS A COOL GUY, AND BECAUSE WE'RE MARRIED, WE'RE ALWAYS TOGETHER, AND THAT'S COOL TOO.
IF YOU WERE ME...
...WOULDN'T YOU FALL FOR HIM?
I GUESS YOU'RE RIGHT...
SNIFF SNIFF...
NOW THAT HE KNOWS HOW I FEEL ABOUT HIM, IT'S OVER.

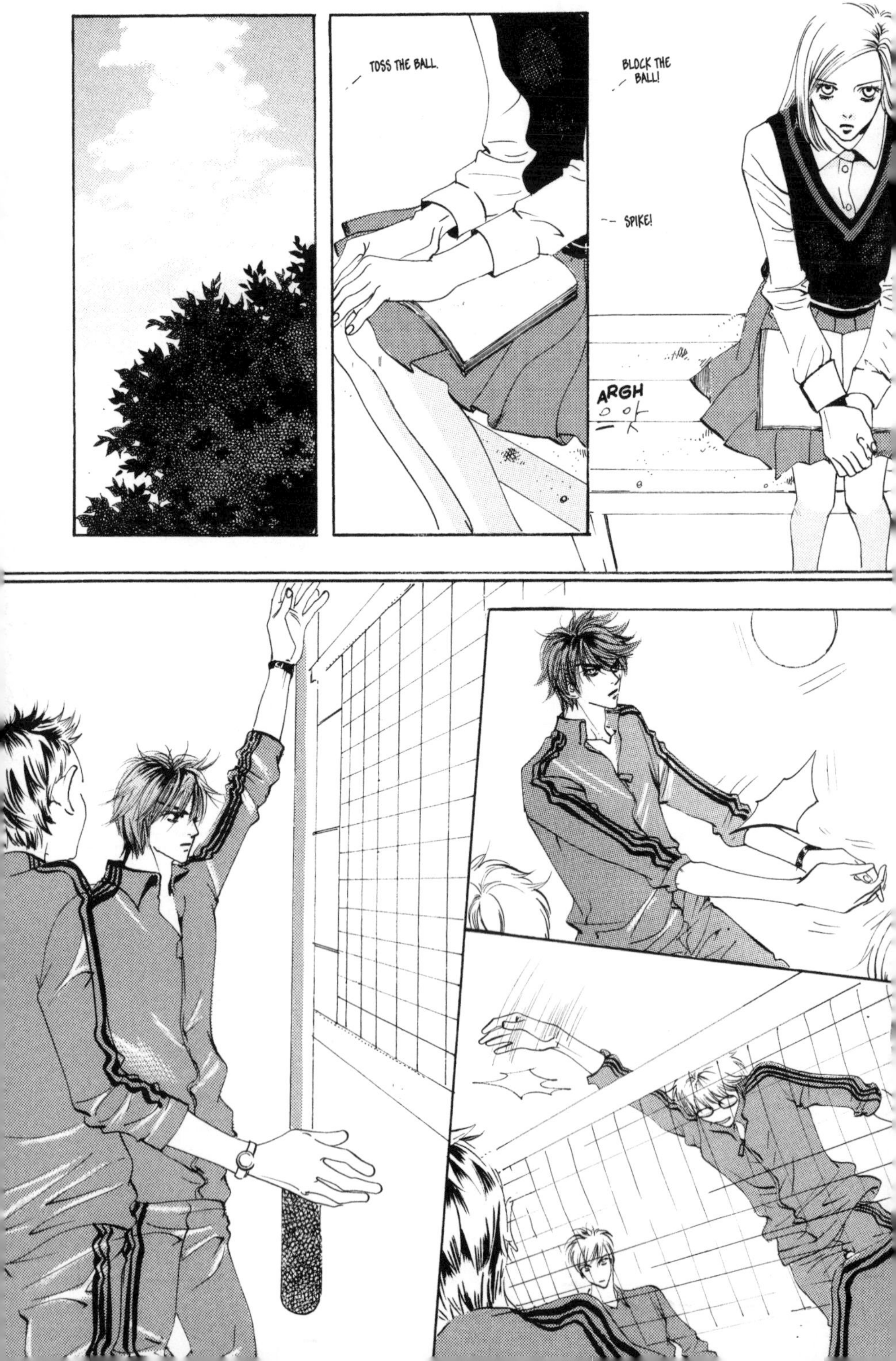
TOSS THE BALL.
BLOCK THE BALL!
SPIKE!
ARGH
으악

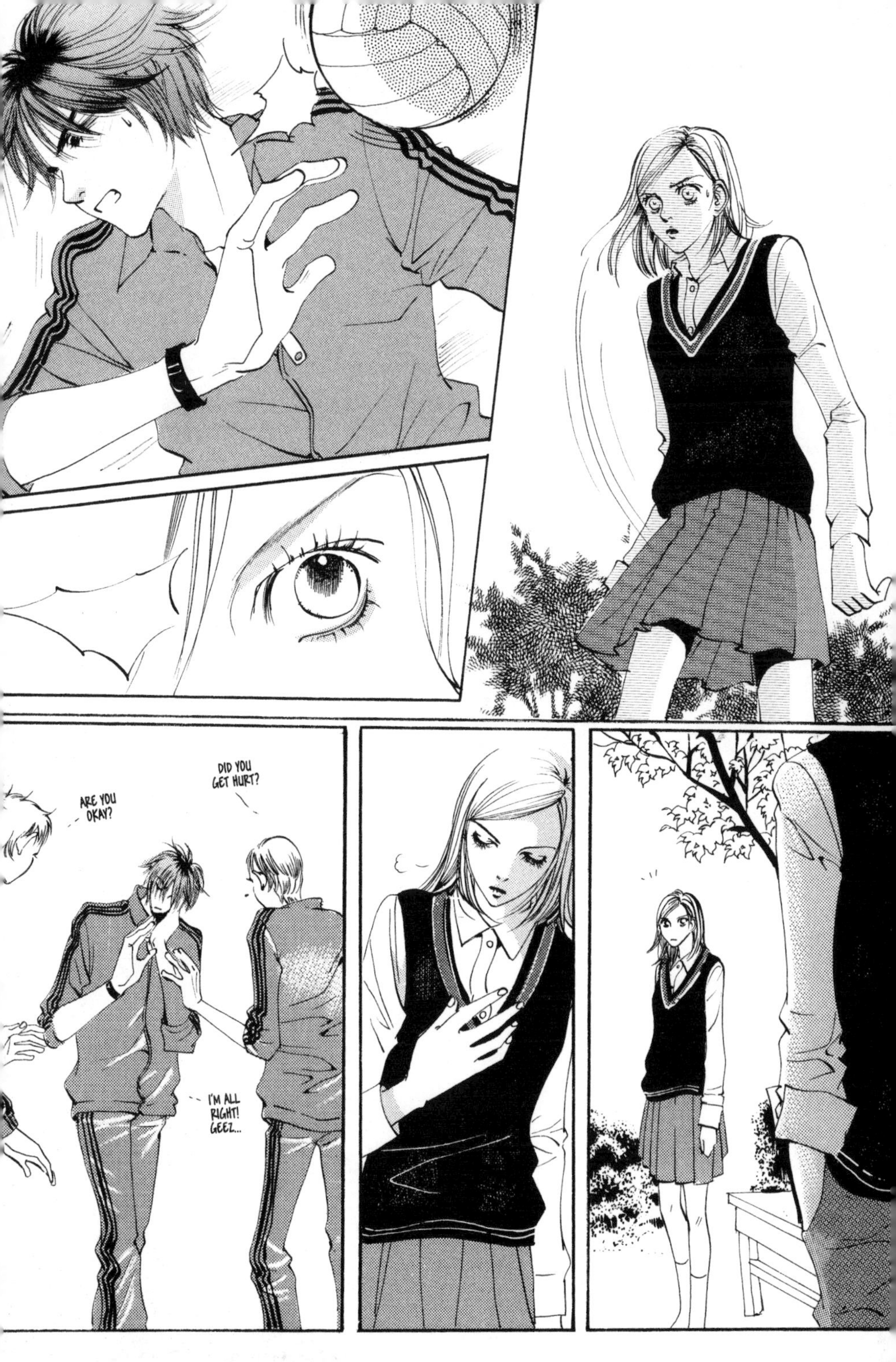
ARE YOU OKAY?
DID YOU GET HURT?
I'M ALL RIGHT! GEEZ...

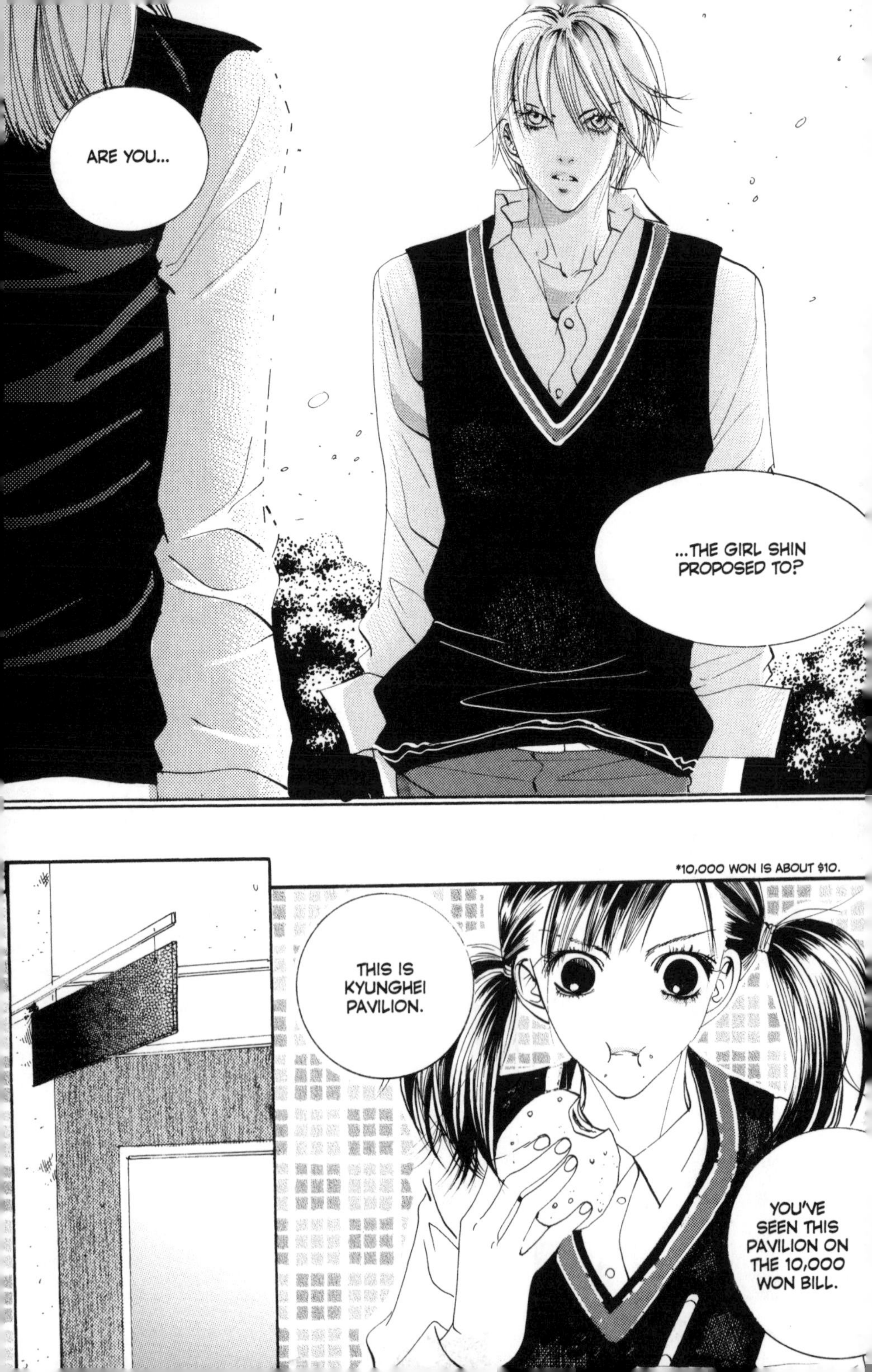
ARE YOU...
...THE GIRL SHIN PROPOSED TO?
THIS IS KYUNGHEI PAVILION.
YOU'VE SEEN THIS PAVILION ON THE 10,000 WON BILL.

*10,000 WON IS ABOUT $10.

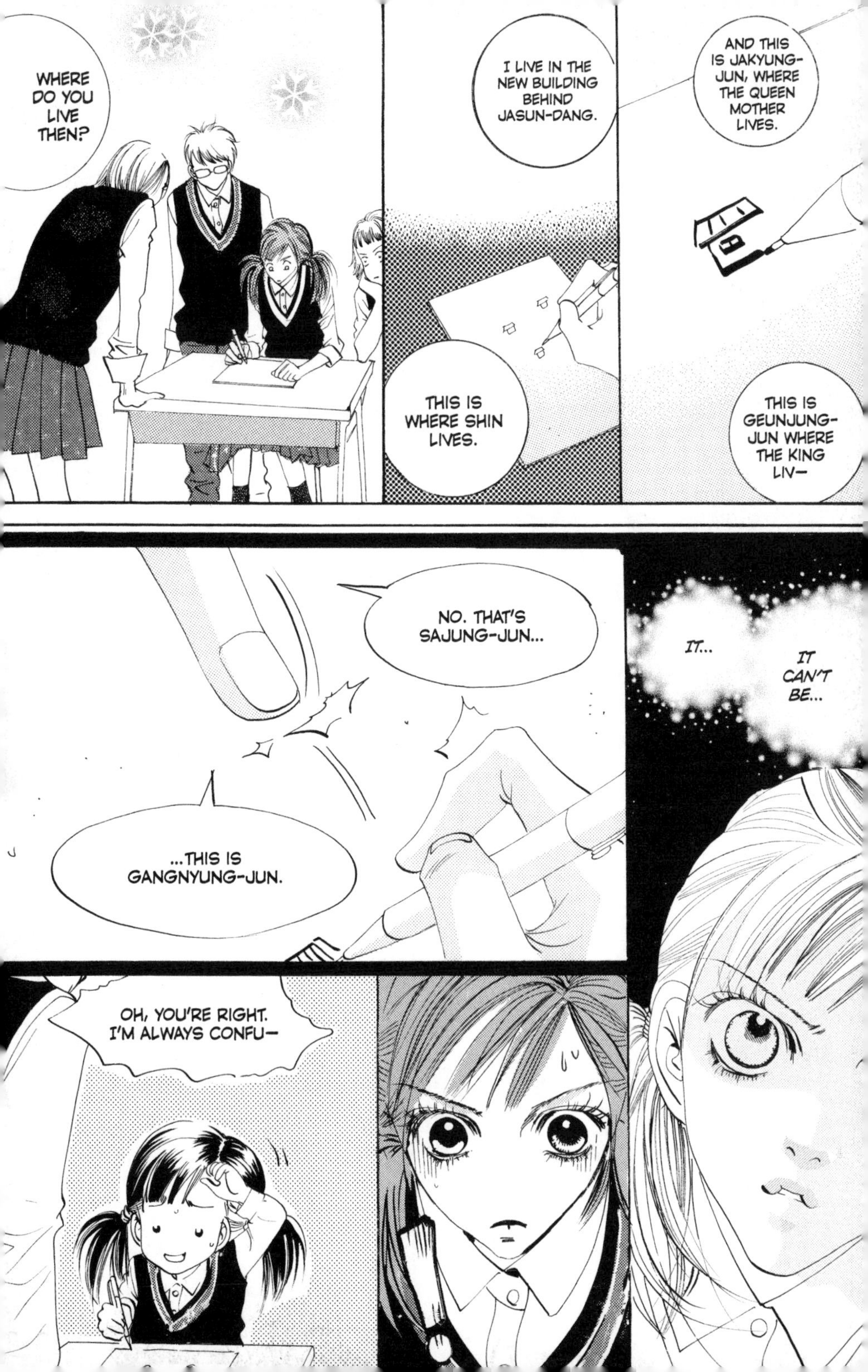
WHERE DO YOU LIVE THEN?
I LIVE IN THE NEW BUILDING BEHIND JASUN-DANG.
THIS IS WHERE SHIN LIVES.
AND THIS IS JAKYUNG-JUN, WHERE THE QUEEN MOTHER LIVES.
THIS IS GEUNJUNG-JUN WHERE THE KING LIV—
NO. THAT'S SAJUNG-JUN...
...THIS IS GANGNYUNG-JUN.
OH, YOU'RE RIGHT. I'M ALWAYS CONFU—
IT...
IT CAN'T BE...

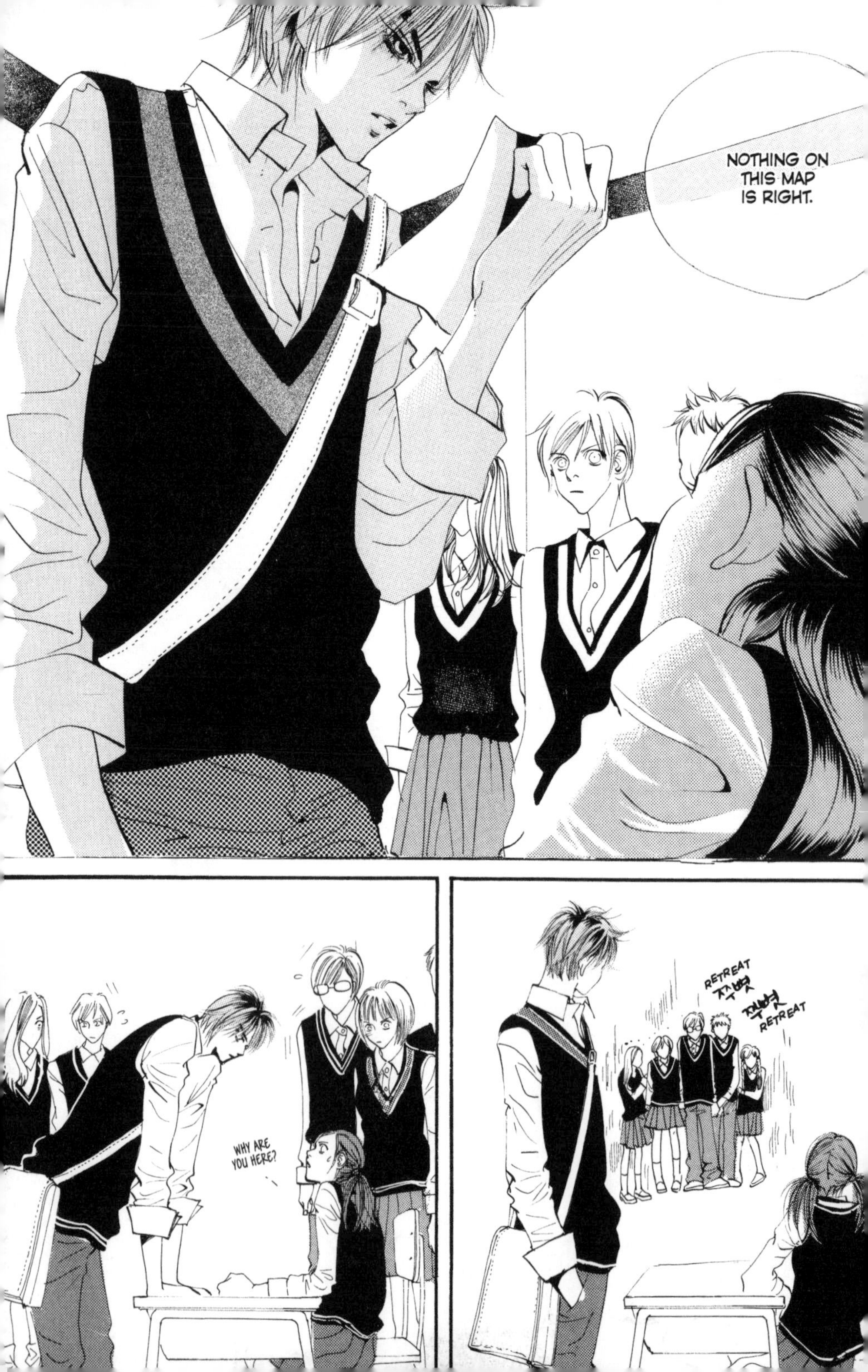
NOTHING ON THIS MAP IS RIGHT.
WHY ARE YOU HERE?
RETREAT
RETREAT

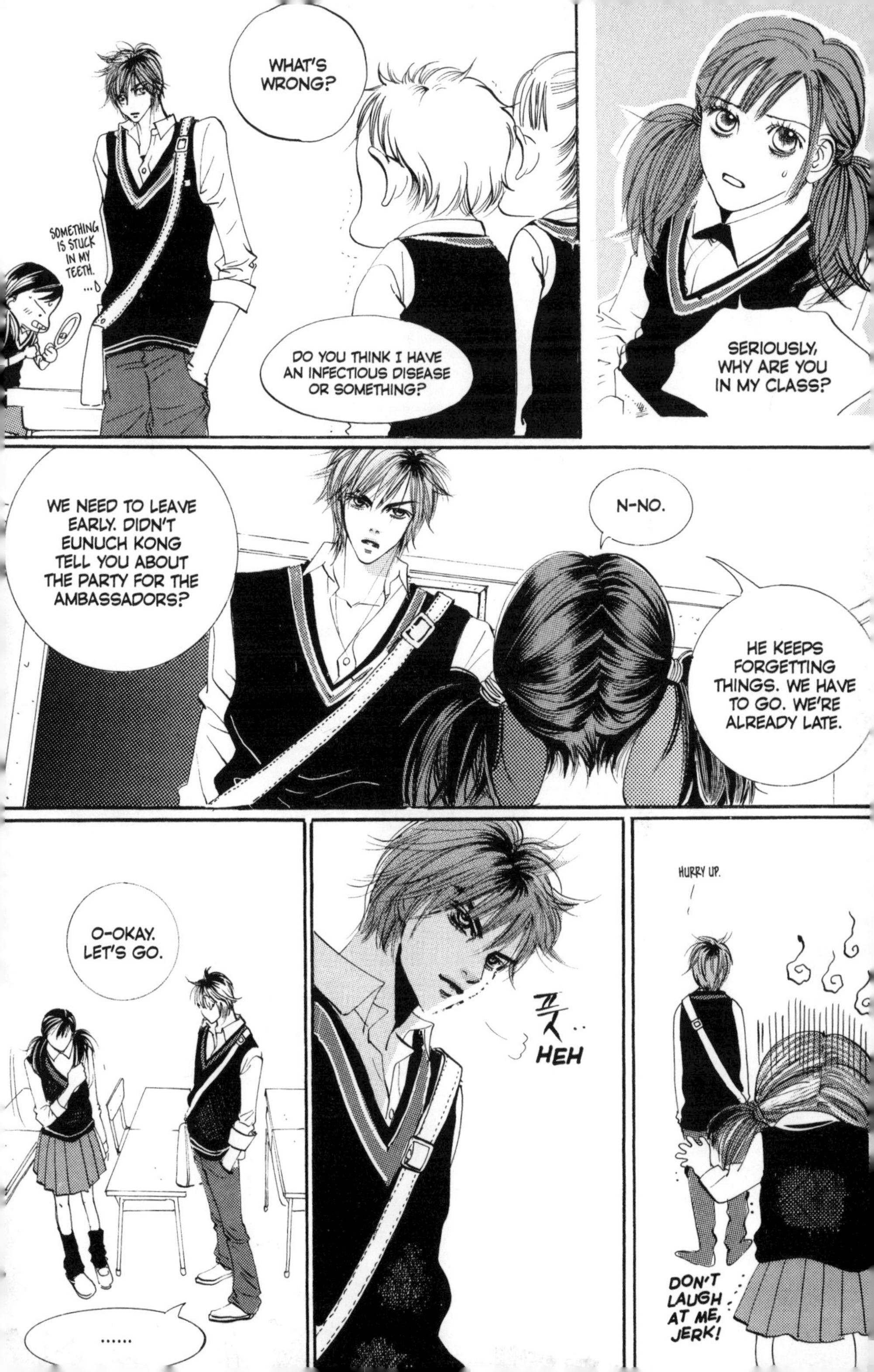
SOMETHING IS STUCK IN MY TEETH.
...
WHAT'S WRONG?
DO YOU THINK I HAVE AN INFECTIOUS DISEASE OR SOMETHING?
SERIOUSLY, WHY ARE YOU IN MY CLASS?
WE NEED TO LEAVE EARLY. DIDN'T EUNUCH KONG TELL YOU ABOUT THE PARTY FOR THE AMBASSADORS?
N-NO.
HE KEEPS FORGETTING THINGS. WE HAVE TO GO. WE'RE ALREADY LATE.
O-OKAY. LET'S GO.
......
HEH
HURRY UP.
DON'T LAUGH AT ME, JERK!

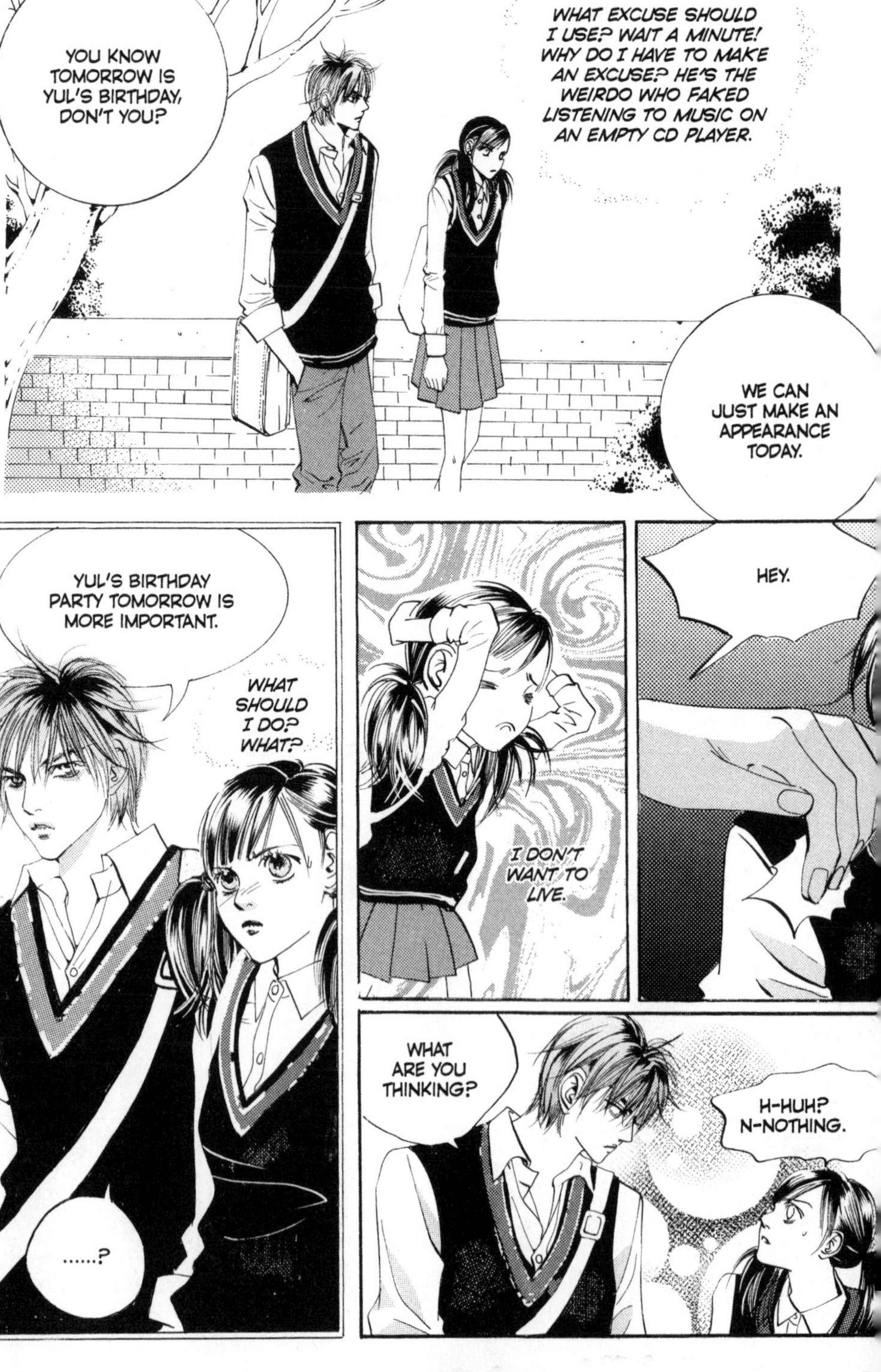
YOU KNOW TOMORROW IS YUL'S BIRTHDAY, DON'T YOU?
WHAT EXCUSE SHOULD I USE? WAIT A MINUTE! WHY DO I HAVE TO MAKE AN EXCUSE? HE'S THE WEIRDO WHO FAKED LISTENING TO MUSIC ON AN EMPTY CD PLAYER.
WE CAN JUST MAKE AN APPEARANCE TODAY.
YUL'S BIRTHDAY PARTY TOMORROW IS MORE IMPORTANT.
WHAT SHOULD I DO? WHAT?
......?
I DON'T WANT TO LIVE.
HEY.
WHAT ARE YOU THINKING?
H-HUH? N-NOTHING.

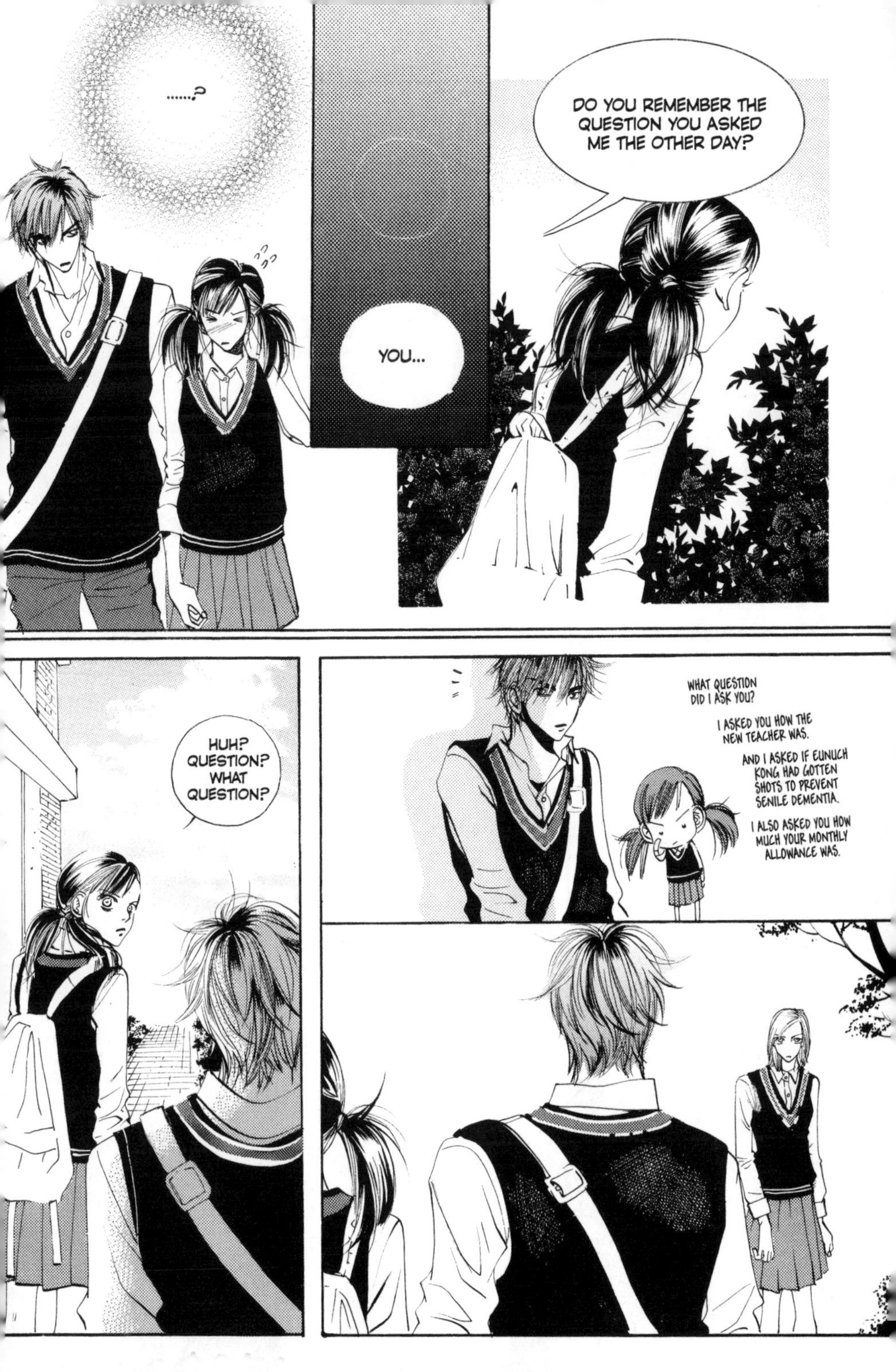
......?
YOU...
DO YOU REMEMBER THE QUESTION YOU ASKED ME THE OTHER DAY?
HUH? QUESTION? WHAT QUESTION?
WHAT QUESTION DID I ASK YOU?
I ASKED YOU HOW THE NEW TEACHER WAS.
AND I ASKED IF EUNUCH KONG HAD GOTTEN SHOTS TO PREVENT SENILE DEMENTIA.
I ALSO ASKED YOU HOW MUCH YOUR MONTHLY ALLOWANCE WAS.

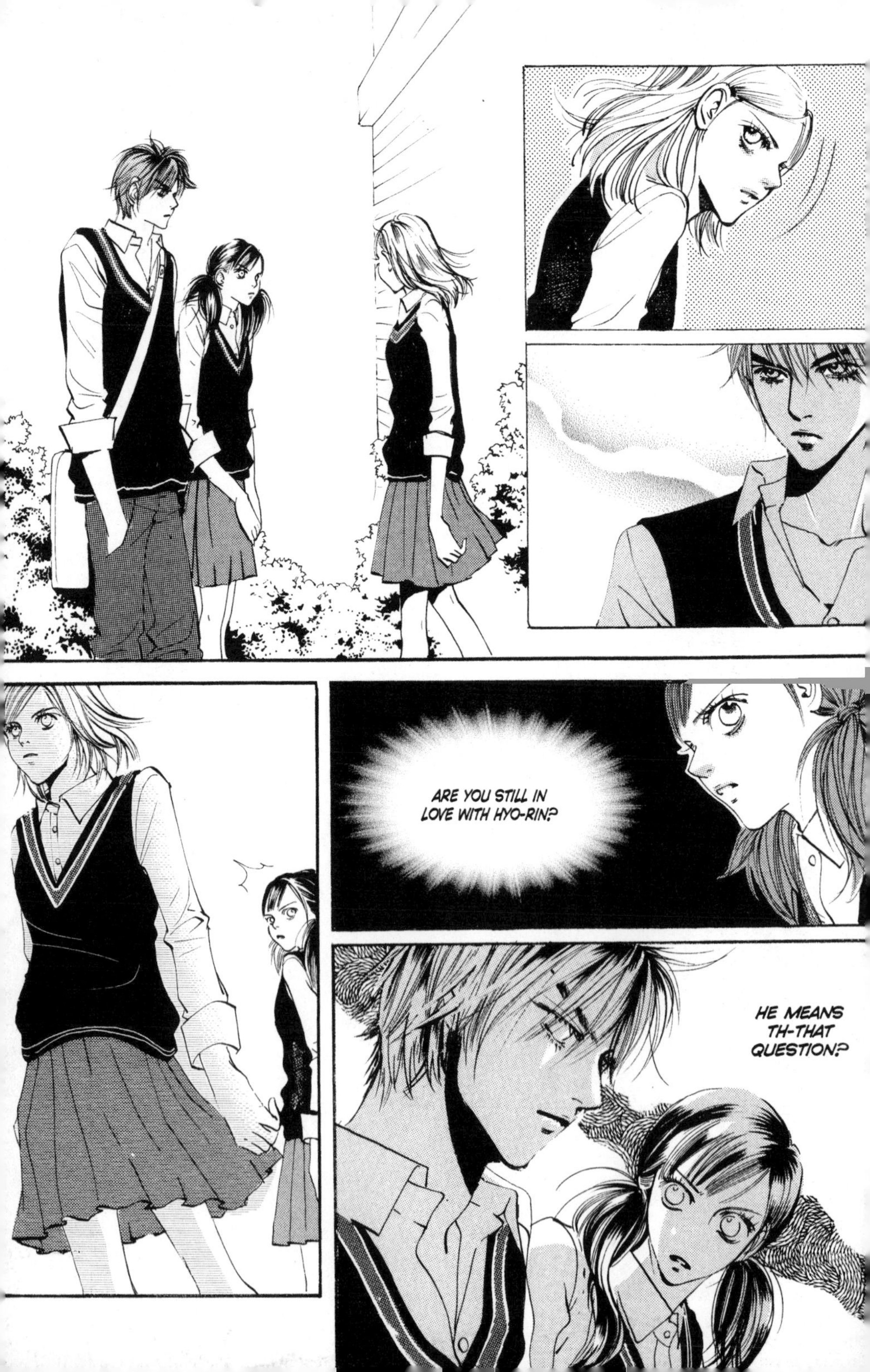
ARE YOU STILL IN LOVE WITH HYO-RIN?
HE MEANS TH-THAT QUESTION?

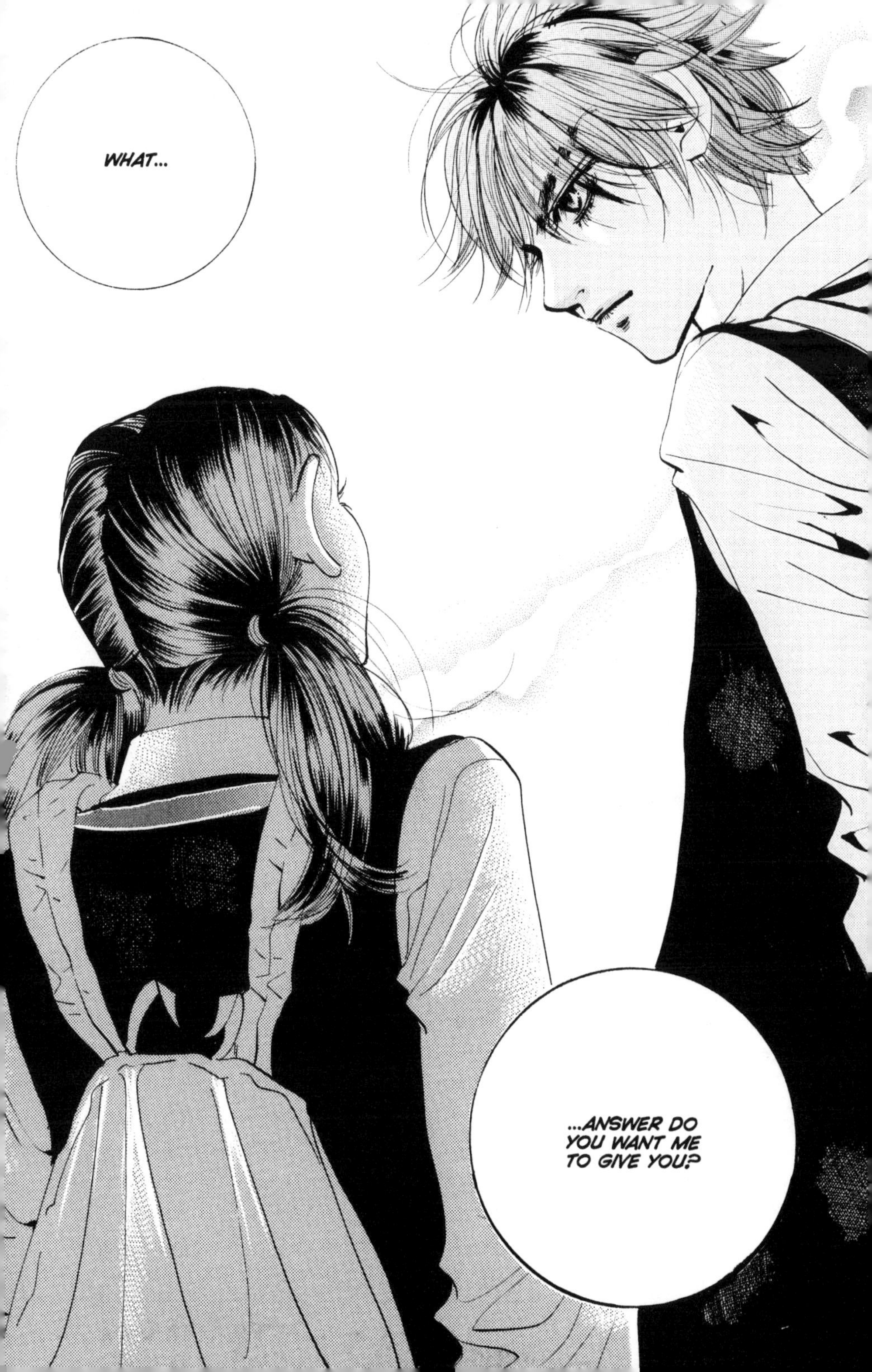
WHAT...
...ANSWER DO YOU WANT ME TO GIVE YOU?

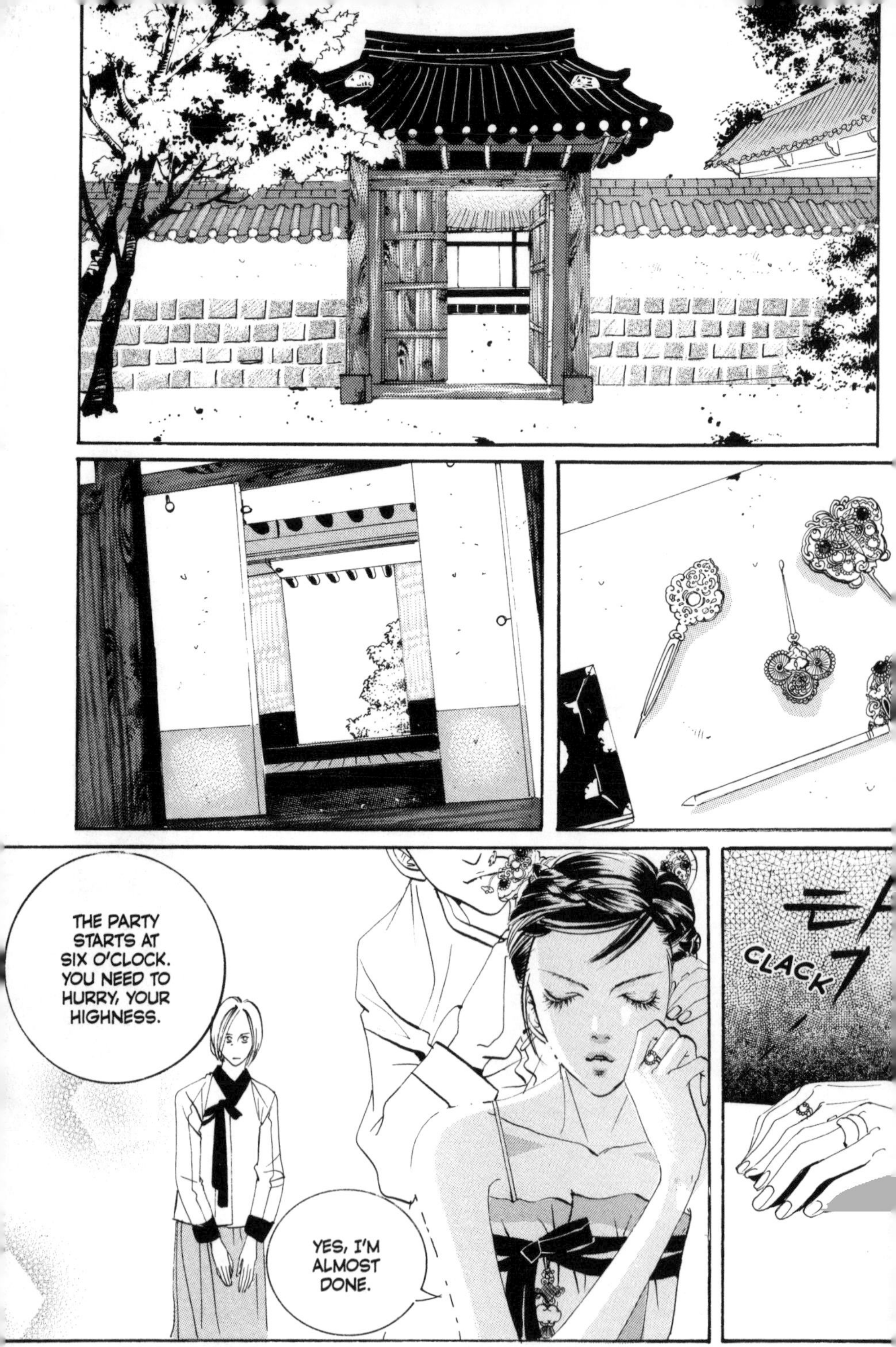
THE PARTY STARTS AT SIX O'CLOCK. YOU NEED TO HURRY, YOUR HIGHNESS.
YES, I'M ALMOST DONE.
CLACK

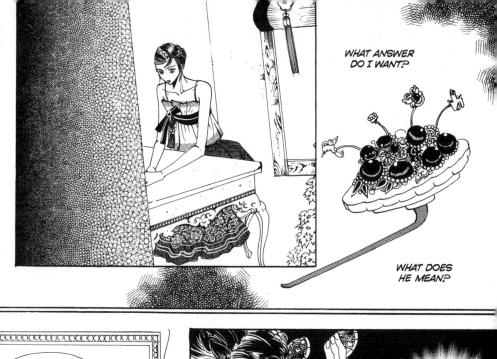

WHAT ANSWER
DO I WANT?

WHAT DOES
HE MEAN?

......

AT LEAST
NOW I KNOW
FOR SURE
THAT HE
HEARD ME.

SIGH...

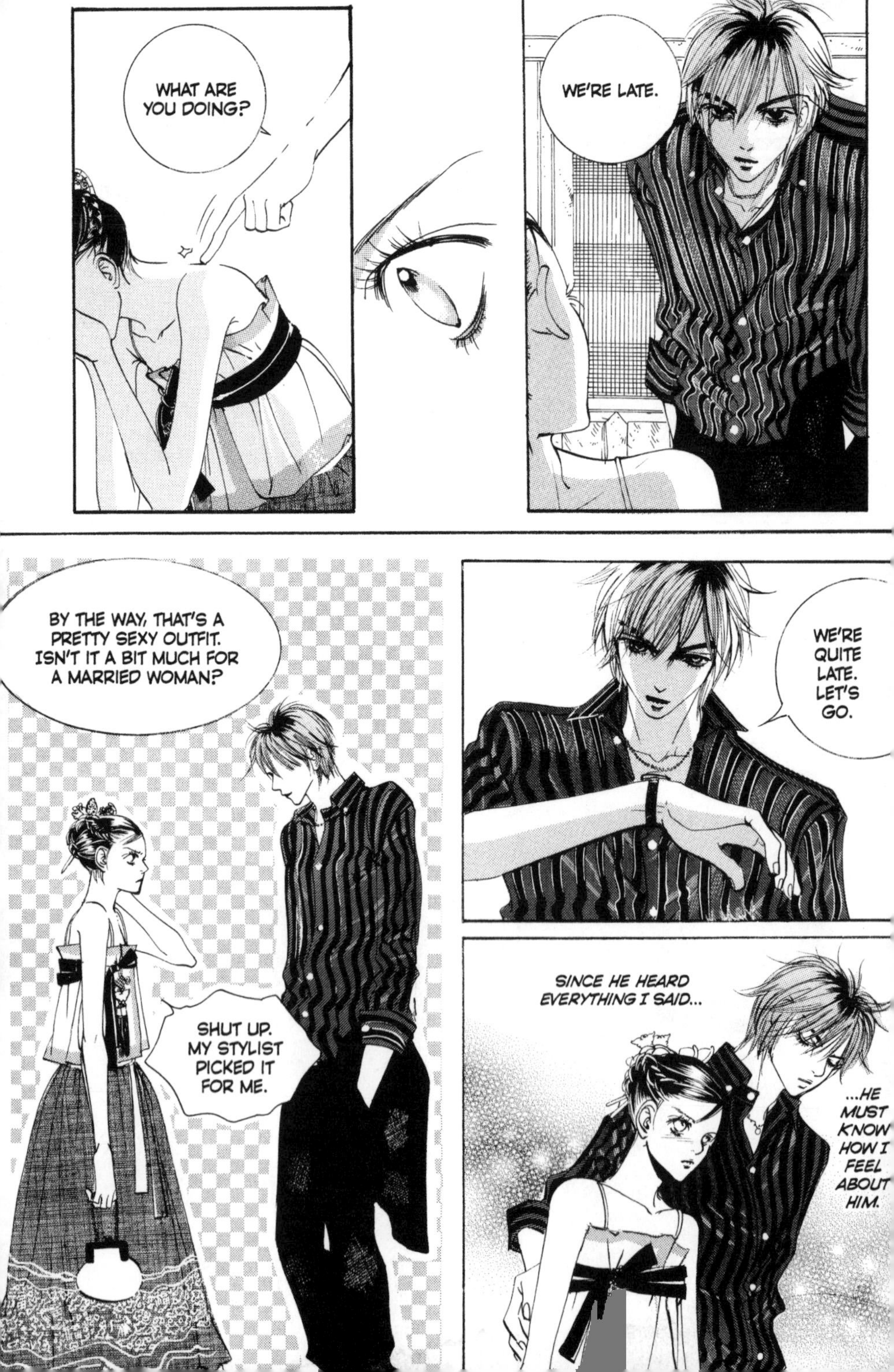
WHAT ARE YOU DOING?
WE'RE LATE.
BY THE WAY, THAT'S A PRETTY SEXY OUTFIT. ISN'T IT A BIT MUCH FOR A MARRIED WOMAN?
SHUT UP. MY STYLIST PICKED IT FOR ME.
WE'RE QUITE LATE. LET'S GO.
SINCE HE HEARD EVERYTHING I SAID...
...HE MUST KNOW HOW I FEEL ABOUT HIM.

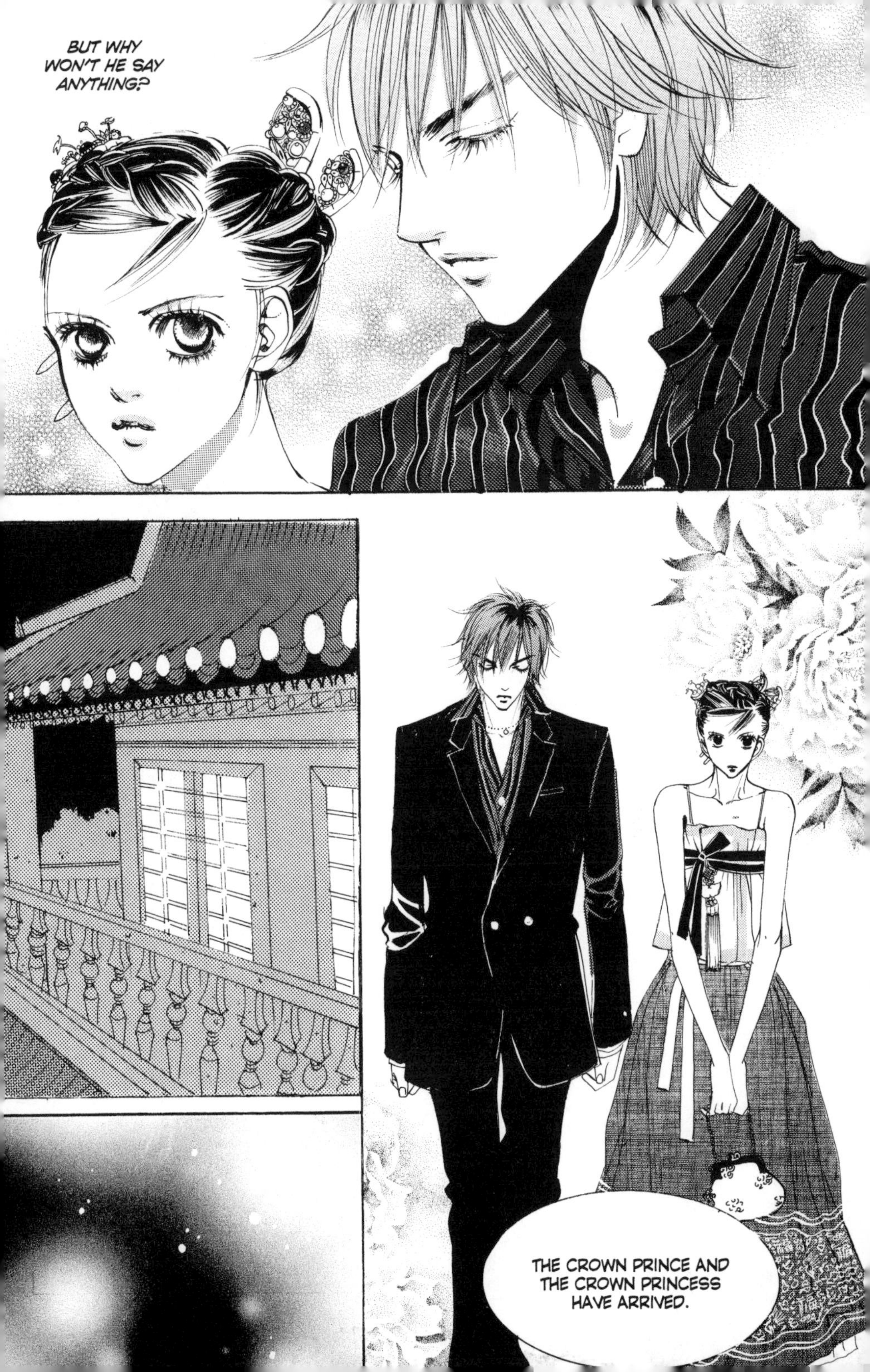
BUT WHY WON'T HE SAY ANYTHING?
THE CROWN PRINCE AND THE CROWN PRINCESS HAVE ARRIVED.

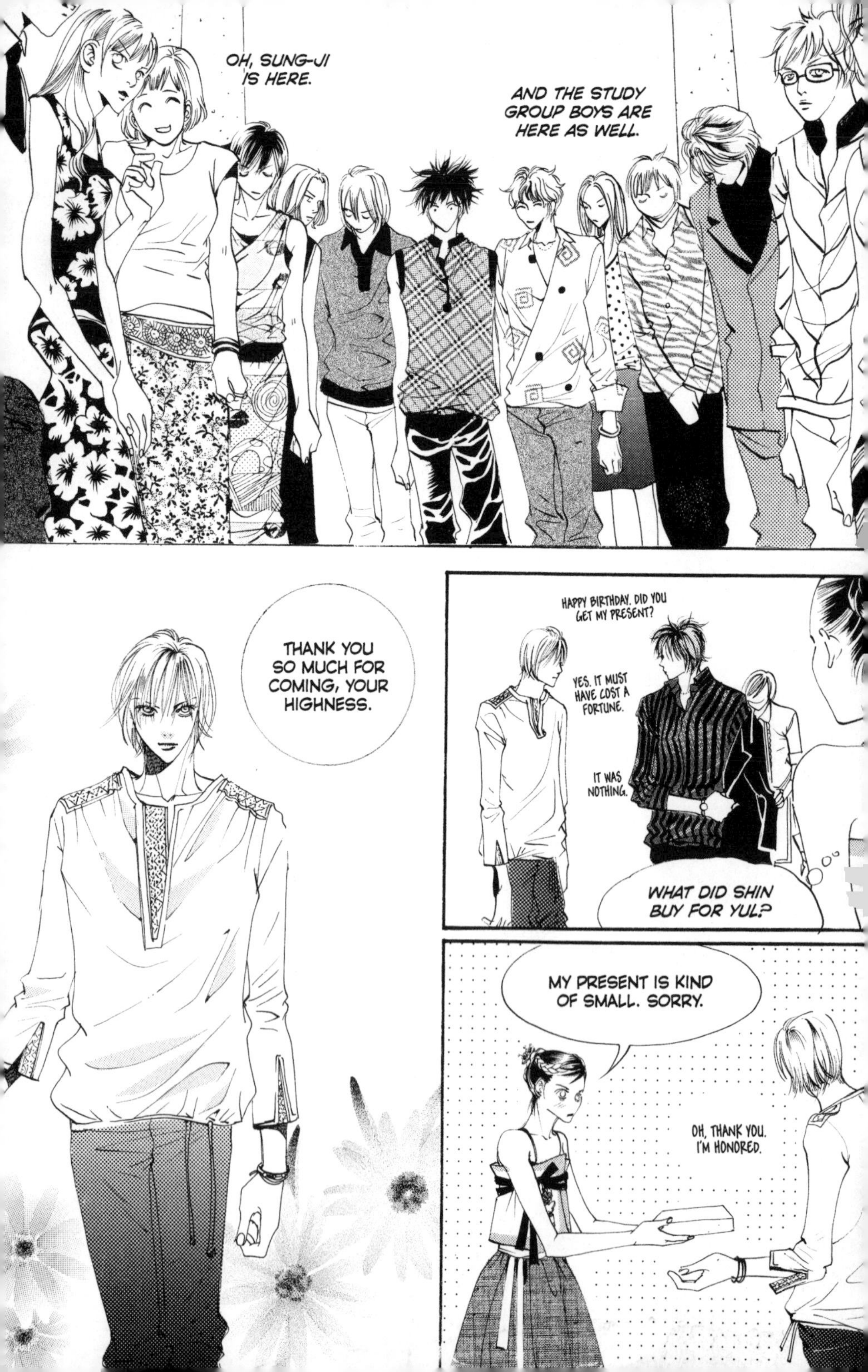
OH, SUNG-JI IS HERE.
AND THE STUDY GROUP BOYS ARE HERE AS WELL.
THANK YOU SO MUCH FOR COMING, YOUR HIGHNESS.
HAPPY BIRTHDAY. DID YOU GET MY PRESENT?
YES. IT MUST HAVE COST A FORTUNE.
IT WAS NOTHING.
WHAT DID SHIN BUY FOR YUL?
MY PRESENT IS KIND OF SMALL. SORRY.
OH, THANK YOU. I'M HONORED.

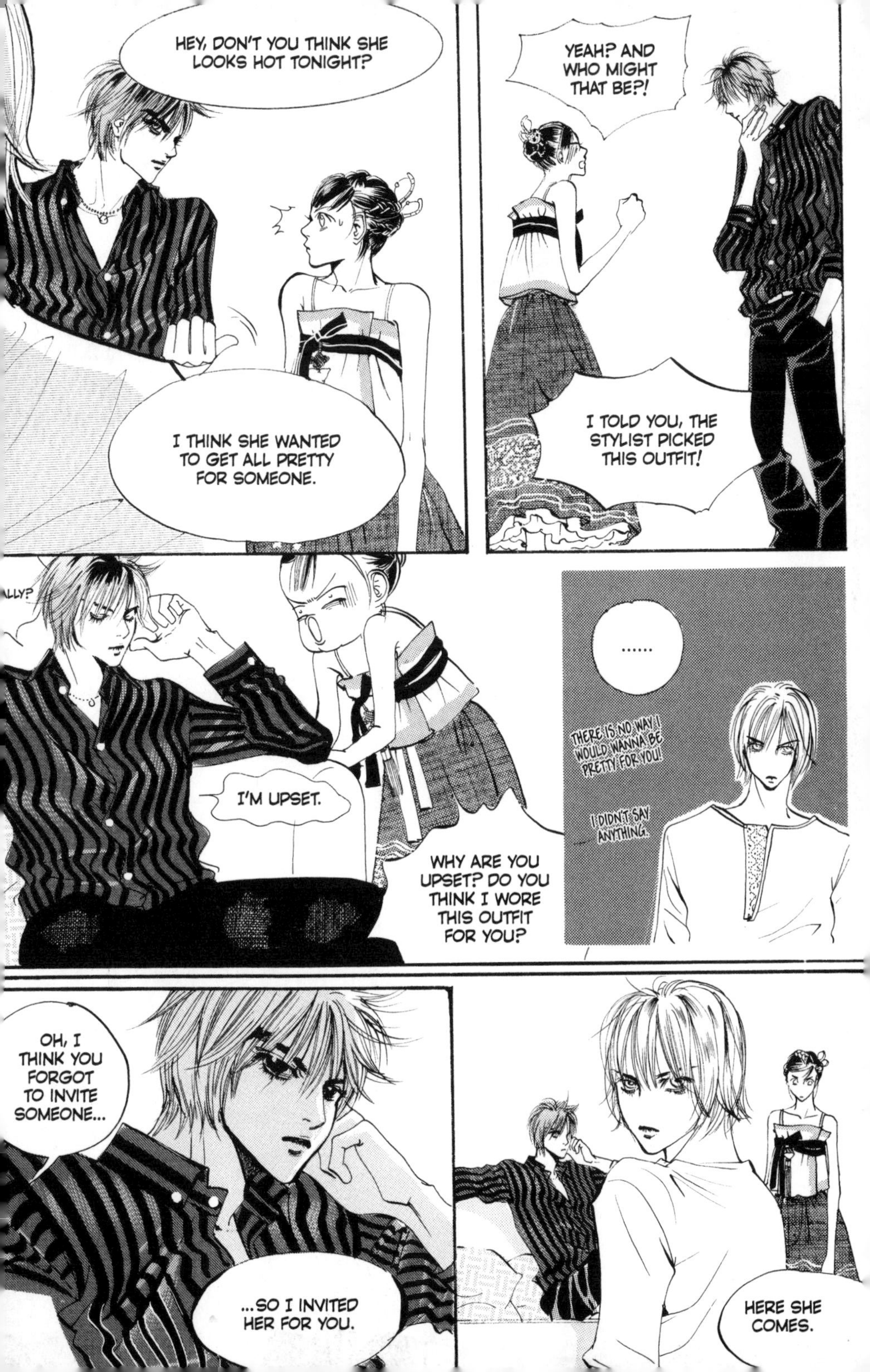
HEY, DON'T YOU THINK SHE LOOKS HOT TONIGHT?
I THINK SHE WANTED TO GET ALL PRETTY FOR SOMEONE.
YEAH? AND WHO MIGHT THAT BE?!
I TOLD YOU, THE STYLIST PICKED THIS OUTFIT!
ALLY?
I'M UPSET.
WHY ARE YOU UPSET? DO YOU THINK I WORE THIS OUTFIT FOR YOU?
......
THERE IS NO WAY I WOULD WANNA BE PRETTY FOR YOU!
I DIDN'T SAY ANYTHING.
OH, I THINK YOU FORGOT TO INVITE SOMEONE...
...SO I INVITED HER FOR YOU.
HERE SHE COMES.

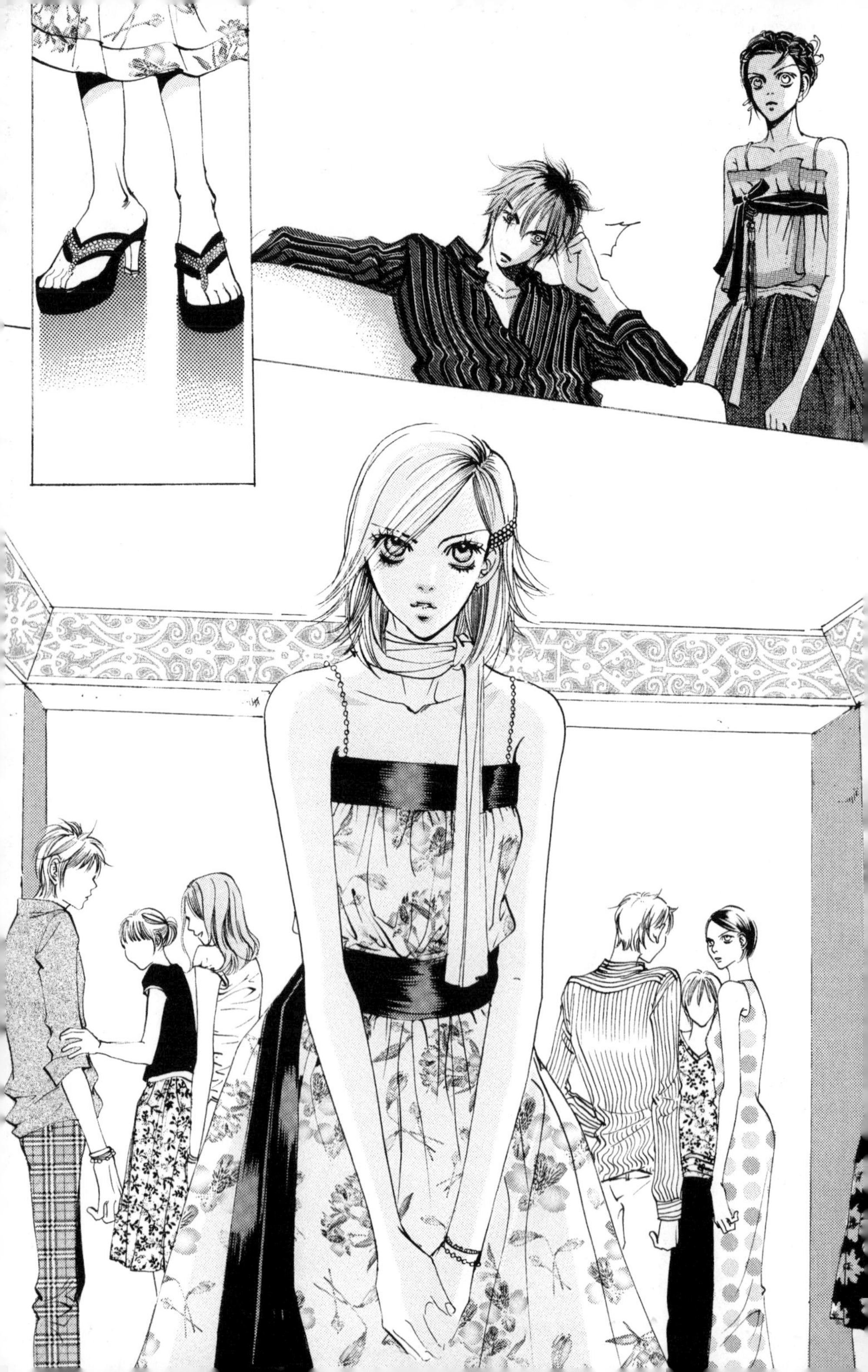

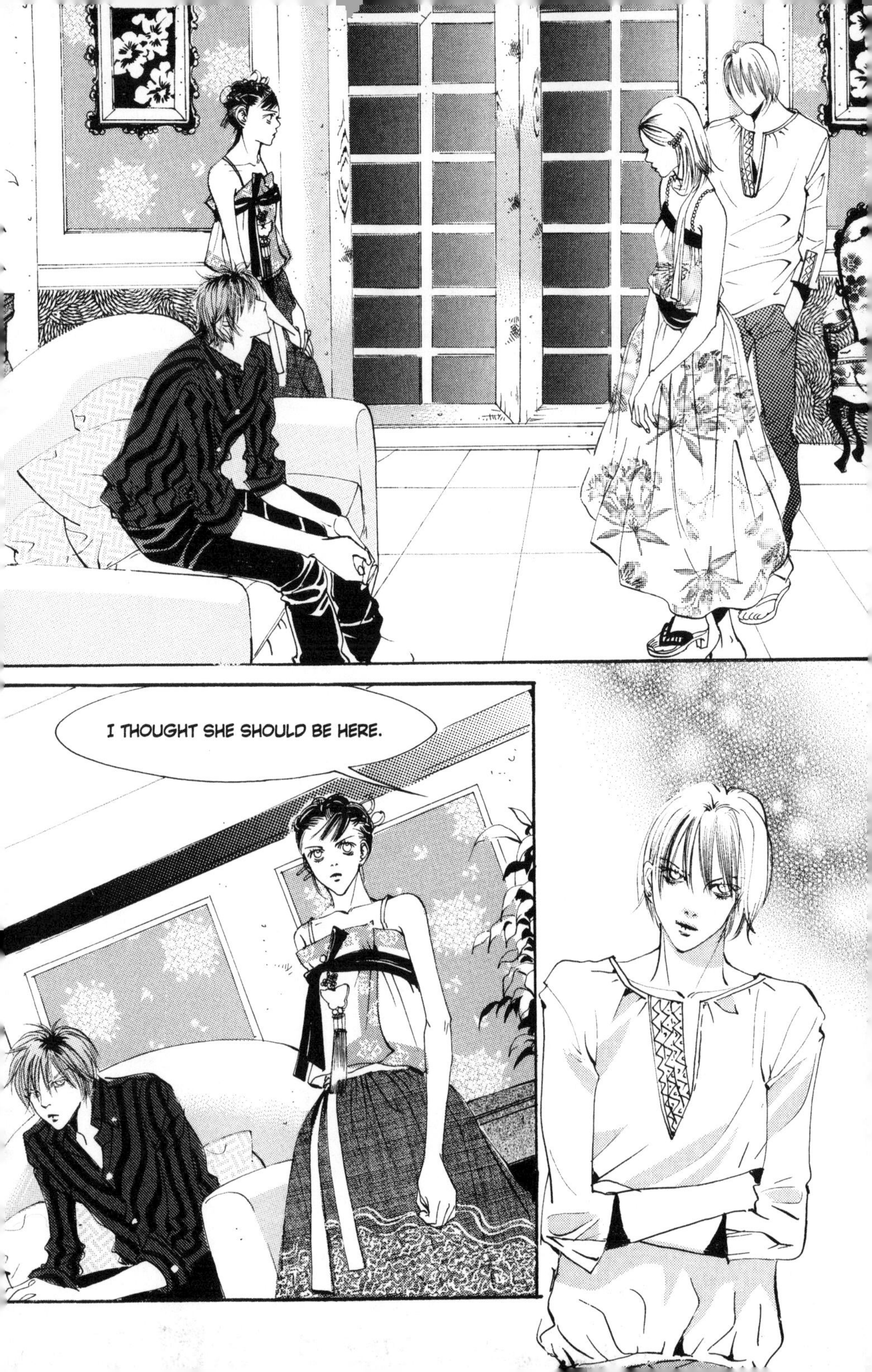
I THOUGHT SHE SHOULD BE HERE.

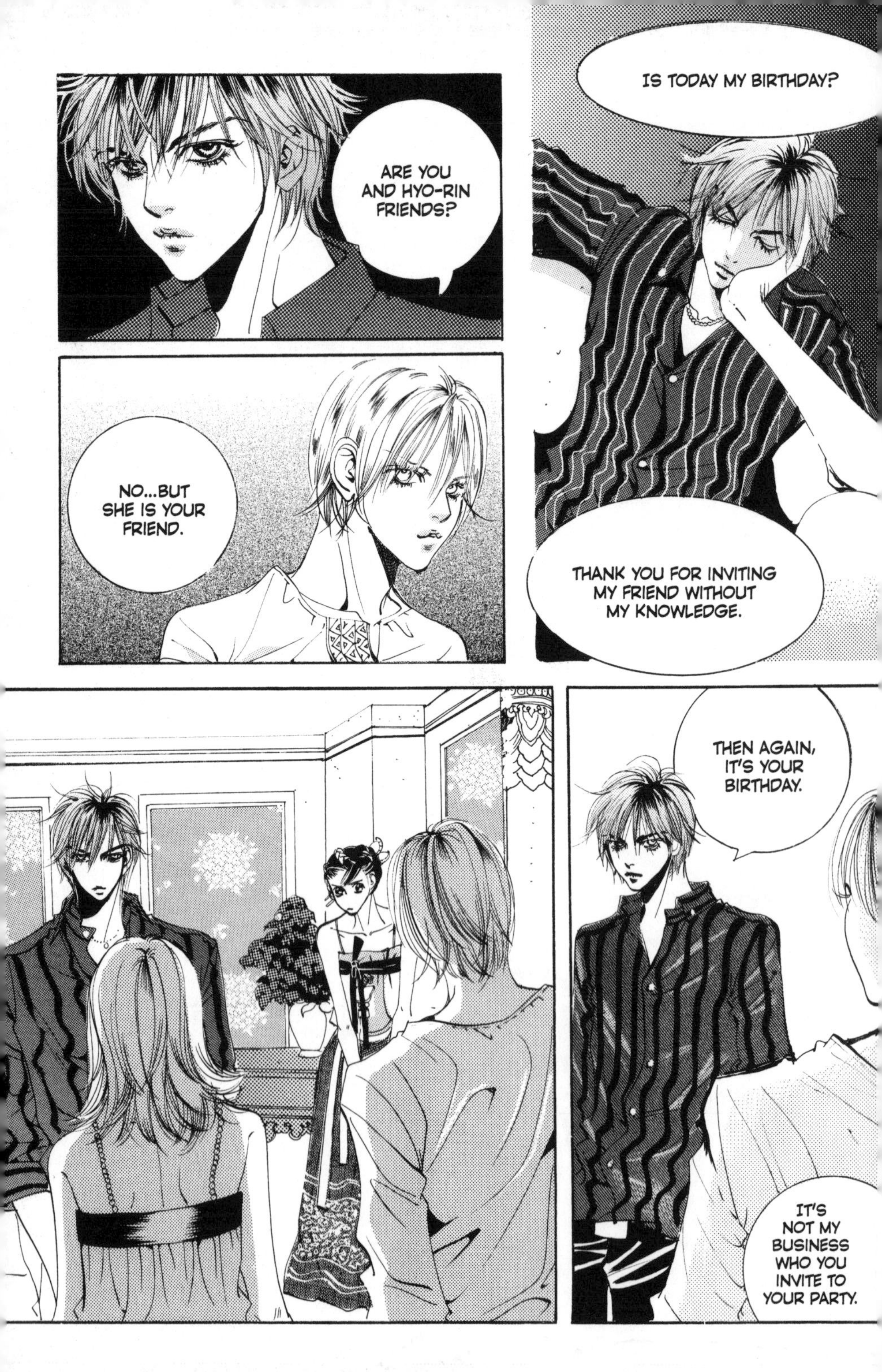
ARE YOU AND HYO-RIN FRIENDS?
NO...BUT SHE IS YOUR FRIEND.
IS TODAY MY BIRTHDAY?
THANK YOU FOR INVITING MY FRIEND WITHOUT MY KNOWLEDGE.
THEN AGAIN, IT'S YOUR BIRTHDAY.
IT'S NOT MY BUSINESS WHO YOU INVITE TO YOUR PARTY.

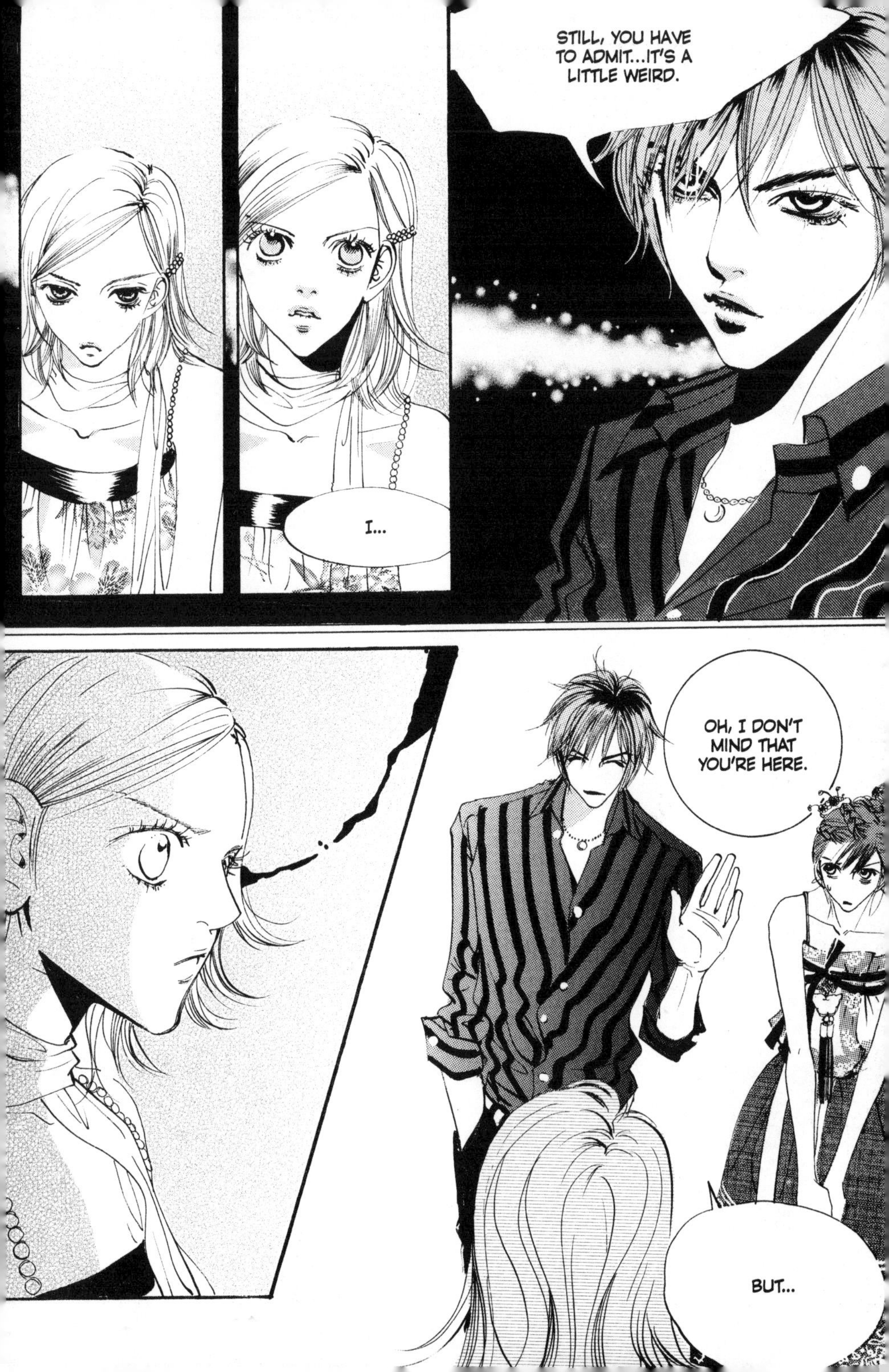
I...
STILL, YOU HAVE TO ADMIT...IT'S A LITTLE WEIRD.
OH, I DON'T MIND THAT YOU'RE HERE.
BUT...

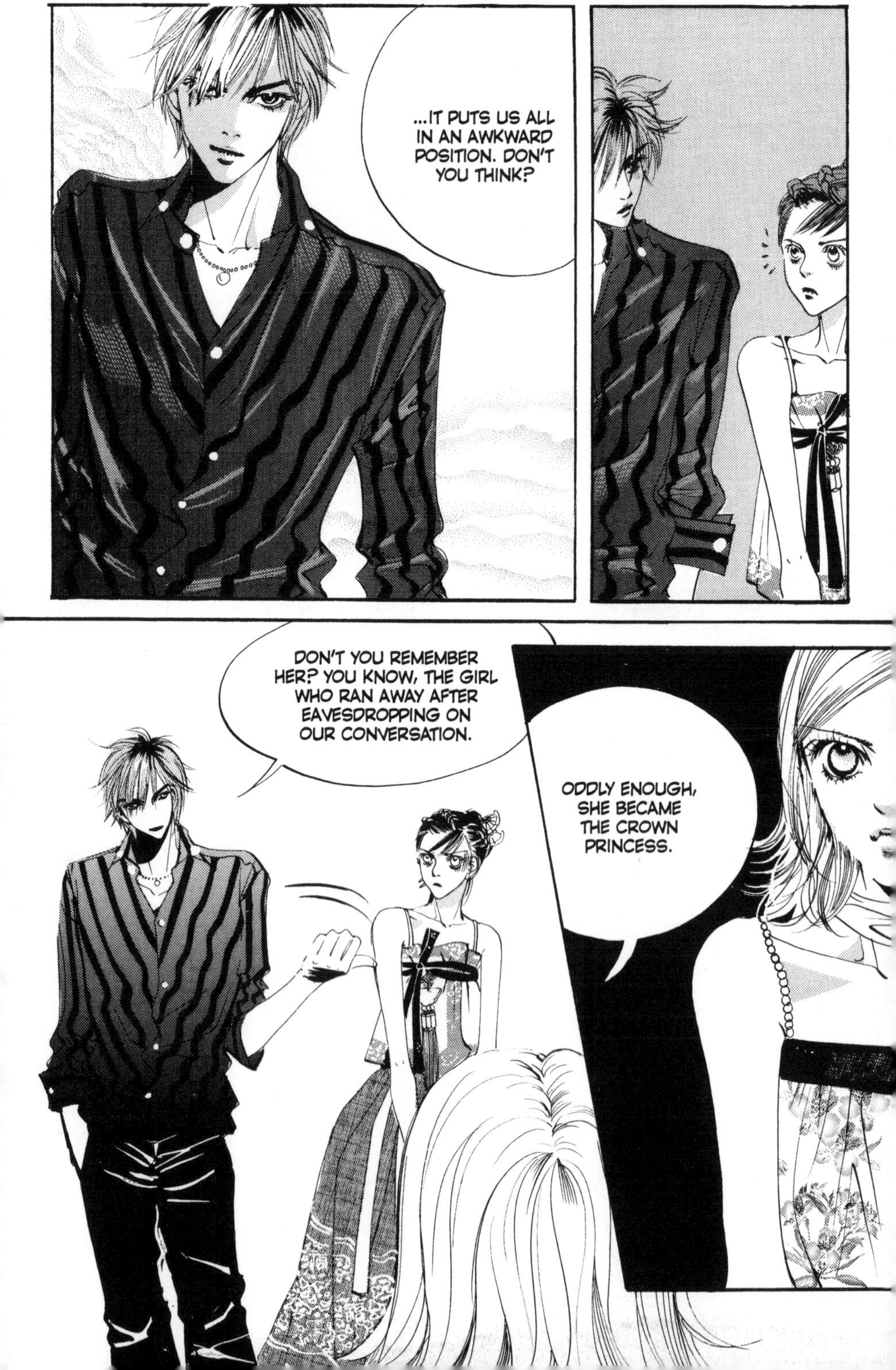
...IT PUTS US ALL IN AN AWKWARD POSITION. DON'T YOU THINK?
DON'T YOU REMEMBER HER? YOU KNOW, THE GIRL WHO RAN AWAY AFTER EAVESDROPPING ON OUR CONVERSATION.
ODDLY ENOUGH, SHE BECAME THE CROWN PRINCESS.

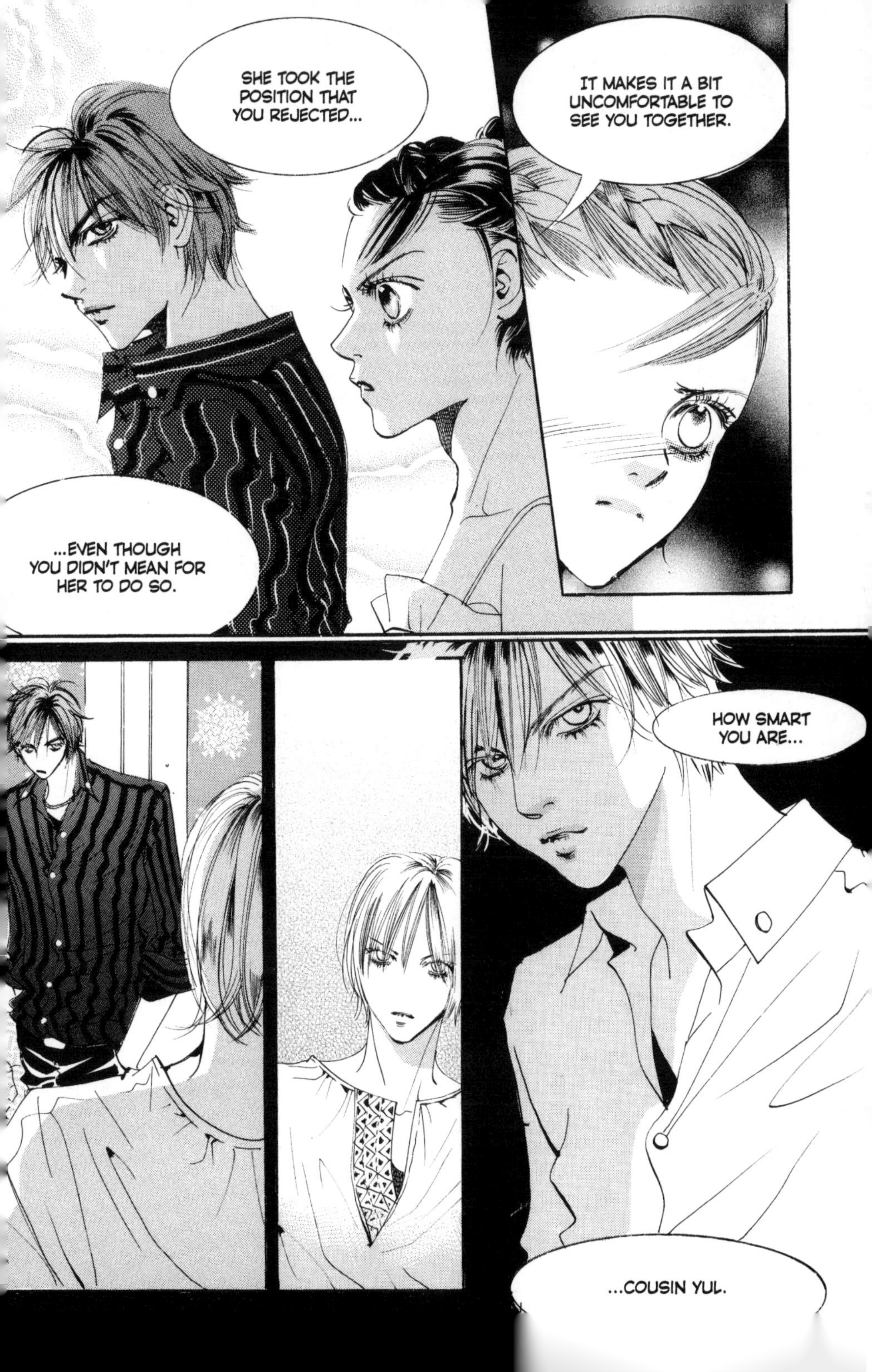
SHE TOOK THE POSITION THAT YOU REJECTED...
IT MAKES IT A BIT UNCOMFORTABLE TO SEE YOU TOGETHER.
...EVEN THOUGH YOU DIDN'T MEAN FOR HER TO DO SO.
HOW SMART YOU ARE...
...COUSIN YUL.

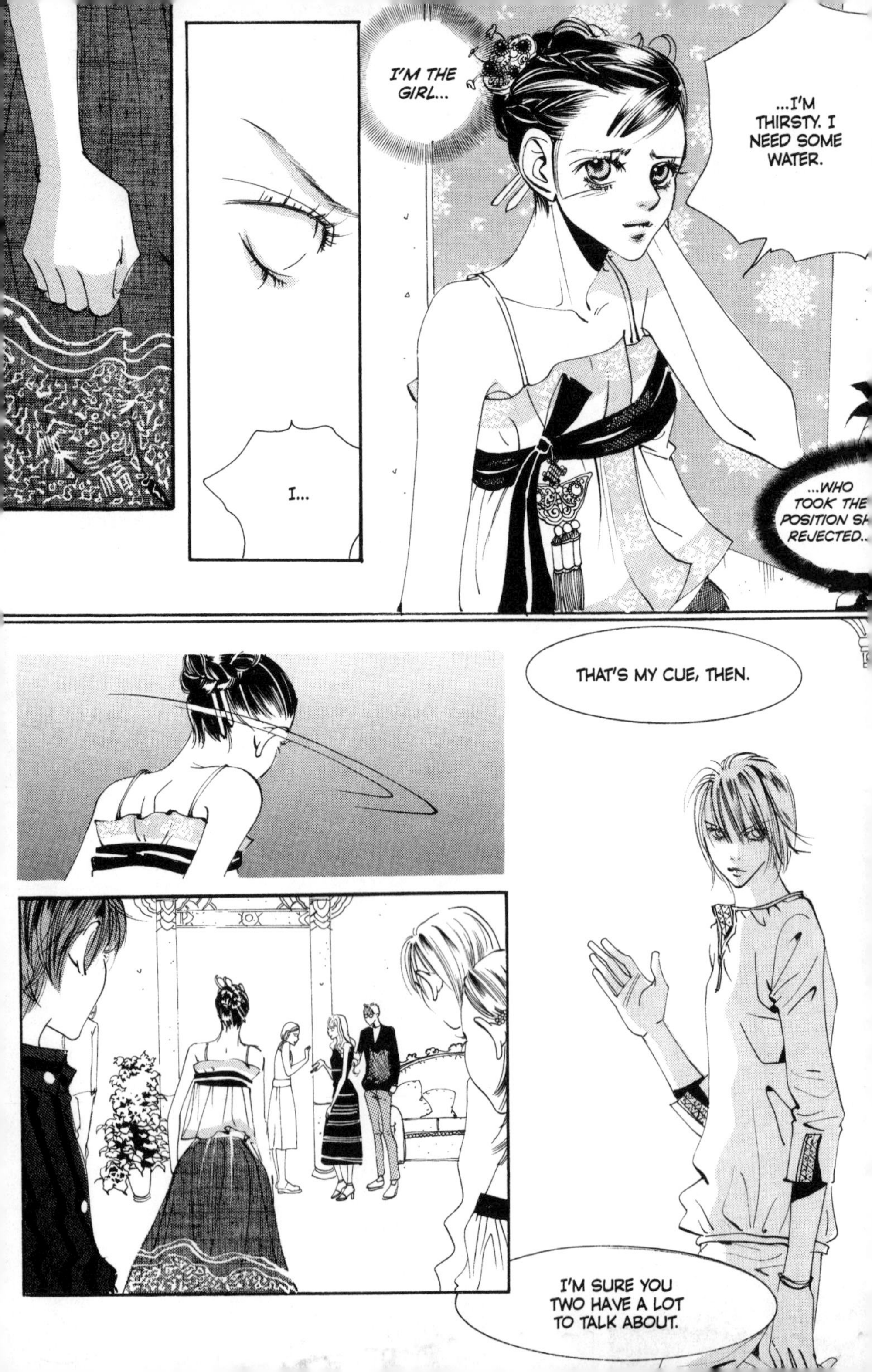
I...
I'M THE GIRL...
...I'M THIRSTY. I NEED SOME WATER.
...WHO TOOK THE POSITION SH REJECTED..
THAT'S MY CUE, THEN.
I'M SURE YOU TWO HAVE A LOT TO TALK ABOUT.

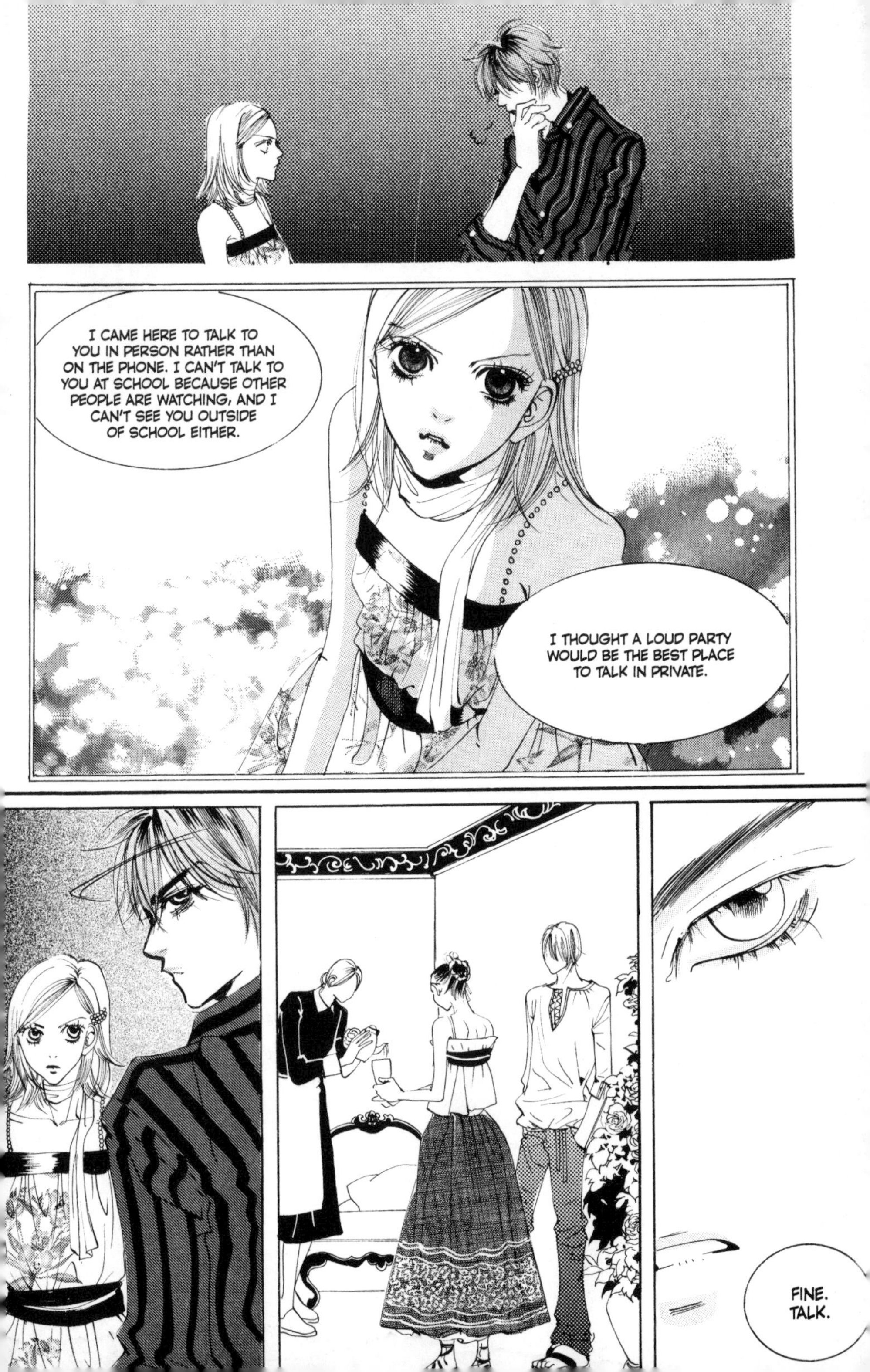
I CAME HERE TO TALK TO YOU IN PERSON RATHER THAN ON THE PHONE. I CAN'T TALK TO YOU AT SCHOOL BECAUSE OTHER PEOPLE ARE WATCHING, AND I CAN'T SEE YOU OUTSIDE OF SCHOOL EITHER.
I THOUGHT A LOUD PARTY WOULD BE THE BEST PLACE TO TALK IN PRIVATE.
FINE. TALK.

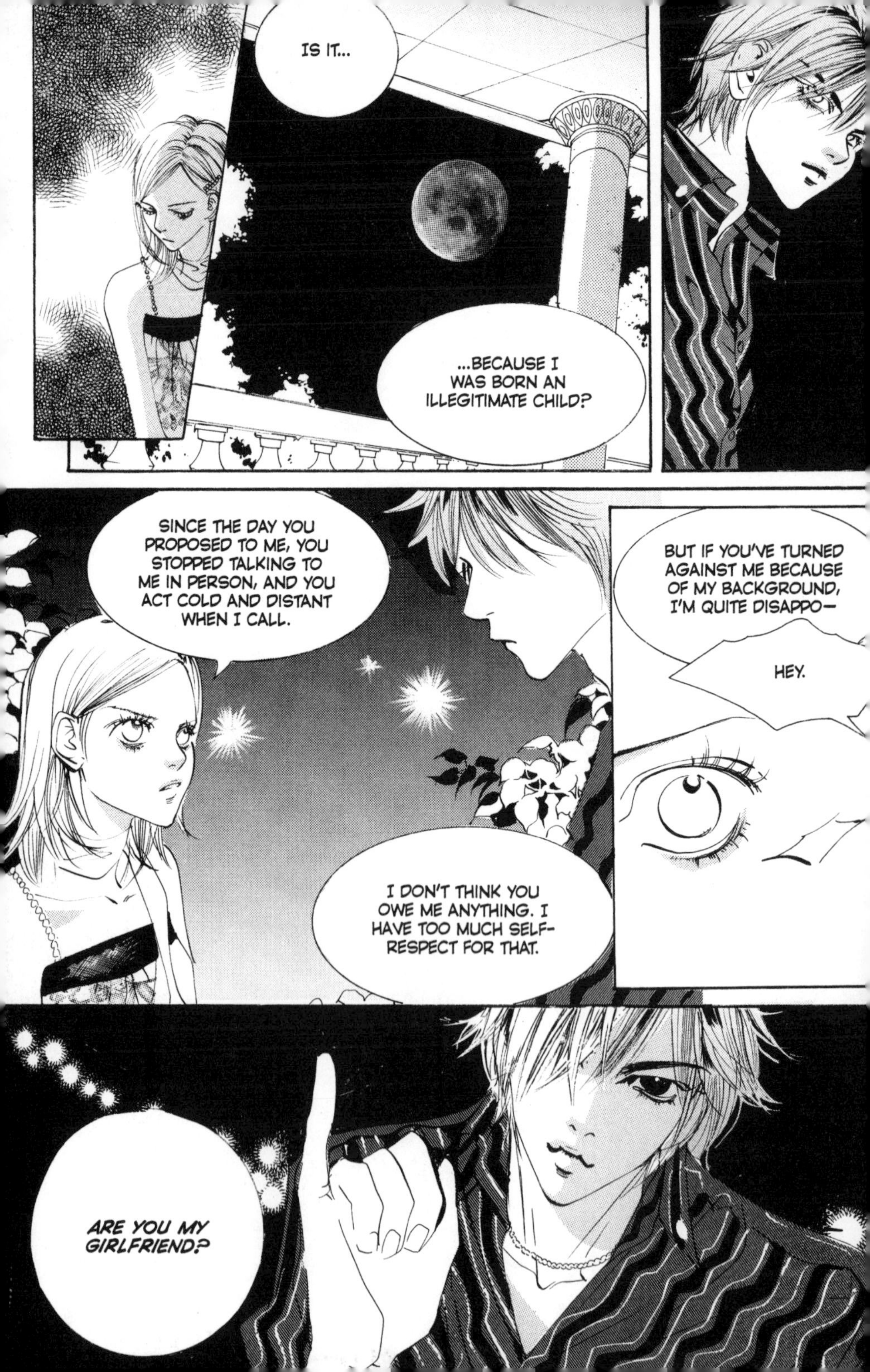
IS IT...
...BECAUSE I WAS BORN AN ILLEGITIMATE CHILD?
SINCE THE DAY YOU PROPOSED TO ME, YOU STOPPED TALKING TO ME IN PERSON, AND YOU ACT COLD AND DISTANT WHEN I CALL.
I DON'T THINK YOU OWE ME ANYTHING. I HAVE TOO MUCH SELF-RESPECT FOR THAT.
BUT IF YOU'VE TURNED AGAINST ME BECAUSE OF MY BACKGROUND, I'M QUITE DISAPPO—
HEY.
ARE YOU MY GIRLFRIEND?

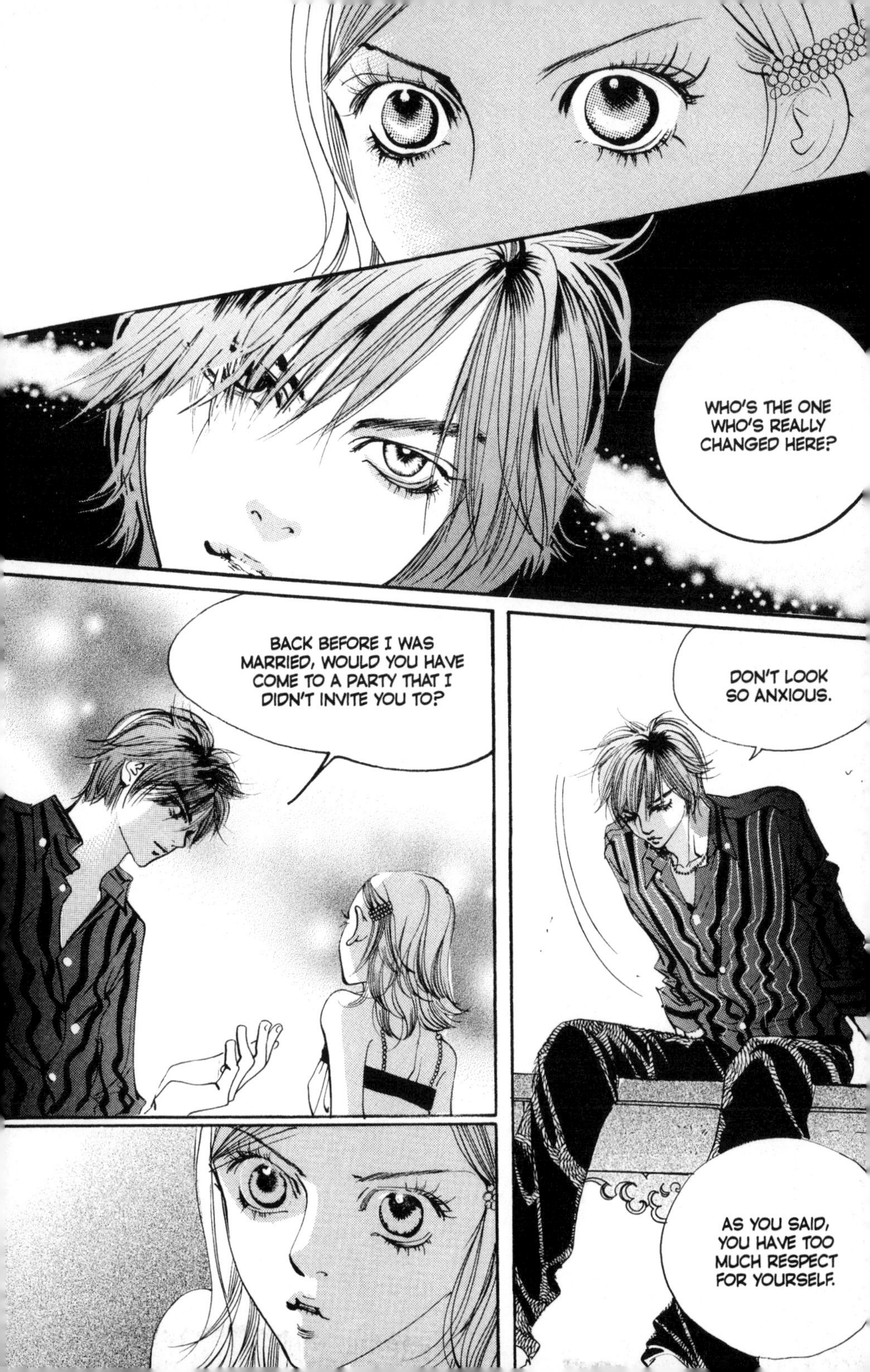
WHO'S THE ONE WHO'S REALLY CHANGED HERE?
BACK BEFORE I WAS MARRIED, WOULD YOU HAVE COME TO A PARTY THAT I DIDN'T INVITE YOU TO?
DON'T LOOK SO ANXIOUS.
AS YOU SAID, YOU HAVE TOO MUCH RESPECT FOR YOURSELF.

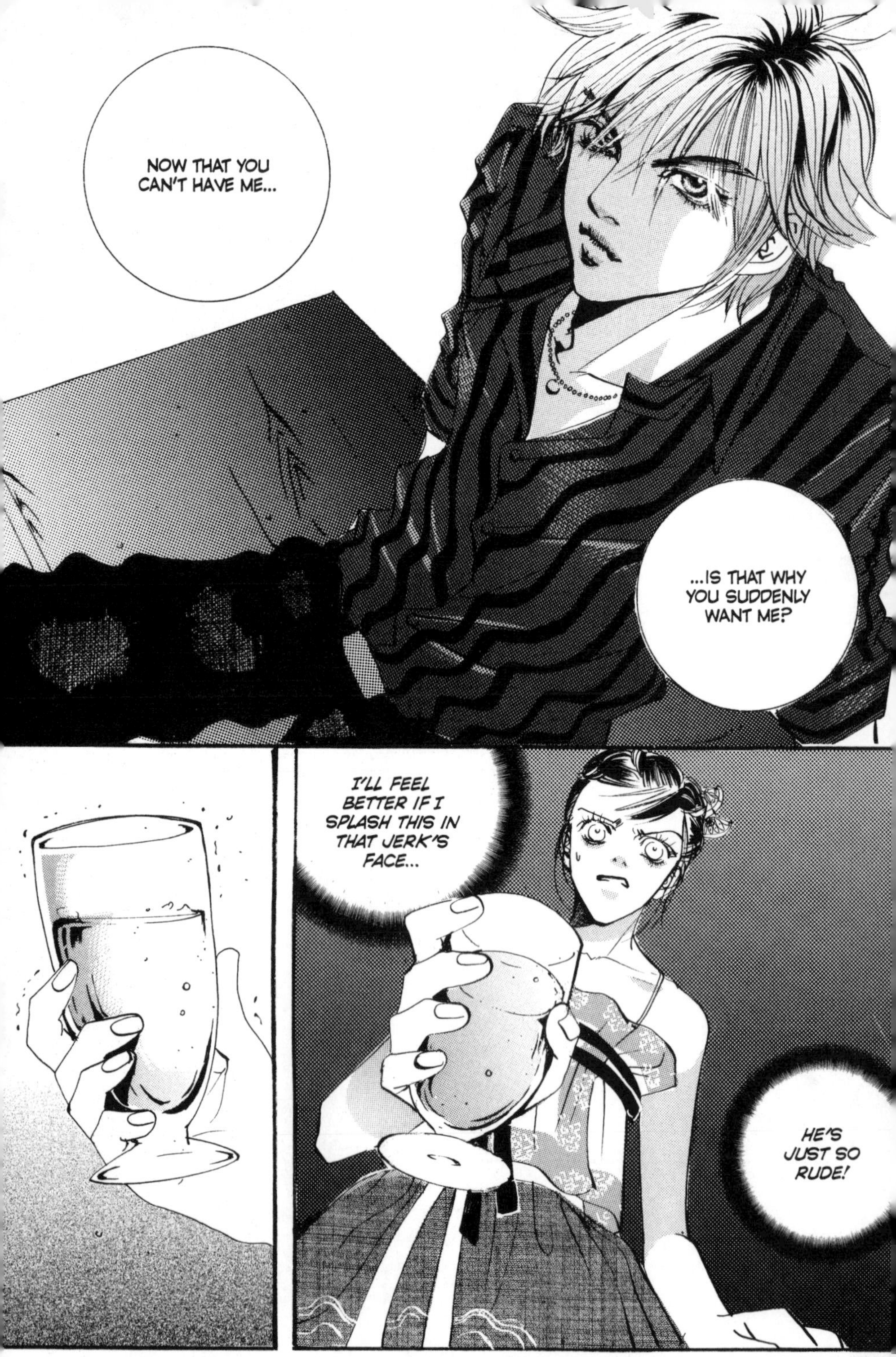
NOW THAT YOU CAN'T HAVE ME...
...IS THAT WHY YOU SUDDENLY WANT ME?
I'LL FEEL BETTER IF I SPLASH THIS IN THAT JERK'S FACE...
HE'S JUST SO RUDE!

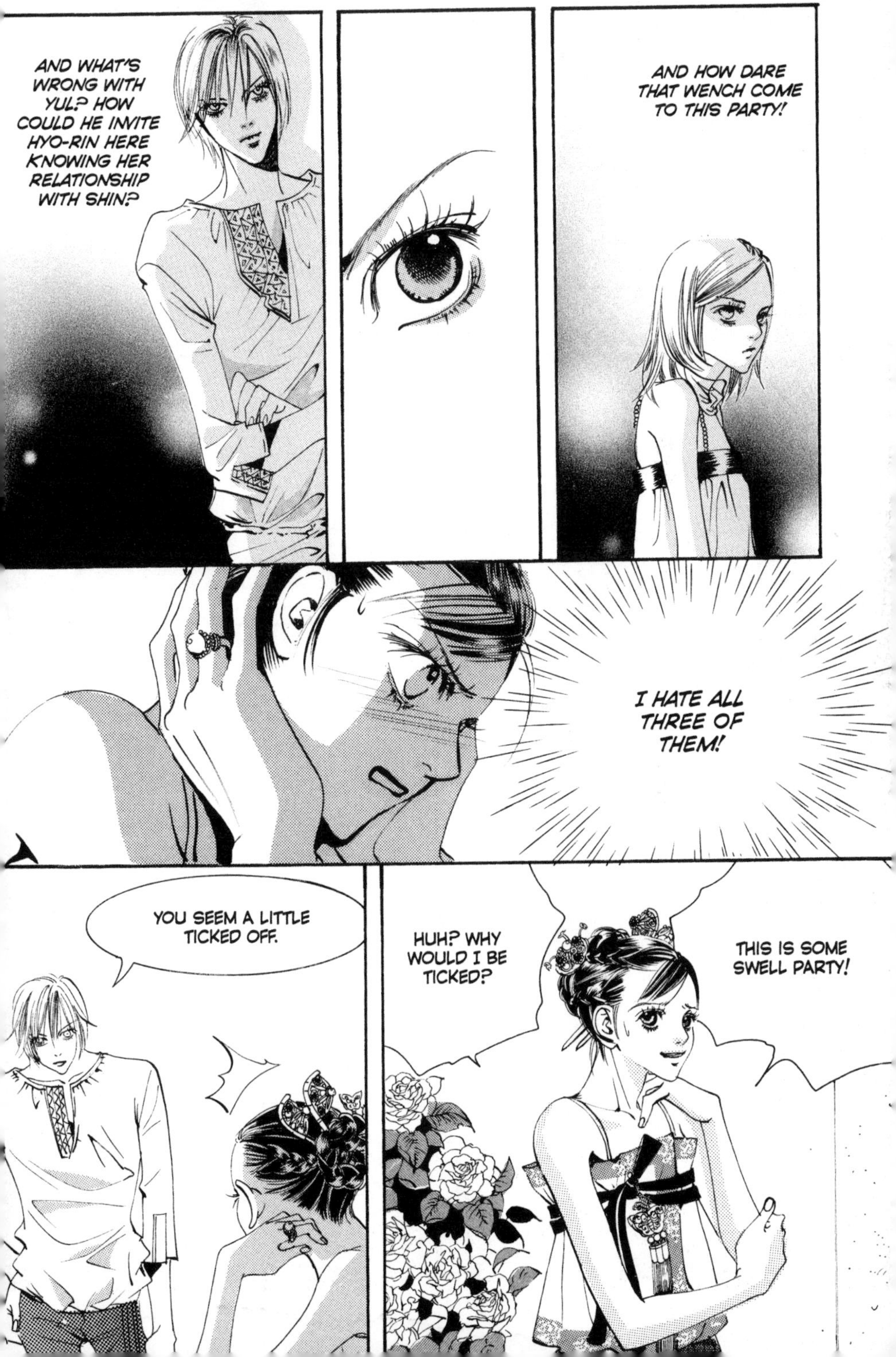
AND WHAT'S WRONG WITH YUL? HOW COULD HE INVITE HYO-RIN HERE KNOWING HER RELATIONSHIP WITH SHIN?
AND HOW DARE THAT WENCH COME TO THIS PARTY!
I HATE ALL THREE OF THEM!
YOU SEEM A LITTLE TICKED OFF.
HUH? WHY WOULD I BE TICKED?
THIS IS SOME SWELL PARTY!

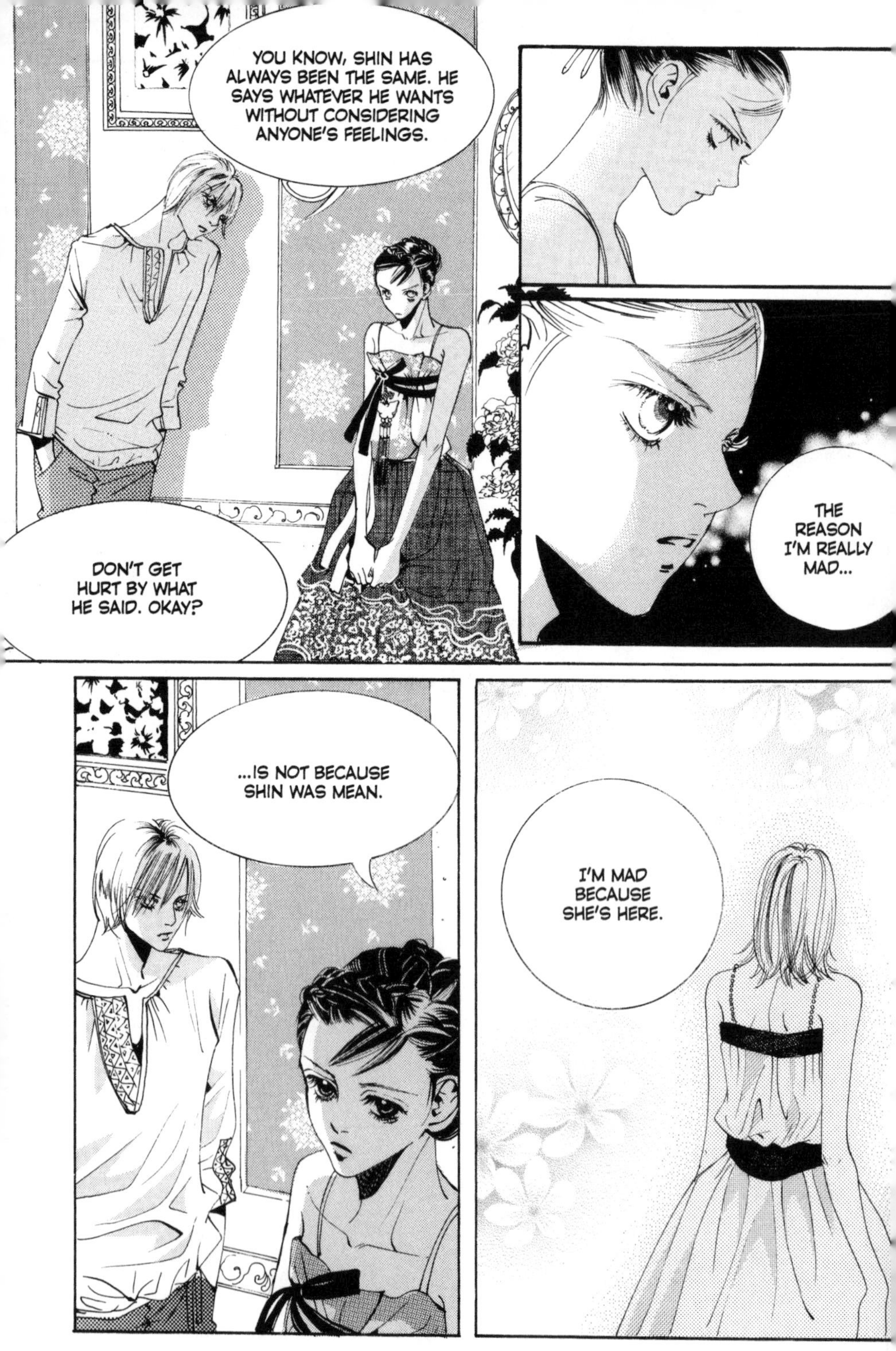
YOU KNOW, SHIN HAS ALWAYS BEEN THE SAME. HE SAYS WHATEVER HE WANTS WITHOUT CONSIDERING ANYONE'S FEELINGS.
DON'T GET HURT BY WHAT HE SAID. OKAY?
THE REASON I'M REALLY MAD...
...IS NOT BECAUSE SHIN WAS MEAN.
I'M MAD BECAUSE SHE'S HERE.

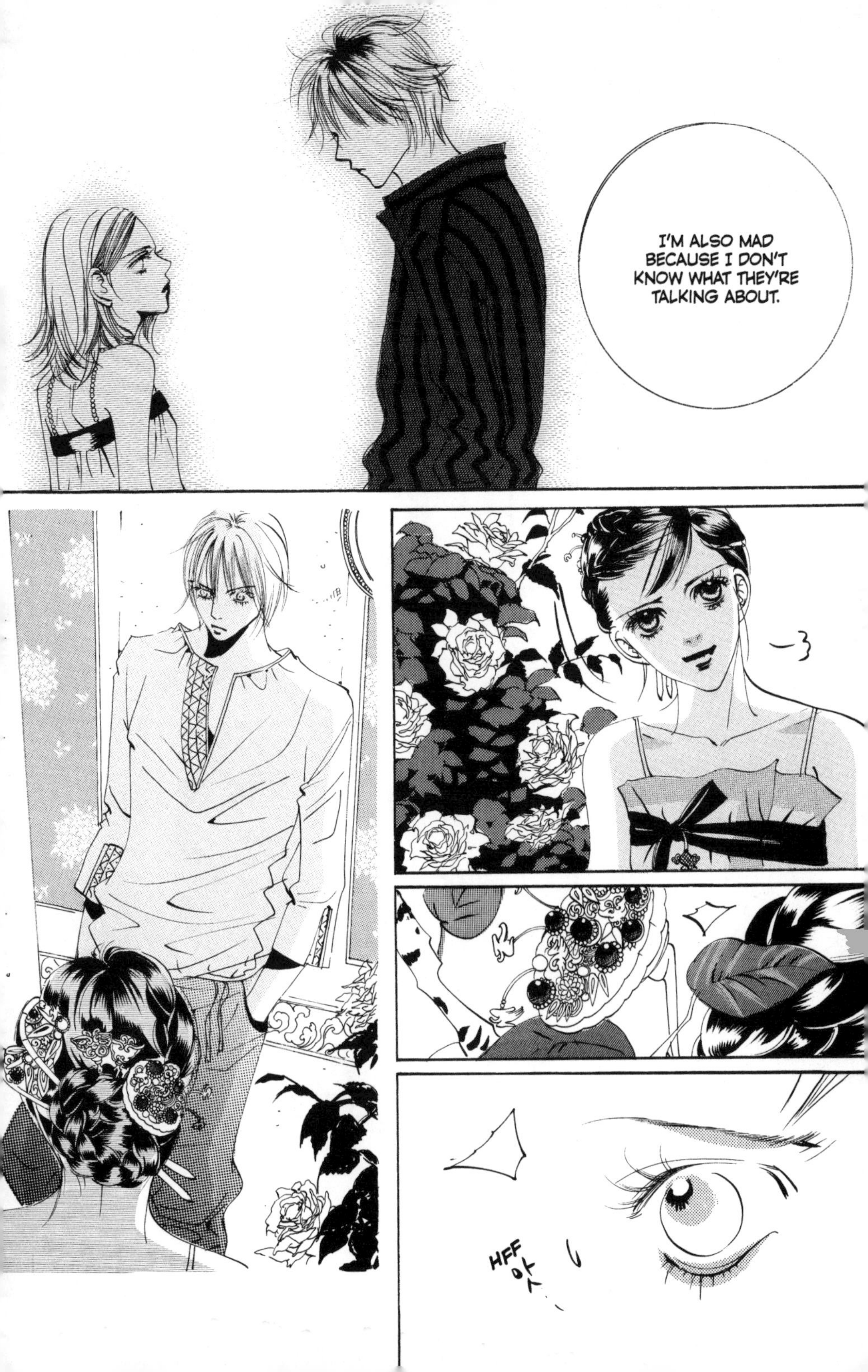
I'M ALSO MAD BECAUSE I DON'T KNOW WHAT THEY'RE TALKING ABOUT.
HFF

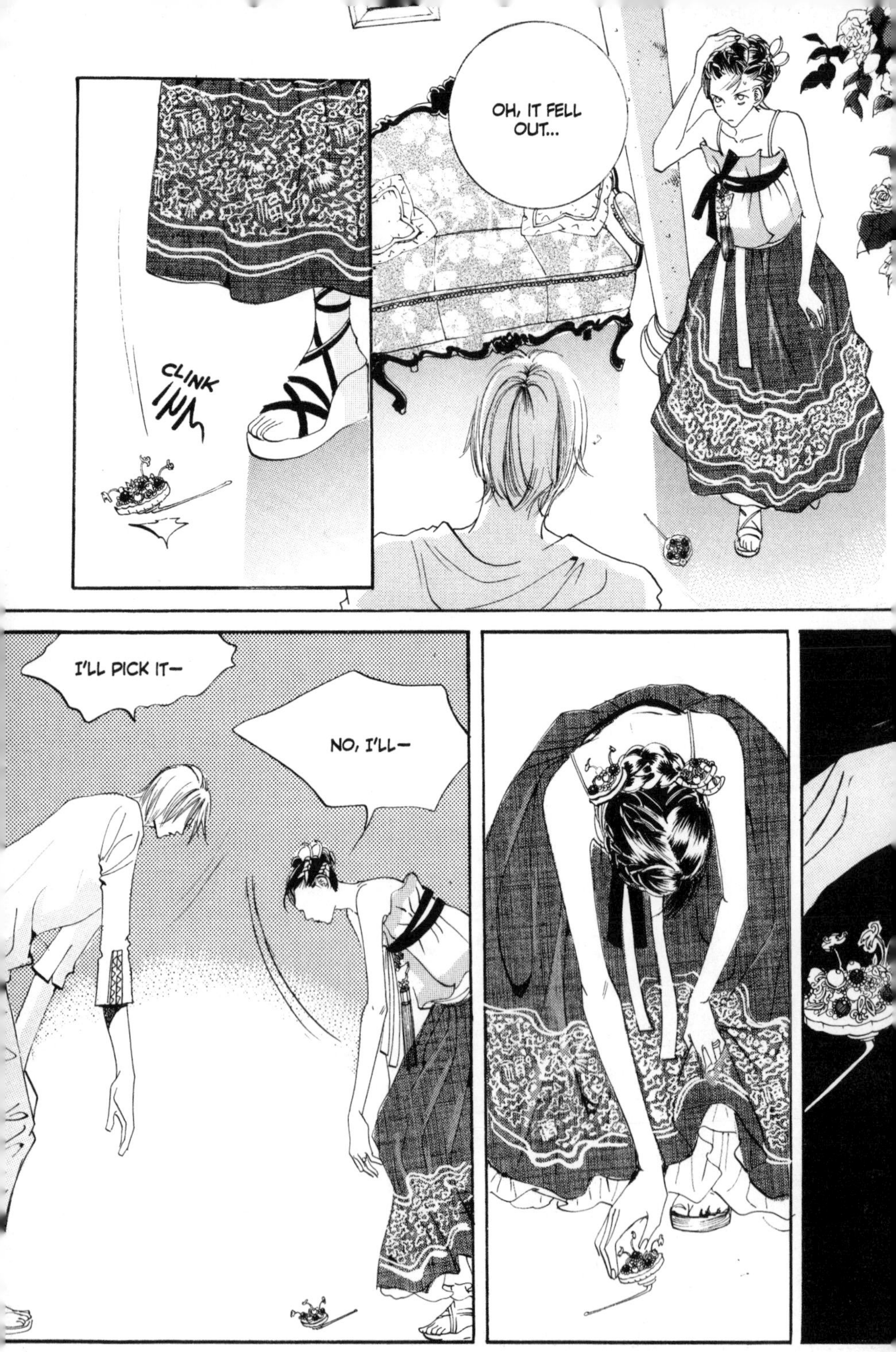

CLINK
OH, IT FELL OUT...
I'LL PICK IT—
NO, I'LL—

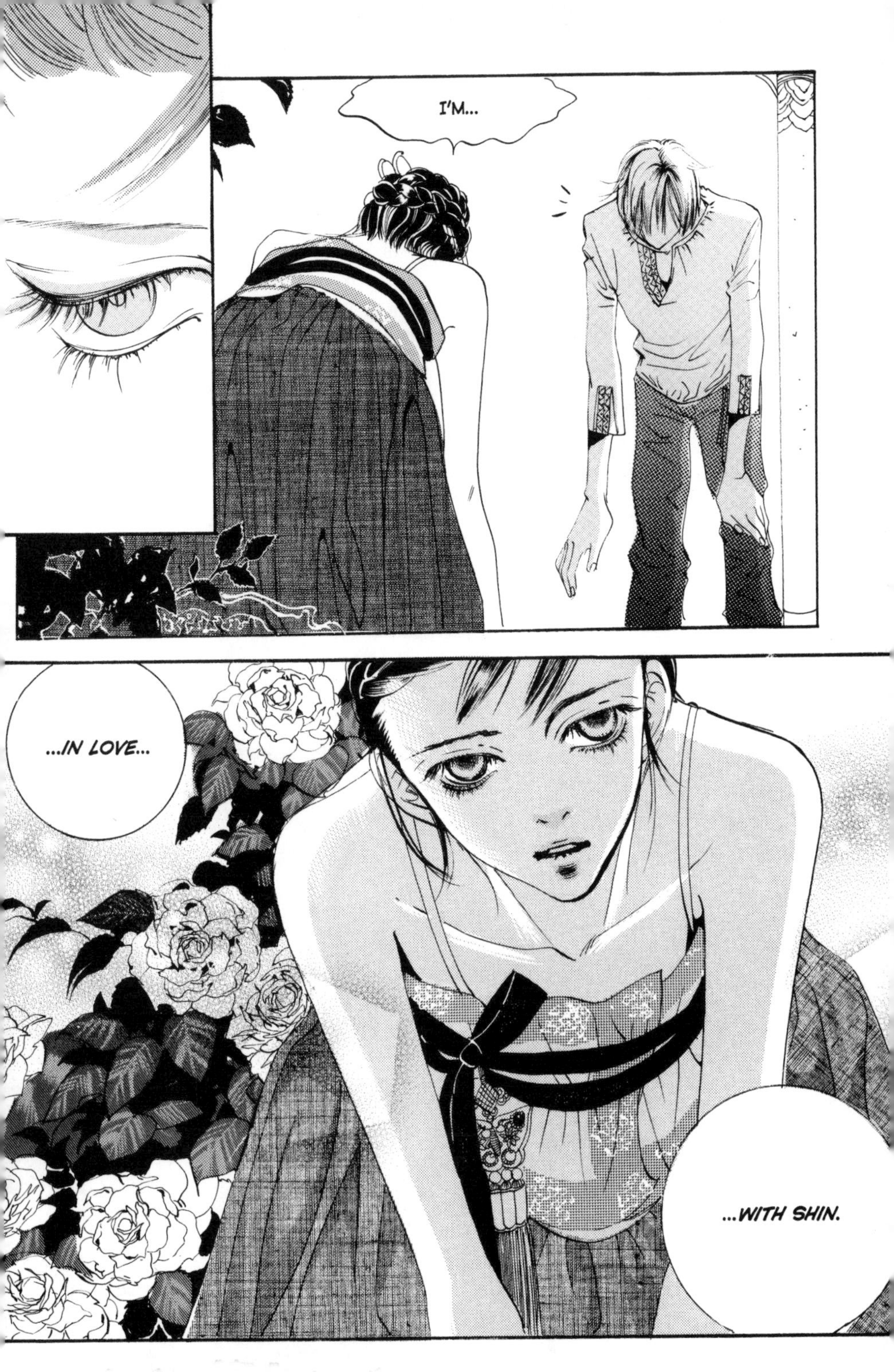
I'M...
...IN LOVE...
...WITH SHIN.

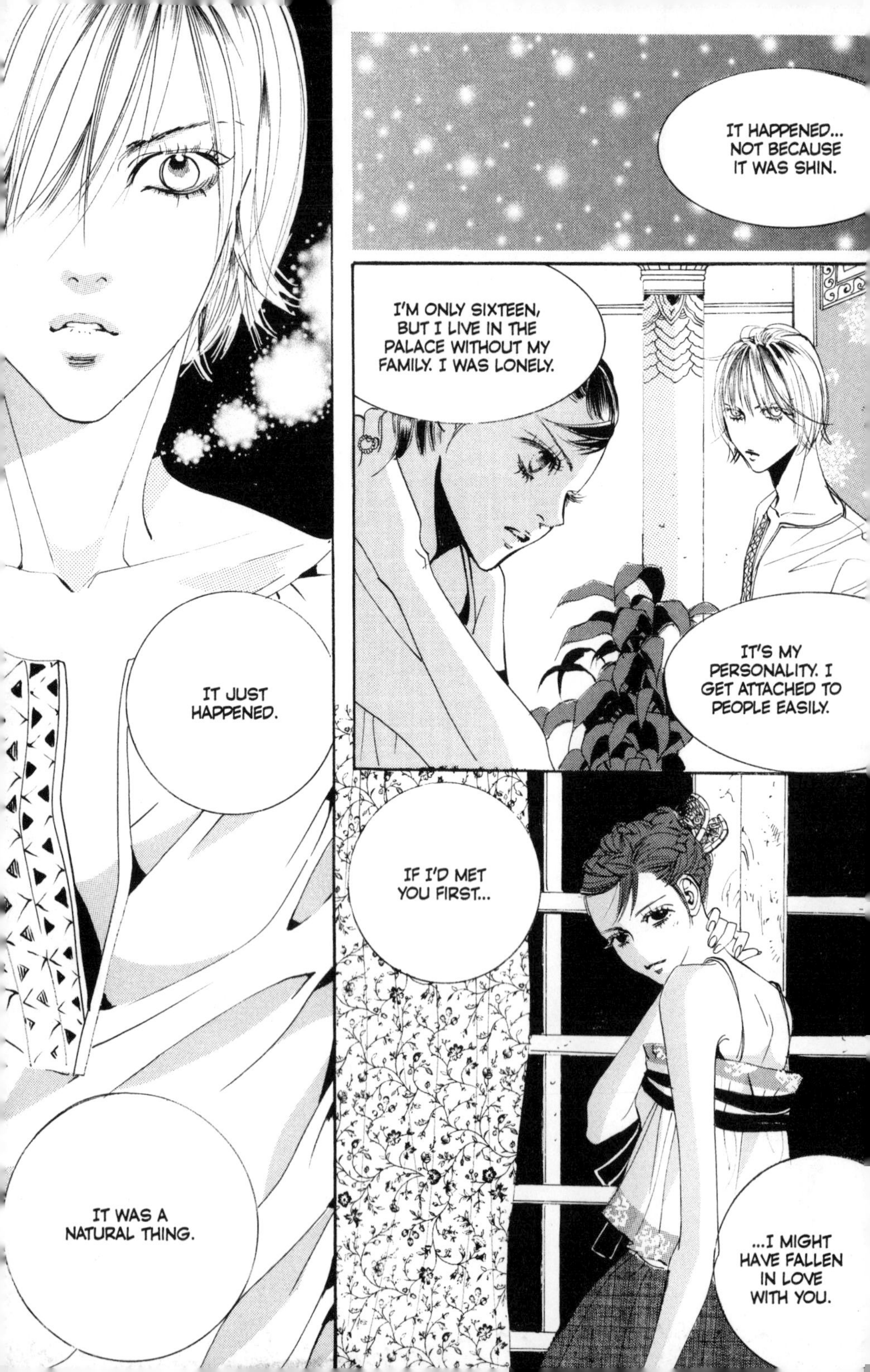
IT JUST HAPPENED.
IT WAS A NATURAL THING.
IT HAPPENED... NOT BECAUSE IT WAS SHIN.
I'M ONLY SIXTEEN, BUT I LIVE IN THE PALACE WITHOUT MY FAMILY. I WAS LONELY.
IT'S MY PERSONALITY. I GET ATTACHED TO PEOPLE EASILY.
IF I'D MET YOU FIRST...
...I MIGHT HAVE FALLEN IN LOVE WITH YOU.

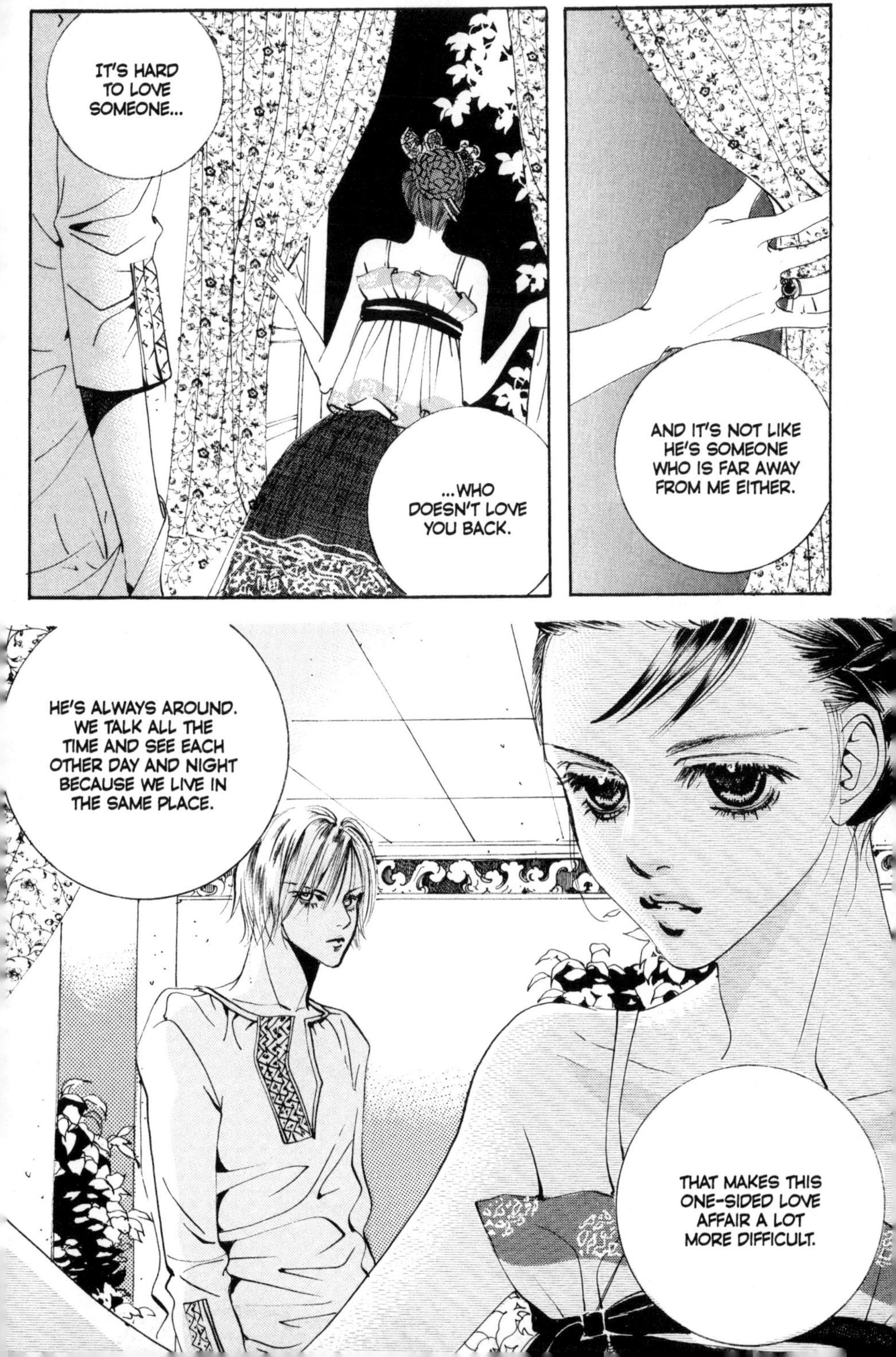
IT'S HARD TO LOVE SOMEONE...
...WHO DOESN'T LOVE YOU BACK.
AND IT'S NOT LIKE HE'S SOMEONE WHO IS FAR AWAY FROM ME EITHER.
HE'S ALWAYS AROUND. WE TALK ALL THE TIME AND SEE EACH OTHER DAY AND NIGHT BECAUSE WE LIVE IN THE SAME PLACE.
THAT MAKES THIS ONE-SIDED LOVE AFFAIR A LOT MORE DIFFICULT.

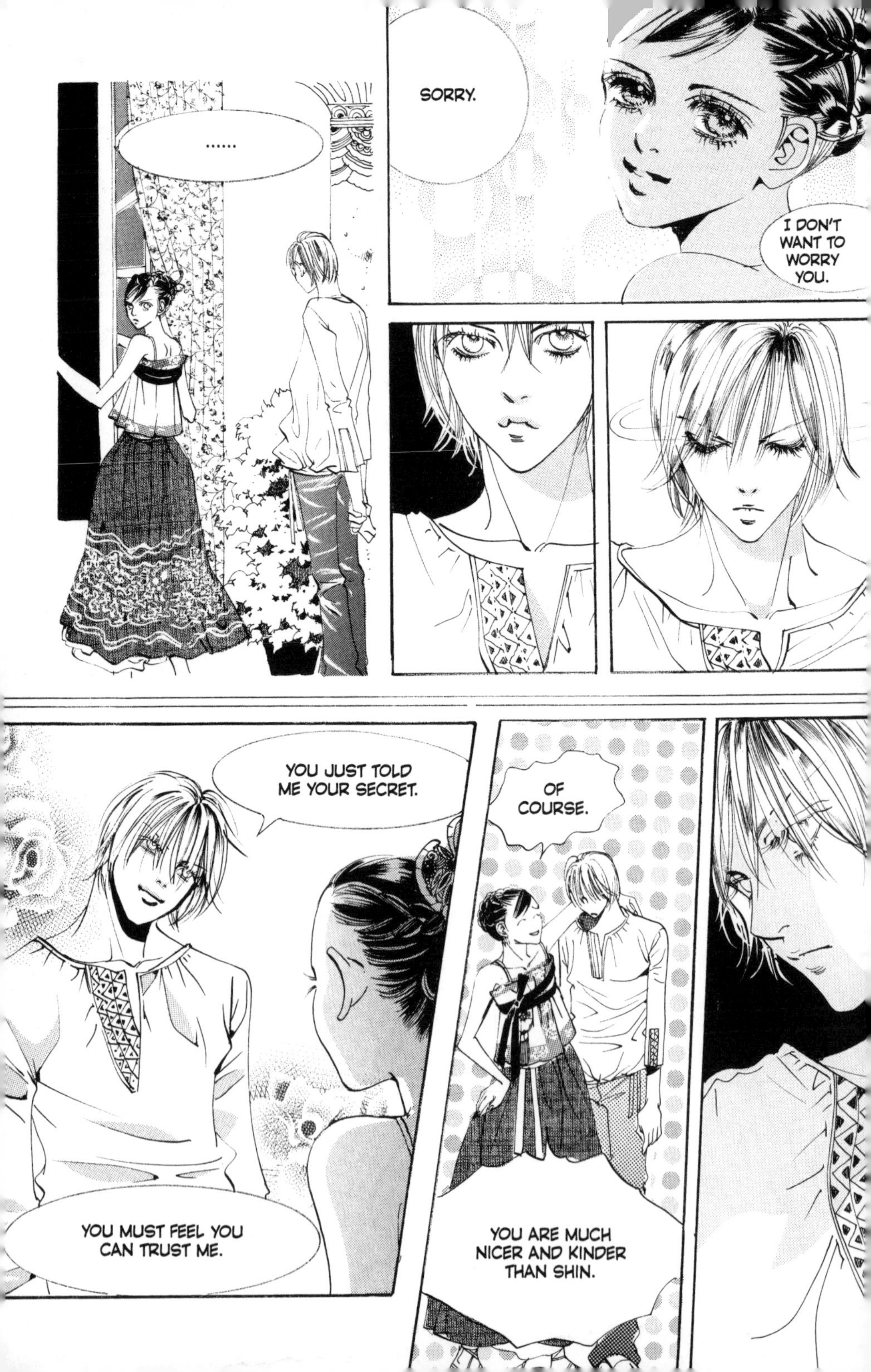
......
SORRY.
I DON'T WANT TO WORRY YOU.
YOU JUST TOLD ME YOUR SECRET.
YOU MUST FEEL YOU CAN TRUST ME.
OF COURSE.
YOU ARE MUCH NICER AND KINDER THAN SHIN.

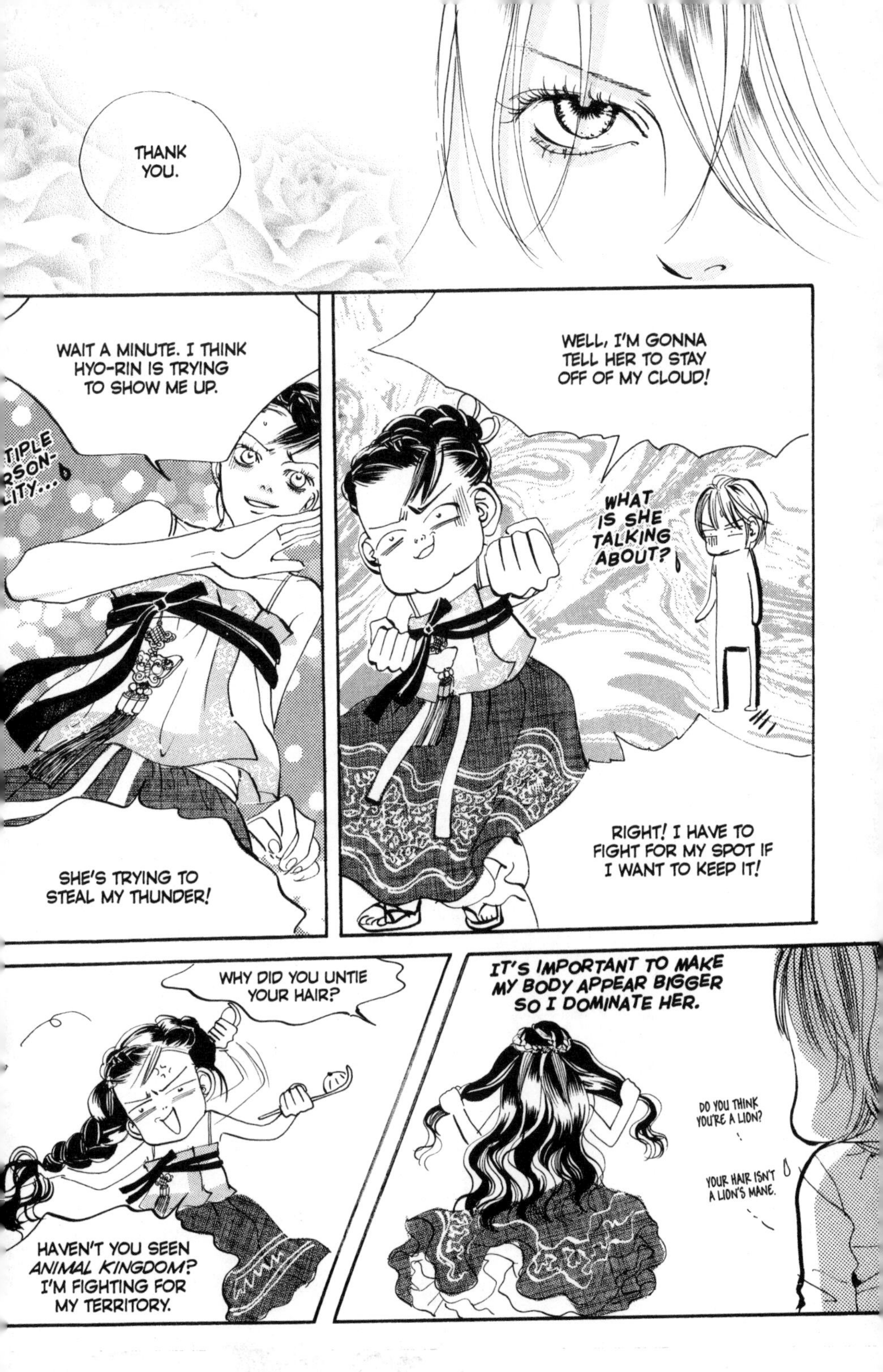
THANK YOU.
WAIT A MINUTE. I THINK HYO-RIN IS TRYING TO SHOW ME UP.
TIPLE RSON- LITY...
SHE'S TRYING TO STEAL MY THUNDER!
WELL, I'M GONNA TELL HER TO STAY OFF OF MY CLOUD!
WHAT IS SHE TALKING ABOUT?
RIGHT! I HAVE TO FIGHT FOR MY SPOT IF I WANT TO KEEP IT!
WHY DID YOU UNTIE YOUR HAIR?
HAVEN'T YOU SEEN *ANIMAL KINGDOM*? I'M FIGHTING FOR MY TERRITORY.
IT'S IMPORTANT TO MAKE MY BODY APPEAR BIGGER SO I DOMINATE HER.
DO YOU THINK YOU'RE A LION?
YOUR HAIR ISN'T A LION'S MANE.

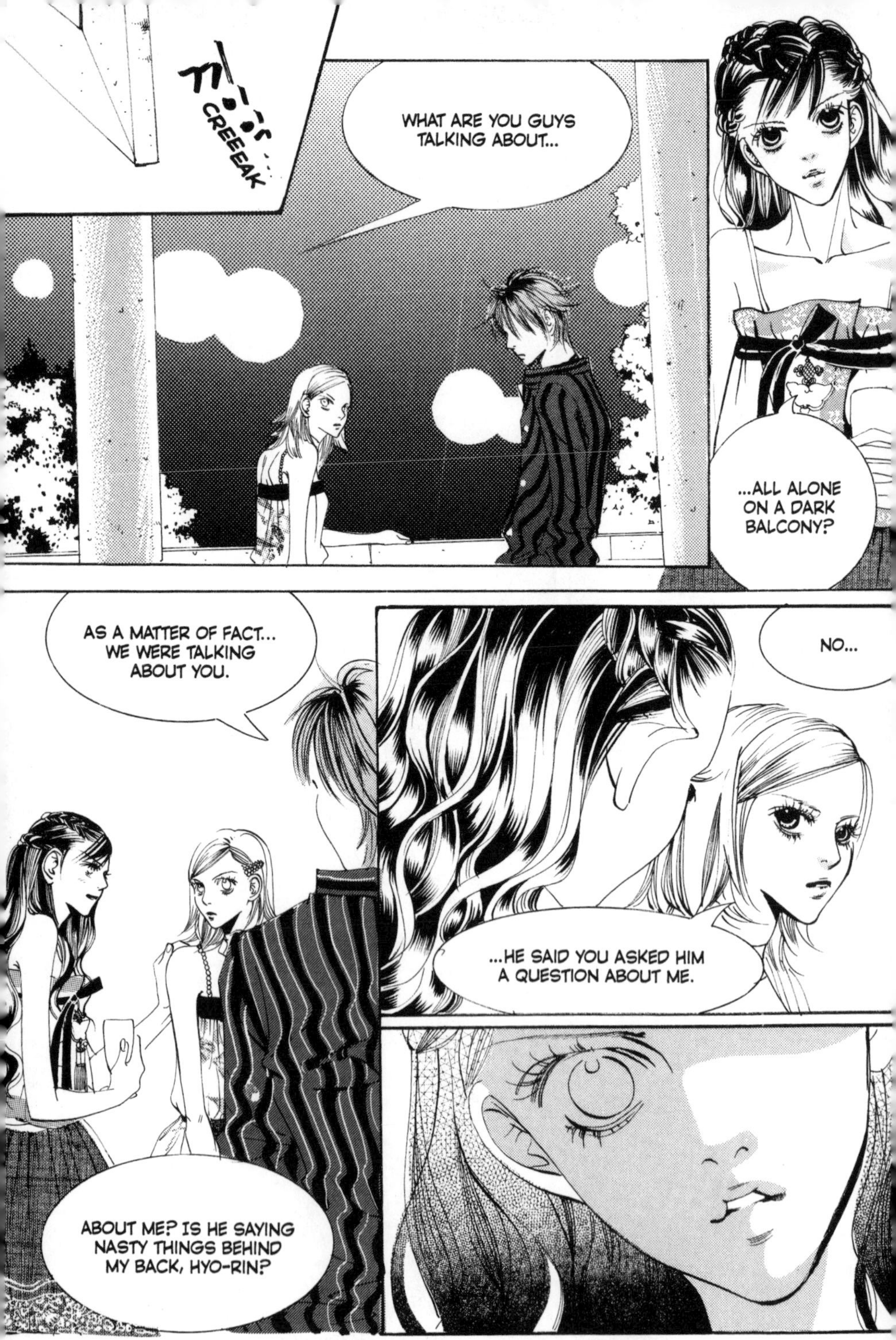
CREEEAK
WHAT ARE YOU GUYS TALKING ABOUT...
...ALL ALONE ON A DARK BALCONY?
AS A MATTER OF FACT... WE WERE TALKING ABOUT YOU.
ABOUT ME? IS HE SAYING NASTY THINGS BEHIND MY BACK, HYO-RIN?
NO...
...HE SAID YOU ASKED HIM A QUESTION ABOUT ME.

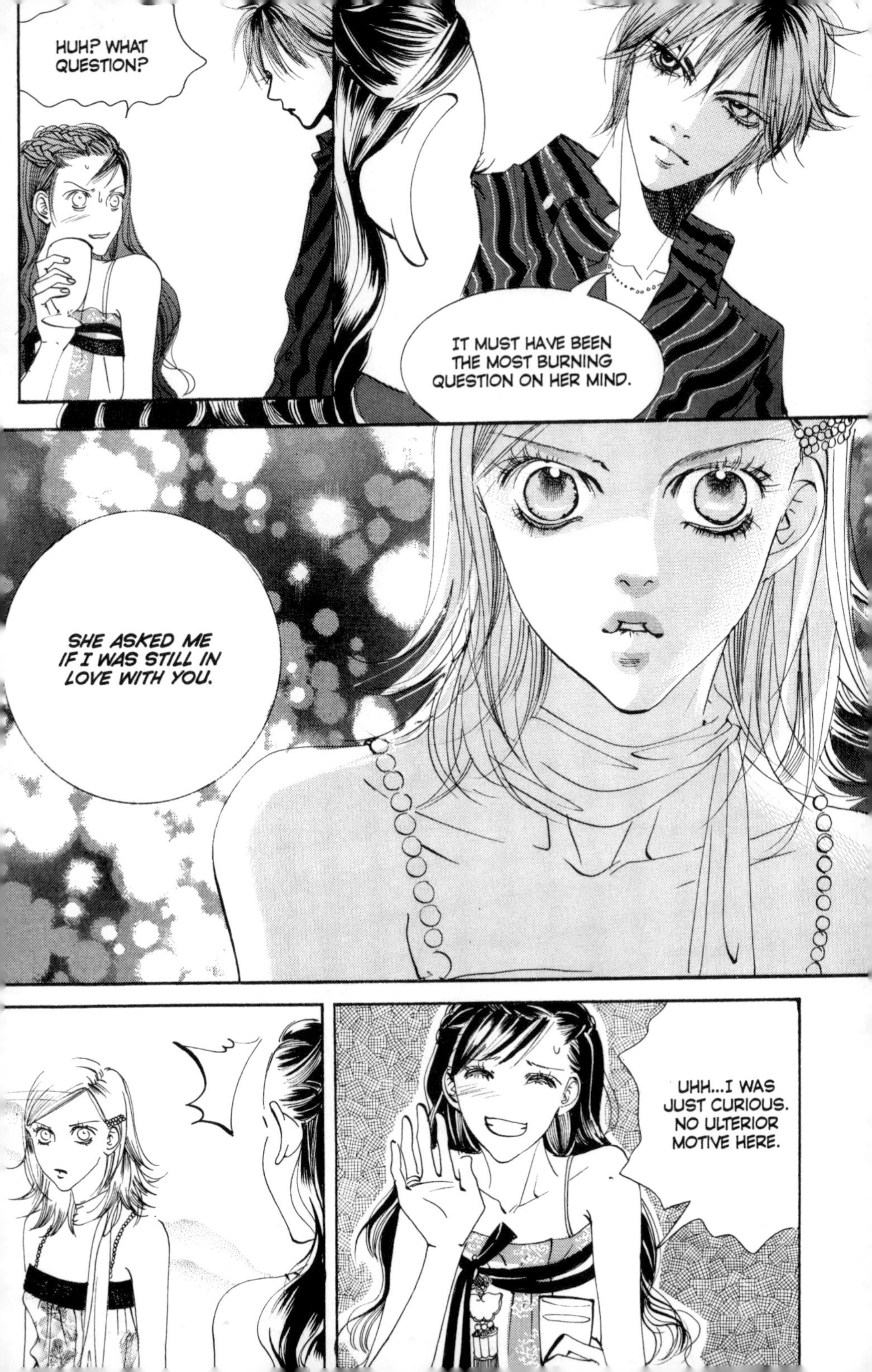
HUH? WHAT QUESTION?
IT MUST HAVE BEEN THE MOST BURNING QUESTION ON HER MIND.
SHE ASKED ME IF I WAS STILL IN LOVE WITH YOU.
UHH...I WAS JUST CURIOUS. NO ULTERIOR MOTIVE HERE.

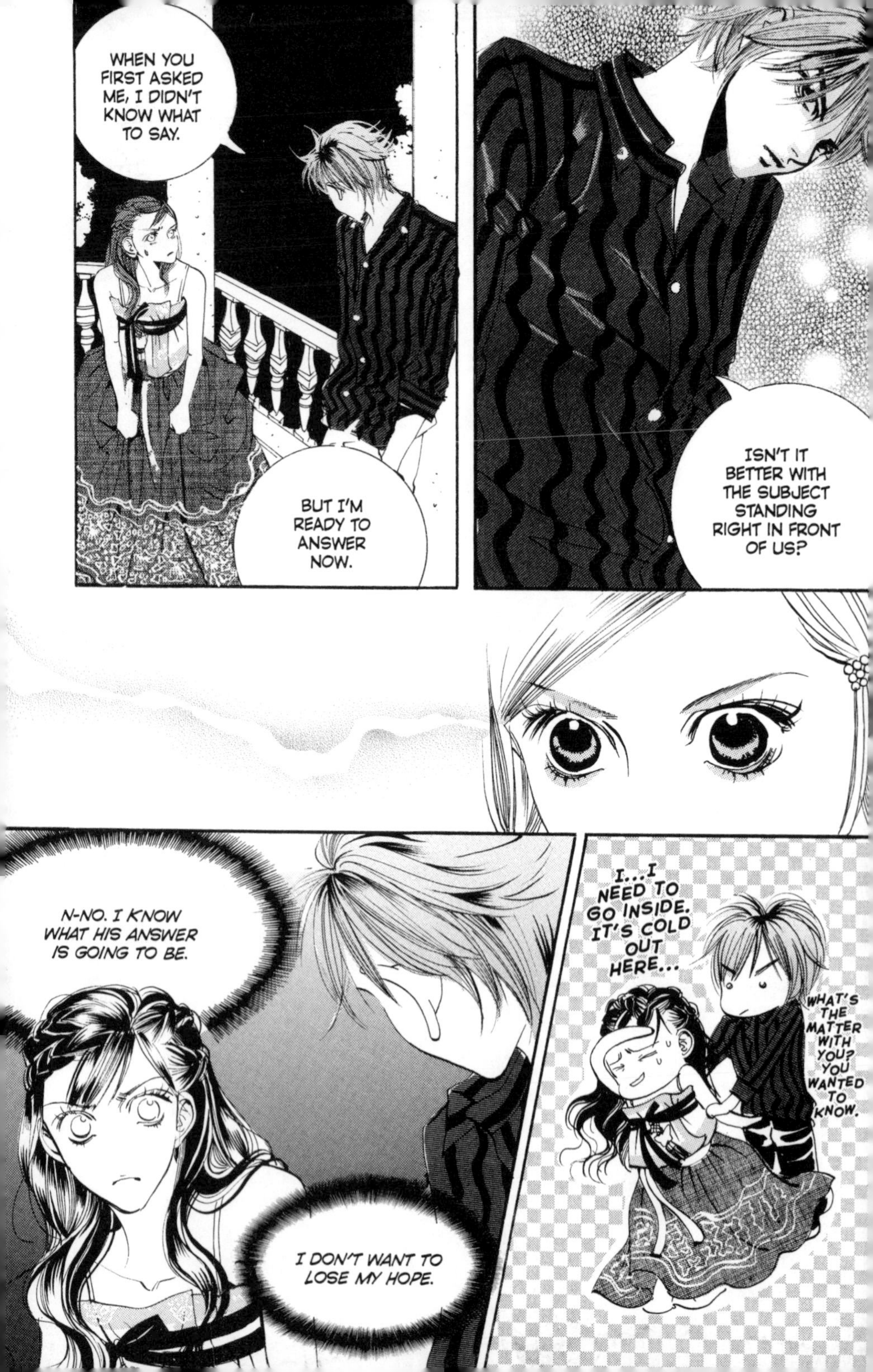
WHEN YOU FIRST ASKED ME, I DIDN'T KNOW WHAT TO SAY.
BUT I'M READY TO ANSWER NOW.
ISN'T IT BETTER WITH THE SUBJECT STANDING RIGHT IN FRONT OF US?
N-NO. I KNOW WHAT HIS ANSWER IS GOING TO BE.
I DON'T WANT TO LOSE MY HOPE.
I...I NEED TO GO INSIDE. IT'S COLD OUT HERE...
WHAT'S THE MATTER WITH YOU? YOU WANTED TO KNOW.

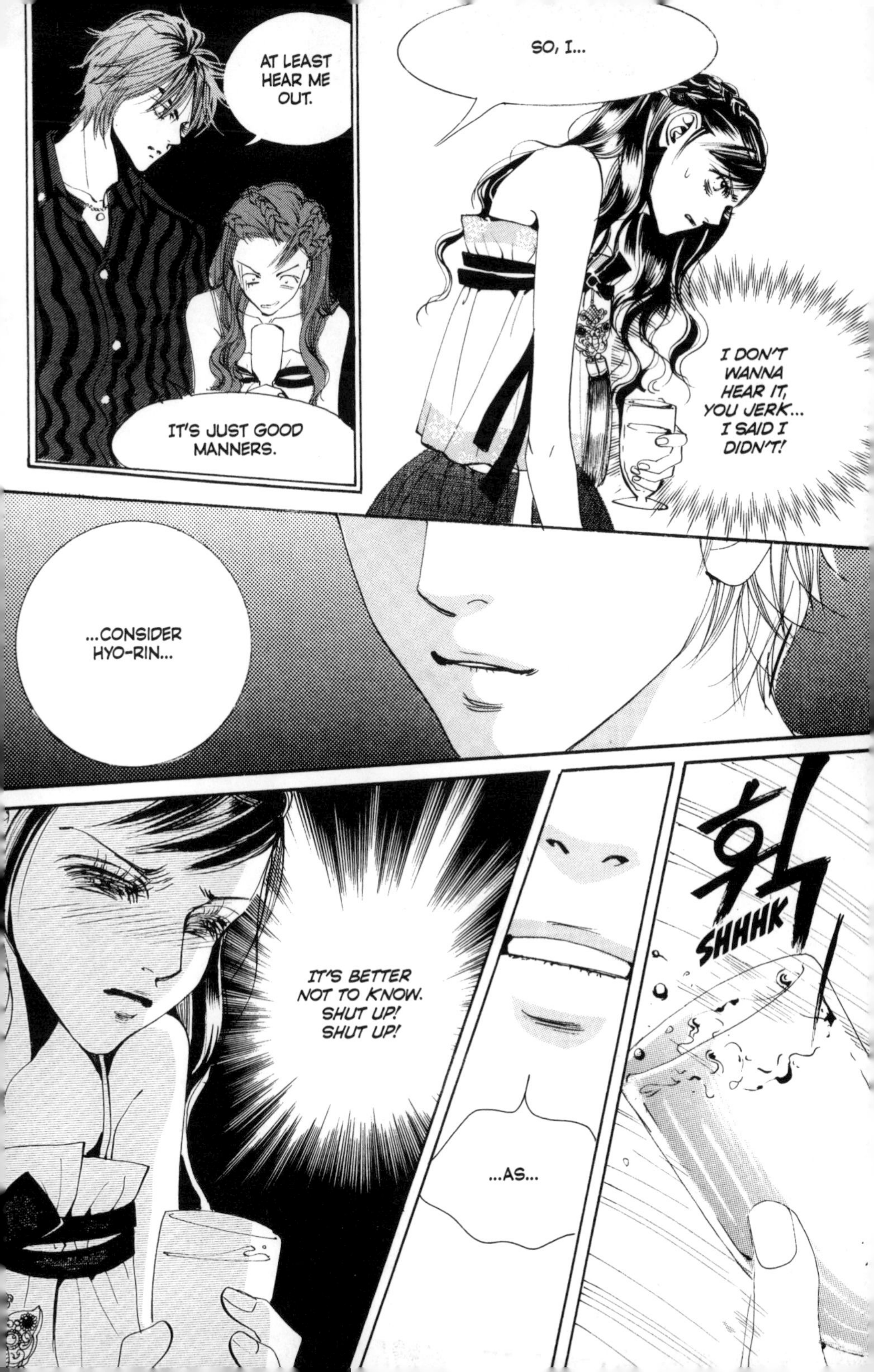
AT LEAST HEAR ME OUT.
IT'S JUST GOOD MANNERS.
SO, I...
I DON'T WANNA HEAR IT, YOU JERK... I SAID I DIDN'T!
...CONSIDER HYO-RIN...
IT'S BETTER NOT TO KNOW. SHUT UP! SHUT UP!
...AS...
SHHHK

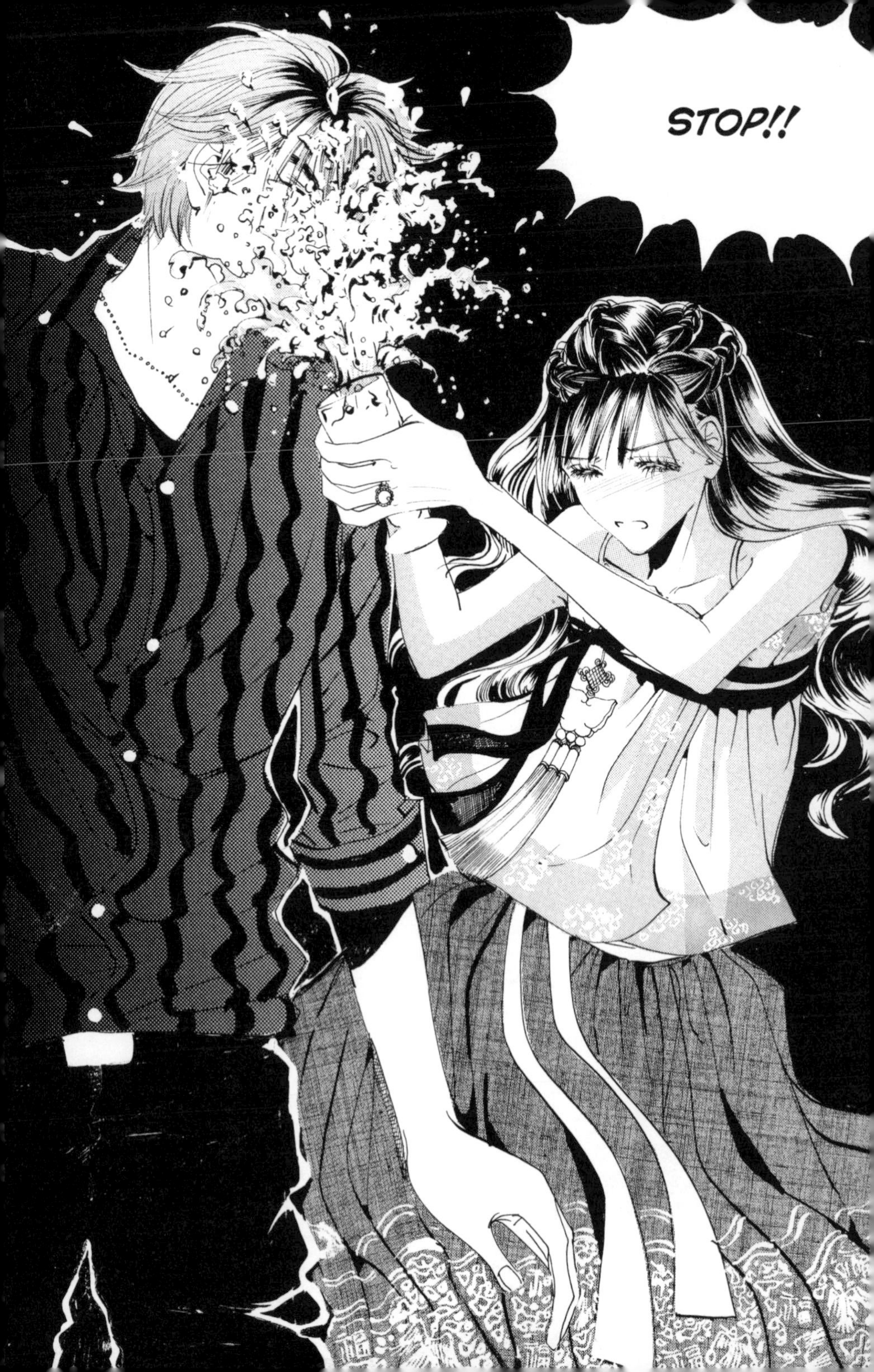
STOP!!

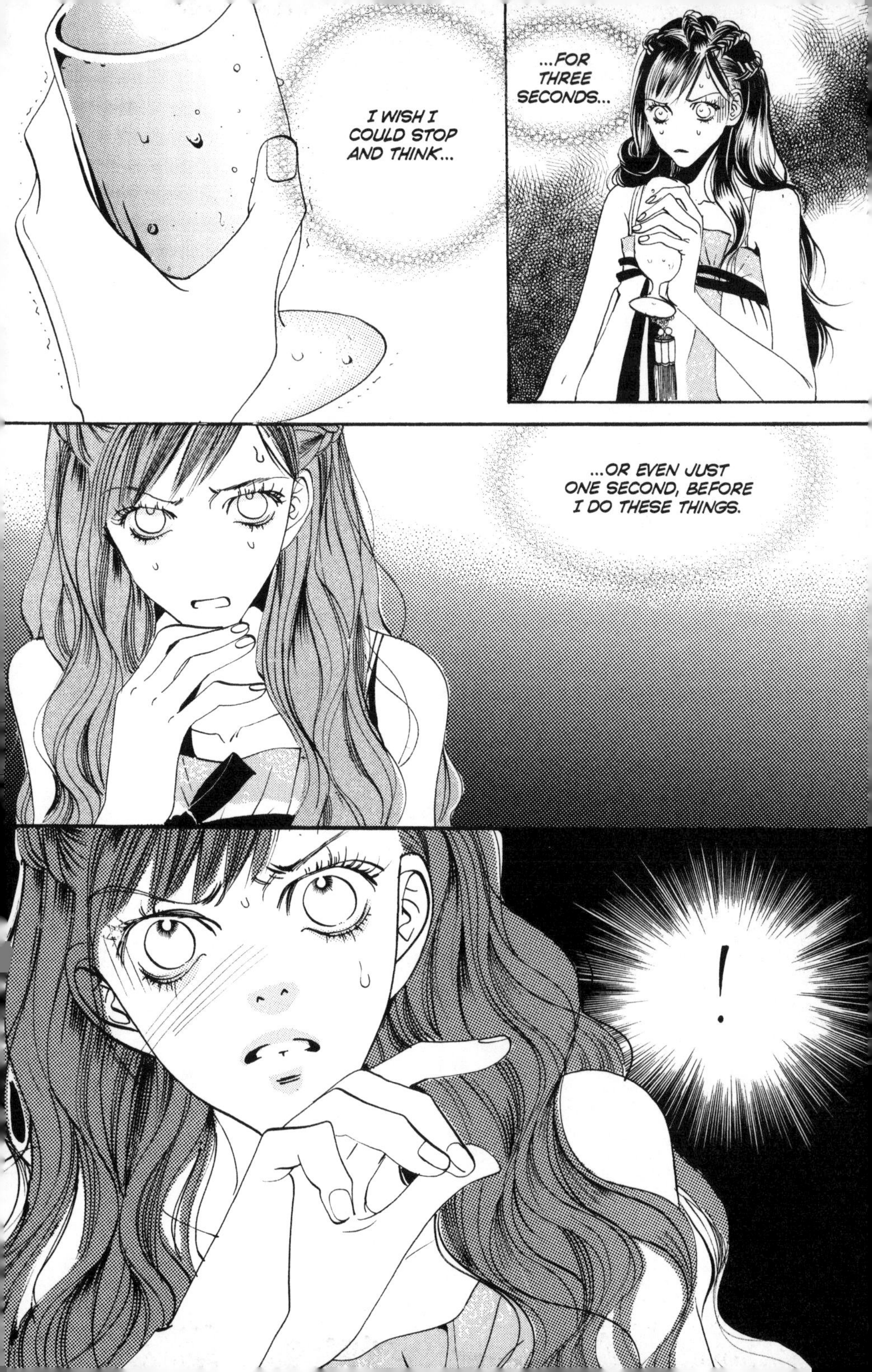
I WISH I COULD STOP AND THINK...
...FOR THREE SECONDS...
...OR EVEN JUST ONE SECOND, BEFORE I DO THESE THINGS.
!

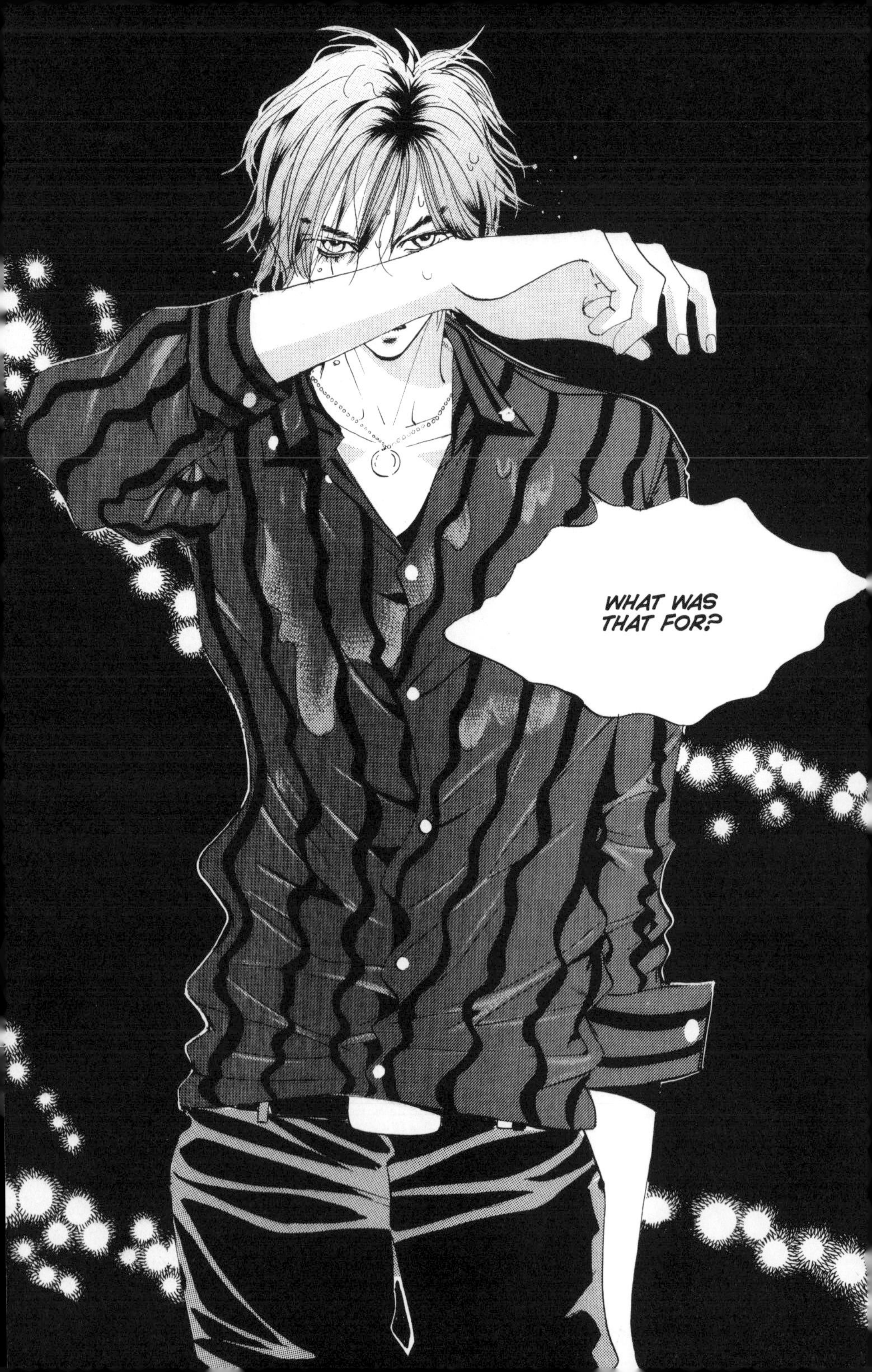
WHAT WAS THAT FOR?

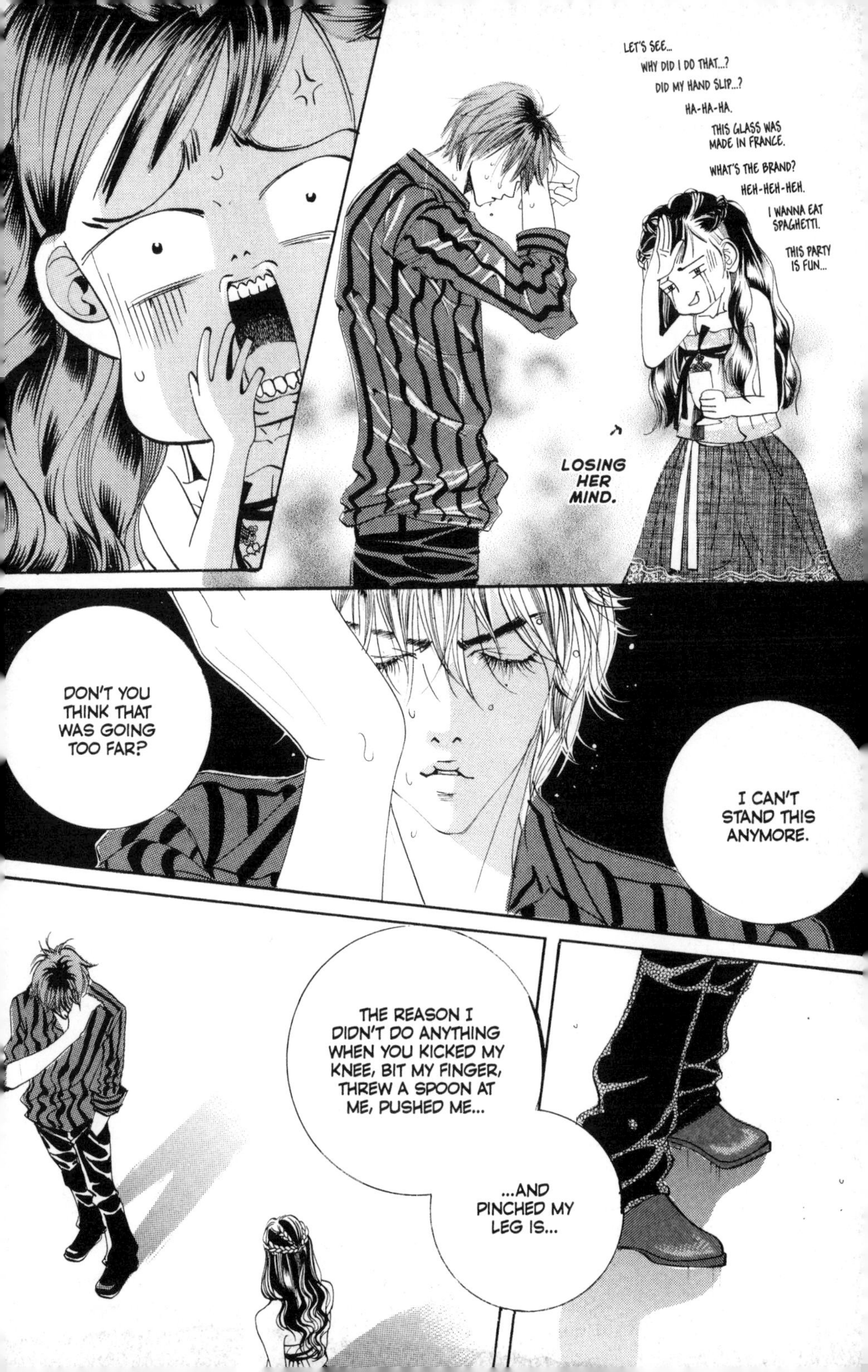
LET'S SEE...
WHY DID I DO THAT...?
DID MY HAND SLIP...?
HA-HA-HA.
THIS GLASS WAS MADE IN FRANCE.
WHAT'S THE BRAND?
HEH-HEH-HEH.
I WANNA EAT SPAGHETTI.
THIS PARTY IS FUN...
LOSING HER MIND.
DON'T YOU THINK THAT WAS GOING TOO FAR?
I CAN'T STAND THIS ANYMORE.
THE REASON I DIDN'T DO ANYTHING WHEN YOU KICKED MY KNEE, BIT MY FINGER, THREW A SPOON AT ME, PUSHED ME...
...AND PINCHED MY LEG IS...

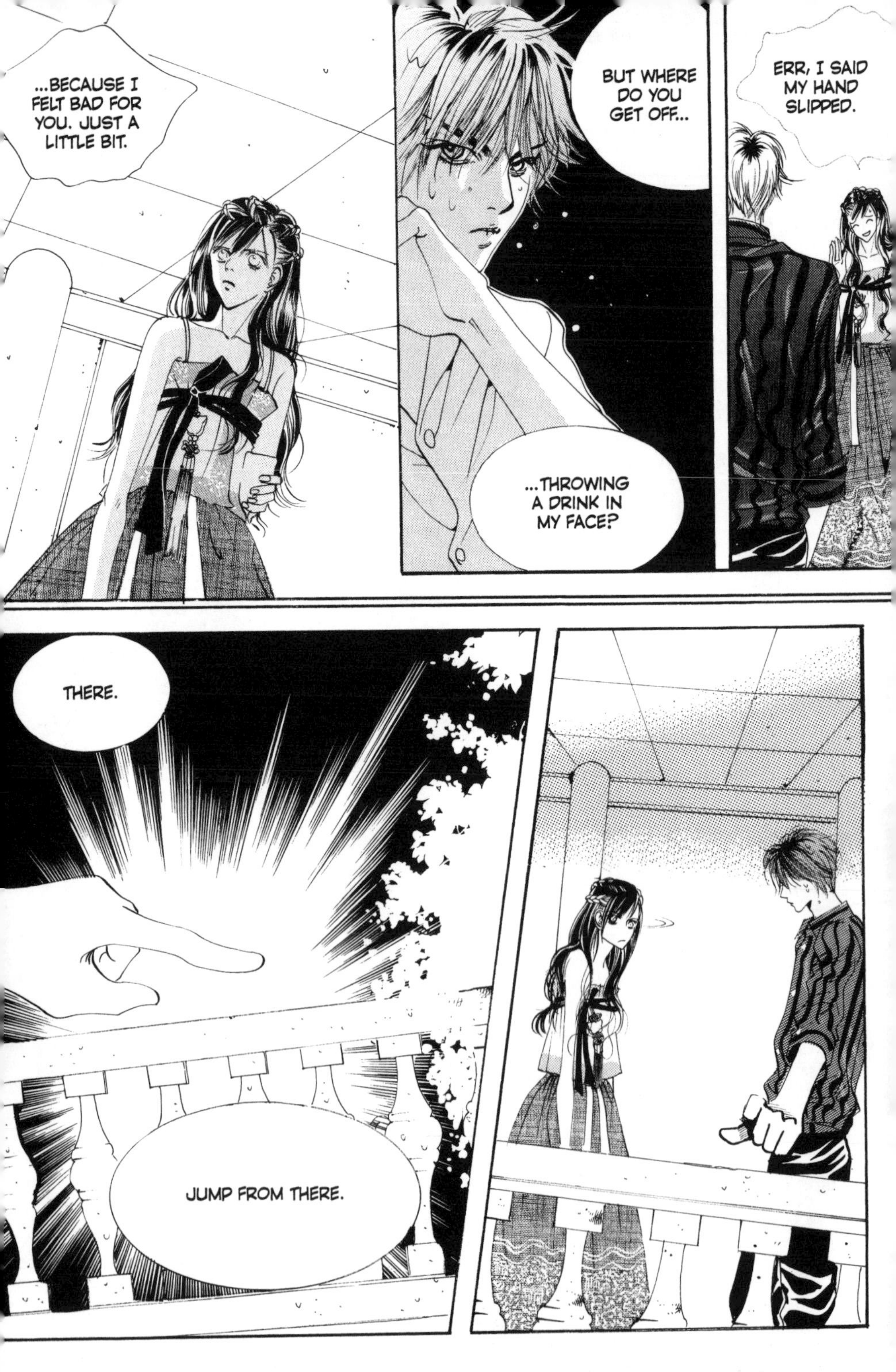
...BECAUSE I FELT BAD FOR YOU. JUST A LITTLE BIT.
BUT WHERE DO YOU GET OFF...
...THROWING A DRINK IN MY FACE?
ERR, I SAID MY HAND SLIPPED.
THERE.
JUMP FROM THERE.

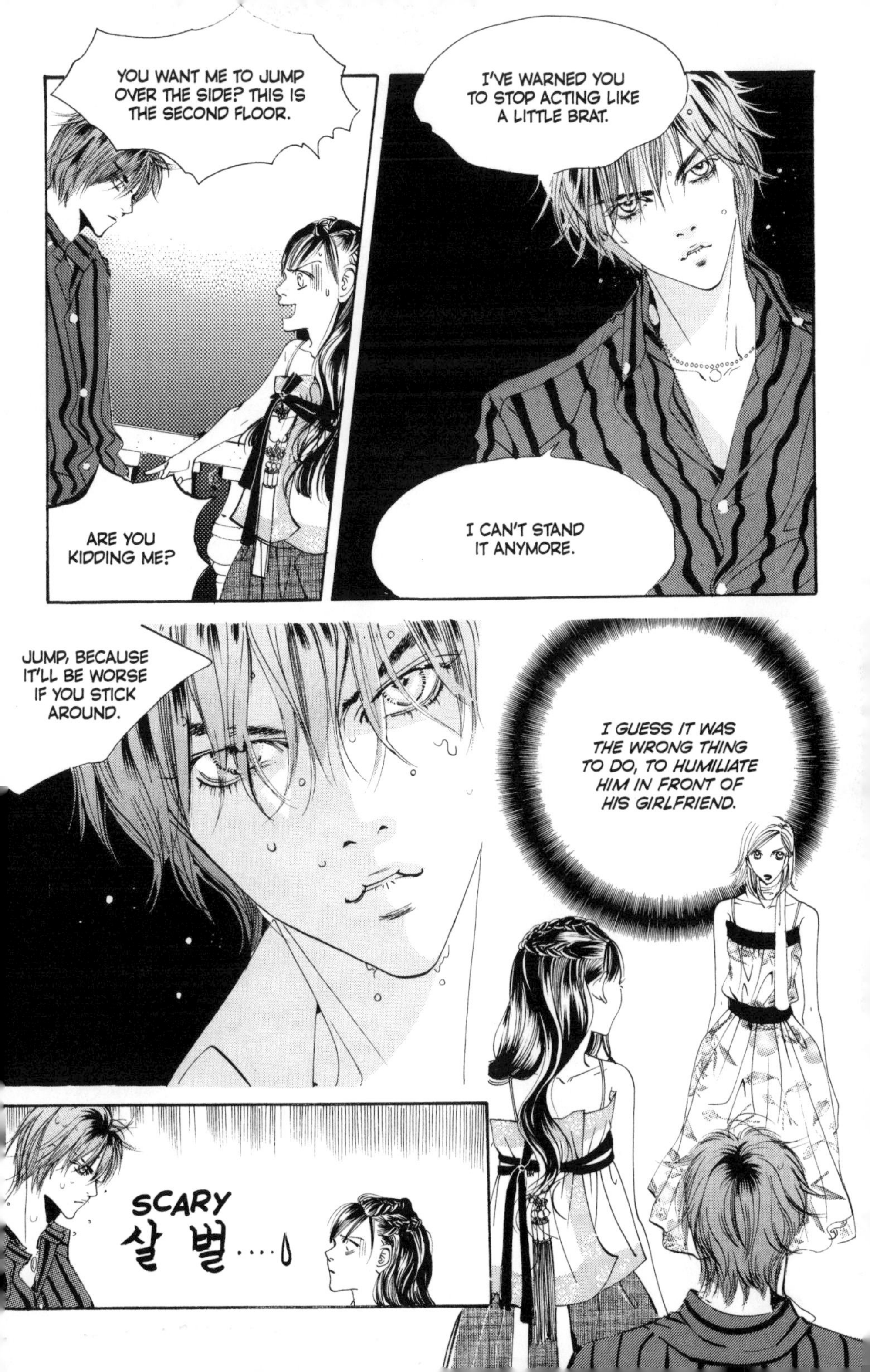
YOU WANT ME TO JUMP OVER THE SIDE? THIS IS THE SECOND FLOOR.
ARE YOU KIDDING ME?
I'VE WARNED YOU TO STOP ACTING LIKE A LITTLE BRAT.
I CAN'T STAND IT ANYMORE.
JUMP, BECAUSE IT'LL BE WORSE IF YOU STICK AROUND.
SCARY
살벌....
I GUESS IT WAS THE WRONG THING TO DO, TO HUMILIATE HIM IN FRONT OF HIS GIRLFRIEND.

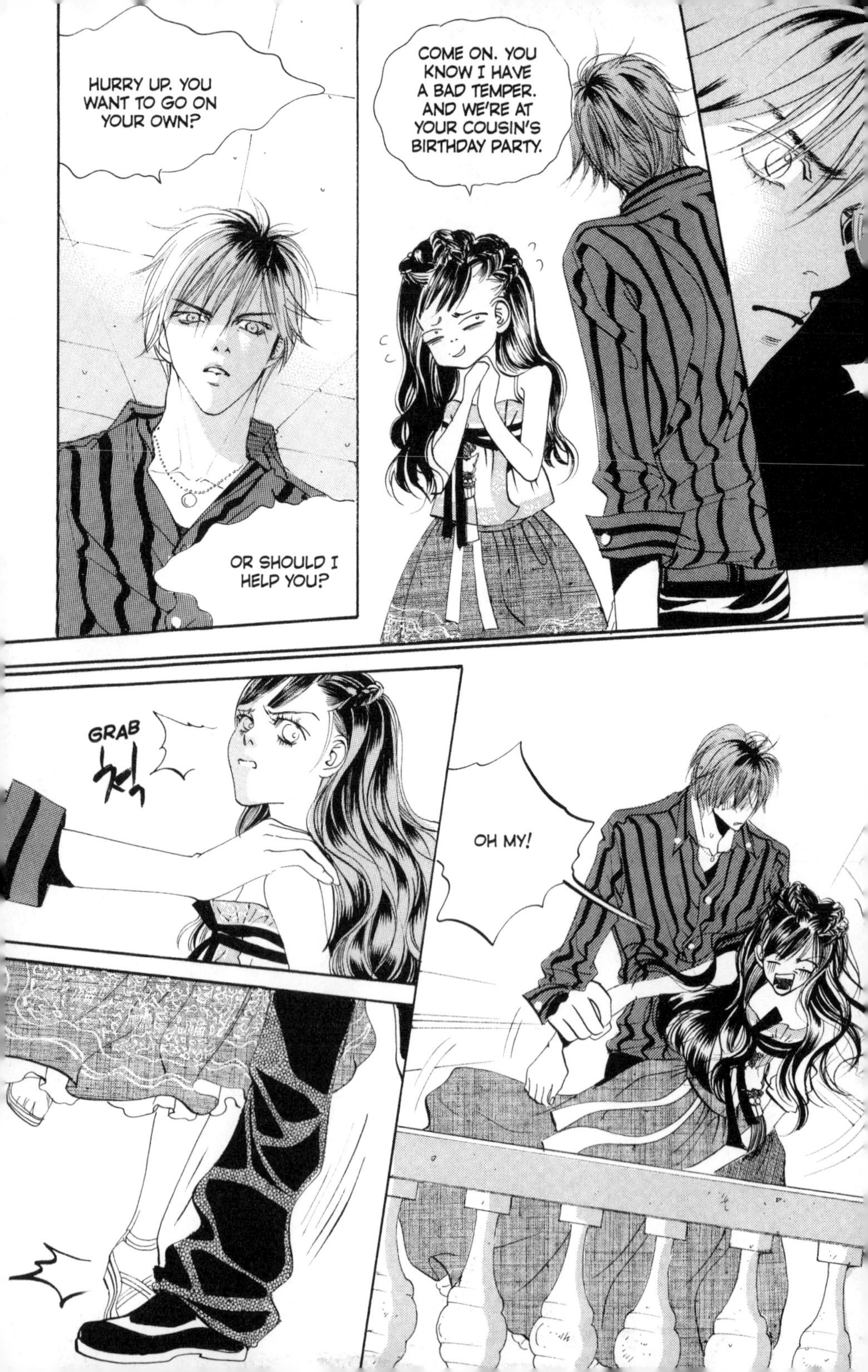
HURRY UP. YOU WANT TO GO ON YOUR OWN?
OR SHOULD I HELP YOU?
COME ON. YOU KNOW I HAVE A BAD TEMPER. AND WE'RE AT YOUR COUSIN'S BIRTHDAY PARTY.
GRAB
척
OH MY!

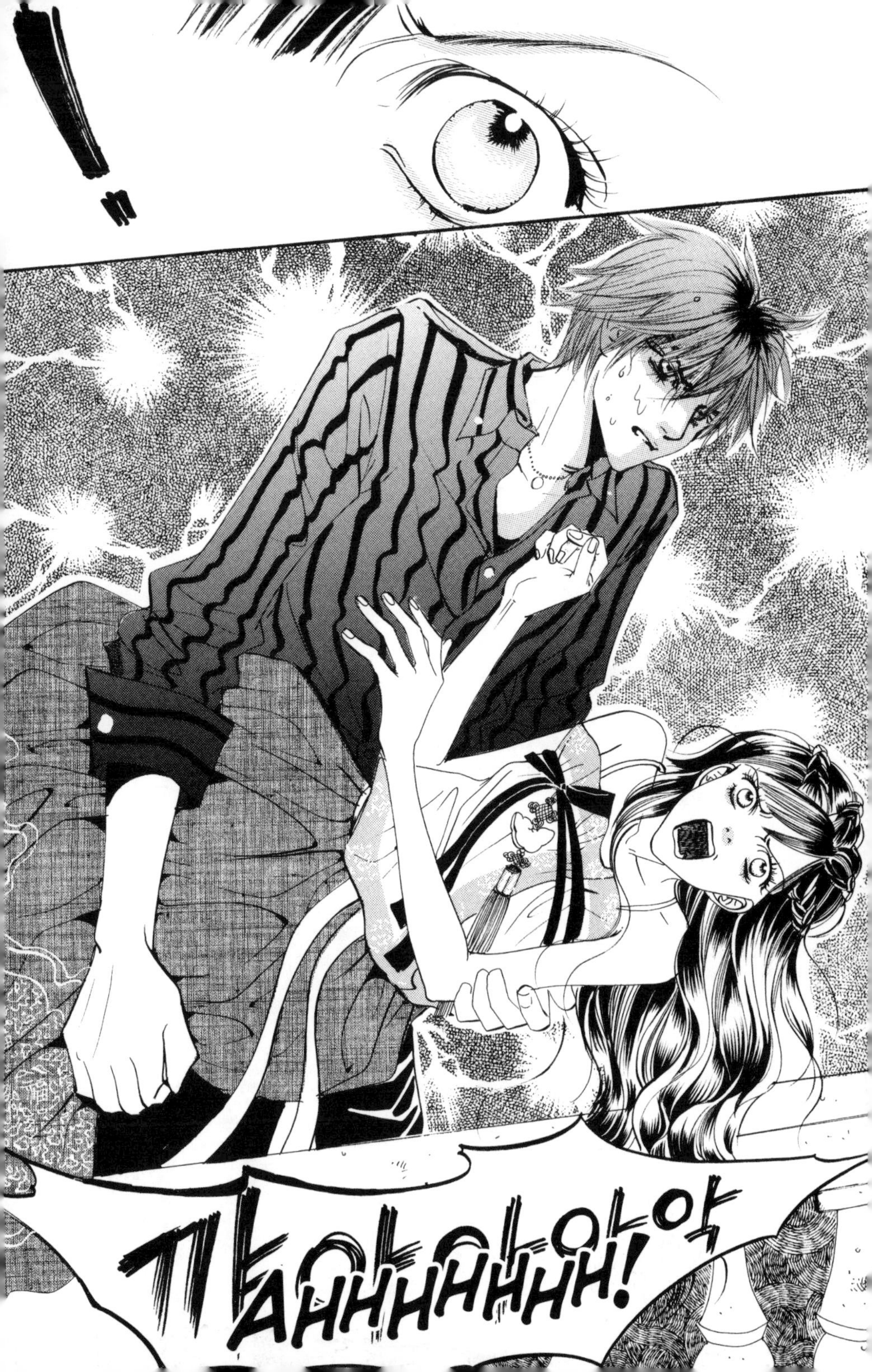
!!
꺄아아아악
AHHHHHHHH!

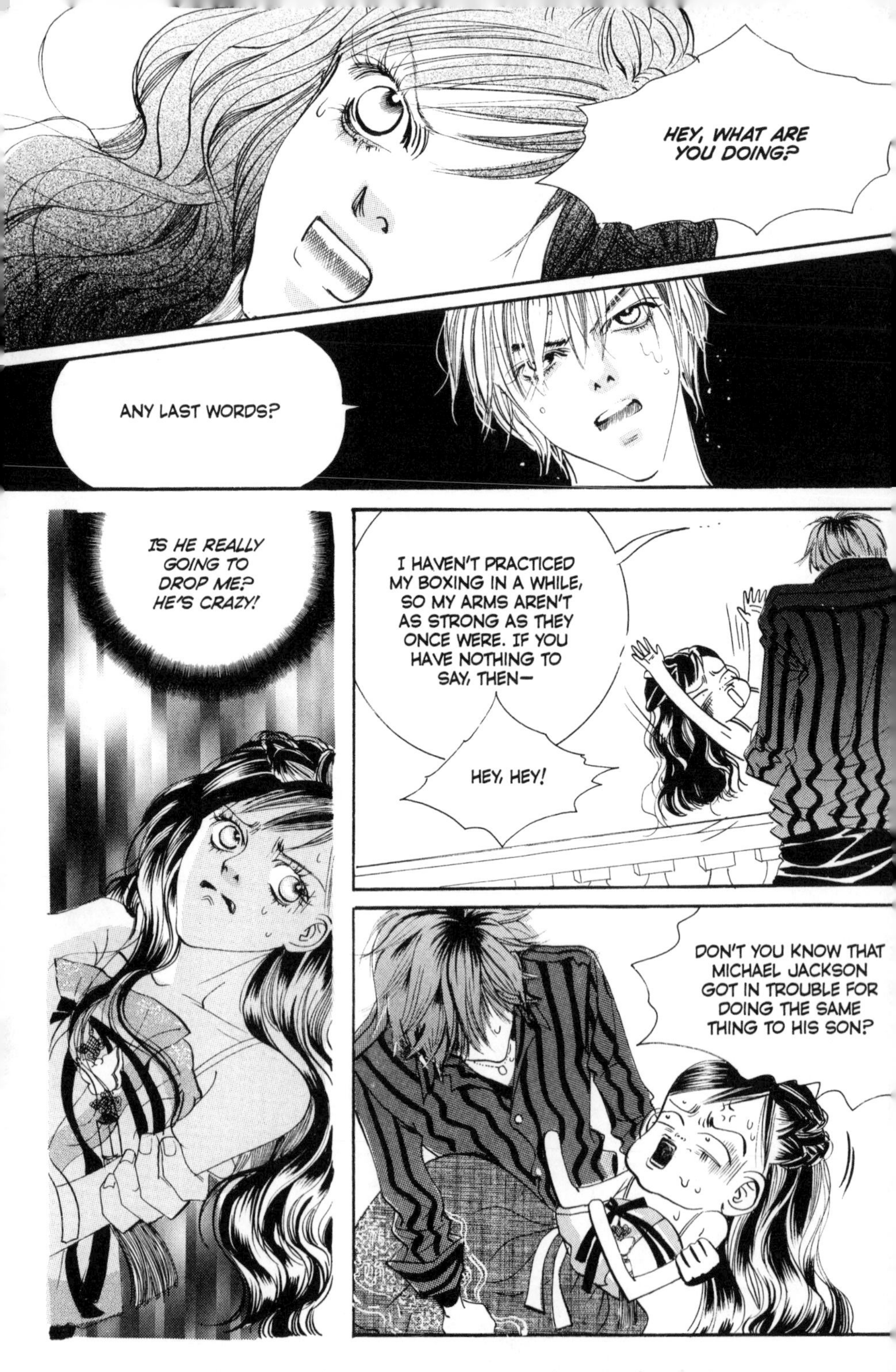
HEY, WHAT ARE YOU DOING?
ANY LAST WORDS?
IS HE REALLY GOING TO DROP ME? HE'S CRAZY!
I HAVEN'T PRACTICED MY BOXING IN A WHILE, SO MY ARMS AREN'T AS STRONG AS THEY ONCE WERE. IF YOU HAVE NOTHING TO SAY, THEN—
HEY, HEY!
DON'T YOU KNOW THAT MICHAEL JACKSON GOT IN TROUBLE FOR DOING THE SAME THING TO HIS SON?

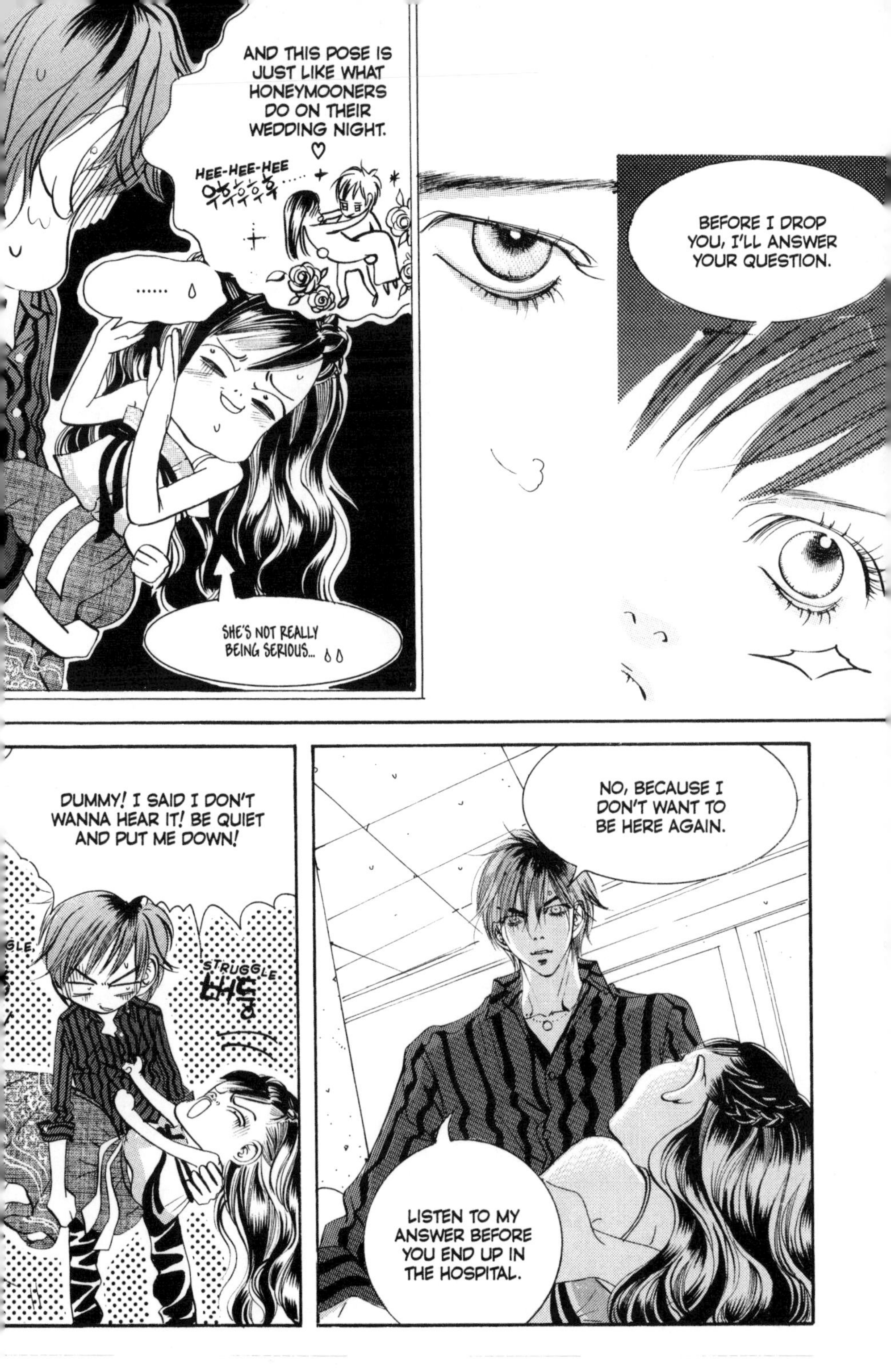

AND THIS POSE IS JUST LIKE WHAT HONEYMOONERS DO ON THEIR WEDDING NIGHT. ♡
HEE-HEE-HEE
......
SHE'S NOT REALLY BEING SERIOUS...
BEFORE I DROP YOU, I'LL ANSWER YOUR QUESTION.
DUMMY! I SAID I DON'T WANNA HEAR IT! BE QUIET AND PUT ME DOWN!
STRUGGLE
NO, BECAUSE I DON'T WANT TO BE HERE AGAIN.
LISTEN TO MY ANSWER BEFORE YOU END UP IN THE HOSPITAL.

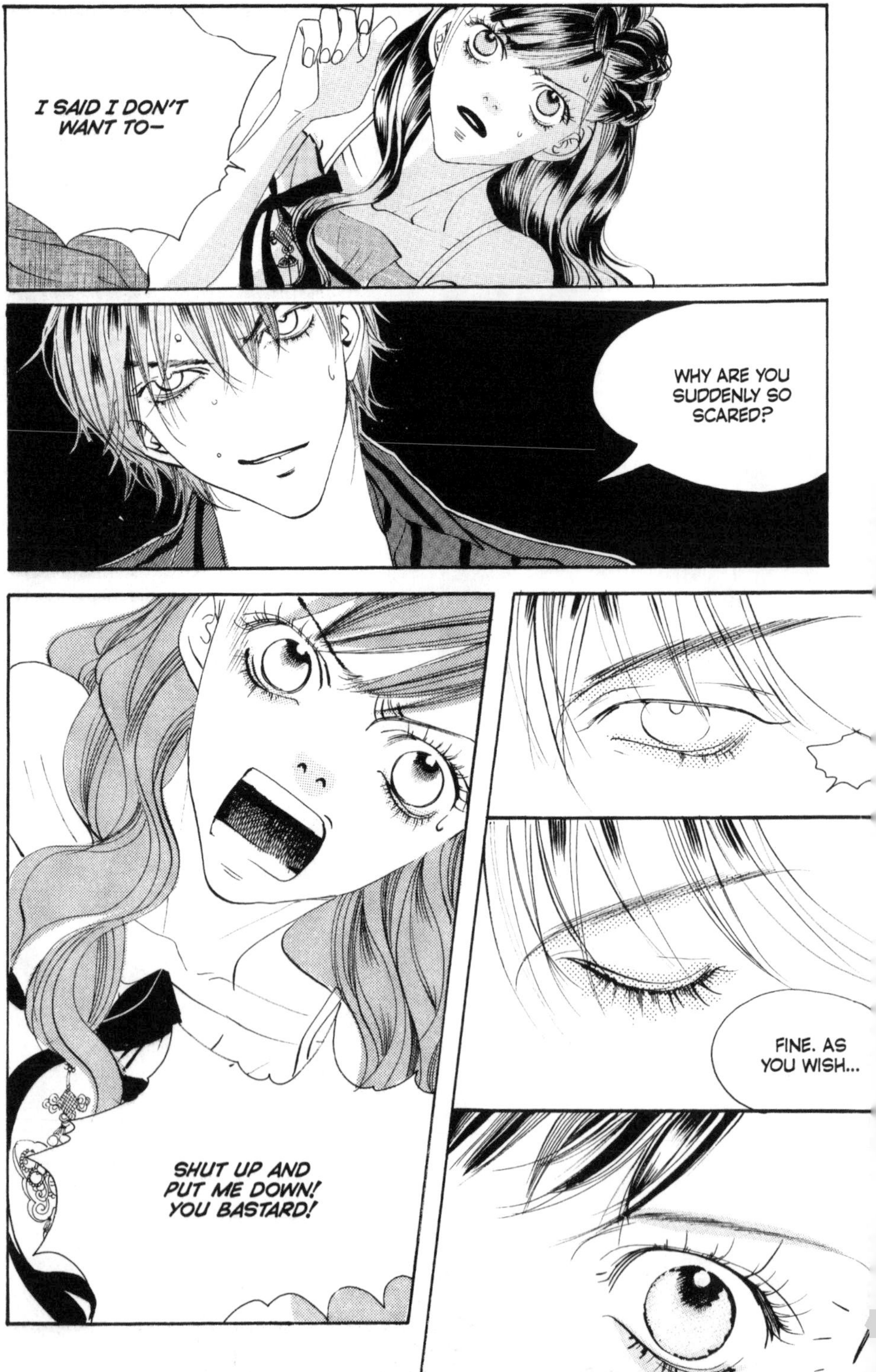
I SAID I DON'T WANT TO—
WHY ARE YOU SUDDENLY SO SCARED?
SHUT UP AND PUT ME DOWN! YOU BASTARD!
FINE. AS YOU WISH...

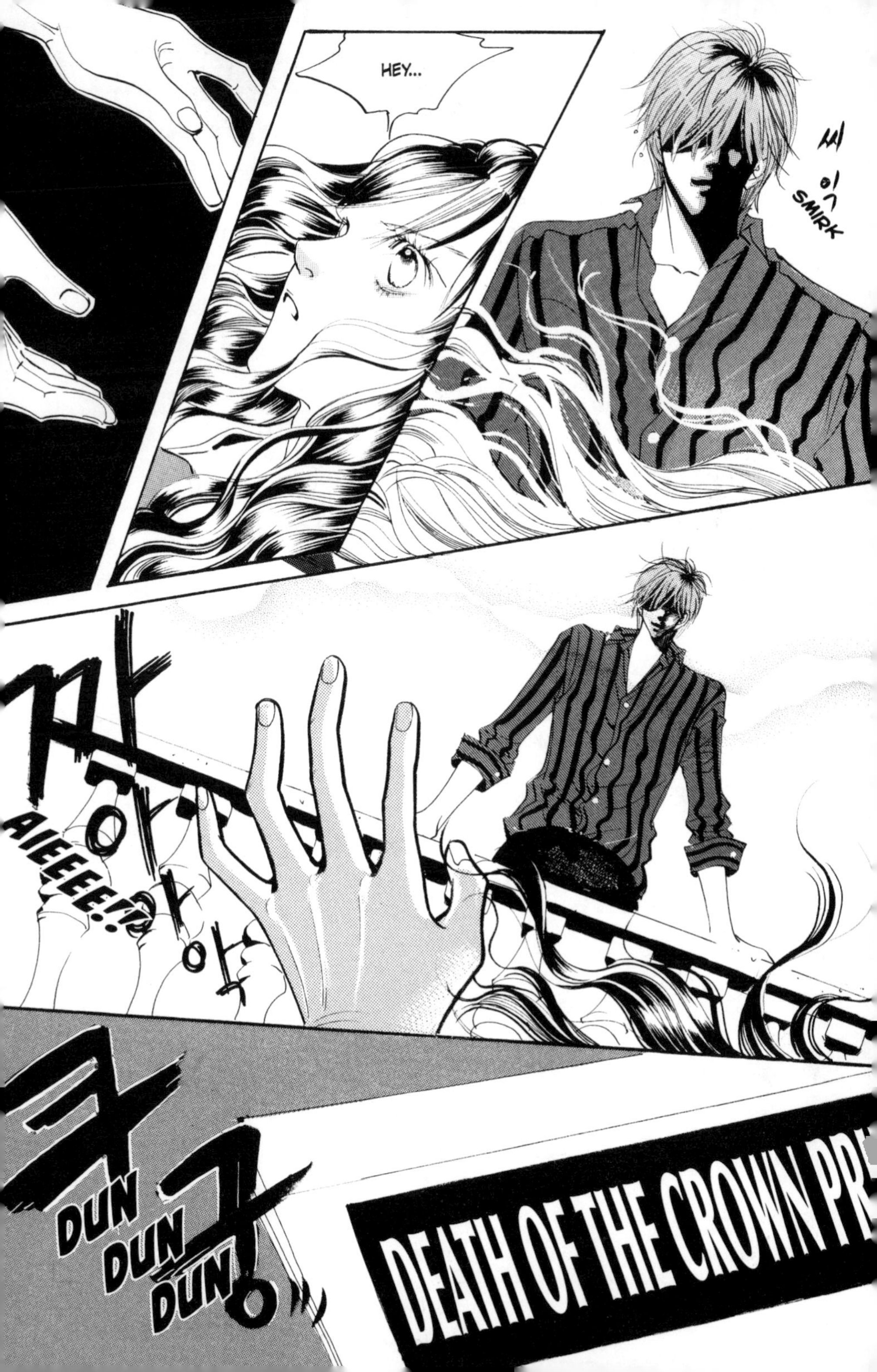
HEY...
씨익
SMIRK
AIEEEEE!?
DUN DUN DUN
DEATH OF THE CROWN PR

TH OF THE CROWN PRINCES

THE CROWN PRINCE KILLED THE CROWN PRINCESS BECAUSE SHE CALLED HIM A "BASTARD."

THE CROWN PRINCE WHO COULDN'T CONTROL HIS TEMPER BROKE DOWN IN TEARS.

Police will investigate whether the crown princess really abused the Crown Prince, as he's insisting.

The prosecution hasn't decided whether the regular law will be applied in this case. If that happens, the royal family will protest the action.

SHOCKING CONFESSION

"WE WERE IN THE WRONG RELATIONSHIP."—Interview with Eunuch Kong

Miss Yun

"I didn't believe the rumor that they were together."

Miss Oh

"The truth is, I'm the one who is in a relationship with Eunuch Kong."

Eunuch Kong who has been in hiding since the shocking confession.

According to the survey by *Wink* newspaper, 95% of the people think the crown princess deserved to die.

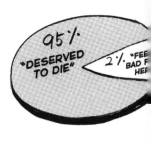

95%
"DESERVED TO DIE"
2%

Margin of error: correct possibility, 2 %; fault possibility, ± 97%

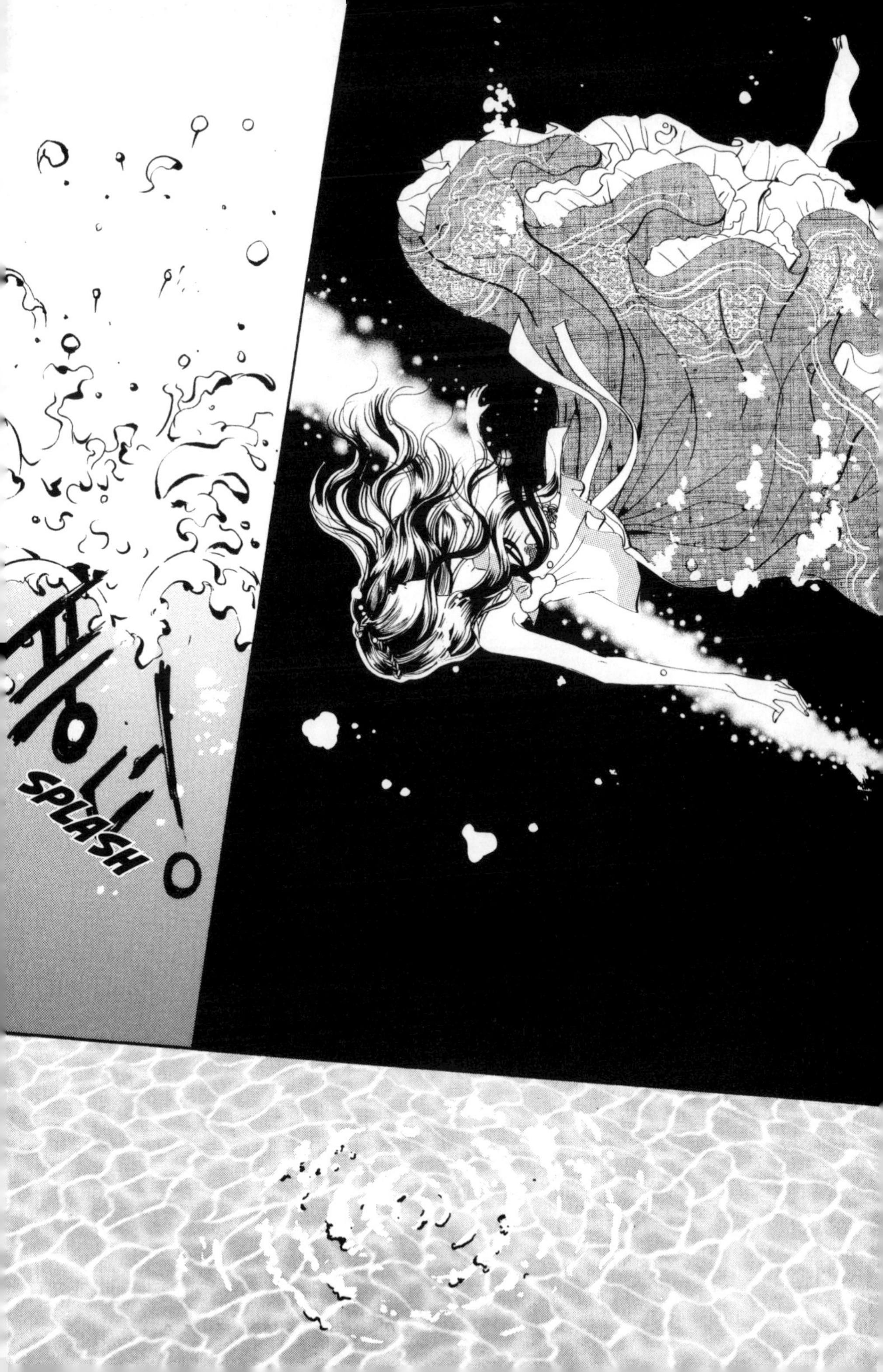
SPLASH

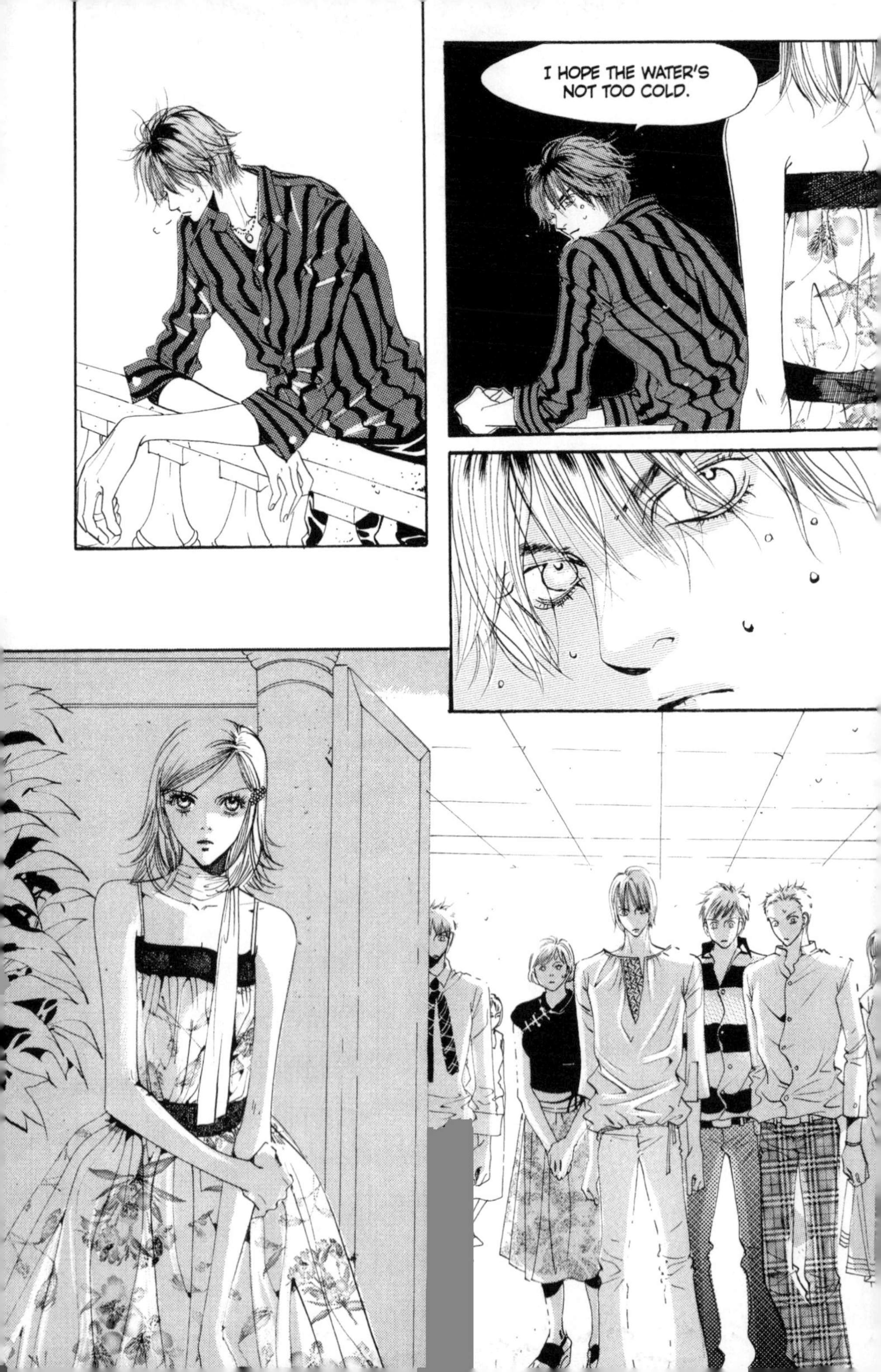
I HOPE THE WATER'S NOT TOO COLD.

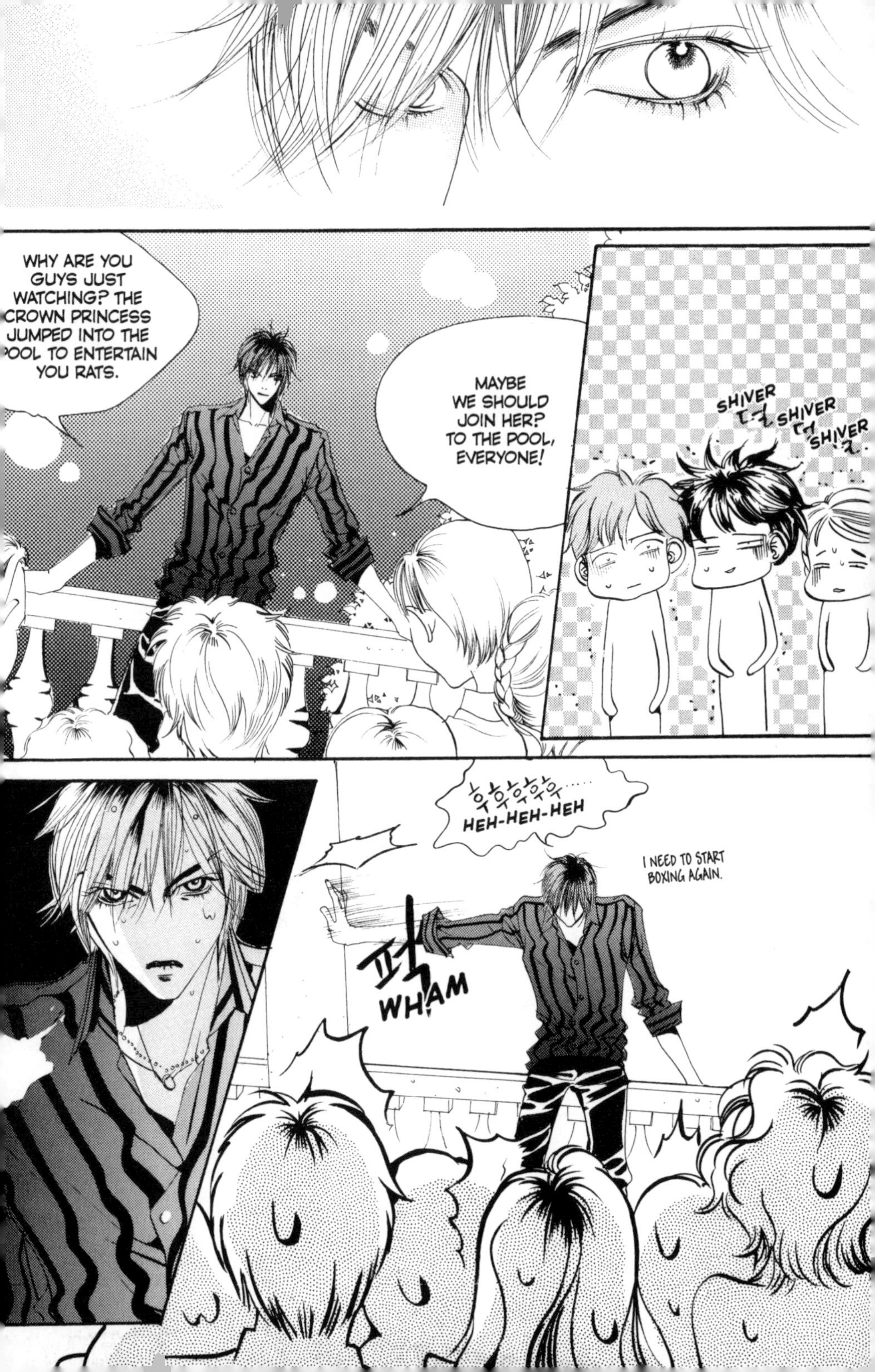
WHY ARE YOU GUYS JUST WATCHING? THE CROWN PRINCESS JUMPED INTO THE POOL TO ENTERTAIN YOU RATS.
MAYBE WE SHOULD JOIN HER? TO THE POOL, EVERYONE!
SHIVER 덜 SHIVER 덜 SHIVER 덜
후후후후후..... HEH-HEH-HEH
I NEED TO START BOXING AGAIN.
퍽 WHAM

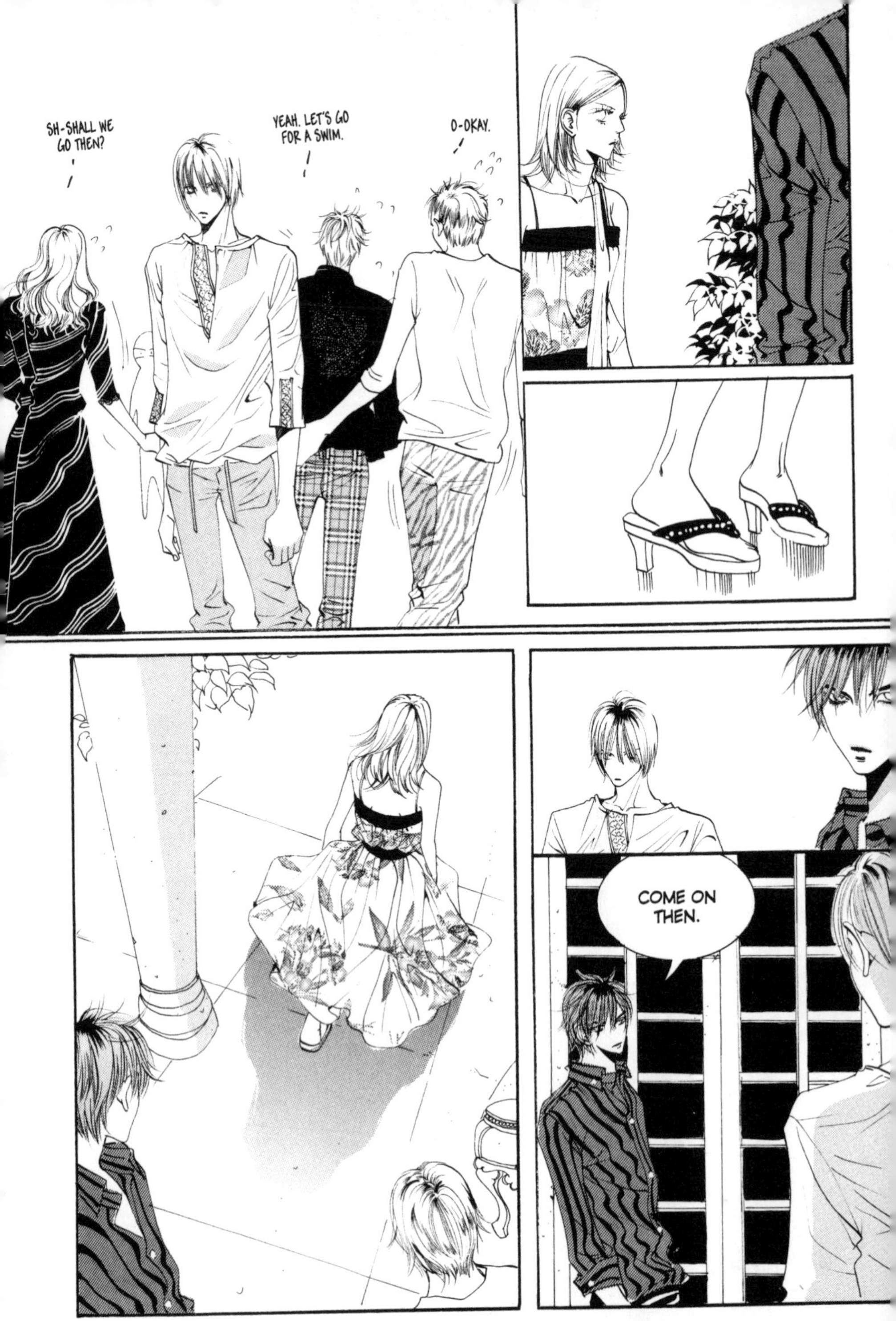
SH-SHALL WE GO THEN?
YEAH. LET'S GO FOR A SWIM.
O-OKAY.
COME ON THEN.

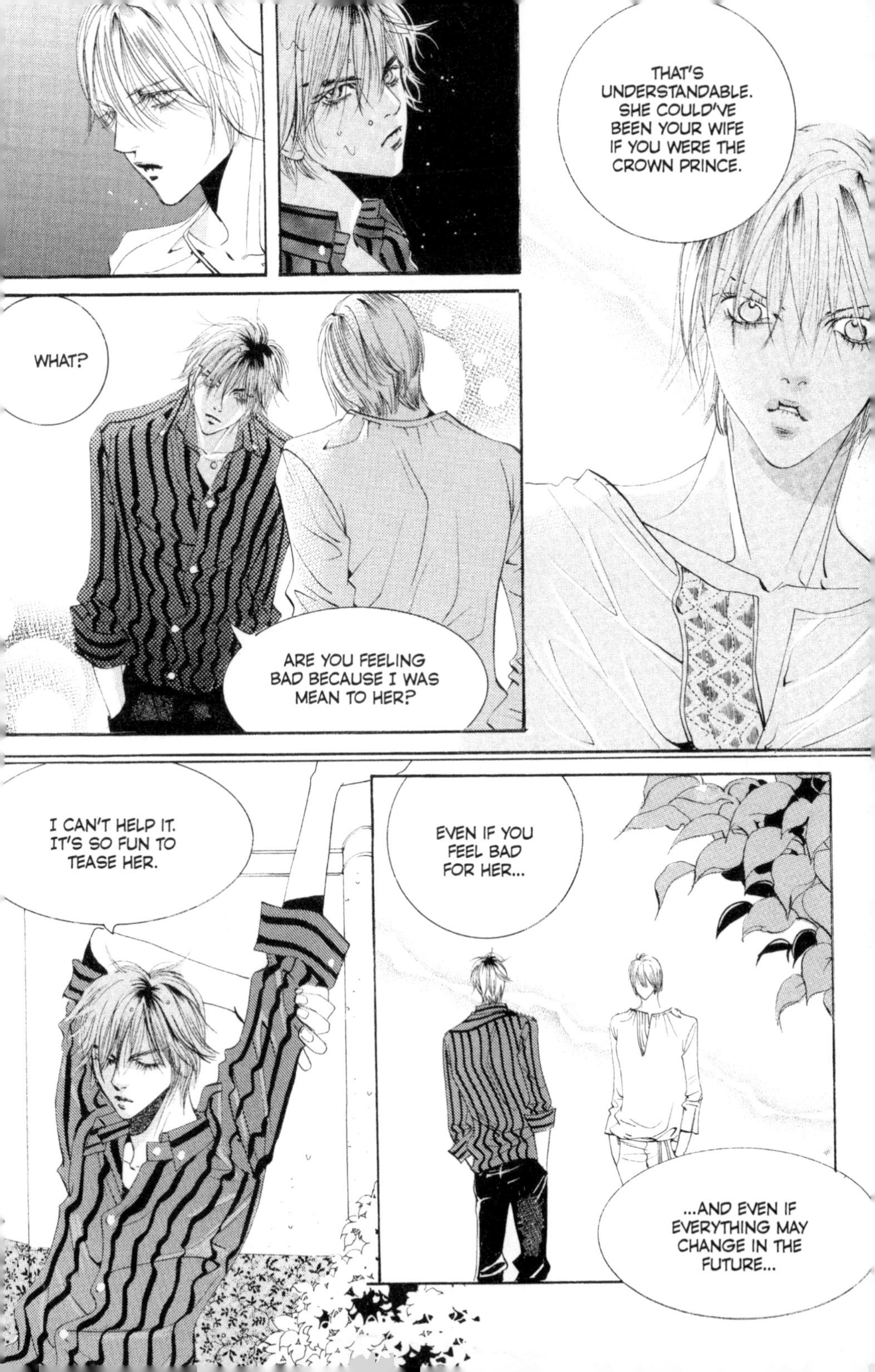
WHAT?
ARE YOU FEELING BAD BECAUSE I WAS MEAN TO HER?
THAT'S UNDERSTANDABLE. SHE COULD'VE BEEN YOUR WIFE IF YOU WERE THE CROWN PRINCE.
I CAN'T HELP IT. IT'S SO FUN TO TEASE HER.
EVEN IF YOU FEEL BAD FOR HER...
...AND EVEN IF EVERYTHING MAY CHANGE IN THE FUTURE...

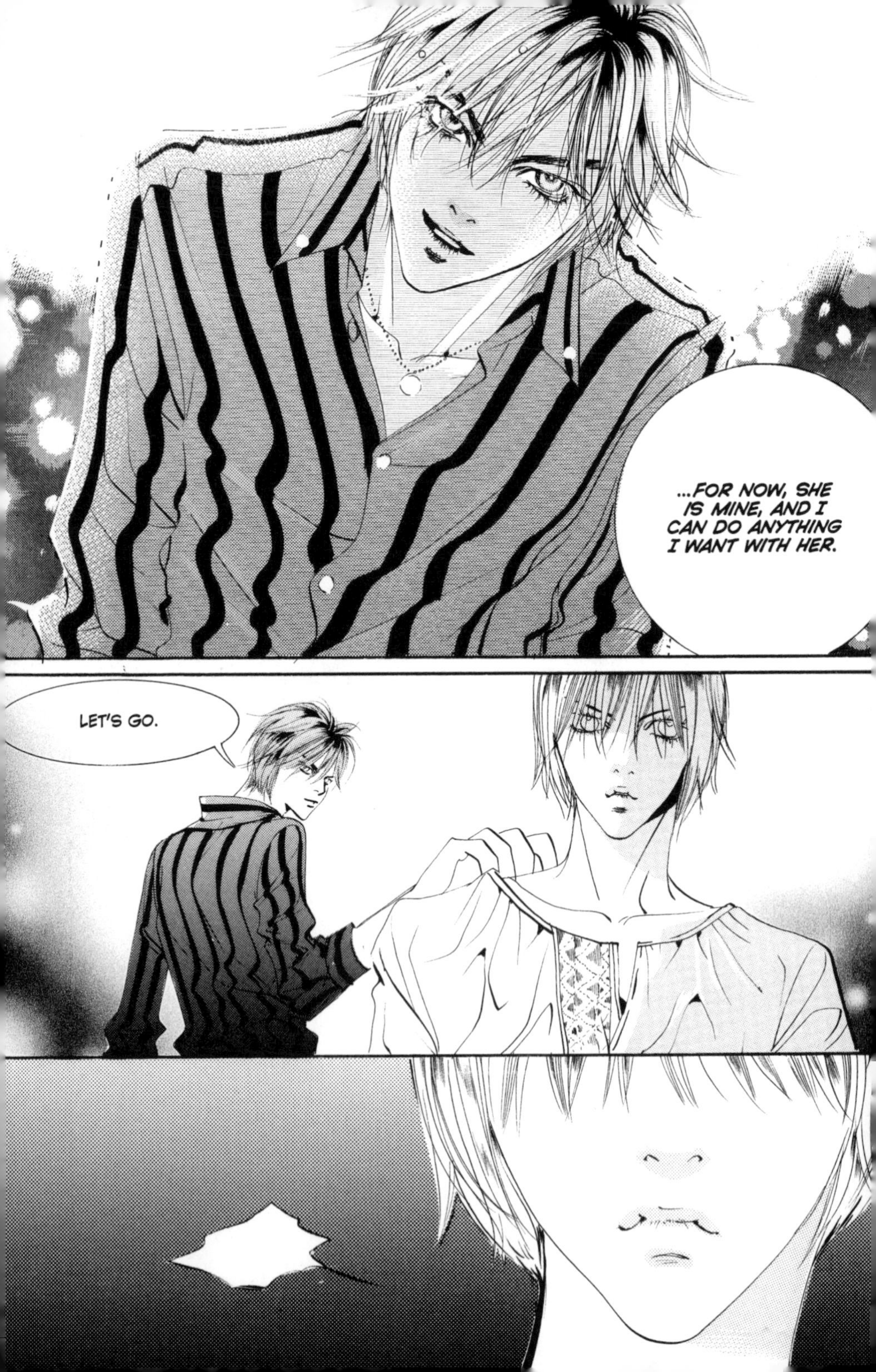
...FOR NOW, SHE IS MINE, AND I CAN DO ANYTHING I WANT WITH HER.
LET'S GO.

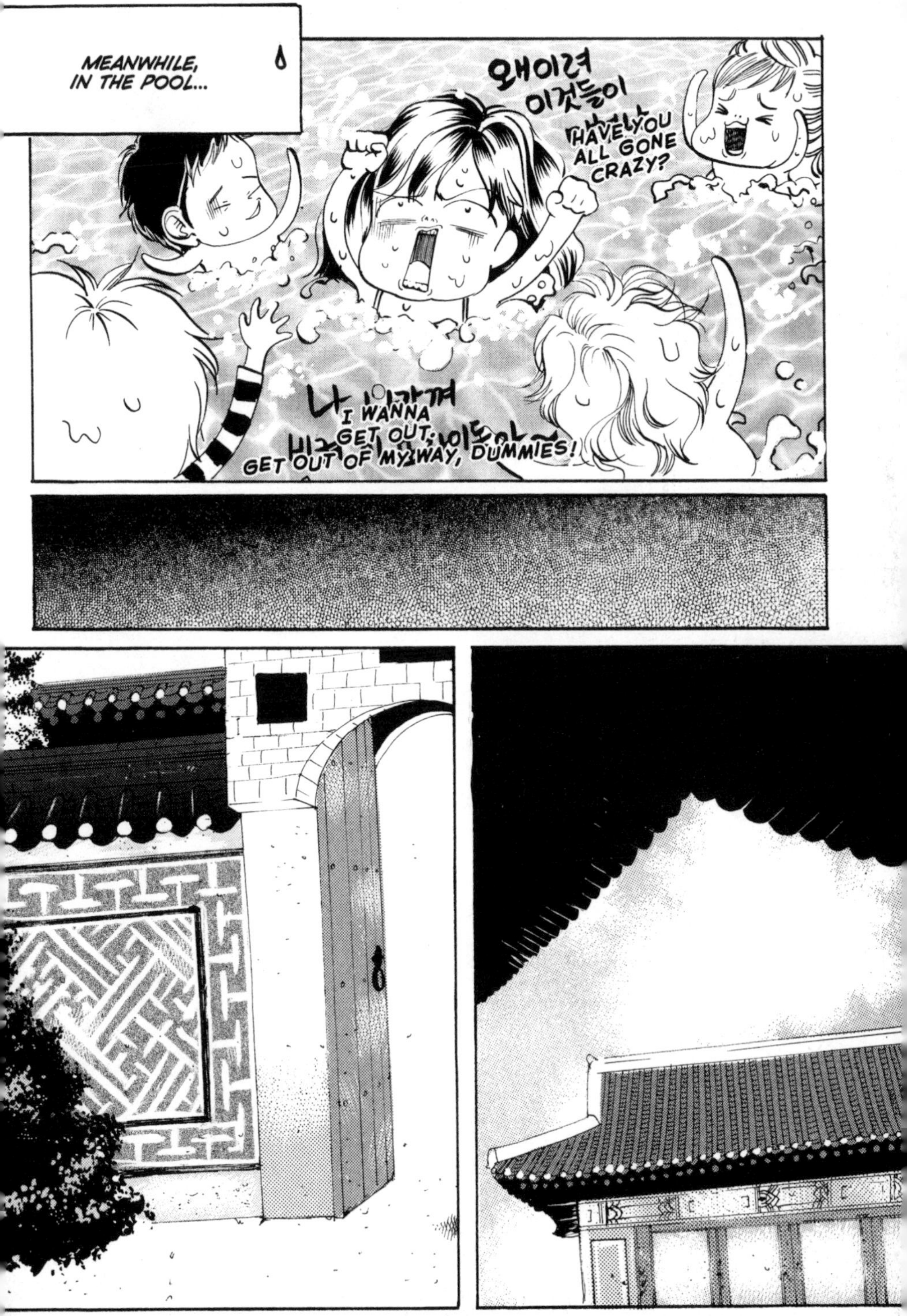
MEANWHILE, IN THE POOL...
왜이려 이것들이
HAVE YOU ALL GONE CRAZY?
I WANNA GET OUT, GET OUT OF MY WAY, DUMMIES!

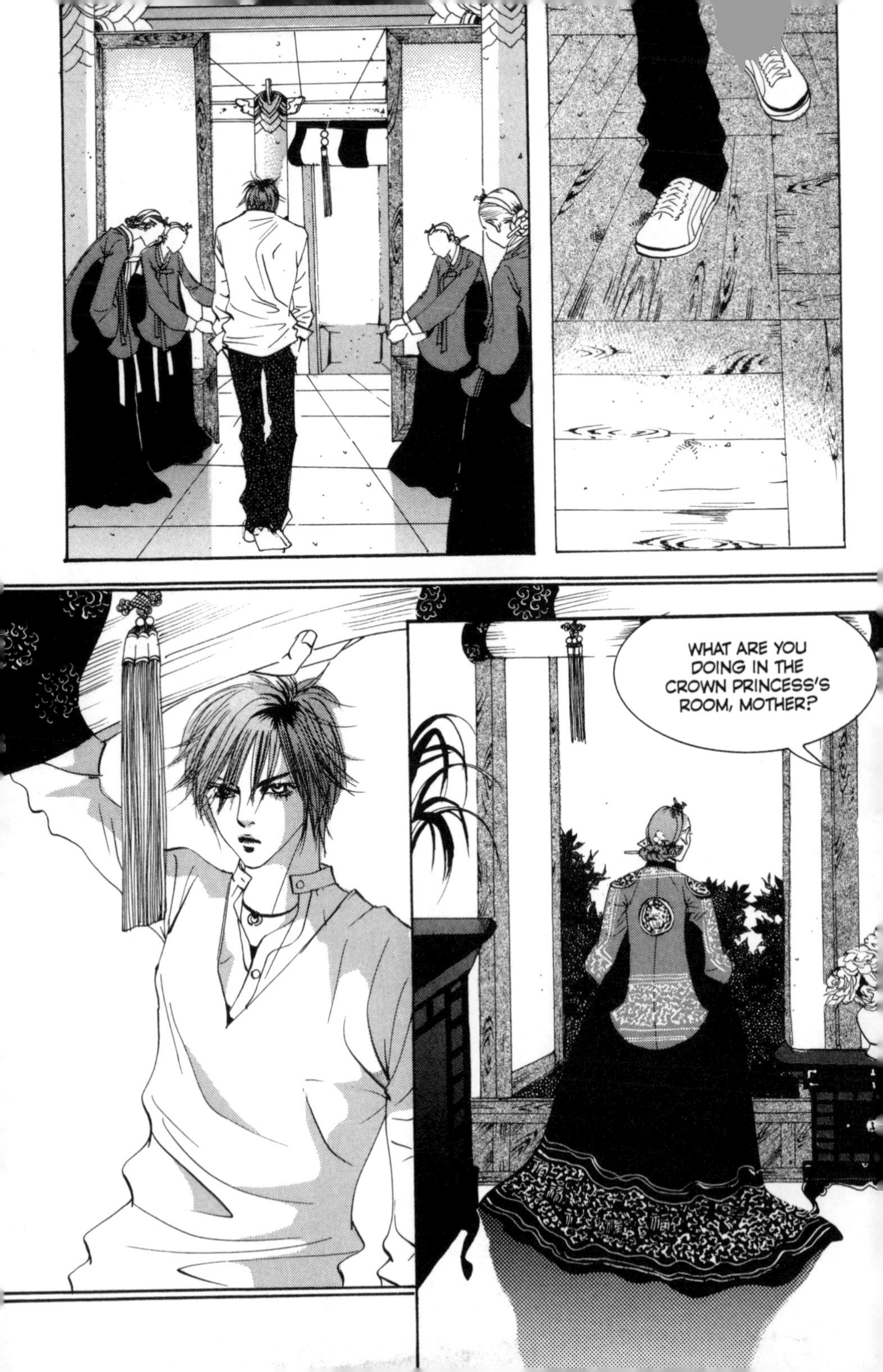
WHAT ARE YOU DOING IN THE CROWN PRINCESS'S ROOM, MOTHER?

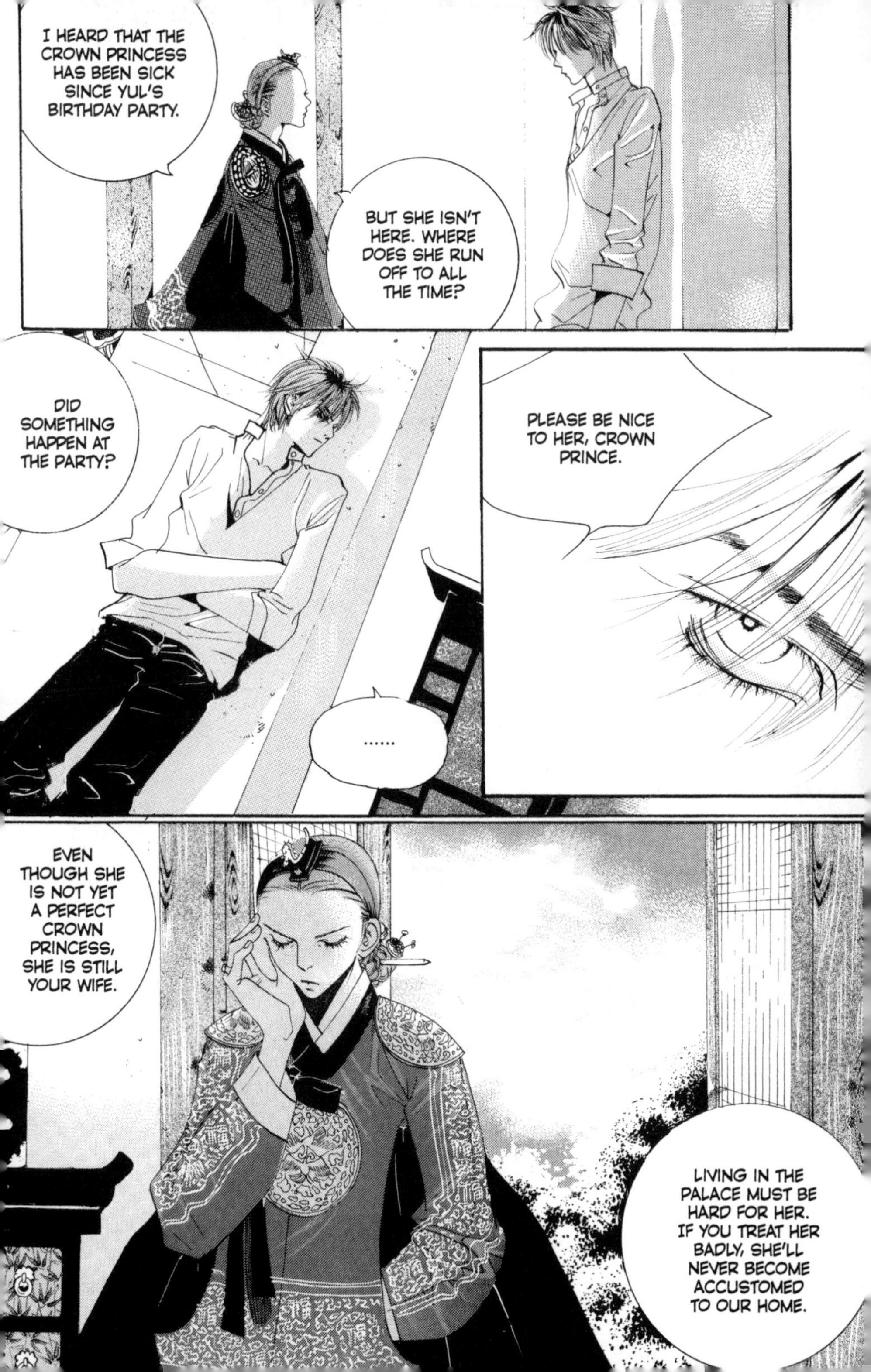
I HEARD THAT THE CROWN PRINCESS HAS BEEN SICK SINCE YUL'S BIRTHDAY PARTY.
BUT SHE ISN'T HERE. WHERE DOES SHE RUN OFF TO ALL THE TIME?
DID SOMETHING HAPPEN AT THE PARTY?
......
PLEASE BE NICE TO HER, CROWN PRINCE.
EVEN THOUGH SHE IS NOT YET A PERFECT CROWN PRINCESS, SHE IS STILL YOUR WIFE.
LIVING IN THE PALACE MUST BE HARD FOR HER. IF YOU TREAT HER BADLY, SHE'LL NEVER BECOME ACCUSTOMED TO OUR HOME.

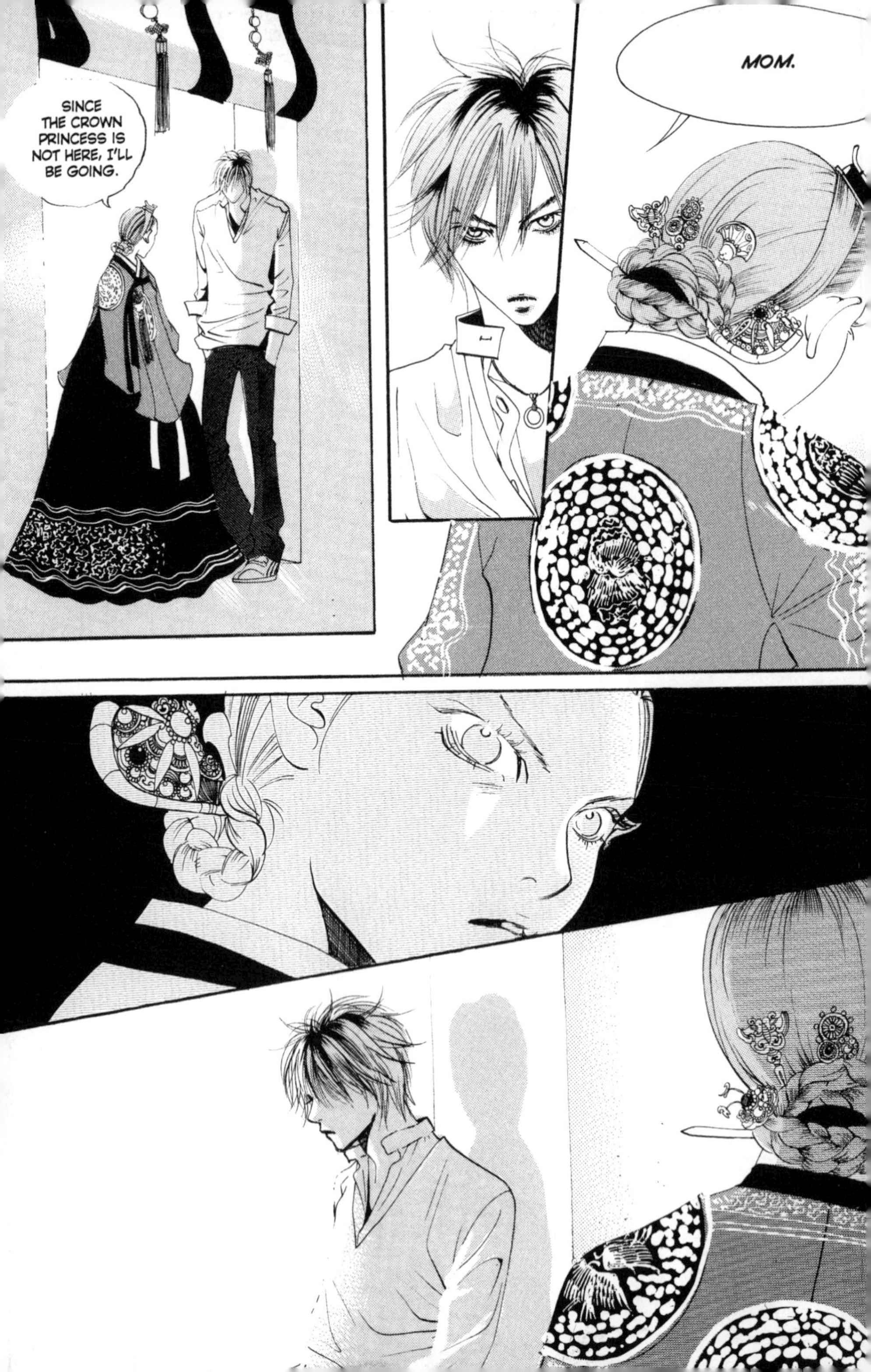
SINCE THE CROWN PRINCESS IS NOT HERE, I'LL BE GOING.
MOM.

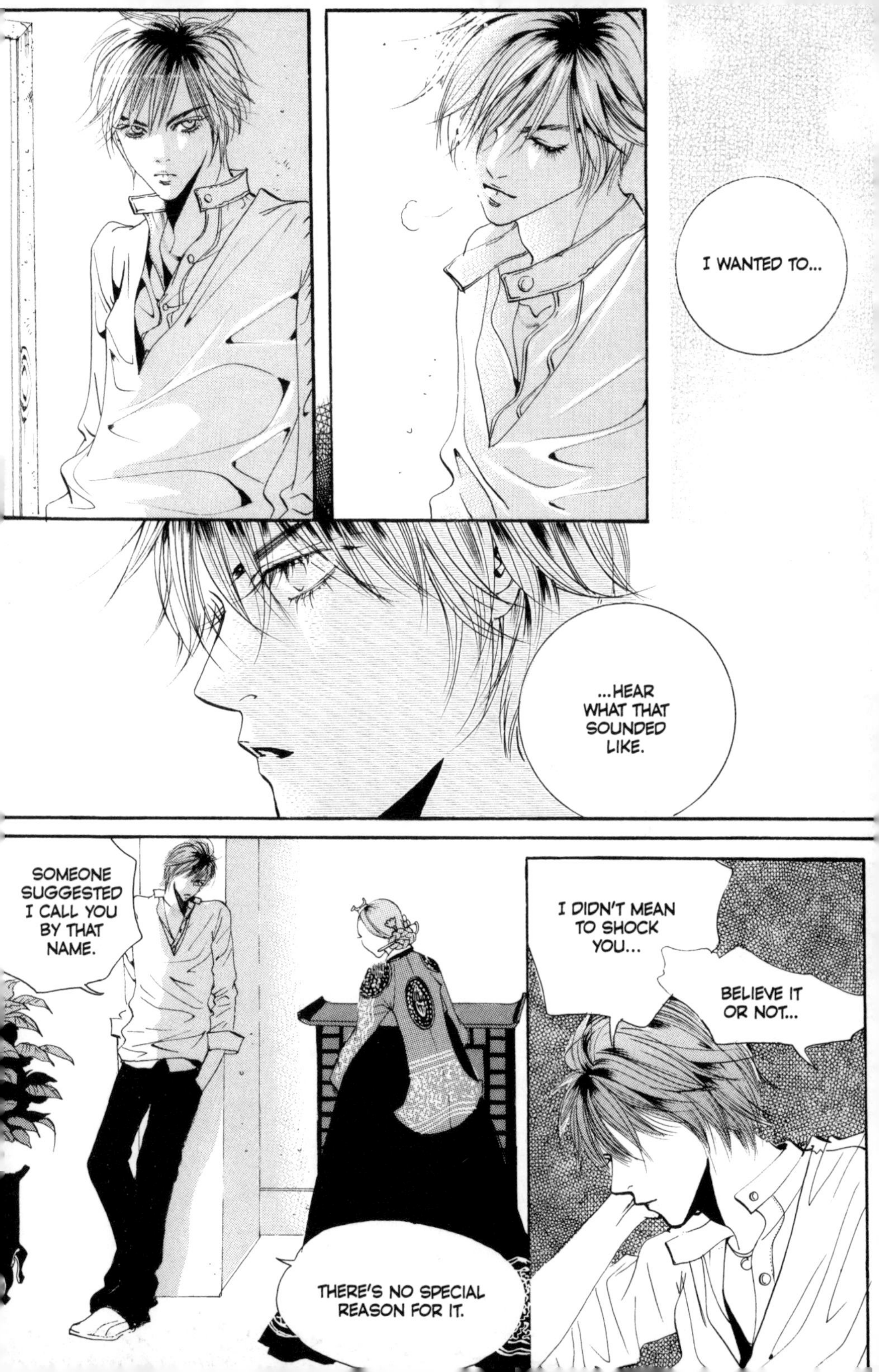
I WANTED TO...
...HEAR WHAT THAT SOUNDED LIKE.
SOMEONE SUGGESTED I CALL YOU BY THAT NAME.
THERE'S NO SPECIAL REASON FOR IT.
I DIDN'T MEAN TO SHOCK YOU...
BELIEVE IT OR NOT...

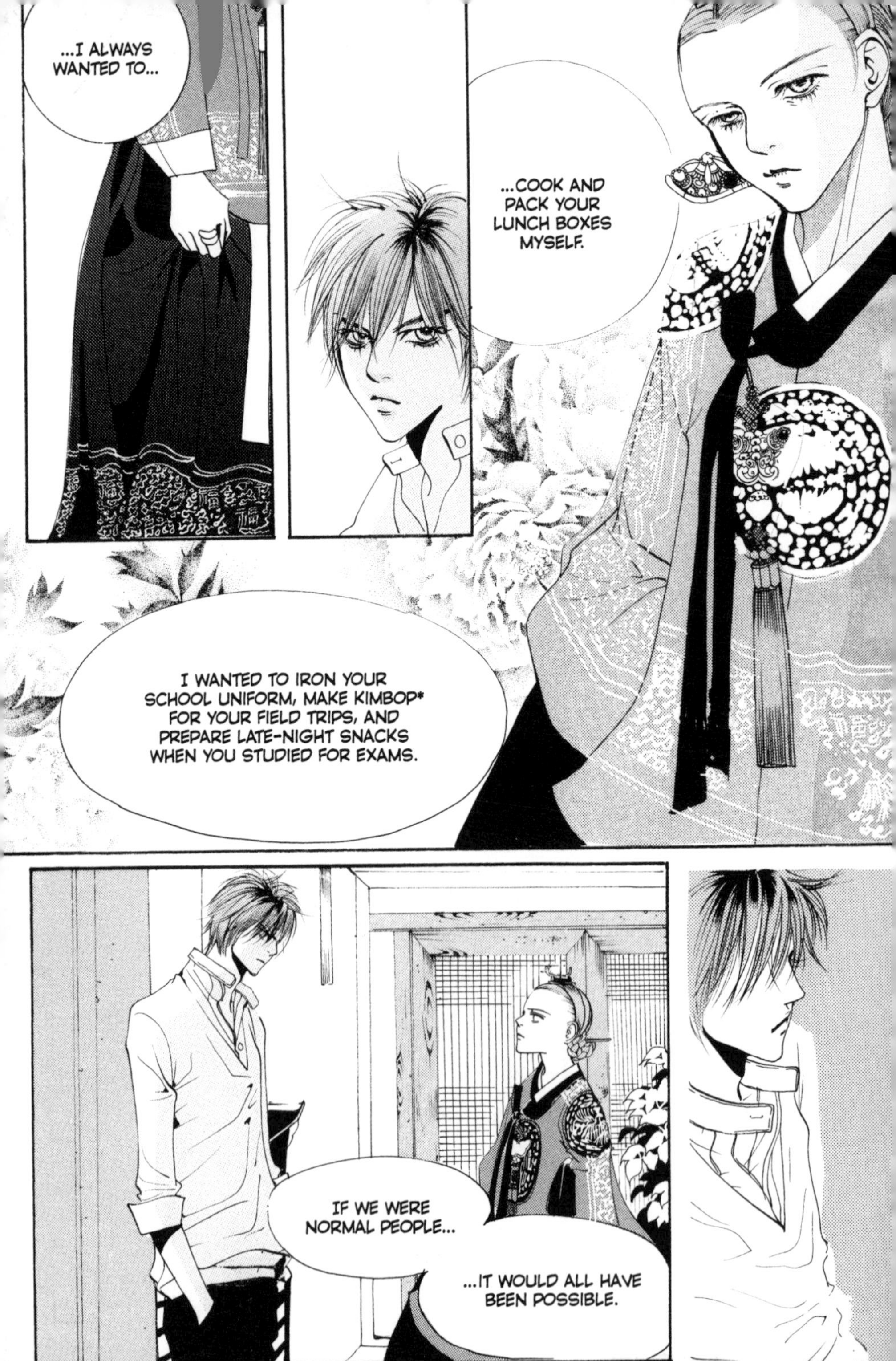
...I ALWAYS WANTED TO...
...COOK AND PACK YOUR LUNCH BOXES MYSELF.
I WANTED TO IRON YOUR SCHOOL UNIFORM, MAKE KIMBOP* FOR YOUR FIELD TRIPS, AND PREPARE LATE-NIGHT SNACKS WHEN YOU STUDIED FOR EXAMS.
IF WE WERE NORMAL PEOPLE...
...IT WOULD ALL HAVE BEEN POSSIBLE.

*KOREAN SEAWEED HAND ROLLS.

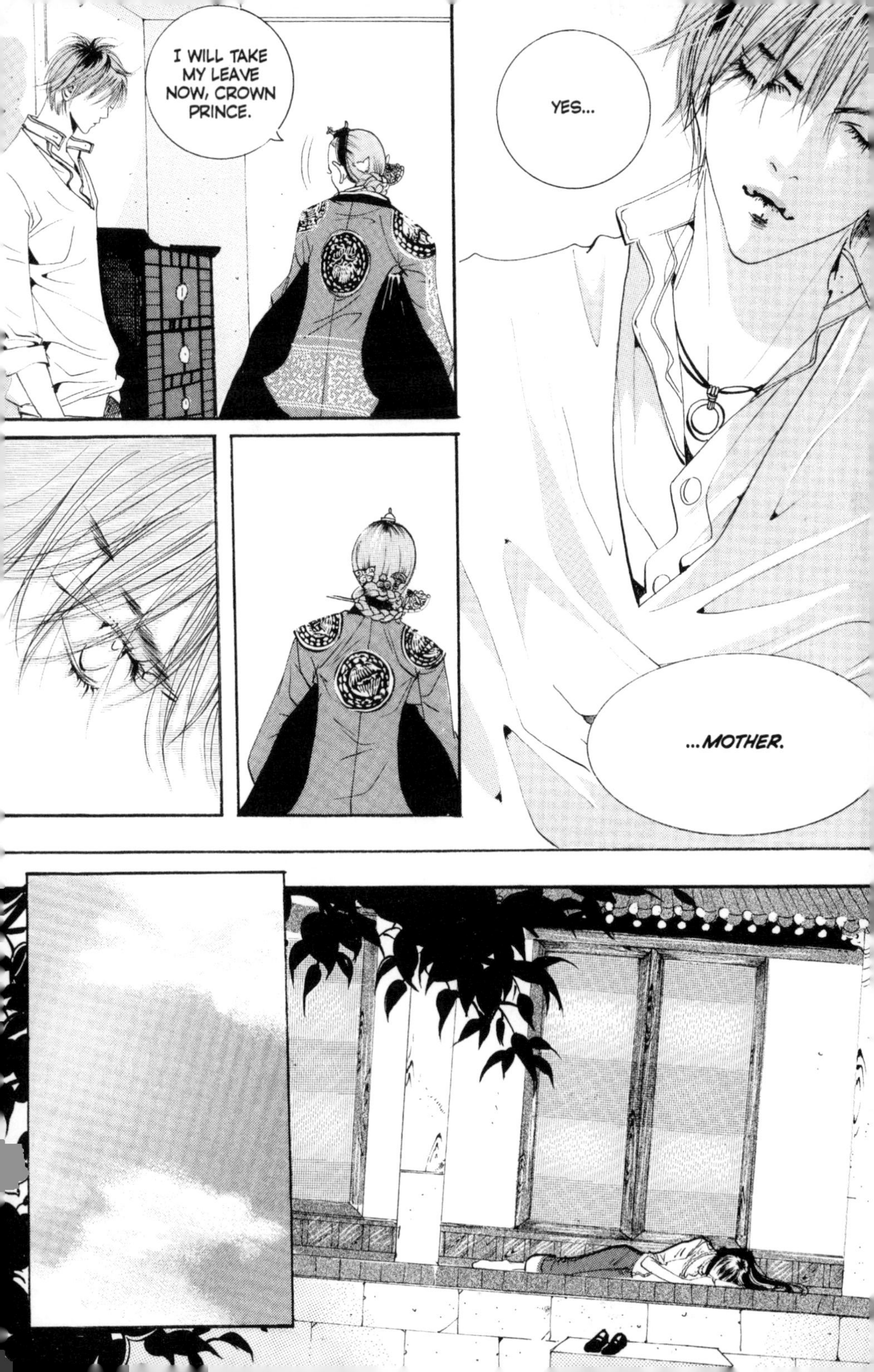
I WILL TAKE MY LEAVE NOW, CROWN PRINCE.
YES...
...MOTHER.

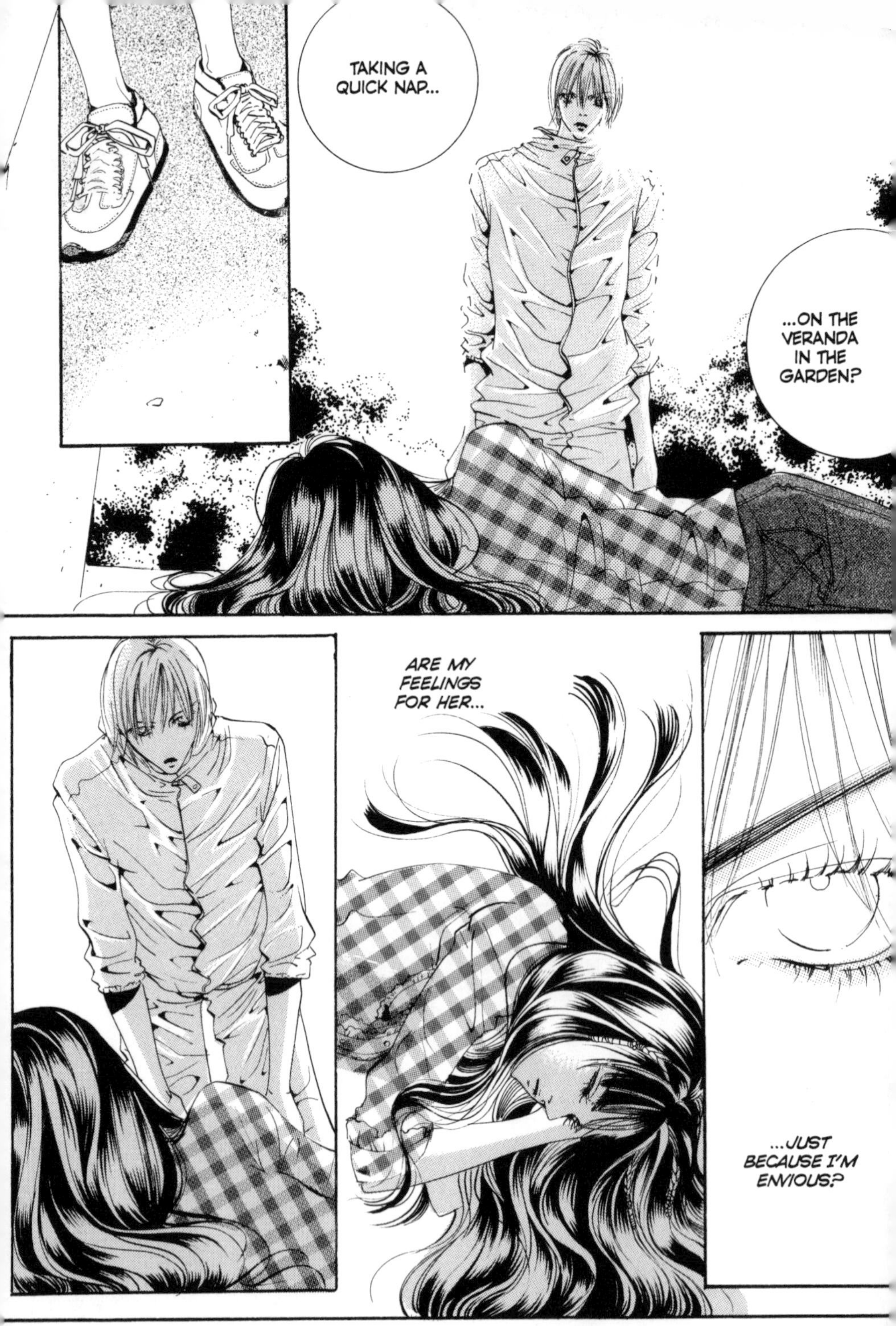
TAKING A QUICK NAP...
...ON THE VERANDA IN THE GARDEN?
ARE MY FEELINGS FOR HER...
...JUST BECAUSE I'M ENVIOUS?

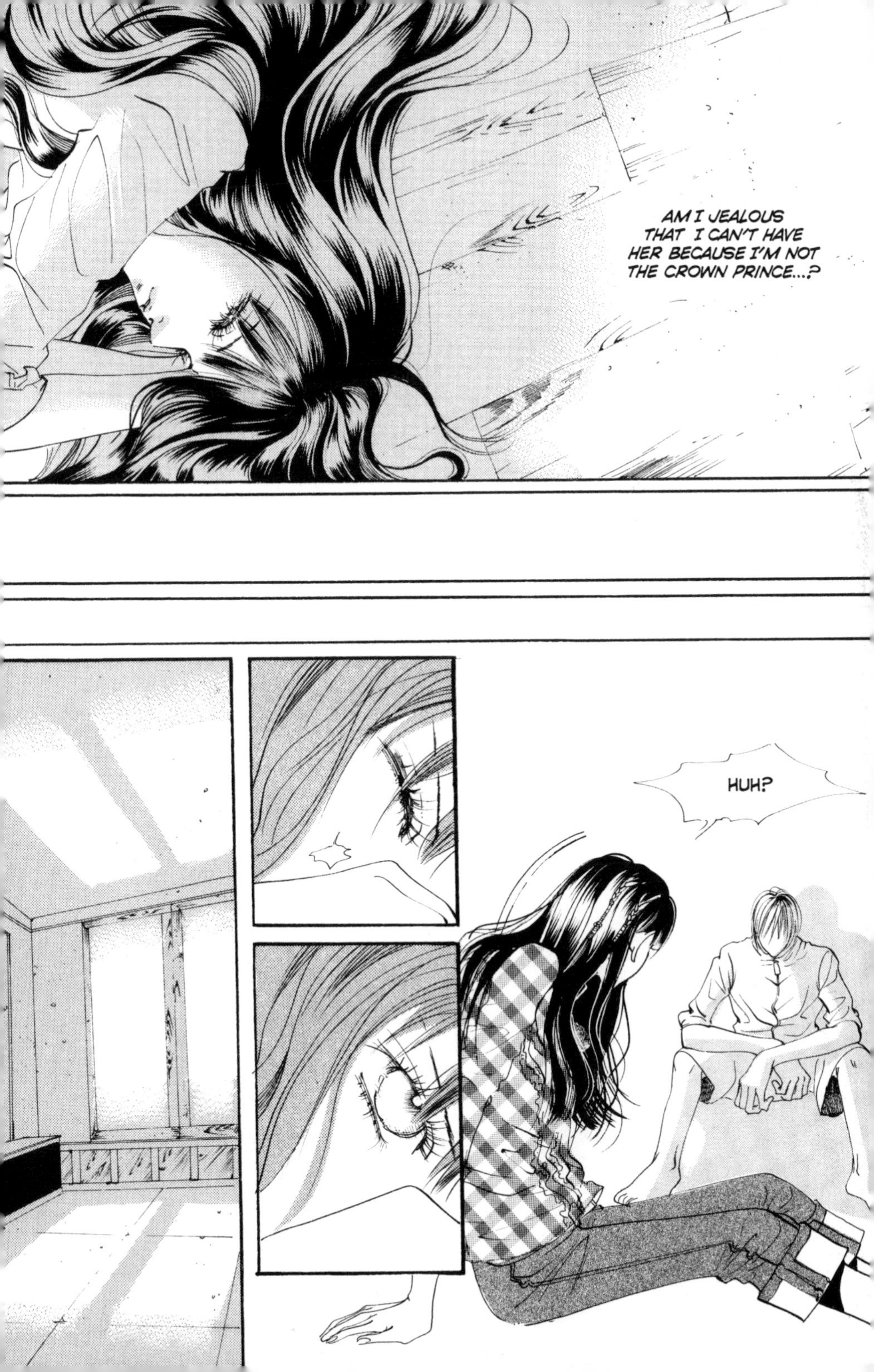
AM I JEALOUS THAT I CAN'T HAVE HER BECAUSE I'M NOT THE CROWN PRINCE...?
HUH?

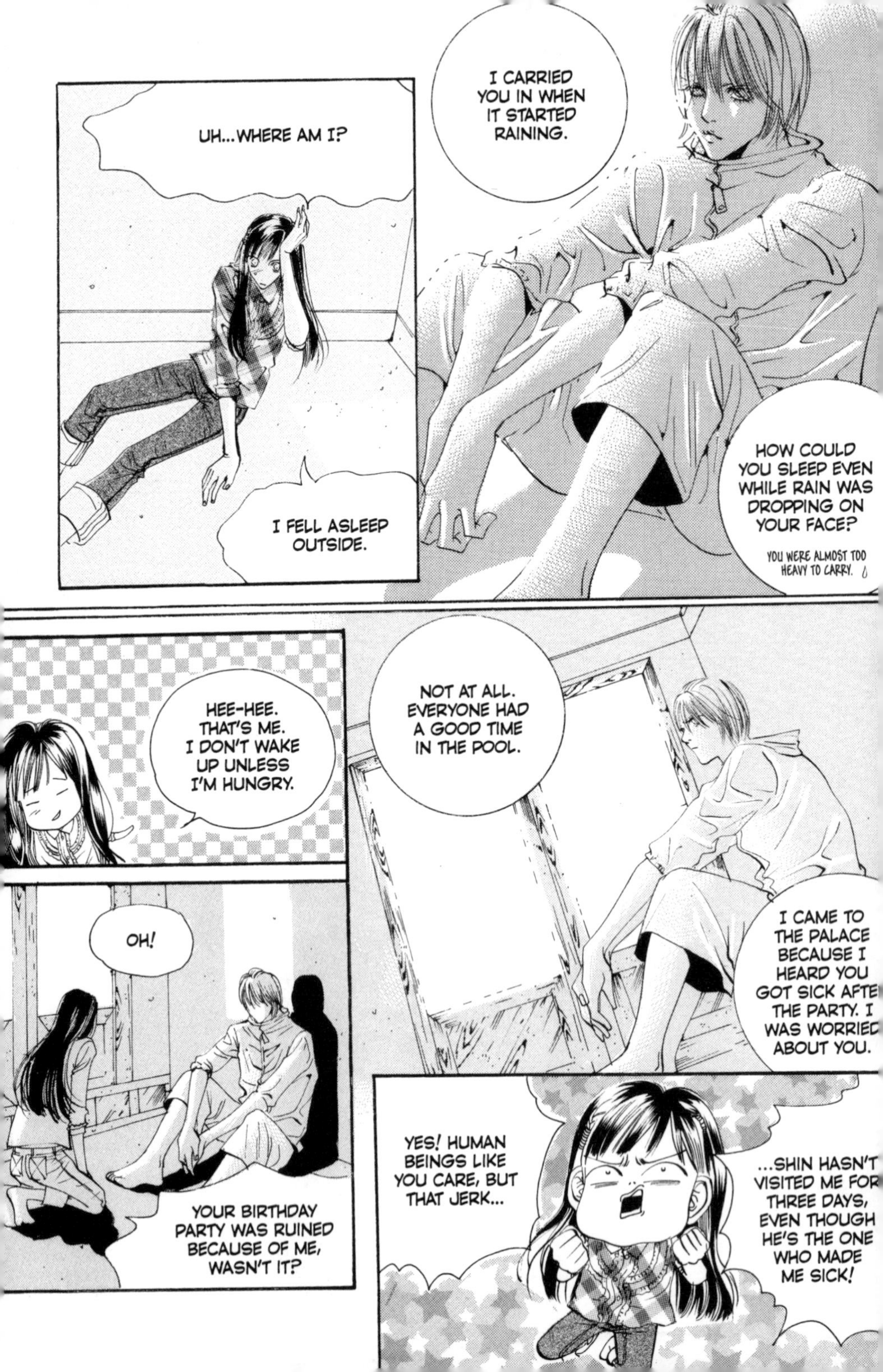
UH...WHERE AM I?
I FELL ASLEEP OUTSIDE.
I CARRIED YOU IN WHEN IT STARTED RAINING.
HOW COULD YOU SLEEP EVEN WHILE RAIN WAS DROPPING ON YOUR FACE?
YOU WERE ALMOST TOO HEAVY TO CARRY.
HEE-HEE. THAT'S ME. I DON'T WAKE UP UNLESS I'M HUNGRY.
OH!
YOUR BIRTHDAY PARTY WAS RUINED BECAUSE OF ME, WASN'T IT?
NOT AT ALL. EVERYONE HAD A GOOD TIME IN THE POOL.
I CAME TO THE PALACE BECAUSE I HEARD YOU GOT SICK AFTE THE PARTY. I WAS WORRIED ABOUT YOU.
YES! HUMAN BEINGS LIKE YOU CARE, BUT THAT JERK...
...SHIN HASN'T VISITED ME FOR THREE DAYS, EVEN THOUGH HE'S THE ONE WHO MADE ME SICK!

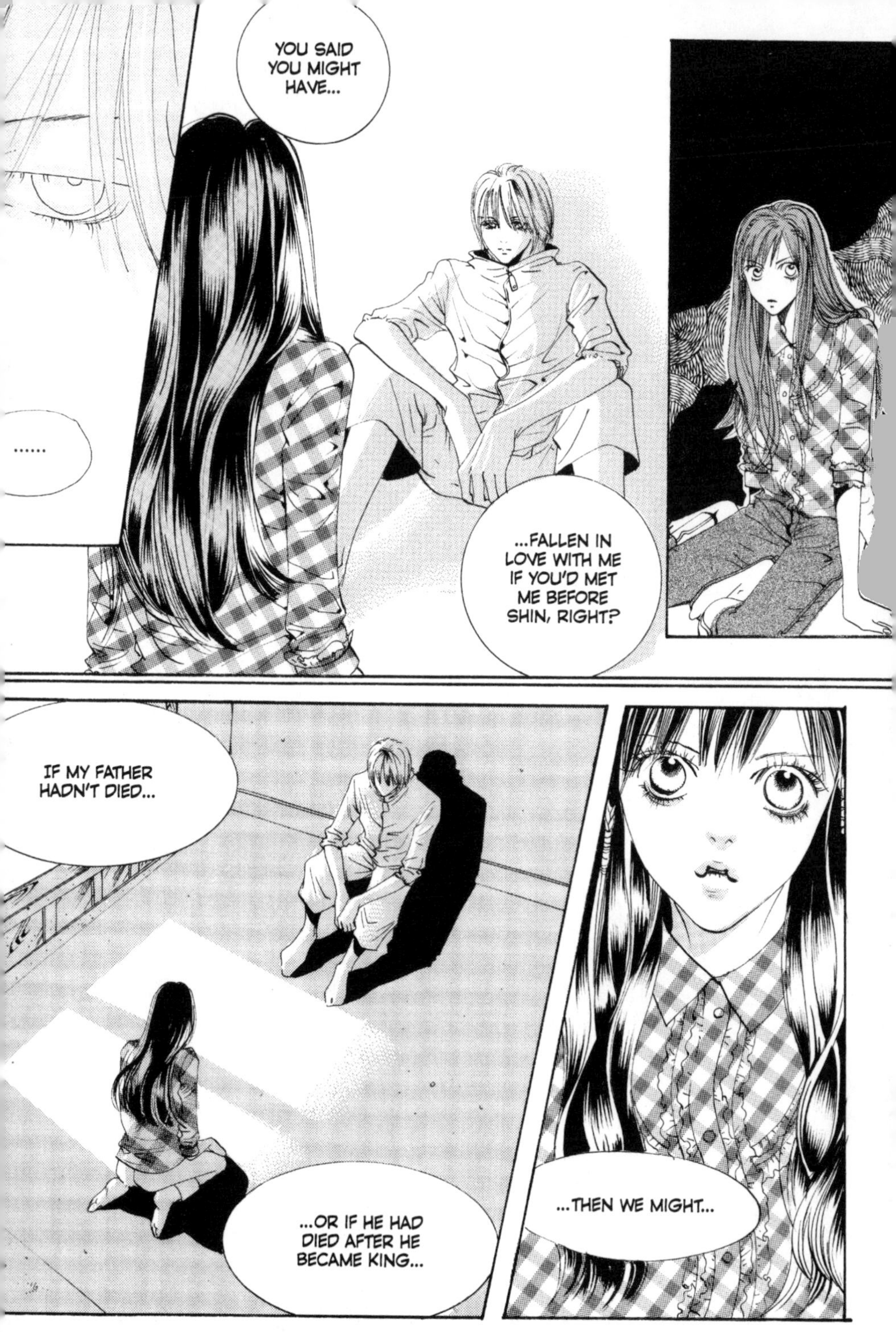
YOU SAID YOU MIGHT HAVE...
...FALLEN IN LOVE WITH ME IF YOU'D MET ME BEFORE SHIN, RIGHT?
......
IF MY FATHER HADN'T DIED...
...OR IF HE HAD DIED AFTER HE BECAME KING...
...THEN WE MIGHT...

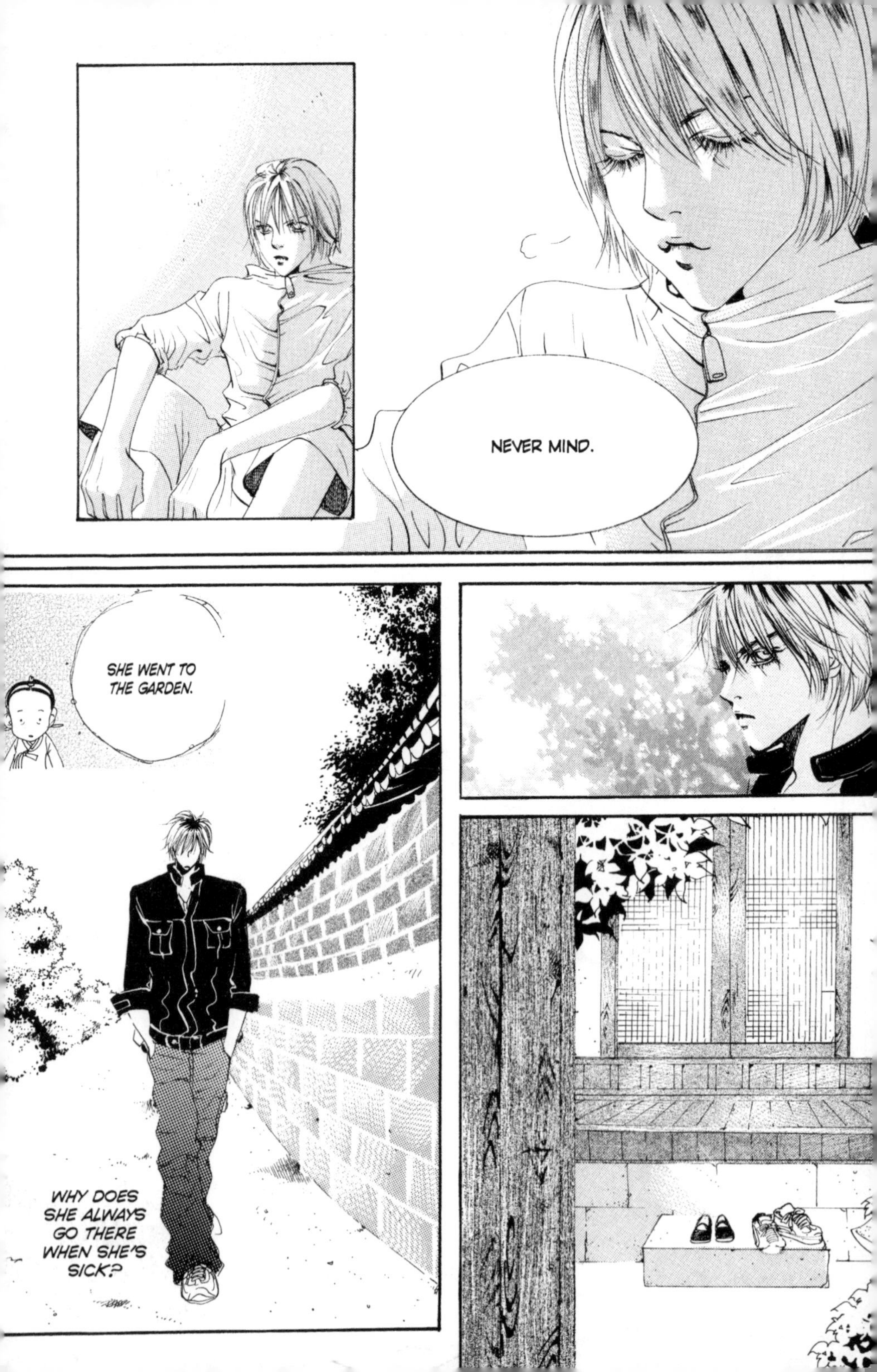
NEVER MIND.
SHE WENT TO THE GARDEN.
WHY DOES SHE ALWAYS GO THERE WHEN SHE'S SICK?

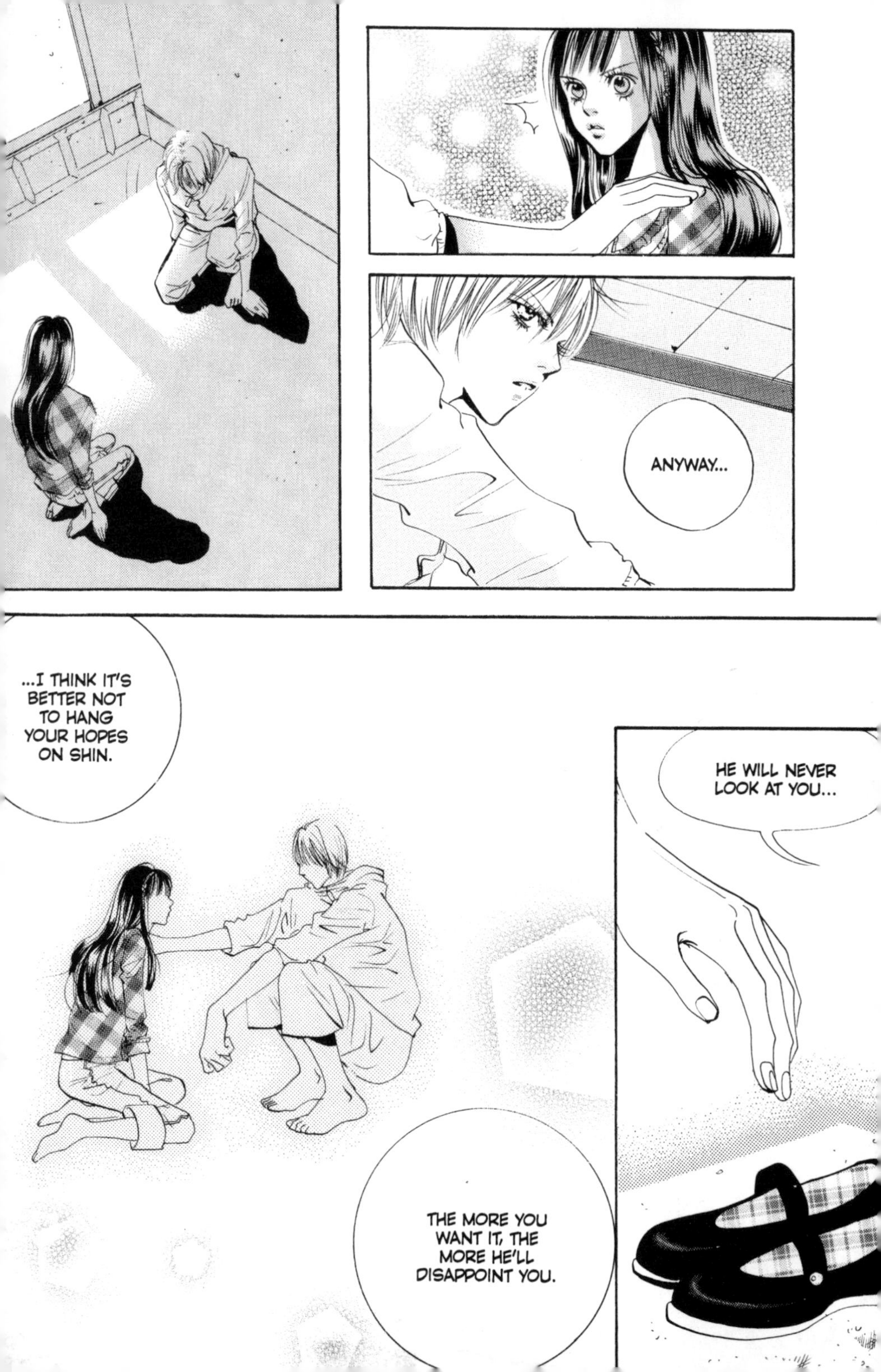
ANYWAY...
...I THINK IT'S BETTER NOT TO HANG YOUR HOPES ON SHIN.
THE MORE YOU WANT IT, THE MORE HE'LL DISAPPOINT YOU.
HE WILL NEVER LOOK AT YOU...

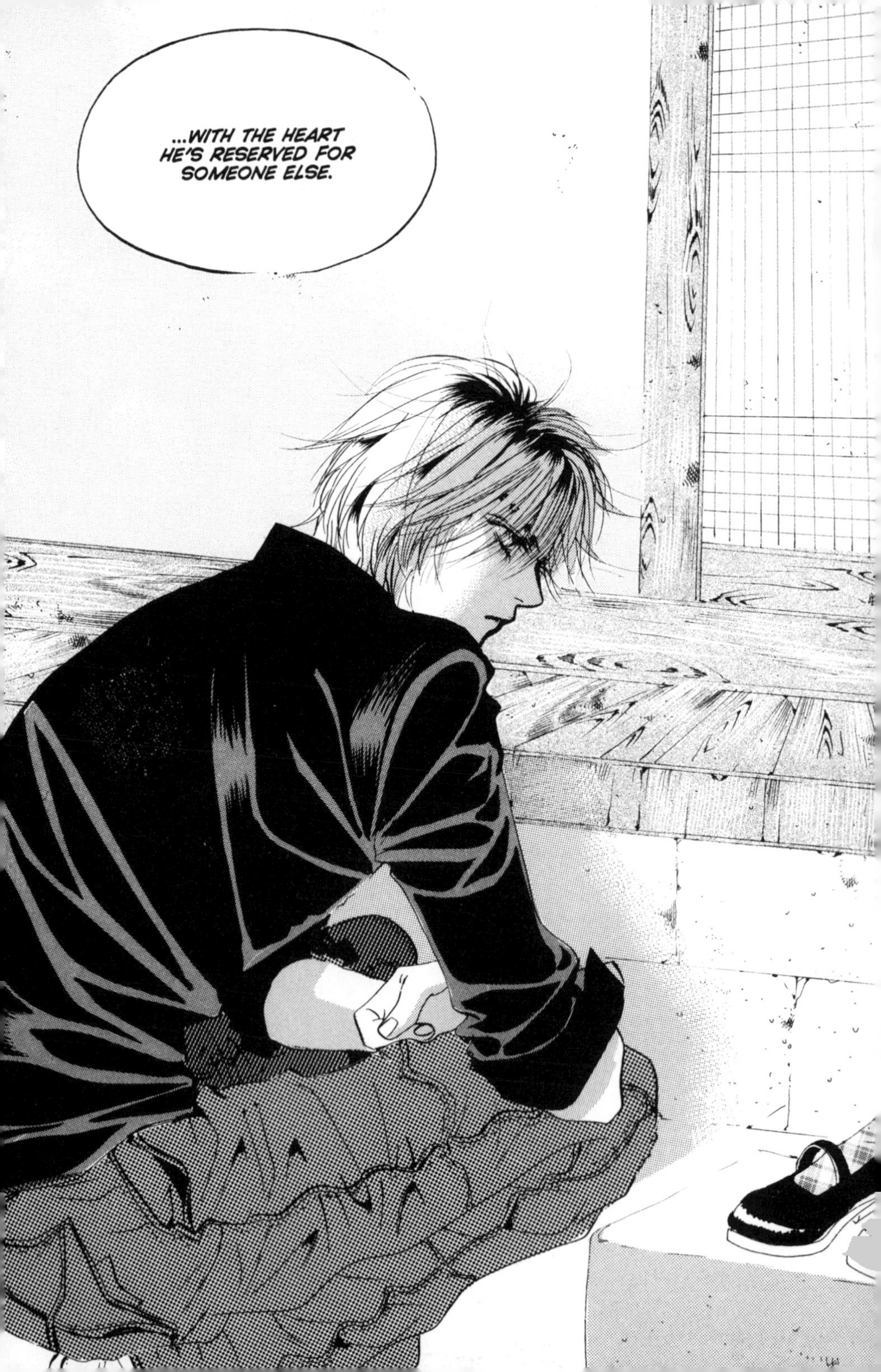
...WITH THE HEART HE'S RESERVED FOR SOMEONE ELSE.

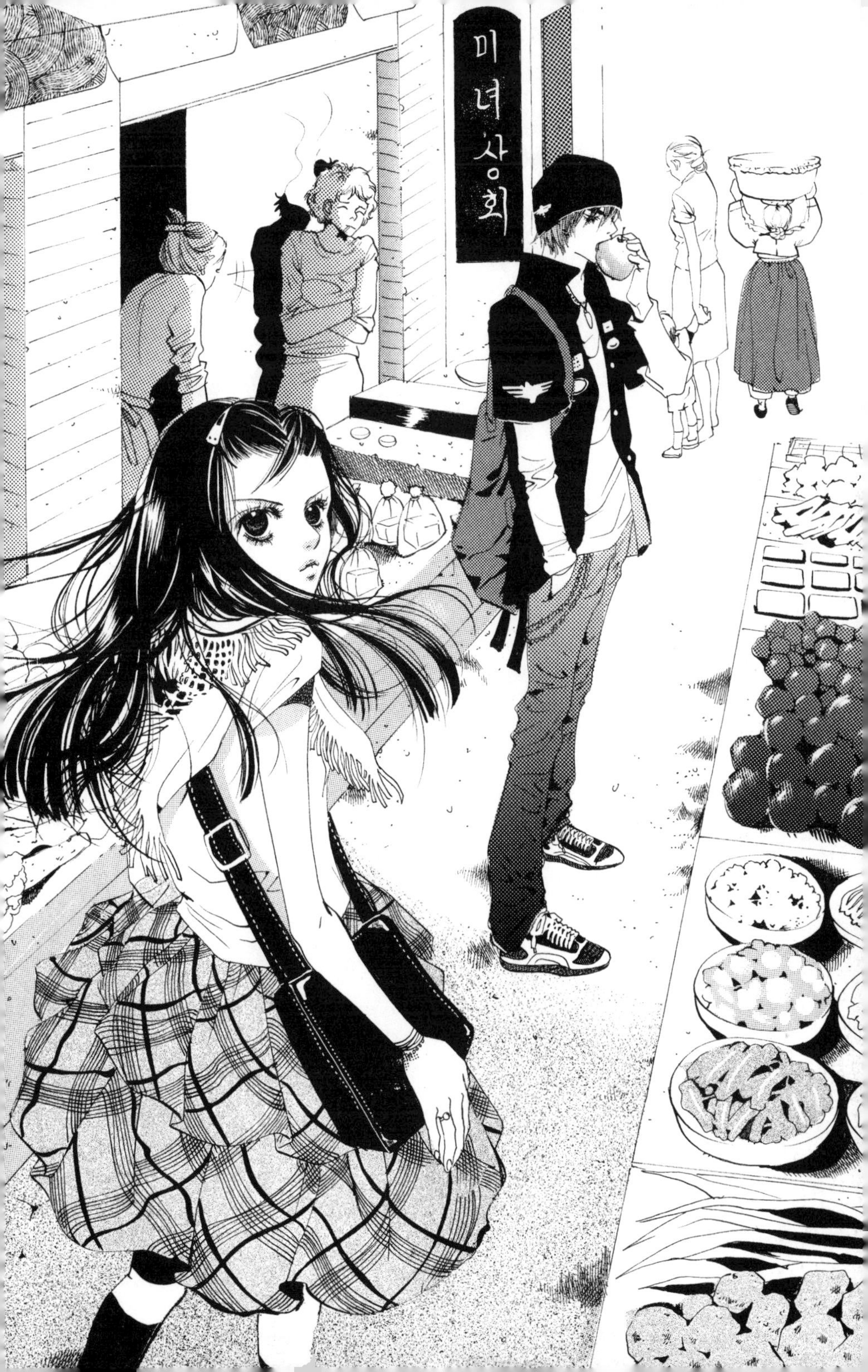
미녀상회

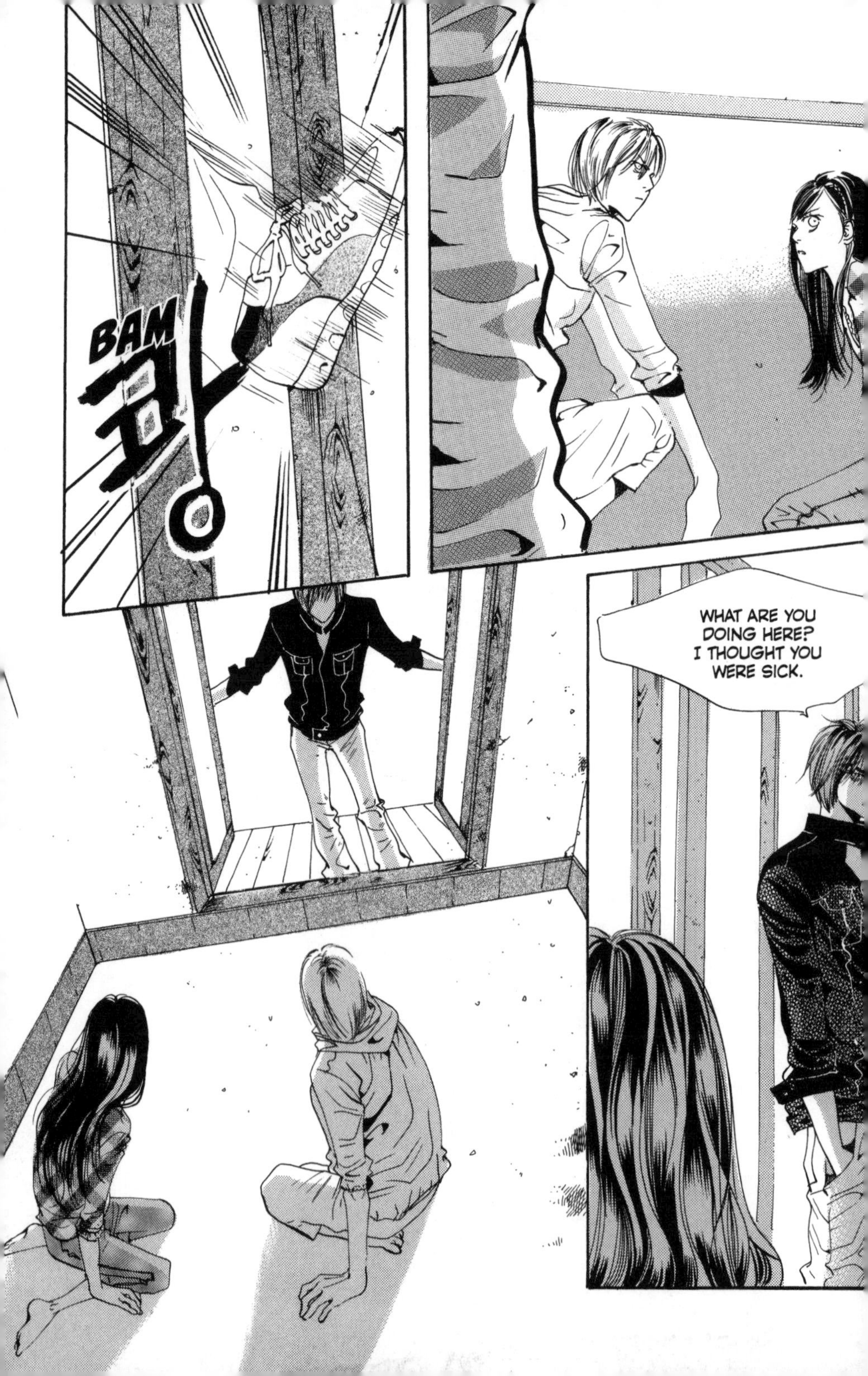
BAM
WHAT ARE YOU DOING HERE? I THOUGHT YOU WERE SICK.

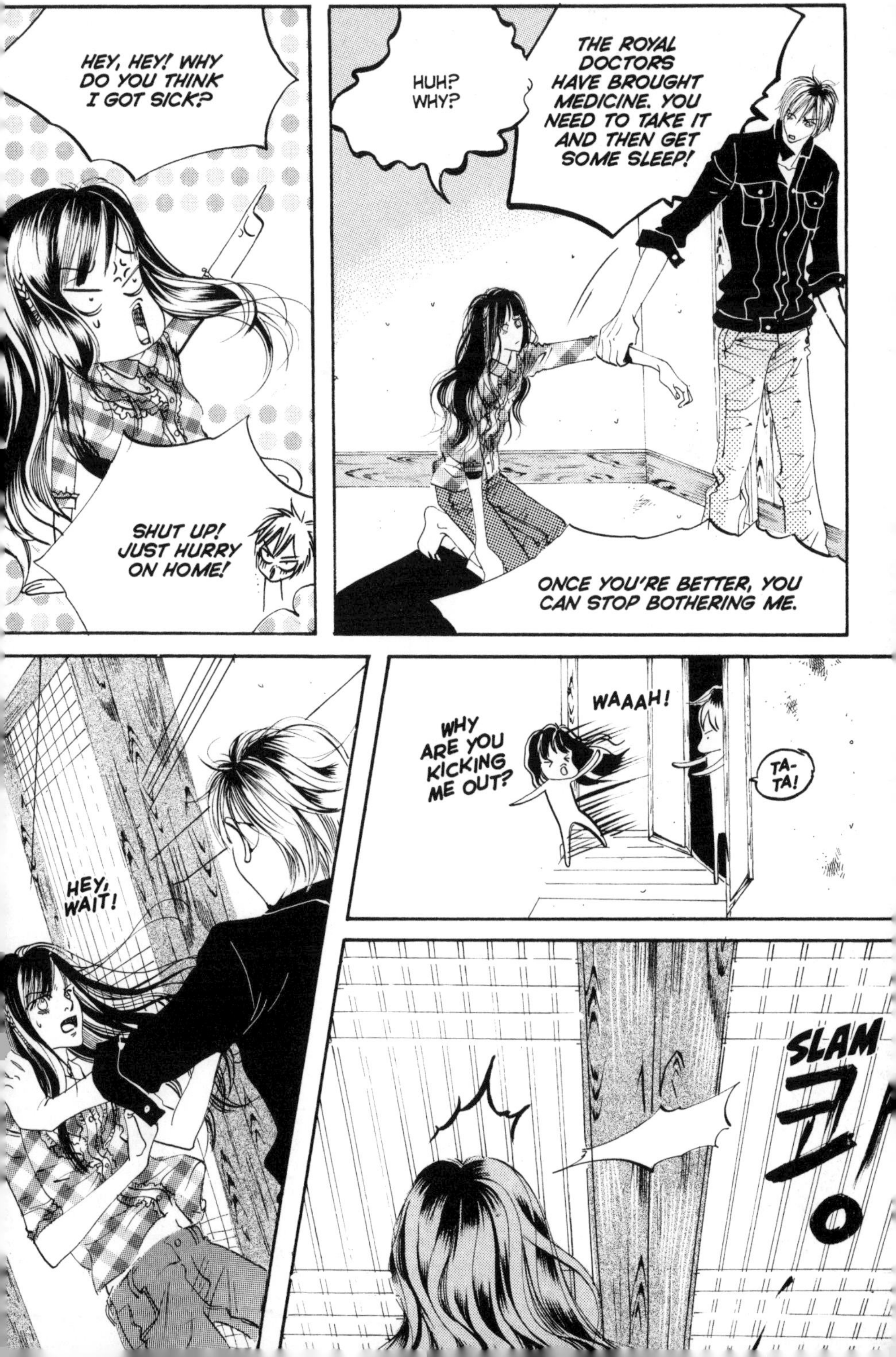
HEY, HEY! WHY DO YOU THINK I GOT SICK?
SHUT UP! JUST HURRY ON HOME!
HUH? WHY?
THE ROYAL DOCTORS HAVE BROUGHT MEDICINE. YOU NEED TO TAKE IT AND THEN GET SOME SLEEP!
ONCE YOU'RE BETTER, YOU CAN STOP BOTHERING ME.
HEY, WAIT!
WHY ARE YOU KICKING ME OUT?
WAAAH!
TA-TA!
SLAM
쾅

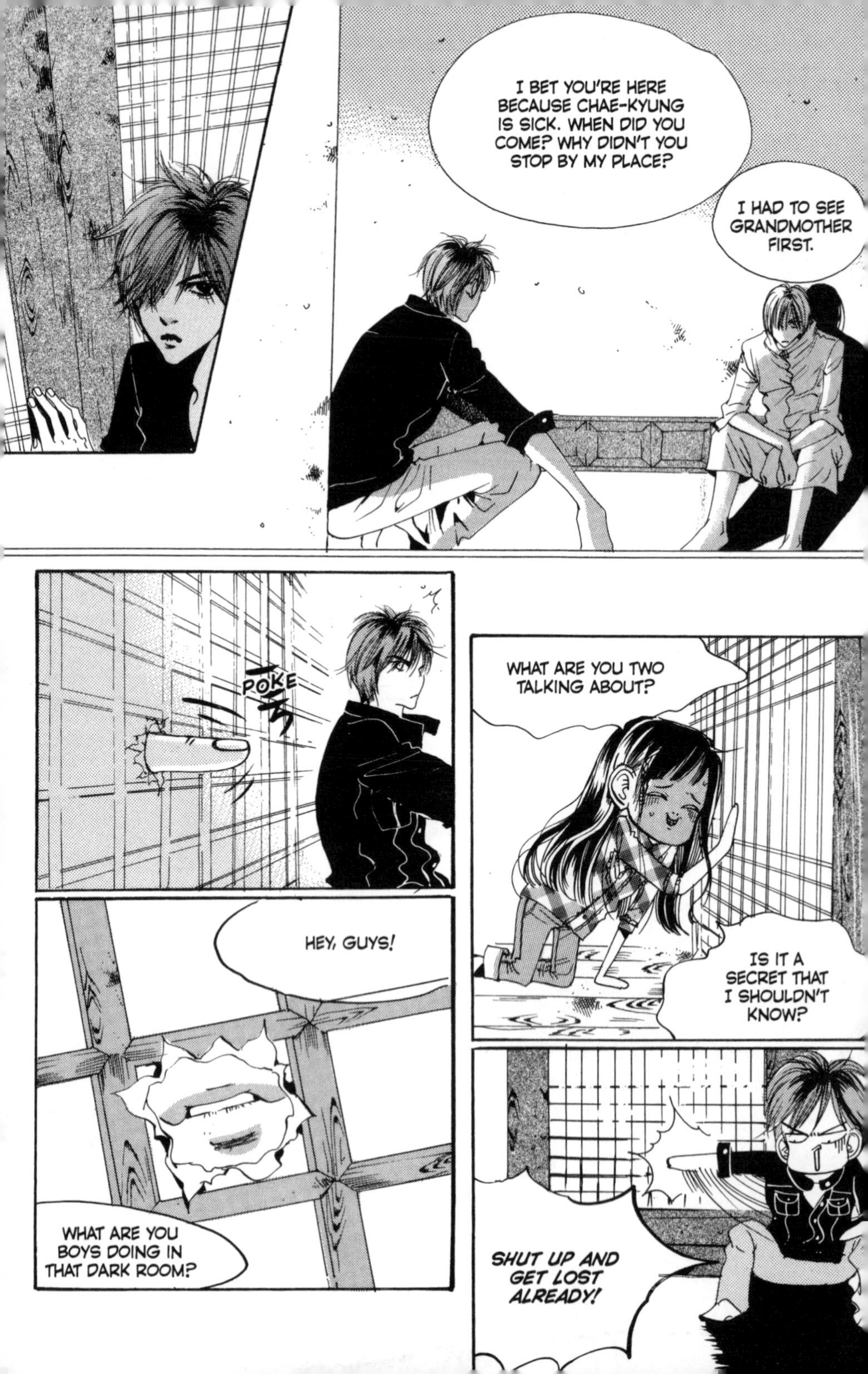
I BET YOU'RE HERE BECAUSE CHAE-KYUNG IS SICK. WHEN DID YOU COME? WHY DIDN'T YOU STOP BY MY PLACE?
I HAD TO SEE GRANDMOTHER FIRST.
POKE
HEY, GUYS!
WHAT ARE YOU BOYS DOING IN THAT DARK ROOM?
WHAT ARE YOU TWO TALKING ABOUT?
IS IT A SECRET THAT I SHOULDN'T KNOW?
SHUT UP AND GET LOST ALREADY!

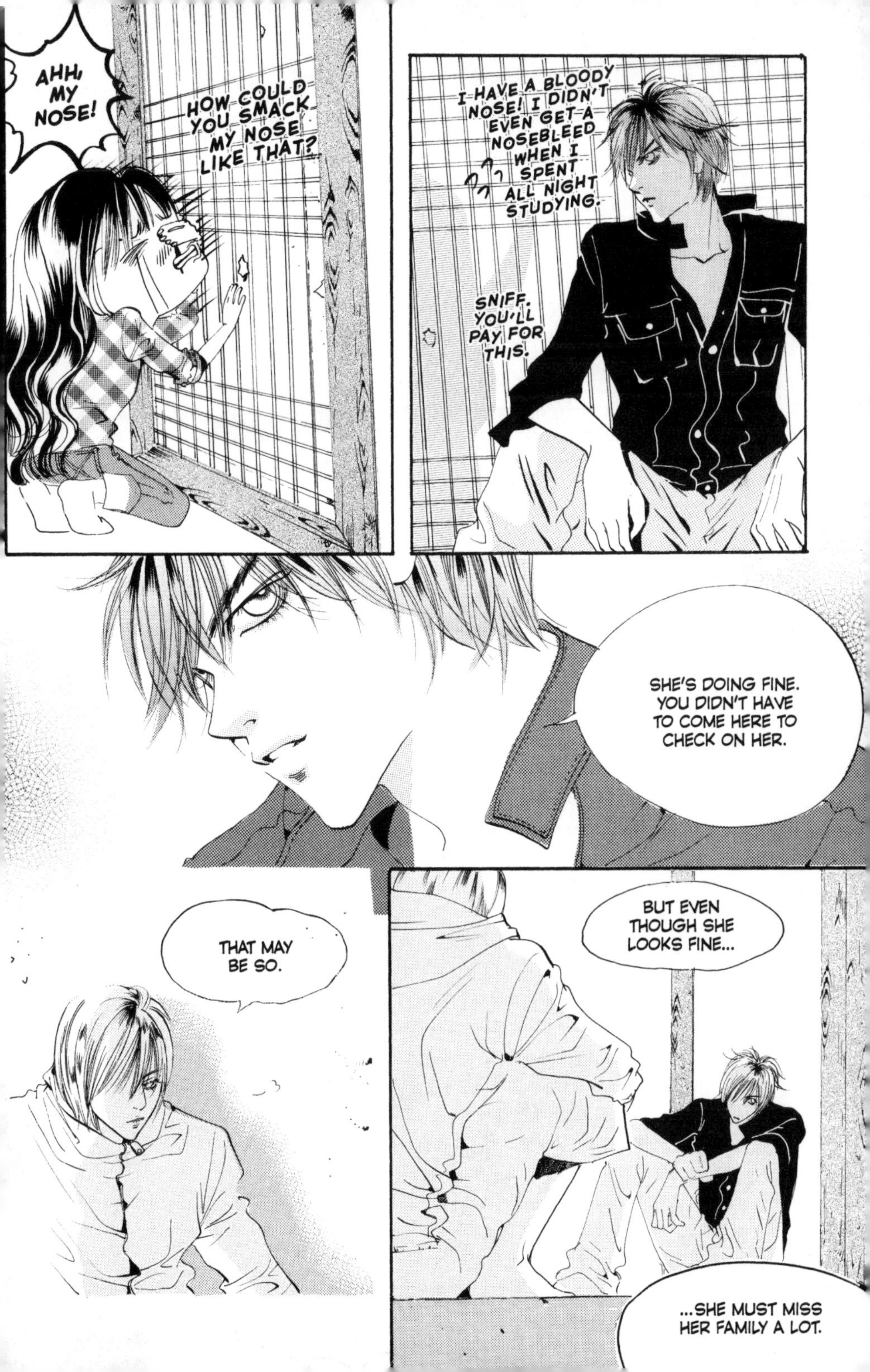
AHH, MY NOSE!
HOW COULD YOU SMACK MY NOSE LIKE THAT?
I HAVE A BLOODY NOSE! I DIDN'T EVEN GET A NOSEBLEED WHEN I SPENT ALL NIGHT STUDYING.
SNIFF. YOU'LL PAY FOR THIS.
SHE'S DOING FINE. YOU DIDN'T HAVE TO COME HERE TO CHECK ON HER.
THAT MAY BE SO.
BUT EVEN THOUGH SHE LOOKS FINE...
...SHE MUST MISS HER FAMILY A LOT.

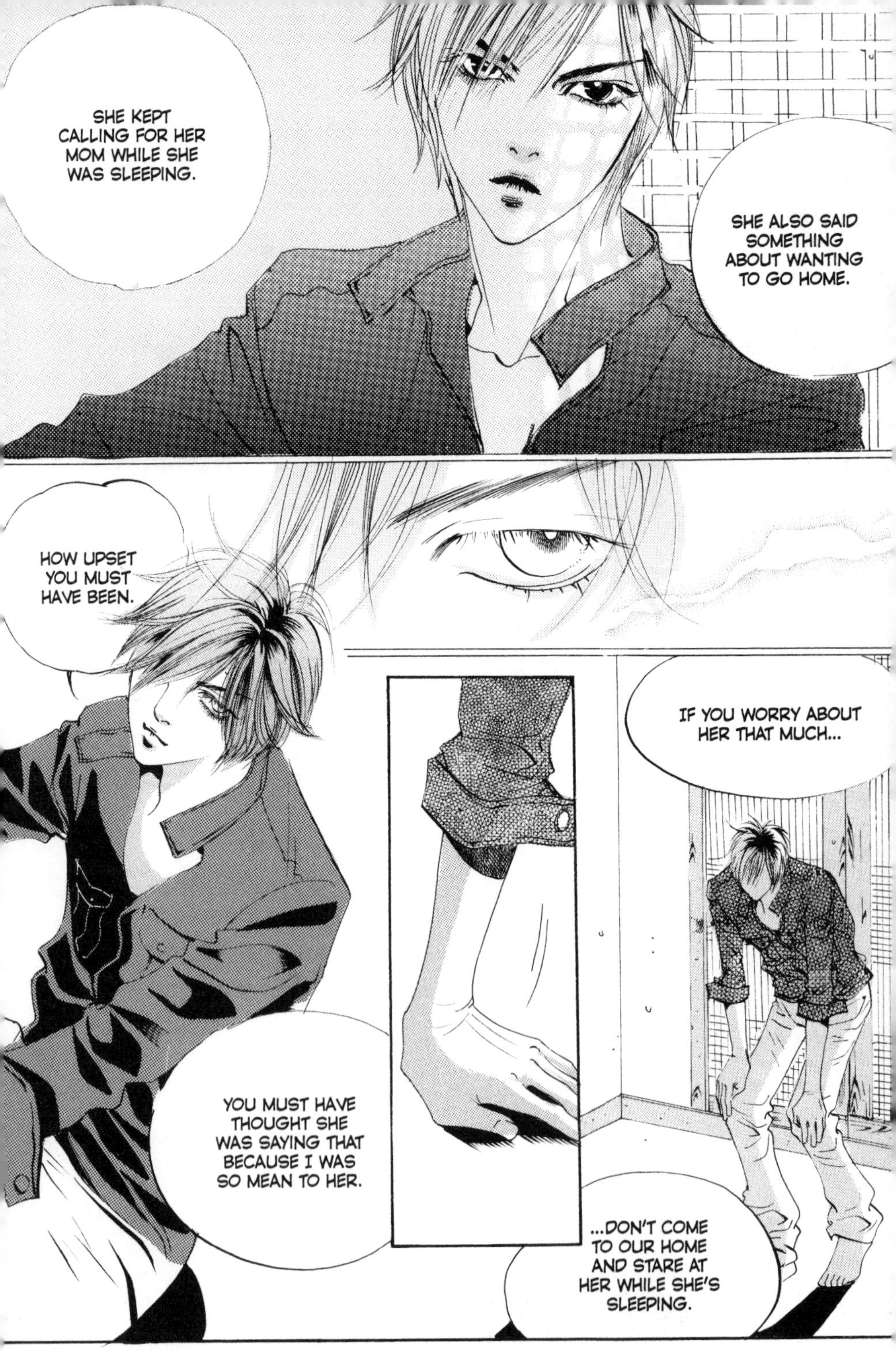
SHE KEPT CALLING FOR HER MOM WHILE SHE WAS SLEEPING.
SHE ALSO SAID SOMETHING ABOUT WANTING TO GO HOME.
HOW UPSET YOU MUST HAVE BEEN.
YOU MUST HAVE THOUGHT SHE WAS SAYING THAT BECAUSE I WAS SO MEAN TO HER.
IF YOU WORRY ABOUT HER THAT MUCH...
...DON'T COME TO OUR HOME AND STARE AT HER WHILE SHE'S SLEEPING.

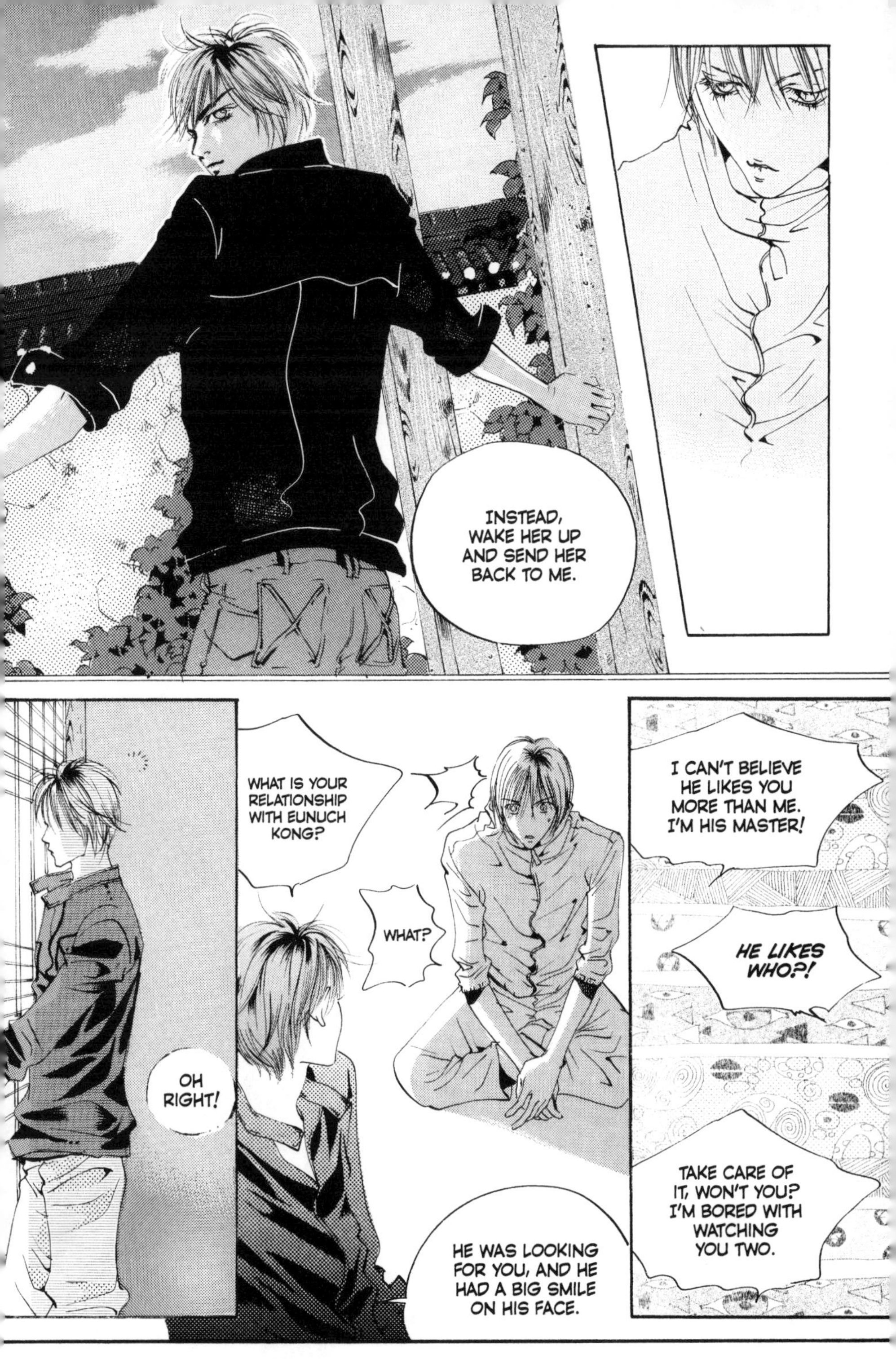
INSTEAD, WAKE HER UP AND SEND HER BACK TO ME.
WHAT IS YOUR RELATIONSHIP WITH EUNUCH KONG?
WHAT?
OH RIGHT!
HE WAS LOOKING FOR YOU, AND HE HAD A BIG SMILE ON HIS FACE.
I CAN'T BELIEVE HE LIKES YOU MORE THAN ME. I'M HIS MASTER!
HE LIKES WHO?!
TAKE CARE OF IT, WON'T YOU? I'M BORED WITH WATCHING YOU TWO.

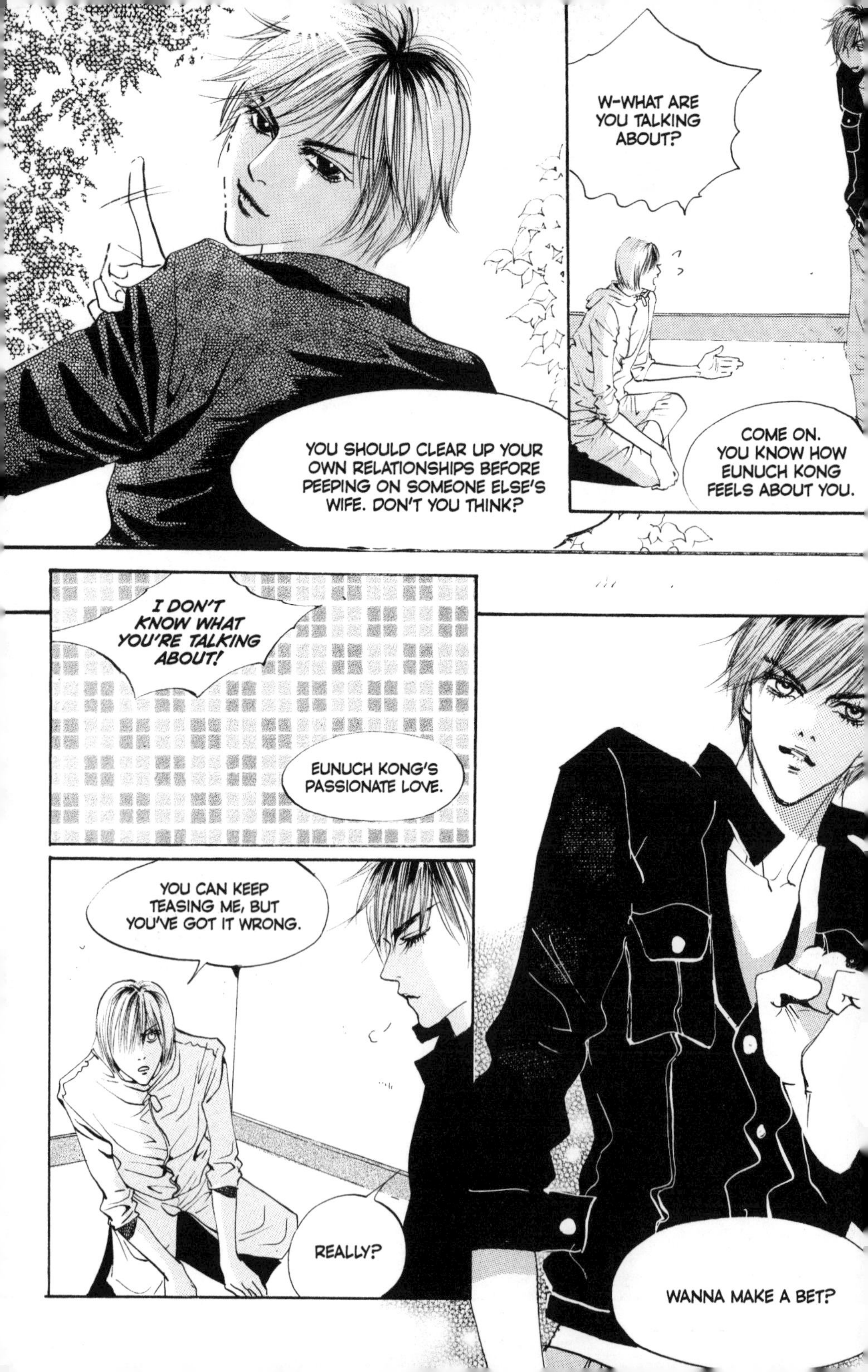
YOU SHOULD CLEAR UP YOUR OWN RELATIONSHIPS BEFORE PEEPING ON SOMEONE ELSE'S WIFE. DON'T YOU THINK?
W-WHAT ARE YOU TALKING ABOUT?
COME ON. YOU KNOW HOW EUNUCH KONG FEELS ABOUT YOU.
I DON'T KNOW WHAT YOU'RE TALKING ABOUT!
EUNUCH KONG'S PASSIONATE LOVE.
YOU CAN KEEP TEASING ME, BUT YOU'VE GOT IT WRONG.
REALLY?
WANNA MAKE A BET?

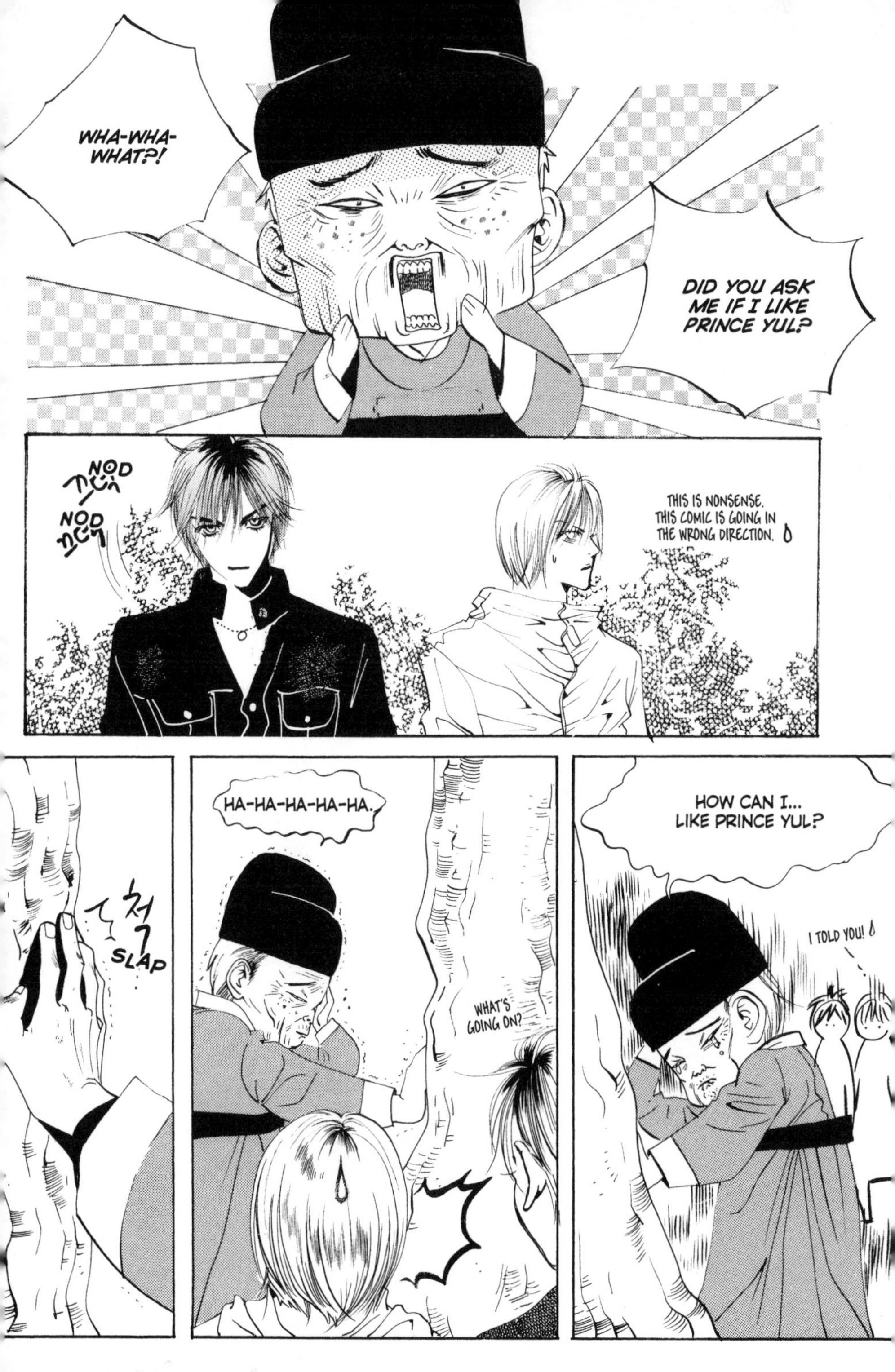
WHA-WHA-WHAT?!
DID YOU ASK ME IF I LIKE PRINCE YUL?
NOD
끄덕
NOD
끄덕
THIS IS NONSENSE. THIS COMIC IS GOING IN THE WRONG DIRECTION.
척
SLAP
HA-HA-HA-HA-HA.
WHAT'S GOING ON?
HOW CAN I... LIKE PRINCE YUL?
I TOLD YOU!

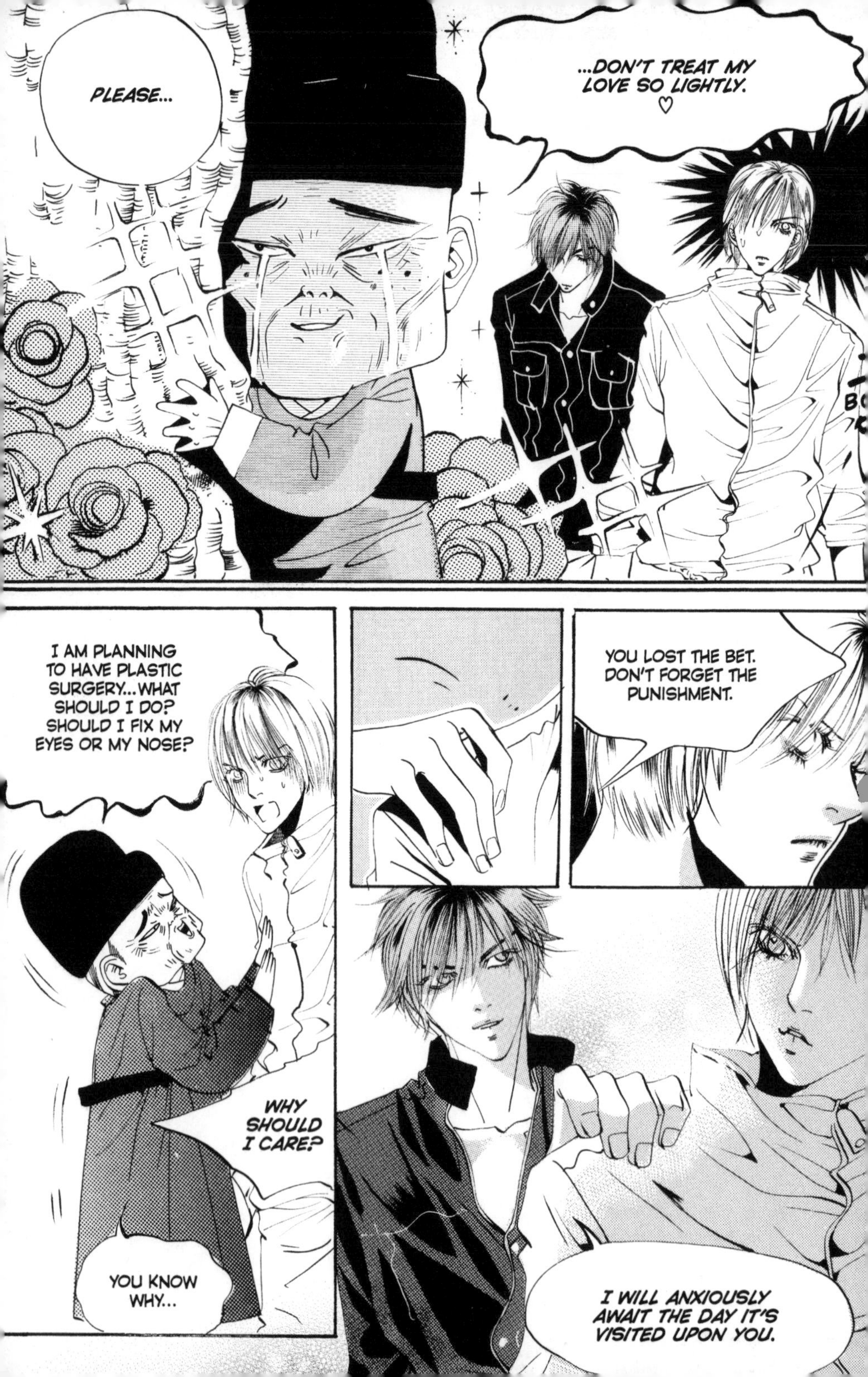
PLEASE...
...DON'T TREAT MY LOVE SO LIGHTLY. ♡
I AM PLANNING TO HAVE PLASTIC SURGERY...WHAT SHOULD I DO? SHOULD I FIX MY EYES OR MY NOSE?
WHY SHOULD I CARE?
YOU KNOW WHY...
YOU LOST THE BET. DON'T FORGET THE PUNISHMENT.
I WILL ANXIOUSLY AWAIT THE DAY IT'S VISITED UPON YOU.

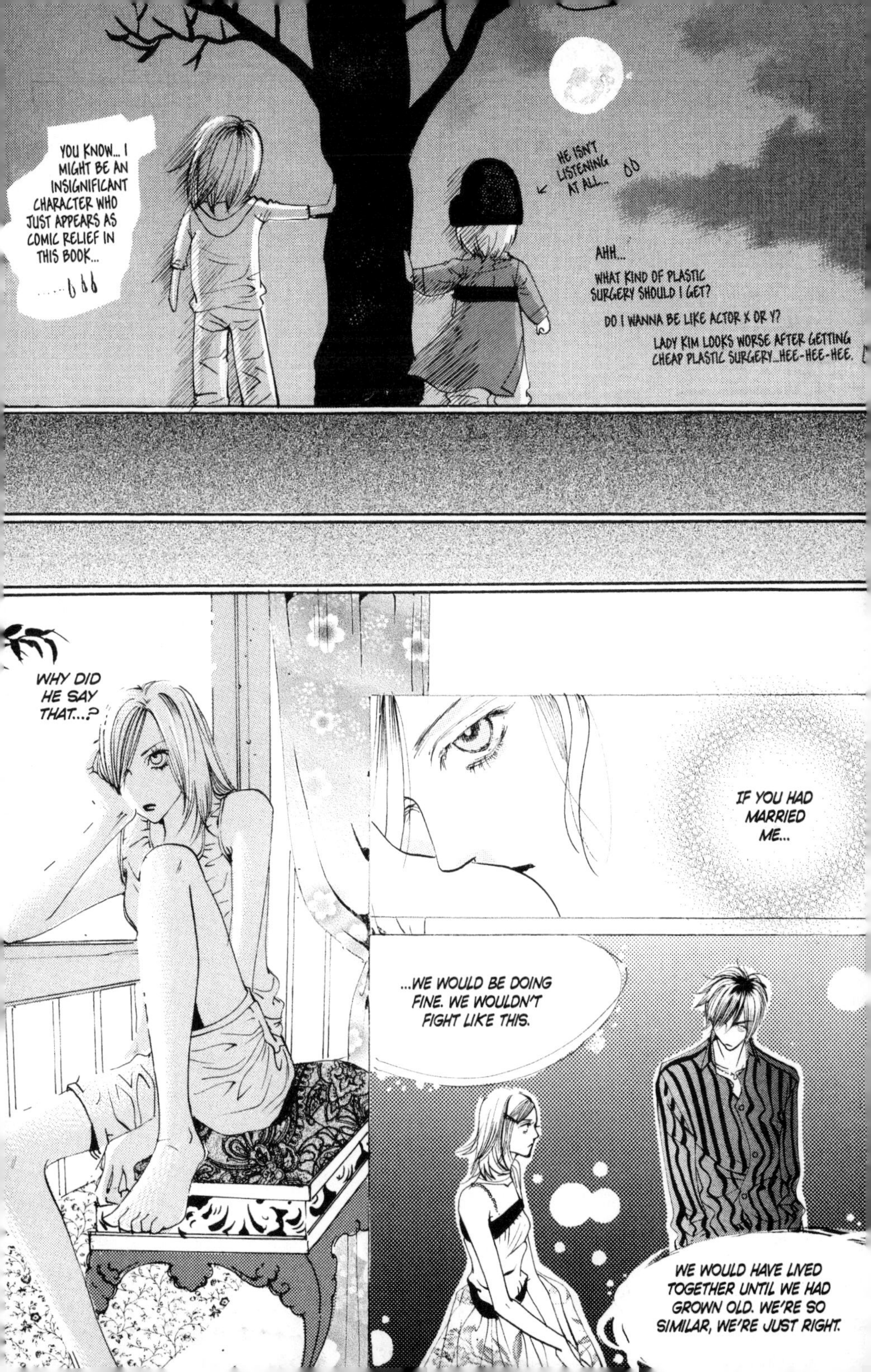
YOU KNOW... I MIGHT BE AN INSIGNIFICANT CHARACTER WHO JUST APPEARS AS COMIC RELIEF IN THIS BOOK...
......
HE ISN'T LISTENING AT ALL...
AHH...
WHAT KIND OF PLASTIC SURGERY SHOULD I GET?
DO I WANNA BE LIKE ACTOR X OR Y?
LADY KIM LOOKS WORSE AFTER GETTING CHEAP PLASTIC SURGERY...HEE-HEE-HEE.
WHY DID HE SAY THAT...?
IF YOU HAD MARRIED ME...
...WE WOULD BE DOING FINE. WE WOULDN'T FIGHT LIKE THIS.
WE WOULD HAVE LIVED TOGETHER UNTIL WE HAD GROWN OLD. WE'RE SO SIMILAR, WE'RE JUST RIGHT.

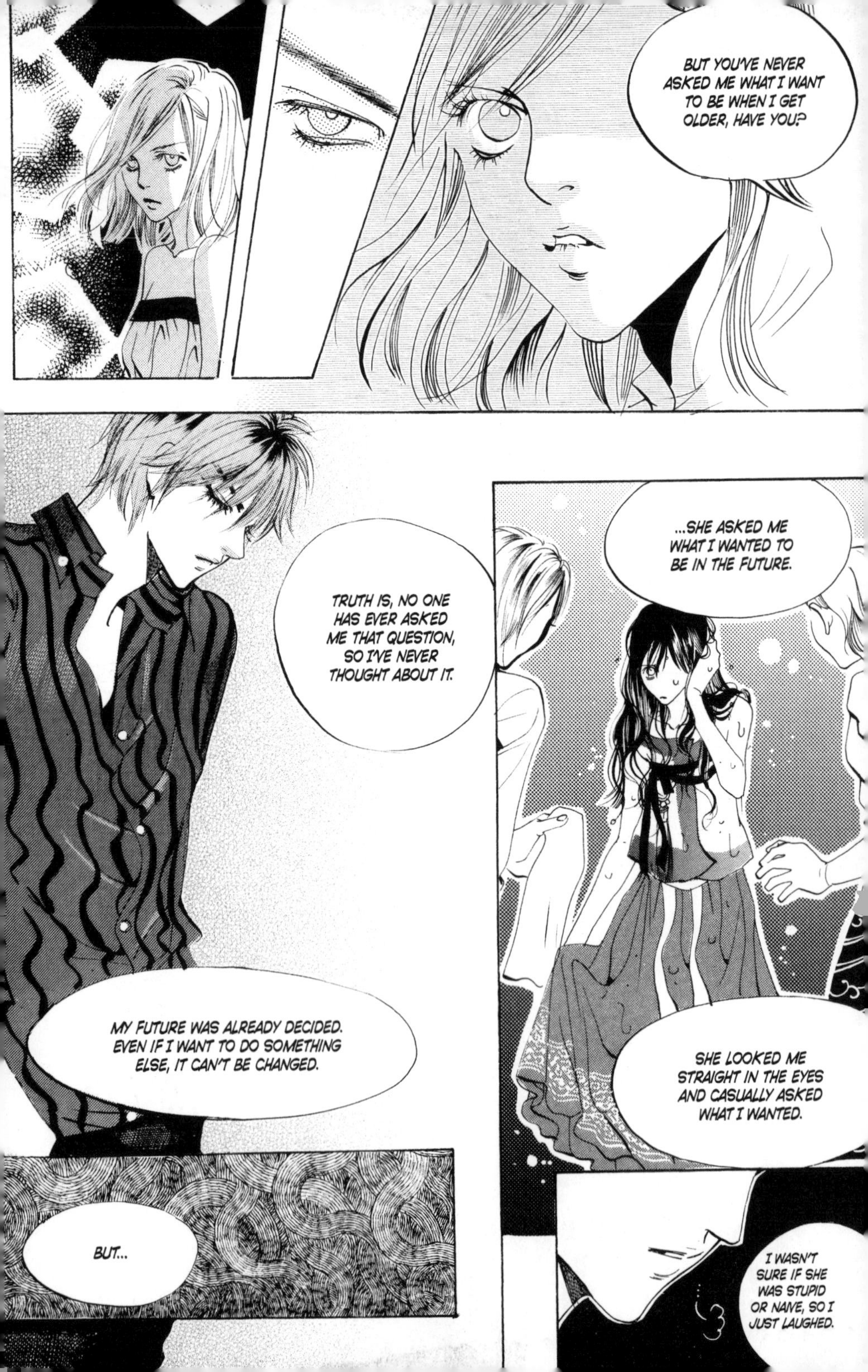
BUT YOU'VE NEVER ASKED ME WHAT I WANT TO BE WHEN I GET OLDER, HAVE YOU?
TRUTH IS, NO ONE HAS EVER ASKED ME THAT QUESTION, SO I'VE NEVER THOUGHT ABOUT IT.
...SHE ASKED ME WHAT I WANTED TO BE IN THE FUTURE.
MY FUTURE WAS ALREADY DECIDED. EVEN IF I WANT TO DO SOMETHING ELSE, IT CAN'T BE CHANGED.
SHE LOOKED ME STRAIGHT IN THE EYES AND CASUALLY ASKED WHAT I WANTED.
BUT...
I WASN'T SURE IF SHE WAS STUPID OR NAIVE, SO I JUST LAUGHED.

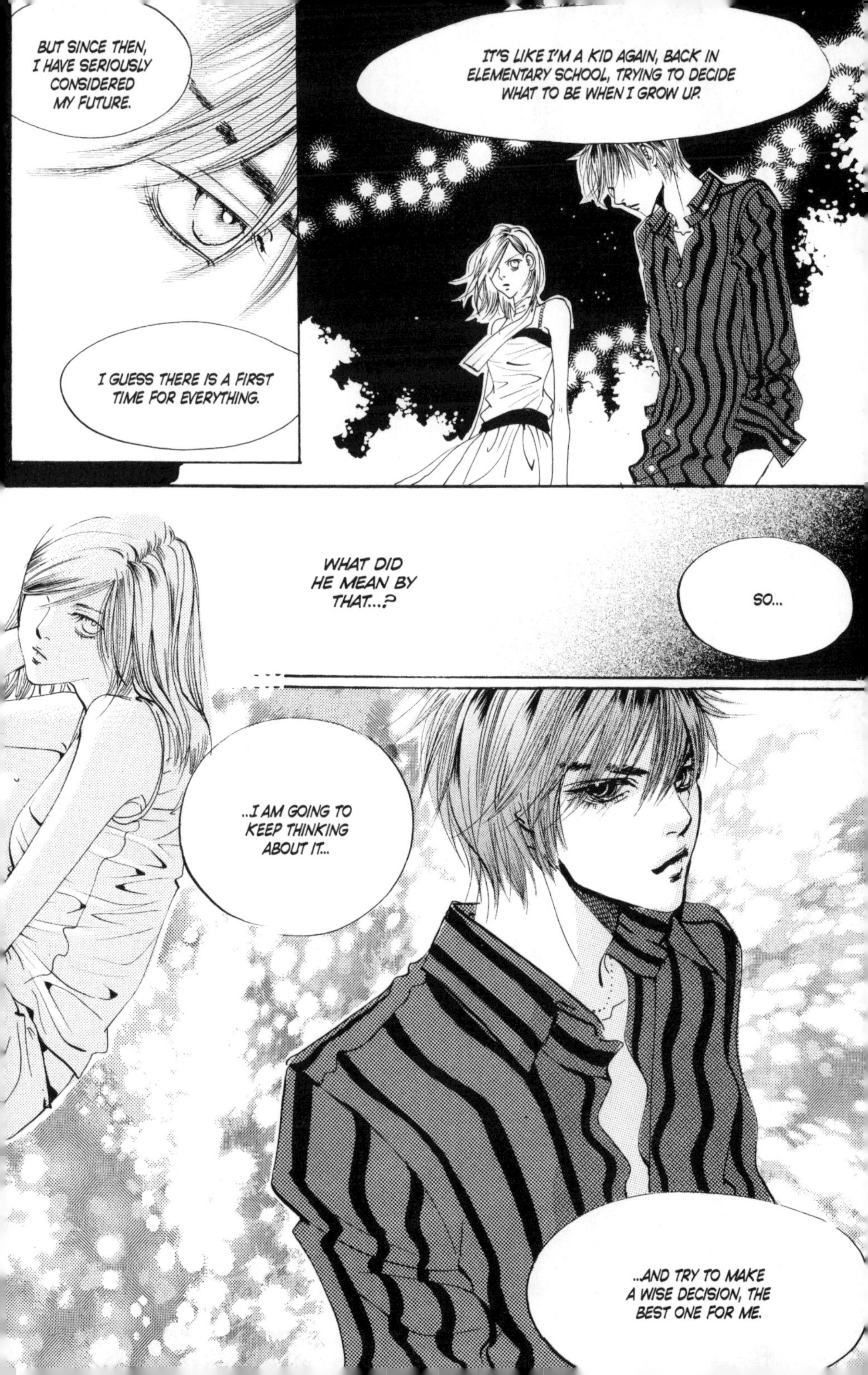
BUT SINCE THEN, I HAVE SERIOUSLY CONSIDERED MY FUTURE.
I GUESS THERE IS A FIRST TIME FOR EVERYTHING.
IT'S LIKE I'M A KID AGAIN, BACK IN ELEMENTARY SCHOOL, TRYING TO DECIDE WHAT TO BE WHEN I GROW UP.
WHAT DID HE MEAN BY THAT...?
SO...
...I AM GOING TO KEEP THINKING ABOUT IT...
...AND TRY TO MAKE A WISE DECISION, THE BEST ONE FOR ME.

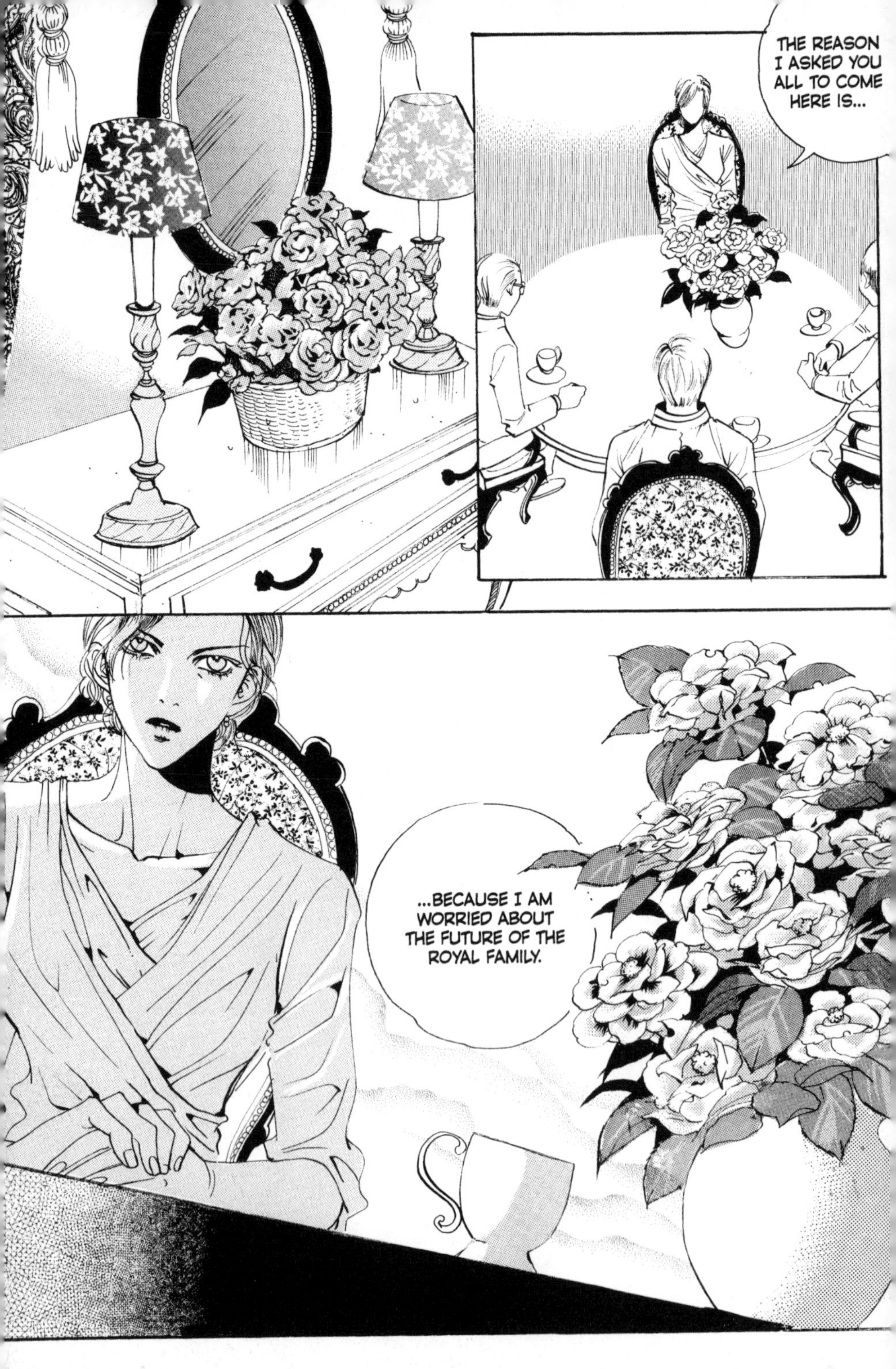
THE REASON I ASKED YOU ALL TO COME HERE IS...
...BECAUSE I AM WORRIED ABOUT THE FUTURE OF THE ROYAL FAMILY.

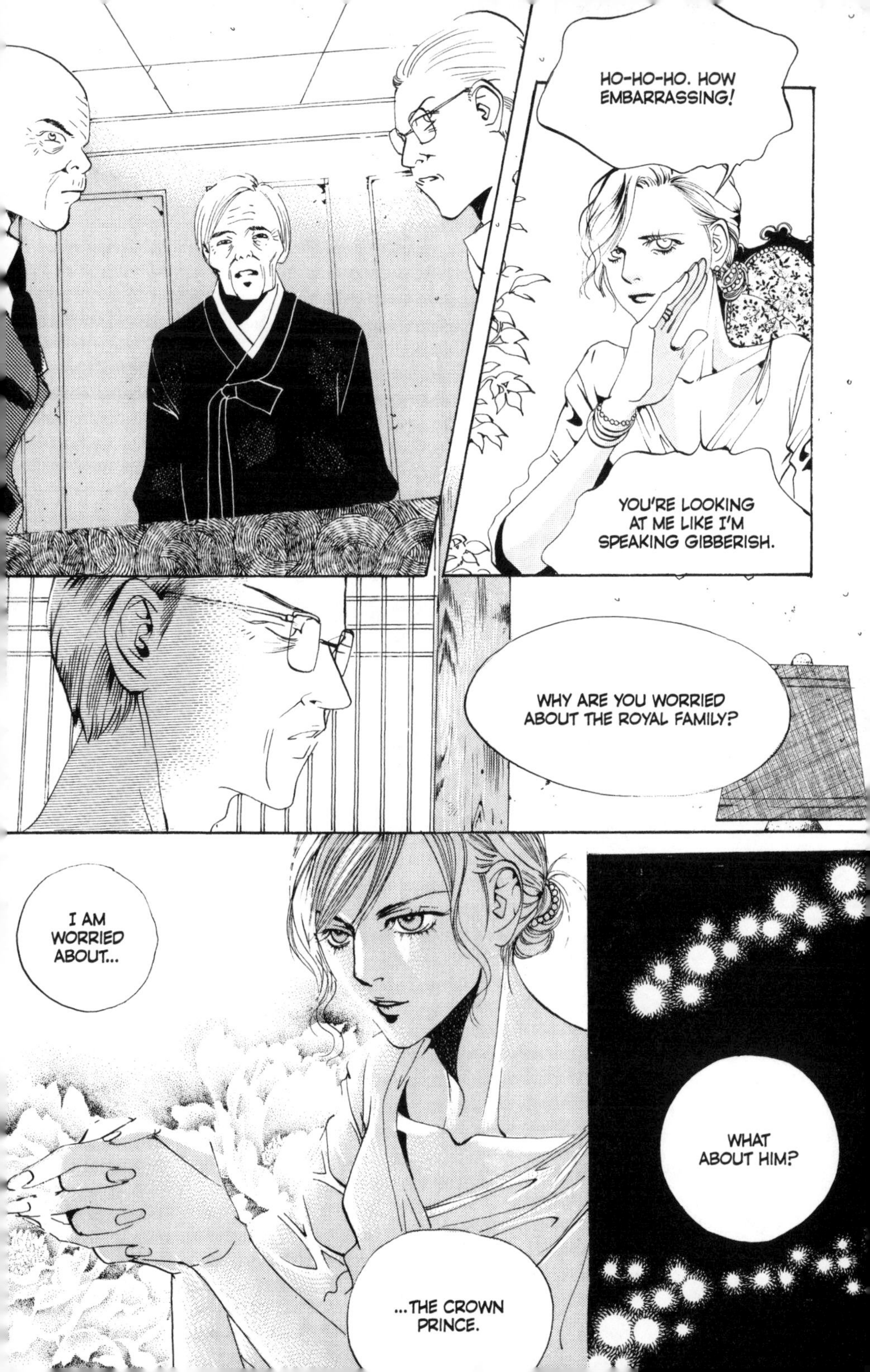
HO-HO-HO. HOW EMBARRASSING!
YOU'RE LOOKING AT ME LIKE I'M SPEAKING GIBBERISH.
WHY ARE YOU WORRIED ABOUT THE ROYAL FAMILY?
I AM WORRIED ABOUT...
...THE CROWN PRINCE.
WHAT ABOUT HIM?

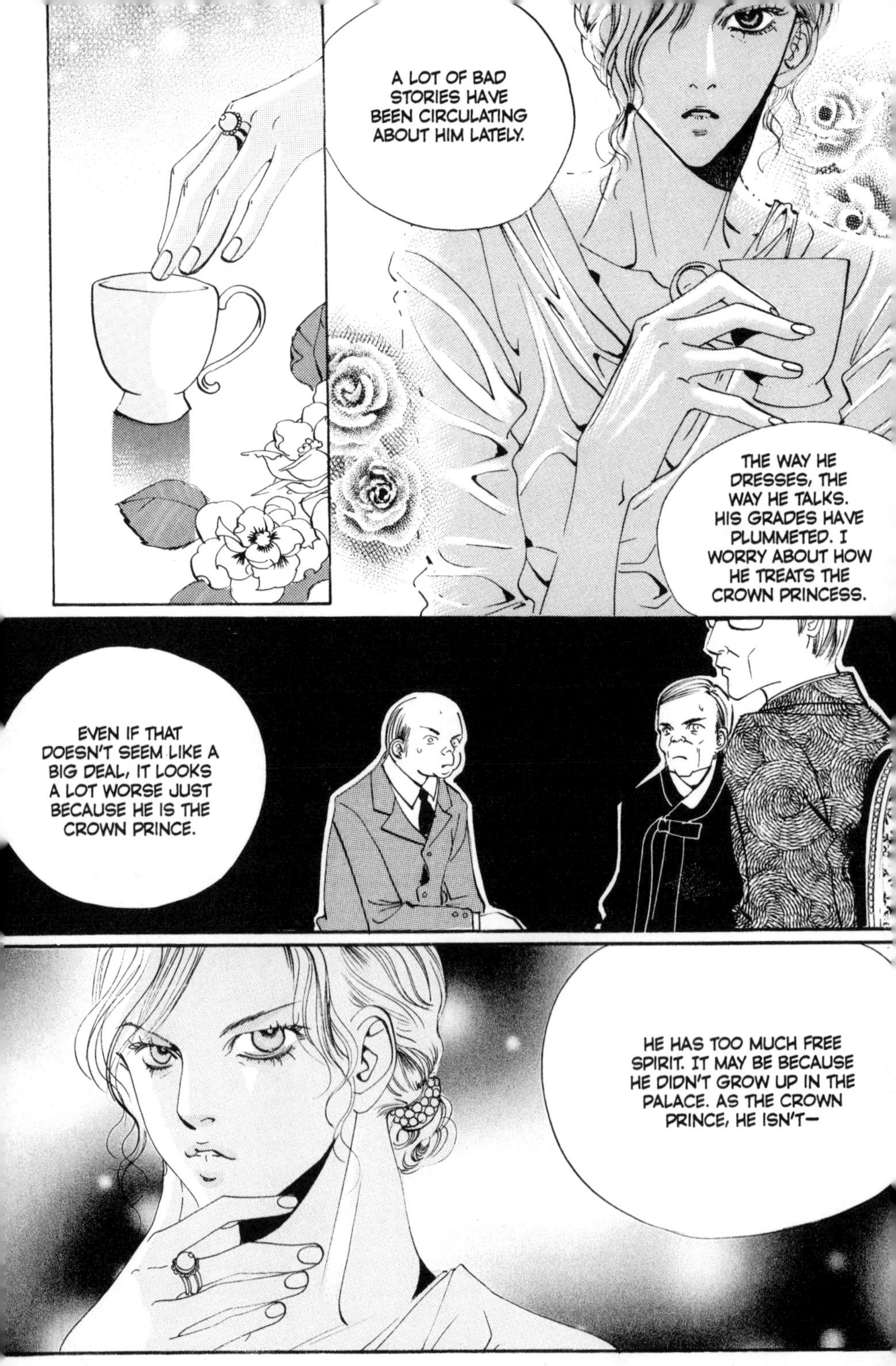
A LOT OF BAD STORIES HAVE BEEN CIRCULATING ABOUT HIM LATELY.
THE WAY HE DRESSES, THE WAY HE TALKS. HIS GRADES HAVE PLUMMETED. I WORRY ABOUT HOW HE TREATS THE CROWN PRINCESS.
EVEN IF THAT DOESN'T SEEM LIKE A BIG DEAL, IT LOOKS A LOT WORSE JUST BECAUSE HE IS THE CROWN PRINCE.
HE HAS TOO MUCH FREE SPIRIT. IT MAY BE BECAUSE HE DIDN'T GROW UP IN THE PALACE. AS THE CROWN PRINCE, HE ISN'T—

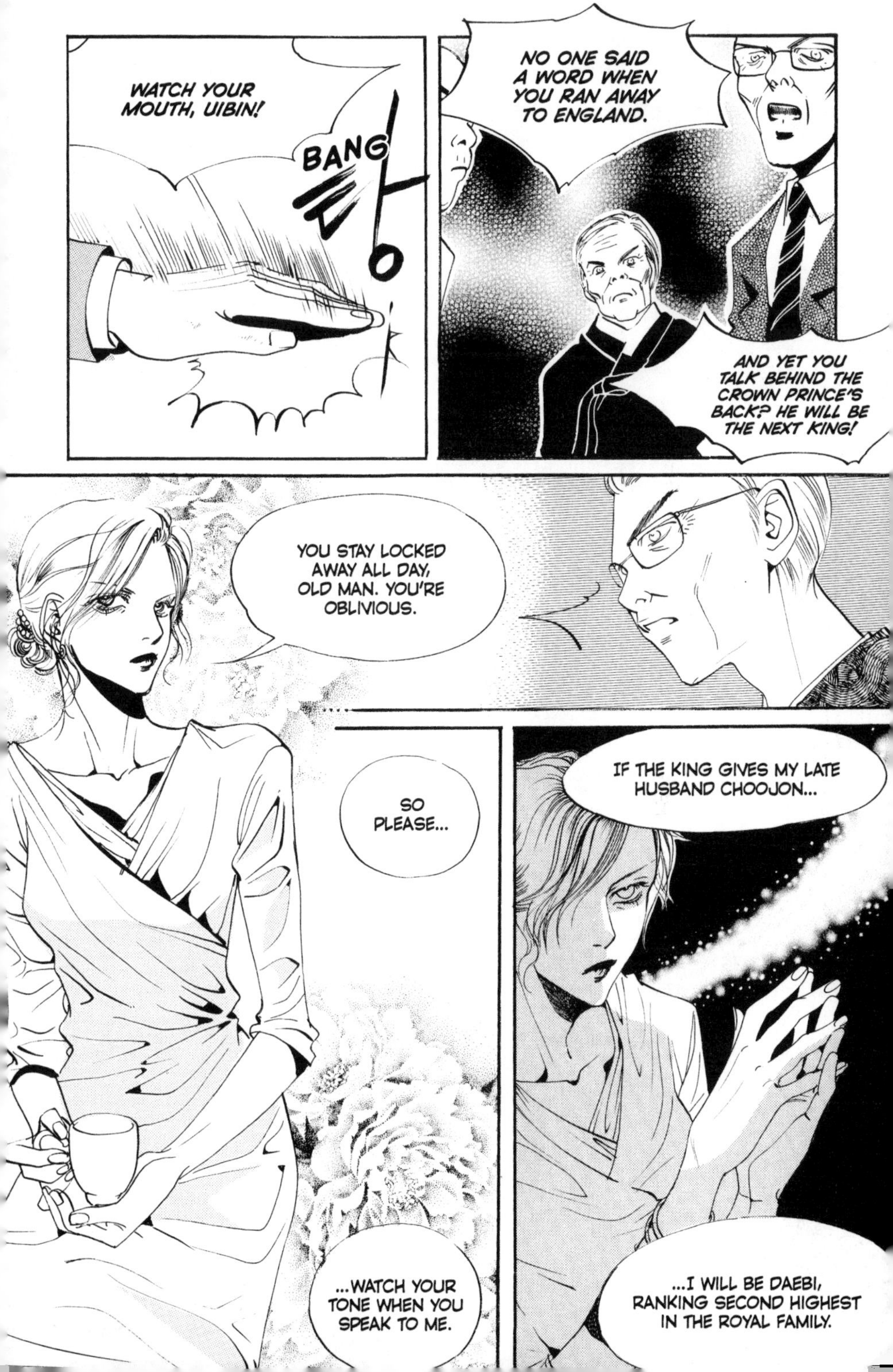
WATCH YOUR MOUTH, UIBIN!
BANG
NO ONE SAID A WORD WHEN YOU RAN AWAY TO ENGLAND.
AND YET YOU TALK BEHIND THE CROWN PRINCE'S BACK? HE WILL BE THE NEXT KING!
YOU STAY LOCKED AWAY ALL DAY, OLD MAN. YOU'RE OBLIVIOUS.
SO PLEASE...
...WATCH YOUR TONE WHEN YOU SPEAK TO ME.
IF THE KING GIVES MY LATE HUSBAND CHOOJON...
...I WILL BE DAEBI, RANKING SECOND HIGHEST IN THE ROYAL FAMILY.

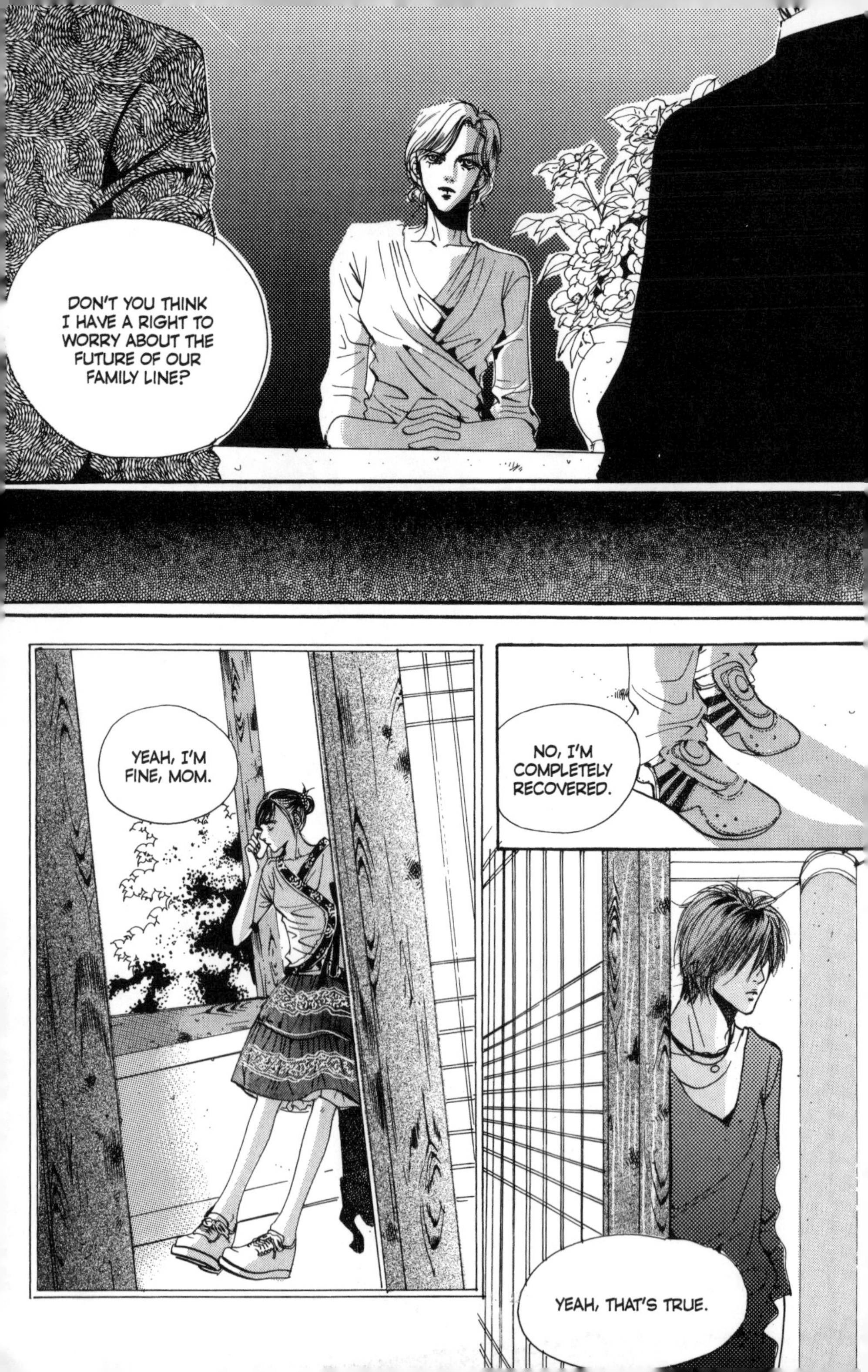
DON'T YOU THINK I HAVE A RIGHT TO WORRY ABOUT THE FUTURE OF OUR FAMILY LINE?
YEAH, I'M FINE, MOM.
NO, I'M COMPLETELY RECOVERED.
YEAH, THAT'S TRUE.

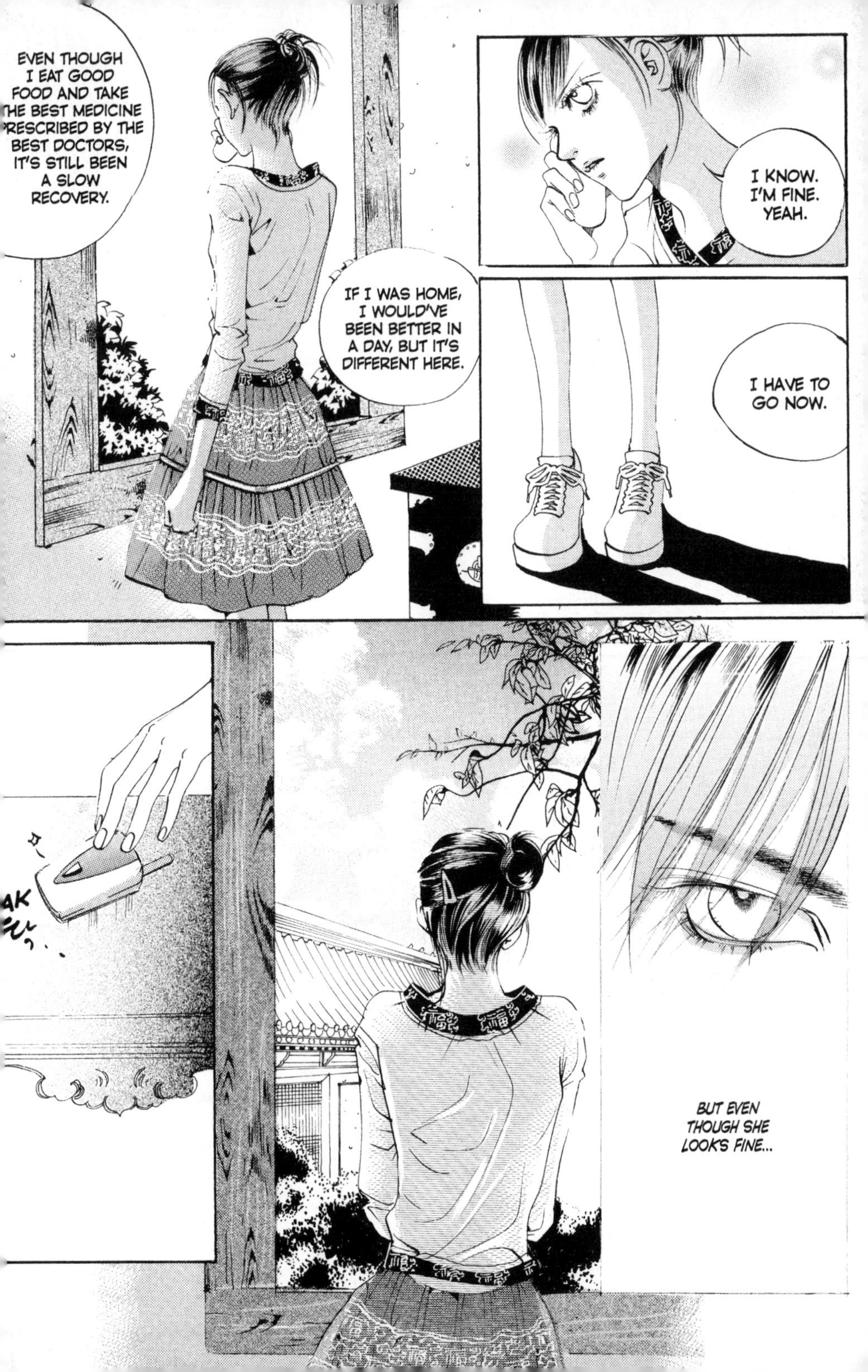
EVEN THOUGH I EAT GOOD FOOD AND TAKE THE BEST MEDICINE PRESCRIBED BY THE BEST DOCTORS, IT'S STILL BEEN A SLOW RECOVERY.
IF I WAS HOME, I WOULD'VE BEEN BETTER IN A DAY, BUT IT'S DIFFERENT HERE.
I KNOW. I'M FINE. YEAH.
I HAVE TO GO NOW.
AK
BUT EVEN THOUGH SHE LOOKS FINE...

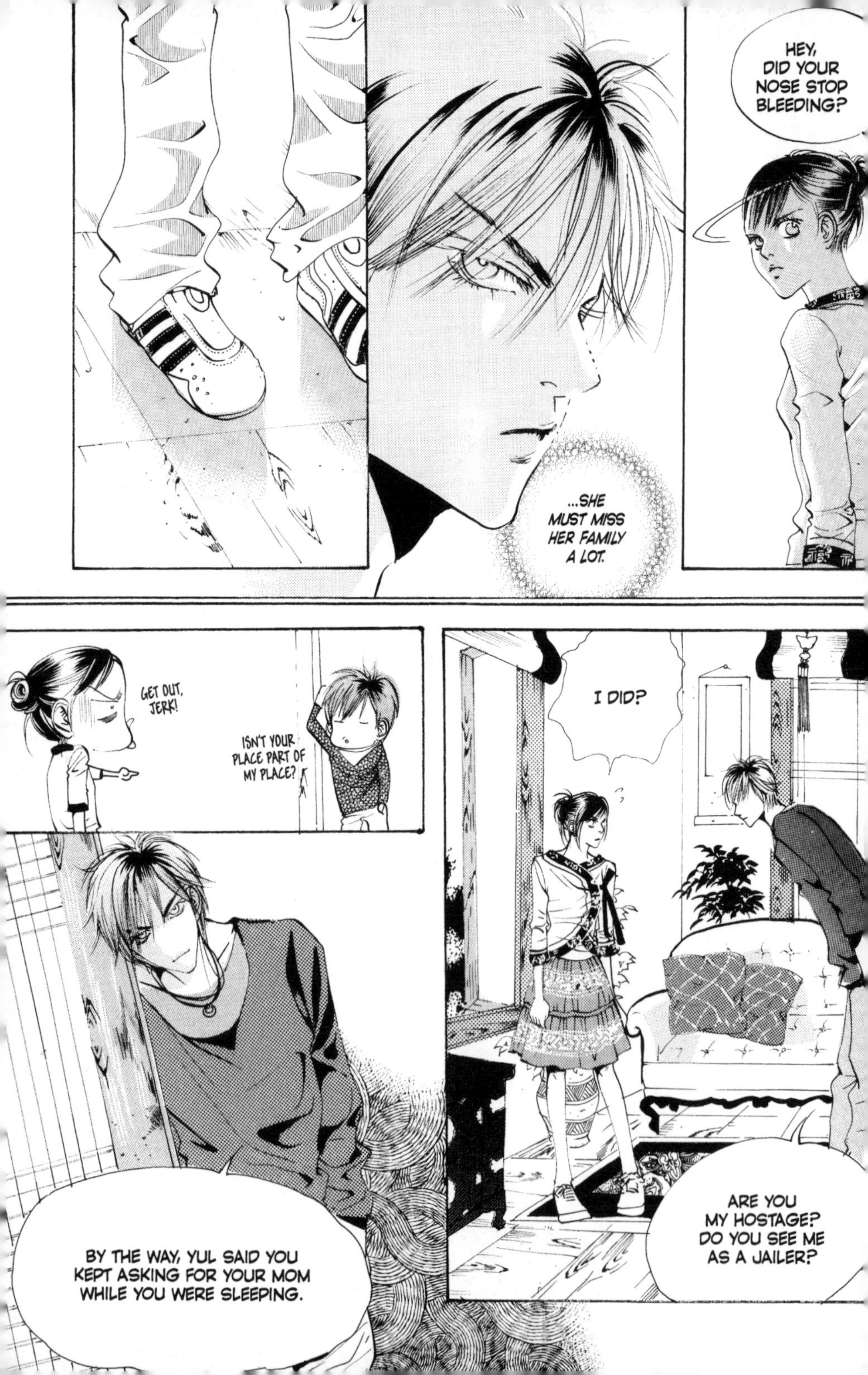
...SHE MUST MISS HER FAMILY A LOT.
HEY, DID YOUR NOSE STOP BLEEDING?
GET OUT, JERK!
ISN'T YOUR PLACE PART OF MY PLACE?
BY THE WAY, YUL SAID YOU KEPT ASKING FOR YOUR MOM WHILE YOU WERE SLEEPING.
I DID?
ARE YOU MY HOSTAGE? DO YOU SEE ME AS A JAILER?

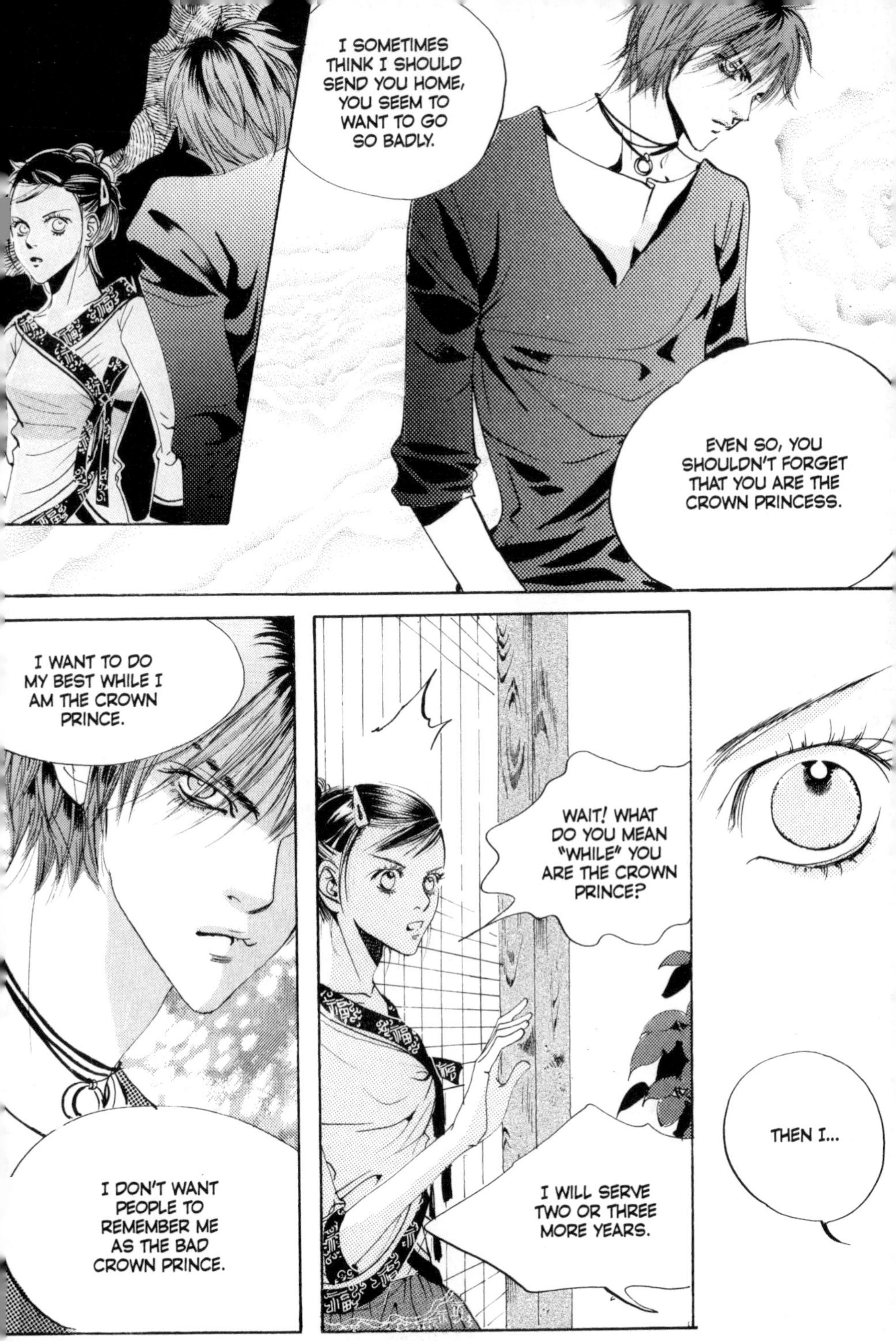
I SOMETIMES THINK I SHOULD SEND YOU HOME, YOU SEEM TO WANT TO GO SO BADLY.
EVEN SO, YOU SHOULDN'T FORGET THAT YOU ARE THE CROWN PRINCESS.
I WANT TO DO MY BEST WHILE I AM THE CROWN PRINCE.
I DON'T WANT PEOPLE TO REMEMBER ME AS THE BAD CROWN PRINCE.
WAIT! WHAT DO YOU MEAN "WHILE" YOU ARE THE CROWN PRINCE?
I WILL SERVE TWO OR THREE MORE YEARS.
THEN I...

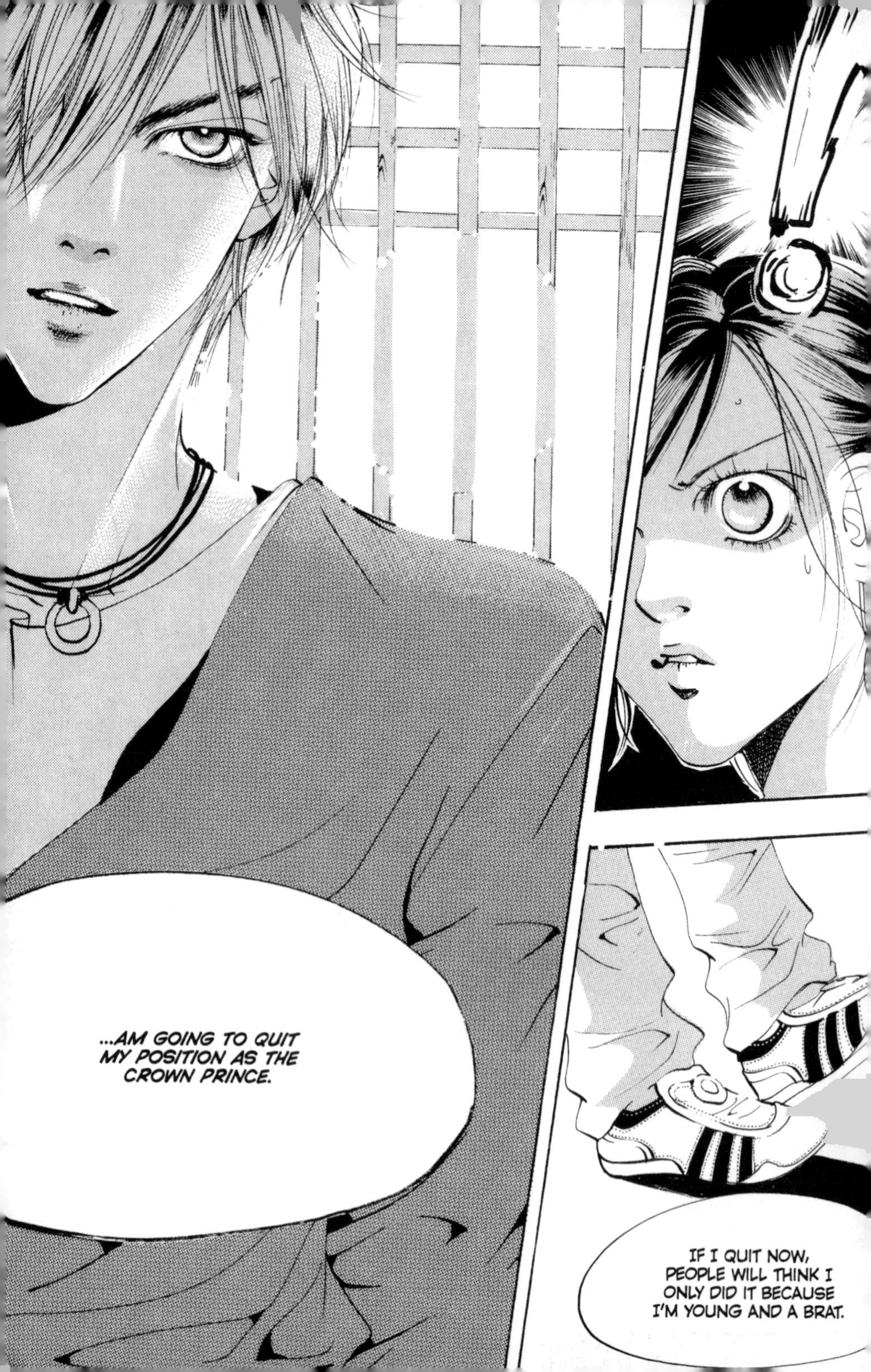
...AM GOING TO QUIT MY POSITION AS THE CROWN PRINCE.
IF I QUIT NOW, PEOPLE WILL THINK I ONLY DID IT BECAUSE I'M YOUNG AND A BRAT.

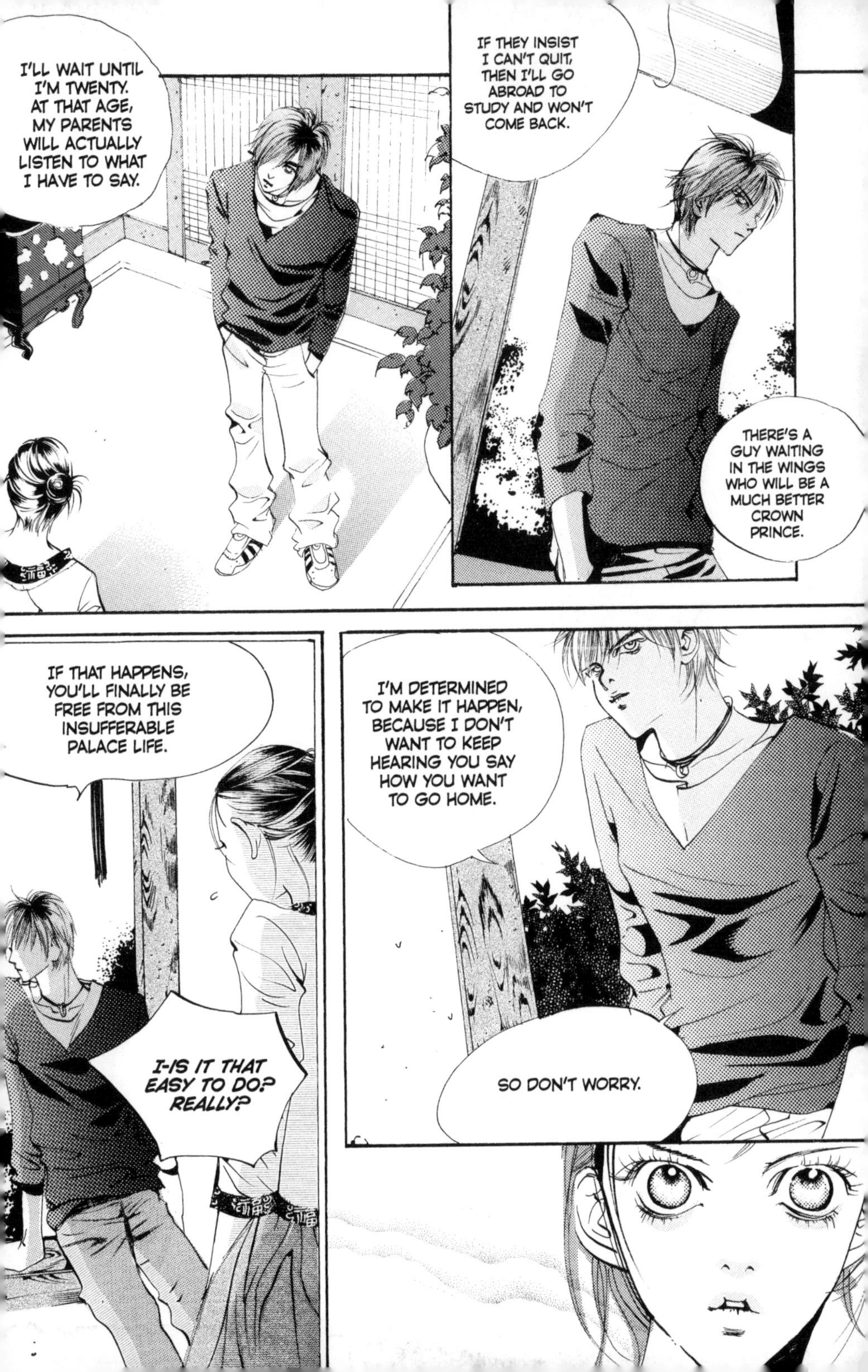
I'LL WAIT UNTIL I'M TWENTY. AT THAT AGE, MY PARENTS WILL ACTUALLY LISTEN TO WHAT I HAVE TO SAY.
IF THEY INSIST I CAN'T QUIT, THEN I'LL GO ABROAD TO STUDY AND WON'T COME BACK.
THERE'S A GUY WAITING IN THE WINGS WHO WILL BE A MUCH BETTER CROWN PRINCE.
IF THAT HAPPENS, YOU'LL FINALLY BE FREE FROM THIS INSUFFERABLE PALACE LIFE.
I-IS IT THAT EASY TO DO? REALLY?
I'M DETERMINED TO MAKE IT HAPPEN, BECAUSE I DON'T WANT TO KEEP HEARING YOU SAY HOW YOU WANT TO GO HOME.
SO DON'T WORRY.

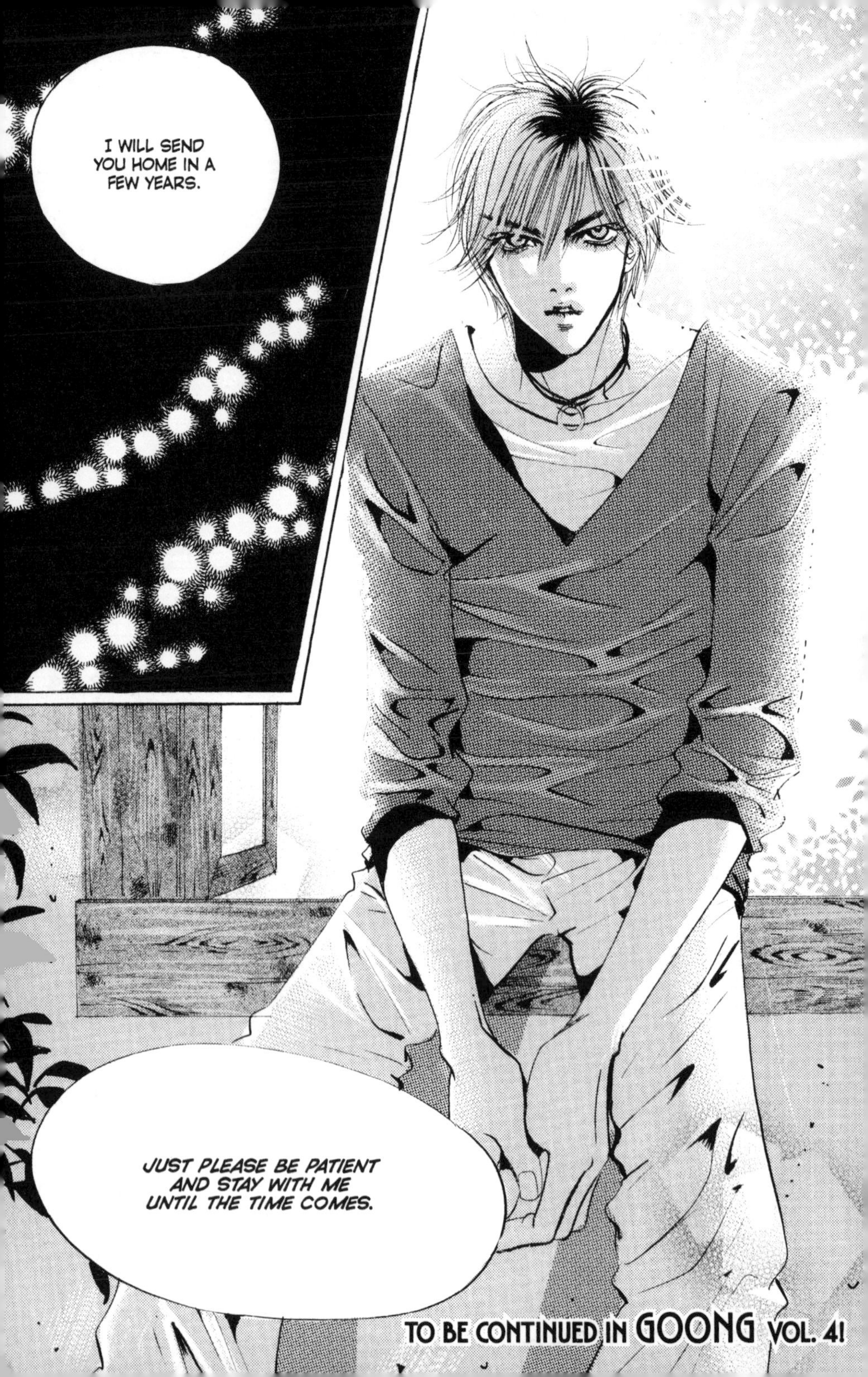
I WILL SEND YOU HOME IN A FEW YEARS.
JUST PLEASE BE PATIENT AND STAY WITH ME UNTIL THE TIME COMES.
TO BE CONTINUED IN GOONG VOL. 4!

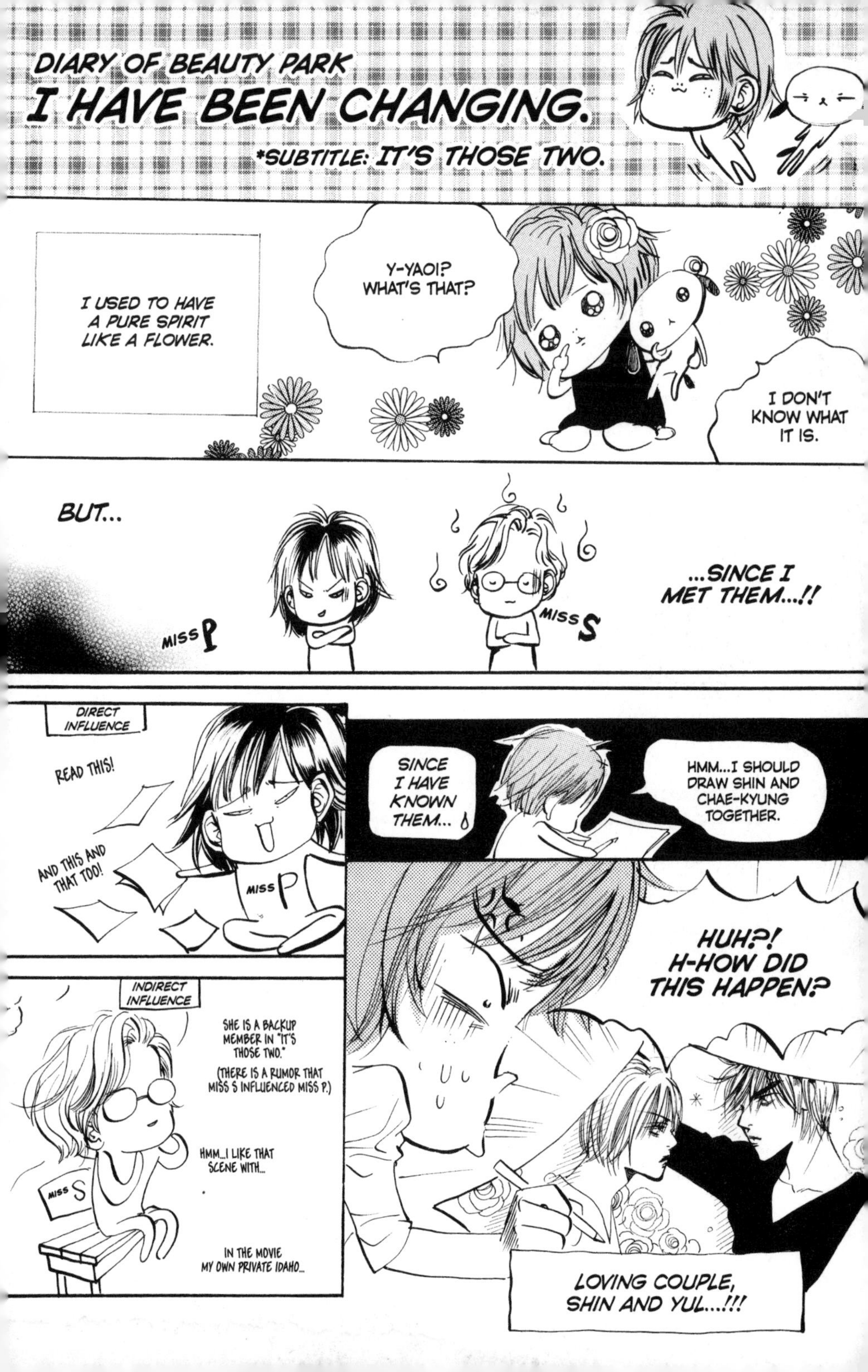
DIARY OF BEAUTY PARK
I HAVE BEEN CHANGING.
*SUBTITLE: IT'S THOSE TWO.
I USED TO HAVE A PURE SPIRIT LIKE A FLOWER.
Y-YAOI? WHAT'S THAT?
I DON'T KNOW WHAT IT IS.
BUT...
MISS P
MISS S
...SINCE I MET THEM...!!
DIRECT INFLUENCE
READ THIS!
AND THIS AND THAT TOO!
MISS P
INDIRECT INFLUENCE
SHE IS A BACKUP MEMBER IN "IT'S THOSE TWO."
(THERE IS A RUMOR THAT MISS S INFLUENCED MISS P.)
HMM...I LIKE THAT SCENE WITH...
IN THE MOVIE MY OWN PRIVATE IDAHO...
MISS S
SINCE I HAVE KNOWN THEM...
HMM...I SHOULD DRAW SHIN AND CHAE-KYUNG TOGETHER.
HUH?! H-HOW DID THIS HAPPEN?
LOVING COUPLE, SHIN AND YUL...!!!

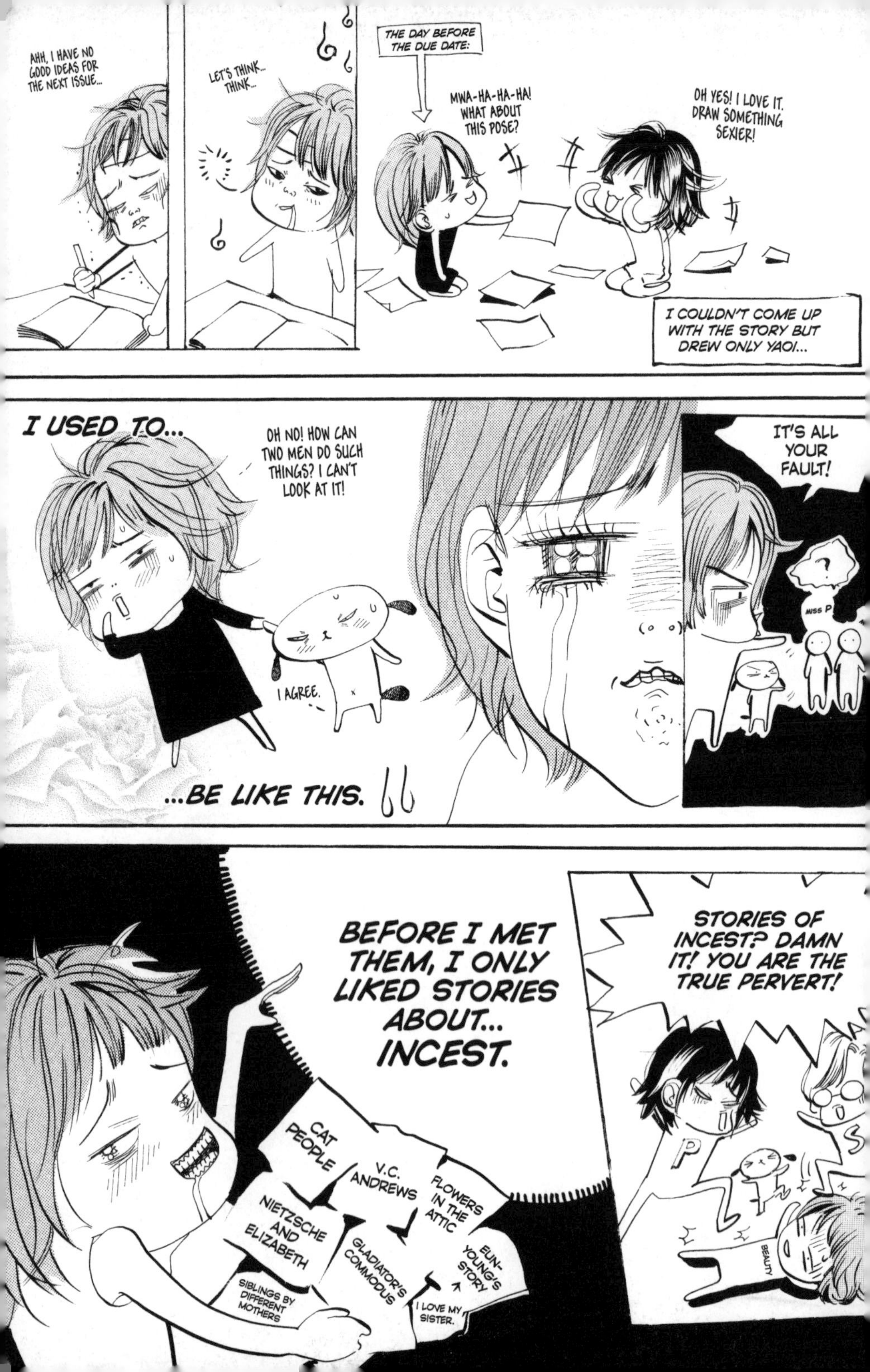
AHH, I HAVE NO GOOD IDEAS FOR THE NEXT ISSUE...
LET'S THINK... THINK...
THE DAY BEFORE THE DUE DATE:
MWA-HA-HA-HA! WHAT ABOUT THIS POSE?
OH YES! I LOVE IT. DRAW SOMETHING SEXIER!
I COULDN'T COME UP WITH THE STORY BUT DREW ONLY YAOI...
I USED TO...
OH NO! HOW CAN TWO MEN DO SUCH THINGS? I CAN'T LOOK AT IT!
I AGREE.
...BE LIKE THIS.
IT'S ALL YOUR FAULT!
MISS P
BEFORE I MET THEM, I ONLY LIKED STORIES ABOUT... INCEST.
CAT PEOPLE
V.C. ANDREWS
FLOWERS IN THE ATTIC
NIETZSCHE AND ELIZABETH
GLADIATOR'S COMMODUS
EUN-YOUNG'S STORY
SIBLINGS BY DIFFERENT MOTHERS
I LOVE MY SISTER.
STORIES OF INCEST? DAMN IT! YOU ARE THE TRUE PERVERT!
BEAUTY

Words from the Creator

I feel like it's only been a few days since I went to see my editor, Burned Potato, with brief sketches of this comic and asked, "Uh...can I...publish this comic in *Wink* magazine...someday?" And yet, here we are at volume three already! When I go through my published books, I think they all could've been better. Still, even if I have some regrets, I like them and will keep working. I only hope to find a good assistant and make this comic book better with each edition, starting with volume four.

I would like to thank "Darker," who suffers greatly because of my laziness, and editor Deuk-Chool Yun, who just had a beautiful boy after nine tough months. I also would like to thank "Oh Desk" and "Kari," who always look at me with disapproval. I know that's how they express their love for me. Hee-hee-hee! (Yeah? Who says?) I also have to thank "Olgami," who makes the pretty covers for this comic, and "Sekuh." Lastly, I would like to thank everyone who knows me and especially the readers who buy this comic.

SoHee Park

Story and art by SoHee Park

Translation HyeYoung Im
English Adaptation Jamie S. Rich
Lettering Alexis Eckerman

Goong, Vol. 3 © 2003 SoHee Park. All rights reserved. First published in Korea in 2003 by Seoul Cultural Publishers, Inc. English translation rights arranged by Seoul Cultural Publishers, Inc.

English translation © 2008 Hachette Book Group, Inc.

All rights reserved. Except as permitted under the U.S. Copyright Act of 1976, no part of this publication may be reproduced, distributed, or transmitted in any form or by any means, or stored in a database or retrieval system, without the prior written permission of the publisher.

The characters and events in this book are fictitious. Any similarity to real persons, living or dead, is coincidental and not intended by the author.

Yen Press
Hachette Book Group
237 Park Avenue, New York, NY 10017

Visit our Web sites at www.HachetteBookGroup.com and www.YenPress.com.

Yen Press is an imprint of Hachette Book Group, Inc. The Yen Press name and logo are trademarks of Hachette Book Group, Inc.

First Yen Press Edition: November 2008

ISBN-10: 0-7595-2872-1
ISBN-13: 978-0-7595-2872-7

10 9 8 7 6 5 4 3 2 1

BVG

Printed in the United States of America